RETURN
TO LOVE

VIVECA CARLYSLE

ARABESQUE

BET
BOOKS

BET Publications, LLC
www.msbet.com
www.arabesquebooks.com

ARABESQUE BOOKS are published by

BET Publications, LLC
c/o BET BOOKS
One BET Plaza
1900 W Place NE
Washington, D.C. 20018-1211

First Printing: September, 1999
10 9 8 7 6 5 4 3 2 1

Printed in the United States of America

RETURN TO LOVE

Trisha shifted around, unable to find a comfortable position. Then she felt more than heard someone near her. She knew Kaliq had joined her but she was afraid of what he would say. She took a deep breath and opened her eyes. He sat inches away, practically devouring her with his gaze.

"Was there something you wanted to tell me?" Trisha asked.

"Actually, I came to make you an offer I don't think you should refuse."

"And that is?"

"Come to Wyoming."

It was almost the same thing he'd said before they broke up. Trisha felt that this was his way of telling her she had another chance, that they could start over again.

"I don't think it's safe here and you need a place to reorganize your life."

Yes, she wanted to go to Wyoming, but not like this. Not as someone he was helping out just as he would a stranger. "I don't know how I could do that."

"It's going to take a lot of work but I think we should give it a shot."

He was so cool and reserved with the offer. She mulled it over in her mind.

"There's just one thing," he added. "Our friends are trying to play matchmaker. They might try to continue to play cupid."

"So what do you suggest?"

"Let them think they're plan worked."

"How do we fool them?"

"Like this."

He leaned over and placed a kiss on her lips.

BOOK YOUR PLACE ON OUR WEBSITE AND MAKE THE ARABESQUE ROMANCE CONNECTION!

We've created a customized website just for our very special Arabesque readers, where you can get the inside scoop on everything that's going on with Arabesque romance novels.

When you come online, you'll have the exciting opportunity to:

- View covers of upcoming books

- Learn about our future publishing schedule (listed by publication month and author)

- Find out when your favorite authors will be visiting a city near you

- Search for and order backlist books

- Check out author bios and background information

- Send e-mail to your favorite authors

- Join us in weekly chats with authors, readers and other guests

- Get writing guidelines

- AND MUCH MORE!

Visit our website at
http://www.arabesquebooks.com

CHAPTER ONE

"Who does Rommel think he is?" Trisha Terrence stared at her business partner Guy Marshall. "How did you let him get so embroiled in our lives?"

"I thought he would help us make some contacts here. But then you wouldn't have dinner with him."

"Oh, so this is my fault. I wouldn't have dinner with him so he's going to ruin our business. I knew he was weird when we met him in Paris."

"I don't know why I didn't think about him buying up my markers."

"I don't know why you didn't tell me they were out there."

She didn't know why she continued to argue with Guy. She'd known he wasn't very strong when it came to wine, women, and song. She just didn't know about the gambling. She walked over to the window and gazed out. Her auburn curls glistened in the sunlight as she turned her head to see what was happening on Carlotta's grounds.

Carlotta's was her dream-come-true Bed & Breakfast that she and Guy had bought and done extensive renovations on to give it a Colonial look. Its winding driveway was a road leading to a stately manor that was hidden from the world by trees. Two white columns framed the doorway to the two-story foyer.

The massive mahogany reservation desk was the first thing you saw when you entered. The plush forest-green carpet blocked out most noise as you walked to your choice of the little elevator or the winding staircase to the second floor. Two bedrooms and baths were set at opposite sides of the hallway to give visitors a feeling of being the only ones on the floor.

"What are we going to do now?"

"I don't know. He called me last night and told me his plans for demanding payment. Then he faxed me the little agreement his lawyer put together when he paid off your gambling debts. I talked to our lawyers this morning and we're legally bound to pay the debt. Even if it means selling Carlotta's."

From the day they'd purchased the inn and renamed it Carlotta's, Trisha thought her dreams were all coming true. She'd spent hours working as a chef in Paris and then New York for this.

She'd worked her way up the ladder in her profession until she'd reached the top and saved every penny she could. Trisha had given up a lot to buy this Bed & Breakfast inn. The biggest thing was love. She'd walked away from a man she'd known for a short time, but whom she'd fallen in love with, and only because he lived in a world so far removed from hers that she had let her fear convince her that they couldn't make it.

Now some person from her past wanted to take it all away. She knew most of the story about Ernie Roman. He'd carved a path from the streets of Chicago to be the owner of three hotels, each with four-star restaurants.

He started by hanging out with jazz musicians in Paris. He'd read about Blacks being accepted in Paris when they were treated badly in the United States and he wanted to see for himself. He didn't have any musical talent so he just hung around and listened to them talk. He heard a young singer from Ohio and talked his way into being her manager. She did well enough to become a minor celebrity, and by the time her star faded from the limelight, he'd met someone who had a minor role in organized crime back in the United States and would take him to his next level of power. One connection led to another and somewhere along the way he learned that money was in real estate. He bought a couple of run-down hotels and fixed them up. Soon he was making a profit. He hired a couple of Cordon Bleu graduates to upgrade the restaurants of the hotels and learned that he could bring in business that way.

When they met in Paris, he knew that Trisha was studying at the Cordon Bleu and he'd offered her a job. But she had her own dreams and had turned him down. He'd hounded her for weeks, with escalating salary offers then veiled threats, but finally got the message and left her alone.

He started calling himself Rommel instead of Roman. She'd heard he did a little loan sharking on the side but until Guy confessed he'd been gambling heavily, she never thought the man would be able to tear down her world.

She didn't know what her next step would be now that she was losing the inn and she needed to talk to someone. So despite her world falling around her, she would keep her monthly shopping date with Jesslyn Owens Rush.

Trisha waited in the lobby of the New York high-rise for her friend. In the four years they'd known each other, they'd met once a month for a day of shopping and lunch and more shopping.

They'd met when the man Trisha was seeing, Kaliq Faulkner, attended a political fund raiser with his friend, Palladin Rush. It was just before Jesslyn was in a devastating car accident and lost her memory for a while. Jesslyn was suspected of industrial espionage and after she'd been cleared, she'd married Palladin Rush.

Trisha and Jesslyn kept in touch. Pennsylvania and New York weren't that far away. They were shopping buddies and New York had the best shopping per square foot than most large cities.

They were also friends who understood each other's passions. It was Jesslyn who held her together when she decided not to follow the man she'd fallen in love with to Wyoming. Had it really been four years since she'd met the dynamic Kaliq Faulkner?

The first time she saw him she felt drawn to him as if he were a magnet. How had the man become part of her life so quickly? She'd guarded her dream so carefully and he bulldozed his way into her life and her heart only a few days after he arrived at the inn.

The valet had assisted him in retrieving his wheelchair from the back seat but he didn't need help getting from the car into the chair. That little action told her immediately he was a very independent man.

He wore a heavy black jacket and black Levis. Although a beret covered his head she could see that he was bald. She could also see that his face wasn't wrinkled so he was bald by choice or heredity. The night before there had been a light dusting of snow and now the January winds brushed it around the wheelchair. She'd seen others like it and wondered why a person would choose that design. The chair didn't have metal arms and the wheels leaned inward.

Trisha chastised herself for staring and returned to her work. The kitchen was buzzing with activity as they prepared the evening meal.

MacPherson's Bed & Breakfast Inn had a continental breakfast, and the guests were on their own for lunch, but dinner was where they allowed the chef to sparkle.

This was her last year working at MacPherson's. She and her partner finally had enough money to buy it and she'd decided to call it Carlotta's Inn. She wanted someplace romantic that served delicious food. It was something she and her mother had talked about all the time she was studying in Paris. A place that served delicious dinners and was far enough off the beaten path to make people think they were in another world.

When all her classmates were dreaming of working in exclusive restaurants, Trisha just wanted something cozy. When all her culinary classmates were talking about writing cookbooks, having their own cooking shows or their own exclusive restaurants, Trisha wanted her place to be a refuge from life in the fast lane.

The first night that Kaliq came down to dinner, he wore a dark brown turtleneck sweater with dark brown slacks. He'd obviously shaved his face and his head. The shaved head was no longer an oddity. In fact, more and more black actors were doing it and getting compliments.

She also noticed several of the waitresses who were off duty stayed around instead of rushing back to their college dorms.

Kaliq didn't encourage them nor did he discourage the attention. He mentioned he had a friend who lived nearby. That he stayed at the inn rather than with his friend was another indication of his independence.

Most of the time he was away from the inn but every now and then Trisha would catch a glimpse of him. He was usually surrounded by women. Some were guests and others were just locals.

She learned he'd been a Foreign Correspondent until something happened to his legs. She found herself watching for him and she scolded herself for having a schoolgirl crush on him.

Somehow he'd found out she was the chef and after a dinner he'd enjoyed he sent her a dozen roses. When he asked for a date, she'd hesitated only for a moment before she accepted. By that time she wanted to know more about the mysterious Mr. Faulkner.

As luck would have it, the stove went out and by the time it was fixed she only had half an hour to get ready. She rushed to her house and got ready in record time. She slipped into a black bra and panties set and then sat down at her vanity and applied her makeup.

She had grown up in Paris and, although her interest was cooking, she had picked up a style as far as fashion was concerned. Tonight Trisha chose an ankle-length maroon velvet dress with a slit up the sides to reveal the black lace slip underneath. She pulled the zipper down enough to step into the dress and then zipped it up and whirled in the mirror to study the effect.

Satisfied it was sexy enough, she went to meet her date. Kaliq drove her to a restaurant that bordered Pennsylvania and New Jersey. "Call it a bus man's holiday," he told her.

He laughed when she ordered chopped steak smothered with cheese and onions. She confessed that she preferred junk food to all the fancy dishes she prepared.

They talked a little about their careers. She learned how he'd been trapped behind enemy lines and his legs had been broken during an escape attempt. Despite being ordered to ignore the situation, his friend Palladin Rush had rescued him.

"That must have been very difficult for him," she said. "You must be very close if he defied his superiors."

"Absolutely, since his nickname was Glacier."

"Does that mean he was cold and unmovable?"

"Exactly."

"But not with you."

"We've been friends since our first year at Harvard. I would never have asked him to make any rescue attempts but I'm damn sure glad he did."

"So am I," she whispered.

The food was superb but Trisha couldn't help imagining how she would change the recipe for her kitchen. It was the peril of being a chef, trying to eat out and not taking the meal apart and mentally trying new combinations. Trisha found it especially difficult since she was planning to open a little bed and breakfast herself. Everything was in place; she was just waiting until the final papers were signed. Of course, if her clientele ever learned that she was more inclined to junk food than the usual fare that she and her staff offered, they might be angry.

"Are you still a journalist?"

"No. I run a summer camp now. Sort of a place where city kids learn about living in wide open spaces and about falcons."

"How do you teach them about falcons?"

"I'm a falconer."

She stopped eating and stared at Kaliq. "A falconer?"

Images of Medieval knights on horseback danced through her head. Heroes bravely standing on a mountain wearing a metallic glove and a falcon perched on the glove.

"How did that come about?"

"Are you trying to say it isn't an honorable profession?" He grinned at her.

"Let's just say it isn't the kind of career my dates usually have."

"And are there lots of dates, Ms. Terrence?"

"Not lately. Most of my time is spent with Guy."

She watched as Kaliq seemed to let that remark meander through his mind before responding. "He's just your partner, right?"

"He's also my friend."

"I'd like to meet him."

She'd sidestepped the issue and avoided making eye contact when she spoke about her plans.

"What kinds of stories did you cover?"

"All kinds. Mostly I went after things that interested me. I wanted to know what divided a country and why. I wanted to know how an American woman can become queen of a nation. I had an insatiable need to learn."

"Did you ever find out why you were so determined?"

"Not really," he said, then changed the subject. "I've talked enough about me. What made you decide to become a chef?"

"In a way it was my mother's dream. She was a terrific cook and wanted to study in Paris."

"What happened?"

"She met my father. He had a great career here in the States and she knew he couldn't give that up."

"What did he do?"

"He was a vice president of a chain of clothing stores. He always said that he didn't see any sense in traveling around the world when he had everything he wanted in New York. He passed away when I was ten. I was an only child."

"Sorry. I was an only child also. I lost my parents while I was in college, so I understand. What did your mother do?"

"She took the insurance money and moved us to Paris. She always wanted to have a bed and breakfast type of business. She worked in a restaurant there and sent me to school."

"Do you speak French?"

"Ah, oui monsieur," she said. "I just don't do it now. I find it pretentious unless the people around me speak it."

"But you didn't stay in France; why not?"

"My mother never wanted to stay away from the United States forever. She had this plan that we'd return and open that bed and breakfast. She subscribed to *Country Inns* magazine and always checked out the property for sale. She passed away before we found the property we wanted. She had cancer. I brought her home and buried her next to my father."

"How long ago?"

"Six years."

They were silent for a few minutes as she remembered what it was like to go from having a family to being an orphan. She knew he was thinking the same thing. A family was so nice. That was probably the reason for his summer camp.

"What do you do now that you're not covering stories all over the world?"

"I live in Wyoming."

"I beg your pardon, Wyoming? First you tell me you're a falconer and now this." She giggled and brushed back the curls that had fallen in her face.

He laughed and then said, "Yes. Wyoming. It's a great state."

"I know, but it's not a place that comes to mind when you're talking to African-Americans."

"You have a point, but I did a story on endangered species for the Sunday *Times* magazine section and one of the places I had to go was Wyoming."

"What endangered species is in Wyoming?"

"The Peregrine Falcon."

He went on to tell her how different it was to hunt

with a falcon rather than a gun. She liked his enthusiasm and she found herself wishing she didn't have
her own plans in place. She would have liked a chance
to see Wyoming through his eyes for two or three
weeks but her heart was set on a wonderful place in
the mountains.

One night he asked her to come to New York. He
was meeting a friend and his new lady. It was going
to be a fund raiser and he wanted her to be his date.

He arrived with a limousine to take them to New
York. Trisha was waiting at her door. She wanted him
to get a look at the outfit she'd chosen tonight. It
was a black tuxedo jacket that was opened to the
waist. She wasn't worried about being topless underneath. To keep her warm she wore a full length sable
coat. It had been a graduation gift from her mother.

The evening was a success and Jesslyn Owens was
a surprise. Although Palladin was well over six feet,
Jesslyn barely cleared five. The two women hit it off
famously.

That night, Kaliq asked her to stay in New York for
the night. They stayed in one of the east side hotels
and the next morning she woke up alone.

At first she was disoriented about where she was
and then she was furious that Kaliq wasn't there with
her.

She was about to take a shower, when the door
opened and Kaliq entered. He had several packages
with the hotel's logo. Inside the bags were a change
of clothes, something to be worn in the daytime rather
than her slinky, sexy look that would have been met
with raised eyebrows if she left the hotel dressed like
that.

After spending the night together, Trisha knew she

was getting in over her head. She wanted to spend as much time with Kaliq as she could. She knew that when he returned to Wyoming it was over for them.

It would take months, maybe years, before she and Guy could build their clientele and reach the goals they'd set for the place. It left no time for any social life, and especially not one that would have to be conducted in two separate states.

She knew a time would come for her to make a decision and she dreaded it. Changing her lifestyle could be too hectic. She'd heard too many stories of women giving up everything for the men they'd wanted, only to find out that the relationship didn't work and they didn't have a man or a career.

Trisha didn't mention it because she didn't want to think about Kaliq asking her to come to Wyoming and she having to refuse. He wasn't the kind of man to take 'no' for an answer. His strong personality would try to bulldoze her into changing her mind. She was equally as strong and she was on a mission.

In some ways she was prolonging the agony and in others, she was enjoying the time they spent together.

When he asked her to come to Wyoming, she confessed.

"I can't. I'm close to a deal I've been waiting for for a long time. I can't leave Pennsylvania now."

He nodded. "I think I'll try to change your mind." Kaliq was true to his word. He never let an opportunity pass as he tried to entice her to his part of the United States; but as she suspected, invitations became ultimatums—until the last night they were together when it became a demand.

"I've made a commitment and I can't change it,

Trisha," Kaliq told her. "I'm asking you to relocate because I can't. I would if I could."

"I know. I'm not trying to be difficult, but I have to stay here."

"Guess we've reached an impasse that neither of us can get by. I'm going to Wyoming tomorrow."

Tears streamed down her face. "We're two people who met at the wrong time and no matter how much it hurts, this wasn't meant to be."

"Don't you think your mother would want you to be happy?"

"Sure. She'd probably say 'he's a fine man, you go girl,' but I'm not the only one involved. I have a partner and he's counting on me. I'm counting on me. Until I do this I'll always wonder if I could. I need to know."

"You just can be so stubborn. I wouldn't want you any other way."

"We do what we must."

"Maybe we'll get another chance someday. I'm not going to do the keep-in-touch thing. If it's going to happen, it will, and if it's not, we're better off not prolonging it."

Trisha Terrence fought back the tears as she listened to Kaliq's decision. She'd known the man less than a month and she had almost been ready to follow him to the wilds of Wyoming. The operative word was *almost*. He was asking her to share his dream but not understanding that she had a dream of her own. Finally he stopped asking and quietly they enjoyed the time they spent.

It was later that she found out about the intrigue that surrounded Jesslyn. She was an amnesiac and suspect in an industrial espionage case. By the time the case had been solved and Jesslyn cleared, she and Trisha had become best friends.

When the time came to decide between a life with Kaliq or her career, Trisha had chosen her career. Love couldn't match the need that burned inside her. She was so close to her dream, she couldn't give it up and move to the wilds of Wyoming. She'd never considered it a Mecca for African-Americans despite Kaliq's raves about the place.

"I hope you haven't been waiting too long." Jesslyn's voice broke through Trisha's reverie. "Did I interrupt something?"

"Just some thoughts about the past. Thanks for stopping them."

Trisha and Jesslyn were an odd couple when it came to height. Jesslyn was barely over five feet tall while Trisha was five feet eight inches in her stocking feet.

Jesslyn, dressed toward the casual side, wore black slacks and a navy peacoat since the September weather had a slight chill to it.

Pennsylvania had already seen its first snowfall and Trisha's outfit was much more dramatic with black boots that came to her knees and an ankle-length fur coat.

Jesslyn shook her head. "If I've told you once I've told you a thousand times, you and Kaliq were perfect for each other. I still say you need to contact him."

Trisha laughed at Jesslyn's overstatement. Kaliq's name came up often during the first year of their friendship and then just faded as Jesslyn stopped mentioning the man's name when she was with Trisha.

It was as if she'd given up hope that the two would ever get back together.

"Why didn't you come up or at least have the concierge notify me you were here?"

"I don't know . . . I guess I needed some time to figure out how to tell you what's happened."

"Uh oh," Jesslyn said. "I think we'd better forget about shopping and let's go up and have a little talk."

"I hate to do this but I'm really frazzled right now. I'm not in the mood to go shopping and that's something to mark in your calendar." She laughed weakly.

Jesslyn searched her friend's sad eyes. She'd only seen her like this once before, when she walked away from Kaliq Faulkner. For several weeks she'd questioned her plans and Jesslyn had seen it in Trisha's eyes. Several months passed before that pain went away.

Jesslyn had always been intuitive and straightforward. Trisha remembered how she'd backed off and let Palladin come after her rather than trying to convince him they could forge a life together.

Unfortunately that hadn't worked with Kaliq. They were too set in completing their own personal dreams to stay together. Or maybe they just didn't love each other enough to make it work.

"I hate to do this, but I'm really . . . I'm not in the mood for shopping."

"We can have a girl's day in."

"What about Palladin and the twins?"

"He's taking them to Radio City Music Hall. He's meeting one of the other fathers in the building and having a 'guy thing.' I think he's jealous of us."

"Aren't the twins a little young for that?"

"He says that even though they're only three, it's

not too early to introduce them to the cultural attributes of the city."

"Translation?"

"He wants to see the Rockettes."

"Won't the twins get restless?"

"They'll fall asleep as soon as they get there. He's going with one of his assistant coaches and his kids from Palladin's hockey team."

"How's the team coming?"

"Good days, bad days, and horrible days. They're on a losing streak right now. They've lost three games in a row. I think that's why they're going to the show. Instead of having a practice session." Jesslyn laughed. "You single people think that married women don't have a life unless their single friends take pity on them and drag them out of the house."

"I'm sorry. I just think taking care of twins is an awesome responsibility."

By the time they got off the elevator, Palladin was just leaving the apartment with a twin on each arm. At six feet four inches he was an impressive sight. His dreads were now shoulder length and the children took pleasure in using them as handles as they came down the hall.

"Did you forget something?" he asked as he leaned over and placed a kiss on Jesslyn's brow.

"No. We had a change in plans. We've decided on girl talk rather than shopping."

"Is there a problem?"

"Take the boys and have fun."

The fact that Jesslyn hadn't answered his question wasn't lost on Palladin. He hoped it was just a "girl talk" thing. Since the birth of the twins their lives had become mundane and he loved it. Jesslyn's gift

basket business was going strong and he'd made a
few smart moves as a venture capitalist. He didn't
need trouble. He leaned forward and kissed Jesslyn's
lips. "Talk to you later. Come on, Vance, Ethan, I
think we're getting a signal that we're not wanted for
a few hours." Then he kissed Trisha on the cheek.
"Maybe you should stay a couple of days." He opened
the door and was gone.

"That man is positively psychic," Trisha said.

"I know. The minute we canceled shopping I knew
he was going to get suspicious, so hang up your coat
and let's get comfortable."

In minutes the two women were seated in the spa-
cious living room. "I see you've changed the place
around since I last saw it."

Trisha scanned the lavish living room with its twelve
foot ceilings. The beige covered walls were just the
place to show off the Impressionist art that Palladin
collected.

The kitchen was a lot bigger than in the apartment
Jesslyn had when they first met but nowhere near the
size Trisha was accustomed to working in.

"Have you tried any of those recipes I sent you?"

"Yes. I tried the honey-glazed biscuits but I have
to say that no matter how I tried to follow it something
went wrong."

"Oh no!"

"Oh, we could eat them and it wasn't that bad, but
they didn't taste like the ones at the inn."

For three years Trisha had been trying to help Jesslyn upgrade her cooking and something always happened. Trisha suspected that her friend was easily
distracted since she didn't live to cook.

"You may not be a great cook, but you know enough to keep your business going."

"Now don't start beating up on yourself. Whatever happens, we'll get through it."

Somehow the cosy feeling of Jesslyn's old apartment had carried over to this one, even though the space was five times larger. Jesslyn seemed to redecorate the place often. Their apartment occupied three floors of the building. On the first floor was the living room with its massive stone fireplace, a dining room that could seat twelve comfortably, and a state-of-the-art kitchen; the master bedroom suite was on the third floor.

The second floor was the guest area and the future bedrooms for the twins. Jesslyn was adamant about giving the twins their own identities. She had refused to have their names rhyme or even let them have the same initials. Currently the twins occupied a room on the same floor as their parents. The former den would serve as a nursery until the boys were old enough to be on their own.

"I'm glad the boys are out of here. I can use the fireplace," Jesslyn told Trisha. "I panic when they're running around and it's on." She turned on the gas-burning fireplace and soon the room was bathed in the heat from the flames.

"You were always the coolest person I know. Clear-headed, problem-solver, and then you had the babies and you lost all of that," Trisha teased and laughed. "You're on a mission to protect them from the rest of the world."

"Tell me about it. Palladin says I came home from the hospital with all these fears about being a good mother. I'll tell you one thing, when you have children you realize how much you don't know about things. Now let me get some wine and fruit and we'll be set."

Trisha took off her boots and put them on the boot rack by the door. She padded back to the sofa, enjoying how the carpet felt under her feet. Jesslyn appeared in the door with a bottle of Pinot Noir wine and two glasses.

She sat on the sofa, handed a glass to Trisha, filled it, and then filled her own glass.

"Okay, what's going on?"

Trisha didn't know where to begin. "So much has happened since I last saw you. I guess the biggest is that I'm going to lose the inn."

"My God! No! What happened?"

Jesslyn knew how much Trisha loved Carlotta's Inn. They usually referred to it as just "the inn." She remembered the first day they opened and got a review that said it was new but it was the place to enjoy great food and spend some time walking over the three acres of land. The inn was a success and it looked as if it would be for years.

Tears filled Trisha's eyes and, despite her willing them not to fall, trickled down her cheeks. She fumbled in her handbag for a tissue and dabbed them away.

"Guy's been gambling heavily and we're in debt. We're going to have to sell."

Jesslyn had met Guy a few times and she couldn't believe a man who loved the business the way he did could gamble it all away. "There's a lien against it and if we don't sell they're going to foreclose."

"Did he always have that problem?" Jesslyn had found Guy a little reserved nothing more.

"I think so. I mean I don't think this is something he just developed. I didn't know about it until he dropped this bombshell last week."

"Could a loan help you out?"

"Probably, but I don't want one. I'm going to just let everything go."

"Trisha you can't. You love that place. It was your dream. You gave up . . ."

Trisha looked up at the ceiling. "Go ahead and say it. I gave up love for the inn."

She always felt that Jesslyn was the only one who understood that making the inn a success came before marrying Kaliq Faulkner. He simply saw it as rejection.

"Why won't you try to save it?"

"I don't know. I don't seem to have the energy to start over again. Maybe I'll just get a job as a chef. I've had several offers from people who stayed at the inn. I think I might make some calls. I've even been offered a chance to stay by the new owner."

"I can't see you doing that."

"You're right. I told him no but I don't think he's listening."

"Do you know him?"

"Yes. I met him in Paris about ten years ago. Then he was just Ernie Roman, a poor guy with a dream to have a five star hotel. Now he calls himself Rommel, and he owns several five-star hotels."

"Why does he want your place?"

"He really wants me to work for him. I've turned him down several times and I guess he felt the only way to get me to be his chef is to buy my inn."

"Why don't you want to work for him? I mean the real reason."

Trisha smiled. She should have known she couldn't fool her friend. "I'm not sure if it's the creepy feeling I get when he looks at me or the rumors that he didn't get his money in a legal manner. I heard that he was little more than a front man for a minor organized crime family."

"Ha! I knew it was something. Your instincts are telling you that this is a bad move. So why don't you fight to keep it?"

"I think it would just be a constant fight to keep him away. He'd always be there lurking in the background just as he did in Florida."

"Was he after an inn or hotel there, too?"

"No. He was after a woman. She didn't want him but after a couple of the men in her life met with accidents, she finally went out with him. She liked to play close to the danger line and he seemed more powerful than he was. After she married him, she became a recluse. She committed suicide two years ago. I always felt that he likes the chase but once you're caught he just tries to destroy you."

"Is there any real proof?"

"No. He covers his tracks pretty well. It's more of a feeling that he's doing something illegal than anything tangible."

"So what's the next step for you?"

"I don't know."

"Well, I know one thing. You can't just tell us what's happening and expect to go back to Pennsylvania without a solution or at least a couple of ideas."

"I didn't bring a change of clothes."

"Great. So we do a little shopping and then we figure out what the next thing is for you to do."

"I almost canceled this trip but something told me that I'd feel better after we talked, and I do."

Trisha slipped her boots on and the two women headed out for some Black Belt style shopping.

Palladin Rush sat in his friend's apartment while he waited for him to get ready for their outing. He'd been a little unsettled about Trisha's demeanor. Something was definitely wrong. He didn't want to interfere with his friends' lives, but he knew two people who needed to be together and were too stubborn to admit it. He reached in his pocket and pulled out his cell phone.

The phone rang four times before someone answered. "Hello," came a deep baritone voice.

"Hello, Kaliq. It's Palladin."

"Hey, what's going on? I haven't heard from you for awhile."

"The twins have been running me ragged. Jesslyn is thinking about hiring a manager and staying home with them."

"What about the nanny you hired?"

"Oh, she's still around. She's on vacation this week and I thought I could fill in."

"No such luck. I still remember what it was like with only one."

Palladin remembered how it was when Kaliq's ex-wife died and he had to take care of Brett. Of course, that was different. Brett was fifteen and not thrilled at having to answer to a man who'd been an absentee father for too long.

"How are things going?"

"Great. I hope to have another good summer session with a group of kids from New York and Chicago next year."

"Anything else on the horizon? Is Daphne still around?"

"Ah . . . No . . . She didn't like Wyoming as much as she thought she would."

"Well, gotta go. I'm taking the boys to Radio City."

"Aren't they a little young for that?"

"Why does everyone keep saying they're too young? I think they'll enjoy the music at least."

"So, when are you coming to visit?"

"Soon."

The men said goodbye and, as Palladin pocketed the cell phone, he smiled. There is only one woman for you my friend, and I think she's beginning to see that she made a bad decision four years ago, he thought.

The roar from the bedroom told him that the boys were ready to head downtown.

CHAPTER TWO

Kaliq Faulkner dropped the phone back into the cradle and ran his hand over his shaved head. Who was Palladin trying to fool? What he really wanted to know was if he was involved with anyone. That meant only one thing. Trisha Terrence was free. How? Why should he care?

He sat behind his massive cherry wood desk and laid out plans for the new addition. Every year since the camp opened he'd expanded the number of boys he could take for the summer. His first group of ten boys arrived two days after they got out of school. Some had never been away from home before and he'd had to deal with a few homesick cases. The falcons eventually won the hearts of all the boys. He'd sent them back to the concrete environment with a new impression of what life could be. He'd also taught them how important the environment should be in their lives.

Only two of the boys had not returned. One had gotten into trouble with the police and could not leave the state. The other boy's family had moved south and he was busy adjusting to another life. He'd written Kaliq that he hoped to come back the next summer. Kaliq tried to concentrate on the papers on his desk but flashes of Trisha interrupted him.

Palladin didn't even have to mention her name, he hadn't realized how much he'd still missed Trisha. She'd been in his life for such a brief time, yet she left an indelible mark on his memories. He'd pushed her to the back of his brain each time he'd been reminded of her. Now his old friend's phone call was making him disregard something he'd learned early in life. The best way to deal with pain was to push it to the back of your mind. Don't bring it out until you could deal with it. Don't bring it out until you could analyze it.

In the four years since he'd seen her, he'd done that with Trisha Terrence. There had been other women in his life but none stayed too long. The ranch took up too much of his time and he had very little left for any other commitment.

Trisha had been different from anyone he'd ever met. She was sure of herself and her goals and wouldn't let anything stop her. He'd had women who wanted the thrill of being involved with a man in a wheelchair. Little antennas told him almost immediately how women saw him. Some were more secretive than others. He could see everything from pity to curiosity in their eyes.

Some women considered him a "trophy" date.

They'd show how good they could be to someone less fortunate. Kaliq had run the gamut of those women. He'd learned to separate the women who wanted just fun and games and the ones who were serious.

Then he'd met Trisha Terrance and found she didn't fit into any mold. She created her own style and he loved it. No! He loved her. If she needed help he'd be there, but he wasn't going to let her know he loved her because he wasn't going to go through the pain of losing her a second time.

As long as she was safe and secure, Kaliq knew that Palladin wouldn't have said anything. She was in trouble and he could help. He just had to find a way to do it without getting involved again.

She was a stubborn woman and probably didn't even want his help.

But a friend sometimes needed to bulldoze his way into helping, whether the person wanted it or not.

That's what had happened to him. After Palladin dragged him kicking and screaming to the rehabilitation center, Kaliq found out there were things he could still do without the use of his legs.

He'd learned to push past the self-pity and get on with the rest of his life. One of the most interesting things he'd learned was that the type of wheelchair you selected sent out several signals. Most men preferred the ones without arms. The wheelchairs that they controlled by pushing the wheels rather than using the motorized panel were a status symbol. The less help the chair gave you the better you felt about being whole.

Kaliq developed into a fair basketball player, but the one thing he loved most was being a falconer.

He'd returned to Wyoming to a sullen sixteen-year-old son who blamed him for almost everything and a dilapidated ranch that consisted of a two-bedroom main house and everything you needed for training falcons.

It had been his dream to bring inner city kids out to see another side of life. Unfortunately, at that time, that dream collided with love when he met Trisha Terrence. She did not pity him or pretend that he wasn't in a wheelchair. She was the chef at this tiny inn in Pennsylvania. They'd met because he'd chosen to stay there rather than with Palladin and Jesslyn. At the time, Jesslyn was suffering from amnesia and was the focus of an investigation involving industrial espionage. Kaliq was charmed by Trisha and they started seeing each other. Why couldn't it have worked?

He pushed his wheelchair over to the window and stared out at the new bunkhouse being built for his expanding summer retreat. How many times had Palladin tried to get him to call her? How many times had Kaliq picked up the phone to do just that? The timing had been wrong for them since the time they'd met. Each of them had a dream. Kaliq wanted the ranch opened so he could teach falconry to inner city kids. He'd grown closer to Brett and he didn't want to lose that. His dream was in Wyoming.

Trisha's dream was in Pennsylvania. She'd been the executive chef at a country inn and was about to invest in her own Bed & Breakfast establishment. It was something she'd been dreaming about since returning from Paris.

Two dreams so opposite and so attainable it would have been wrong for either of them to put that dream on a back burner. He still disliked the way he handled it. He'd asked her to give up her dream because his was closer to fruition. She'd done the only thing she could. She'd refused.

Now perhaps she'd accomplished what she wanted and Palladin thought there was still a chance for them. Kaliq had never been able to think of Trisha without remembering the first time they'd made love.

They'd gone to a fund raiser in New York and then instead of driving her home as they'd planned, they dropped off Palladin and Jesslyn and checked into a hotel.

The next day when the limousine took them to Pennsylvania, they stopped at Trisha's house. She had chosen not to live in the inn although they had offered her a small studio apartment. She had a little bungalow about ten minutes away.

She took his coat, hung it in the closet, and gave him a mini tour of her house. They both liked the open floor plan. There was one large space on the lower level that was the living room, dining room, and kitchen. The master bedroom was upstairs but there was a guest bedroom on the first level.

The cozy little house was filled with books. There were mostly cookbooks but Kaliq spotted a few *New York Times* bestsellers on the shelf. She tended to like mysteries and thrillers. The biggest surprise had been her food choices. Instead of being loaded with gourmet goodies, she had a pretty good staple of junk food, like jams, peanut butter, cookies, and potato chips.

"I know what you're thinking. How can I cook all

those fancy dishes for the hotel and not for me? When I'm in a restaurant I tend to dissect the menu but only because I'm thinking of the guests at the inn. I guess fast food is what I missed most living in Paris," she explained.

"Guy says the same thing."

"Guy?"

"My future business partner. I told you about him. We met in Paris and then a couple of years ago he got a job in a restaurant in Pennsylvania. He looked me up and we started hanging out together."

"Just 'hanging out'?"

"Yes! He's a friend and, as I said, a future business partner. Nothing more."

Trisha said it with such finality that he didn't question it any further. She was sitting in a chair next to him so their faces were close together. Spending the night together had not abated the need he felt to be close to her. He wanted to kiss her, in fact he'd been aching to do that since they first entered the house. He couldn't resist the lure of her full cranberry-colored lips. He touched his mouth gently to hers almost as a test. When she didn't pull away he knew that she wanted it as much as he did.

Trisha's mouth was soft, inviting, and he wondered how many kisses it would take to end his hunger. Something inside of him said there wasn't enough time in the world.

With a low groan Kaliq pulled back. This was always an awkward moment for him. He turned his chair so he could face her completely and crushed her lips with a hard kiss that tried to pull the essence of her to him so he could know just what would make her happy. She tasted like a fresh, slightly tart fruit. Sweet enough to want more, spicy enough to savor, and somewhat forbidden.

Driven by need, he slid his lips from hers and traced the silky texture of her cheeks. He was taken by the smooth, clear, tan skin that was as beautiful up close as it was across a room.

Trisha uttered a small cry of pleasure as she curled her arms around his neck. That caused a burning flare to streak through his loins.

She then stood up and walked behind his chair. She pushed and when it didn't move, she glanced down at him. He lifted the brake and allowed her to push him into the guest bedroom. She didn't turn on the lights. The window was open and the half moon provided all the light he needed.

Once there, Trisha slipped into the adjoining bathroom tossing out a line about getting into something comfortable. This gave Kaliq the time to take his clothes off and get into bed. It wasn't a disparaging move but one that she probably made with any man the first time they were together. It was a little break to give them both the time they needed to take the next step in their relationship.

When she returned, wearing a short hot pink satin nightgown that barely reached her knees. They both had made a decision that this was a serious move and one they both wanted.

"You are one beautiful woman, Trisha Terrence," he said as he watched her climb into bed next to him.

He pulled her over so she lay across his chest. He stroked her neck, then let his mouth follow the same path as his hand, only now with biting kisses.

Breathing raggedly he pulled her the rest of the

way so she lay on top of him. He dug his fingers into her hair and kissed her deeply, parting her lips with his tongue and feeling a desire unlike ever before.

Her soft moans urged him on and he plunged deeper into the ecstacy swirling around them. His hands meandered over her back and down to her thighs. The nightgown fell toward her waist leaving her honey-colored skin bathed in the light from the moon and the open bathroom door.

The satiny feel of her skin under his calloused fingers lit a fire in his body, and the demanding desire to know her in the truest sense of the word pushed him on. He stroked her hips, thighs, and then lifted her body on top of his.

She was slightly startled by his upper body strength but didn't withdraw from the intimate contact. Instead, she sought his mouth with hers.

He imagined he was like one of his falcons who had flown as high as he could and now was swooping back to earth, free falling through the sky without regard to how he would land.

As passion consumed them they learned every inch of each other's bodies. He followed her whispers of desire and tried to kiss her until the raging fire inside cooled, but to no avail. Each kiss carried him to a more passionate plane until once again it was raging out of control.

His breath was reduced to gasps and his body covered with a thin sheen of perspiration as he continued in his determination to bring Trisha to the same level of ecstasy he had attained. They were perfect partners for each other. Each was so intent on giving that it accelerated the pleasure until he lifted her up and shifted his body so he could bury himself in her warmth.

She slid gently to his side and put her arm across his chest. She let her other hand caress his face and his shaved head. "I love the way black men are beginning to cut their hair off. I think it gives you a look of strength and character."

He showed strong white teeth when he grinned. "Think so? Some people find the look a little intimidating."

"Sure they do. Remember when men started wearing dreads? There were people who thought there was going to be blood in the streets. They thought they were revolutionaries bent on overthrowing the government."

"My buddy wears them and you're right about intimidating."

"But you decided to go in the other direction."

"That's true. I did it because my traveling was just too much to get a decent haircut so it was easier to just cut it all off."

They lay there talking, loving and Kaliq thought it might be the start of a major occurrence in his life. It was true on one hand, but not exactly the major change he'd wanted.

Kaliq was still sitting there an hour later when Brett came in. His son had grown several inches in four years. At twenty, he now stood six feet one inch and weighed one hundred and eighty pounds that was all muscle.

"What's up, Pops?"

"A little blast from the past. I just talked to Palladin. Stop calling me Pops."

"What's wrong with 'Pops'?"

"Nothing's wrong with it. I just don't like it."

"Oh, do these testy feelings have anything to do with your call from New York? Is something wrong?"

"He didn't say. I got the feeling he was on a fishing expedition. He wanted to know about Daphne."

Brett shook his head. He'd known from the minute she arrived that life away from a city wasn't for her. He had to admit she'd tried hard but she was a city girl through and through. She was a counselor visiting the ranch to see if perhaps more boys could stay there and Kaliq could even get financial aid.

Brett had hoped she'd be right for his father. They'd had a commuter relationship for a short period, but a winter in Wyoming had stopped the romance from going any further. They still talked about the boys that were eligible for the camp, but as colleagues not lovers.

She'd suggested that he get government funding so he could expand faster, but Kaliq knew that if the government got involved it would mean an incredible amount of paperwork and bureaucracy. He'd rather deal directly with the parents and churches.

It would be similar to the Fresh Air Fund that took Black kids off city streets for the summer and sent them to live in Vermont with white families, as they tried to promote a better understanding of the races and different lifestyles. It started out with good intentions, but like most government programs that helped the poor, it died out.

"I think he's tired of me being a bachelor."

"You think he's matchmaking?" Brett asked on his way to the kitchen.

"Yeah. It sounded as if Trisha Terrence may be in trouble."

"Who?" Brett stopped and turned around. "Oh no. Don't tell me he thinks you and Trisha Terrence might get back together."

"Brett, you were sixteen when I met her."

"Right, and just because I'm twenty now you think I don't remember how you came back here. You were like a deflated balloon."

"It wasn't an easy decision for either of us."

"She picked her career over you."

"I picked my career over her," Kaliq countered. "One day you'll understand."

"Oh no! Don't start that 'when you fall in love' lecture."

"Okay, okay. I won't. But when it happens to you I'm going to say I told you so."

Father and son had spent a great deal of time talking during the long winters. Brett was aware that Trisha had cast some kind of spell over his father. All the women since Trisha had been compared to her in some way. Yet once she chose her career over his father, Brett thought that was the end of it.

"What happened to her?"

"I don't know. He didn't say anything about Trisha exactly but I know it's something to do with her."

"Don't get your hopes up. Even if she does want to try again, she might be like Daphne."

"I know. It takes a certain kind of woman to adopt the lifestyle of Taharqa."

He'd named his ranch after the Nubian ruler. Taharqa had controlled the largest empire in ancient

Africa for twenty-five years. Brett always told the story
of the warrior to the kids at the camp when they first
arrived. Hopefully it relieved some of the fear and
anxiety of being away from home. Kaliq and Brett
knew that the kids would never admit the fear. He'd
started out with ten inner-city boys and now he hoped
to bring thirty. Two of the older boys would be
returning as temporary ranch hands.

It had been a good life but there was one thing
missing. That special woman still eluded both father
and son.

"Do you think he's right this time?" Brett knew
that there would always be a special place in his
father's heart for Trisha Terrence. He also knew that
if she came here and couldn't stay, that would be the
last hope. Not many women could handle a relationship with a man that couldn't walk. His father was a
special man and he deserved a special woman. Brett
wasn't convinced that Trisha was that woman.

A wave of terror floated over Guy Marshall as he
climbed the stairs to Rommel's office. He'd seen what
could happen to people who tried to squeeze out of
a deal with the man. He couldn't believe he'd been
stupid enough to get caught in the trap. Once before
he'd managed to outwit the loan shark who now
called himself a hotelier. If Rommel ever found out
about that he'd disappear from the face of the earth.

His mind was still fuzzy from all the drinking he'd
done since Rommel had called him. He'd managed
to get himself in a cab and up the stairs to the reception area where he'd been waiting twenty minutes.

At last a secretary appeared and ushered him into

the inner sanctum of Rommel's office. It was paneled in dark, rich wood and had a gas burning fireplace. Above the fireplace was a portrait of a beautiful Black woman wearing a dark green dress and holding long-stemmed red roses. He knew it was Rommel's late wife. He also knew that the portrait wasn't hanging there because of love. She'd been the man's first conquest. She, like Trisha, had said no to him, but he wooed her until she finally went out with him. She turned against her family to marry him and then he treated her like yesterday's news. She'd reportedly committed suicide, but Guy had his doubts. He was smart enough to keep those doubts to himself.

Rows of books lined the shelves and from talking to Rommel, Guy knew he'd read most of them. He prided himself on being a strategist. That's why he was successful.

Rommel entered from a hidden door next to the bookshelves. "So I understand that you want to find a way to keep me from taking over Carlotta's."

"I just want to see if we can work something out. Trisha's worked so hard to get this place . . ."

"And now she's about to lose it because of your gambling debts. I see you're still wearing that bishop. So guilt is pushing you to try to be a knight on a white charger and ride in and rescue the lady. Well forget about it."

"But she . . ." Guy thought about the bishop he wore around his neck. One time in Paris, Rommel had beaten a Grand Master at chess. Rommel had holes bored into the chess piece and had worn it around his neck.

When Guy had beaten Rommel by sacrificing the queen and using the bishop to win, he'd done the same thing as Rommel. He still wore it. He'd even given Trisha one like it for a good luck piece.

"I don't care. If she wants the place she can have it under my terms."

"She doesn't want to work for you . . . or anyone."

"That's what she says now. You know what I think? I'm betting she wants that place more than you think she does."

Guy shook his head. "She's going to just walk away from it."

"Nonsense. It's a perfect business for her."

"Not working for you."

Rommel laughed. "If this is all you came up here for, I suggest you get out. Your speech is so slurred now I can hardly understand you."

His secretary buzzed him and he saw the light on the phone blinking. He ignored it as he continued to tell Guy how easy it had been to get his markers. The secretary buzzed him again and he snatched up the phone.

"What is it?" he barked. He waited a beat then said, "Send him in."

The man who entered was well over six feet and weighed about two hundred fifty pounds. He was almost meek as he approached Rommel, a man just six feet and a solid one hundred seventy-five pounds.

"I can't believe he ended up in the hospital. If this is how he makes collections for me, I'm going to get someone else."

Rommel pushed something on his desk and checked it before walking over to the fireplace. He tapped the painting of his wife and it clicked open. He turned the dial until the safe clicked and then he pulled out a stack of hundred dollar bills. He peeled several off and gave them to the man who left quickly. Rommel peeled off a few more hundreds and tossed them to Guy. They fell on the floor and he grabbed them up.

"Get yourself together and find a way to convince your partner that working for me isn't so bad." He returned the rest of the money to the safe and closed it. He pushed the painting back in place.

"She didn't have it so bad," he said about his wife. "Until she thought she could leave before I told her she could."

Guy nodded and stuffed the money in his pockets. He started for the door but turned back. "You can't blame me if she still says no. I'll see what I can do but you can't blame me."

Rommel watched the man depart. He hated weaklings and yet he thrived on them. They were what made life interesting. All those people who had all the chances, education, and money never learned how to survive.

He waited for his next victim. She opened the door and came in. She was the kind of woman that turned heads. Men wished she could be theirs; women wished they had her looks. She was tall and slender, but not the skinny model style. She had curves in all the right places. The royal blue dress hugged those curves and her makeup was flawless. She was everything most men wanted. He'd met her in London and paid for her to come to the States. She'd gotten a few modeling jobs and a commercial but her career hadn't taken off because of her high pitched voice. The commercial she made didn't call for a speaking part. She'd been after Rommel to get her an acting coach but the novelty was wearing off and he planned to ship her back to England. He wasn't put off by her voice; for Rommel she had only one flaw. She wasn't Trisha Terrence.

Trisha sat in the huge blue crushed velvet chair in Jesslyn's den thinking what a difference a few hours could make. Last night she was going through her usual routine and then her world started to collapsed on her a little more. Last night all she could think about was a hot bath and getting some sleep.

She'd gone through her usual routine of applying cold cream to her face and then climbing into her bath. She let the steam from the tub help the cream bring out the impurities in her skin. She soaked her body in the hot water. She'd never been able to take a bath in tepid water even though her friends warned her about making her skin dry.

Her only guests had left at noon and since none were expected, she'd left early. The night clerk would handle any unexpected visitors and give her a call if she were needed. It had been weeks since she'd been needed.

After a busy day she'd turn the Jacuzzi on and let the pulsing spray beat out the kinks of stress in her body. Tonight she just wanted to get clean and climb into bed.

She dried herself off on a bath sheet and slipped into a long, black silky nightgown.

Only the lamp by the bed was on. As she walked to the bed she was aware something nagged at her brain. She didn't know what it was but it had to do with Carlotta's.

Trisha remembered how she'd selected the name

of the inn. She'd been living in Paris and her mother took her to see an old Alfred Hitchcock movie called "Vertigo." To Trisha's mind the most exotic character in the movie was named Carlotta. She fell in love with the name. Years later when she saw the movie, she was old enough to understand that Carlotta's story was a figment of the villain's imagination but Trisha still loved the name. She tossed and turned and eventually found a comfortable spot in the queen-size bed.

Trisha lay in bed thinking about her dream and the problems that now surrounded it.

She'd made the inn a picturesque setting in the mountains and she was proud of the achievement. If necessary, she could do it all again. Trisha was confident in her ability to survive. What hurt her the most was that she had walked away from love to carve out this dream and now it was gone.

There was no way she'd borrow the money to pay off Guy's debts and there was no way she'd stay and work for Rommel. There had to be another way.

She drifted off to sleep hoping to have the answer when she awakened.

Guy stumbled down the stairs. If Rommel insinuated himself into Trisha's life she'd just become a trinket. How could he let the best thing that ever happened to him get caught in Rommel's web?

It was true that she loved the inn but she had too much respect for herself to be lured into Rommel's trap. He had to find a way to stop him or get Trisha enough money to fight him off. The man had spies everywhere. How else did he end up with his markers?

He staggered out of the club and got in a cab. An hour later he was sketched across his bed sleeping off the liquor. Something had happened when he was in the office with Rommel. Something important that could solve all their problems had happened but he just couldn't remember what it was.

At three in the morning he awakened. His head felt as if there were men with jack hammers tearing up the ground. The pounding was unbearable. He fumbled his way to the bathroom and opened the medicine chest.

He smiled at the large bottle marked "aspirin" but the smile faded when he picked it up and shook it. It was too light to contain what he needed. He opened the bottle and dumped the two remaining tablets in his hand. Then he remembered that he was supposed to buy a new supply before he went to Rommel's.

Guy turned on the faucet and let it run as he tossed the pills in his mouth, then bent down and drank the water straight from the faucet. He turned the water off and went back to bed.

He slept for ten hours. The next time he awoke the headache was still there, but not as painful as before. He took a cold shower, dressed in sweats, and went out for his morning jog. He thought about calling Trisha but he didn't want to talk to her until he had a plan in place to get them out of this mess.

During his jog he remembered what Rommel had done the night before. The man couldn't remember numbers. He always had them written somewhere. The night before when he opened the safe he'd checked his desk first. Guy would bet money that was where the combination to the safe was written. He'd also bet that all his markers were in that safe, along with the phony loan papers. Without them, he could deny the "loan" and Rommel would no longer have a hold on Carlotta's.

He showered and dressed. He had to see Trisha. He had to tell her that there was a way out.

Trisha had awakened excited about going to work until she remembered. Her days owning Carlotta's were numbered. She showered and dressed and headed for the inn.

Once there she pulled out all the records. Something had been bothering her about the cancellations. She thumbed through a few of them and decided to call a few.

"Mrs. Wilson?" she asked and then continued once the woman confirmed she was Mrs. Wilson. "I'm calling from Carlotta's Inn . . ."

"Oh yes. How are the renovations coming? We were sorry to hear that we couldn't spend another weekend there."

"The renovations?"

"Yes. That's what the letter said, that you were remodeling."

"So you did enjoy your stay with us?"

"Absolutely. Please keep me on your mailing list."

"I certainly will."

Trisha dropped the receiver in the cradle. So that was the reason for the cancellations. People thought the inn was being remodeled.

She checked the time of Mrs. Wilson's call to make the reservation. Trisha walked out to the reservation desk and spoke with the clerk. Julie was working her way through college and had been the detail oriented person to handle the reservations for Carlotta's since they opened.

"I was just reviewing the cancellations. They seemed to have called while you were on duty. Did they say anything?"

"No ma'am. They just said they couldn't make it or that their plans changed."

"Really, I just spoke with Mrs. Wilson." Trisha put the registration card down in front of Julie.

The girl stepped back. "I didn't think it would be a problem. I mean we always have people coming by and we're always full."

"Just what does that mean? Why did you tell the woman we were renovating?"

"He said that nothing would happen to you. He said that a couple of people cancelling wouldn't hurt your business."

"Who said it?"

"Mr. Rommel. He just asked me to call five people and tell them there was a sudden need to renovate and to call in a couple of months."

"What did he offer you to do this?"

"Enough money to pay for a full year's tuition."

"Julie, don't you understand that it was wrong?"

"I know ma'am, but I needed the money. There aren't any jobs around that will let me continue school and pay enough for me to live on. Am I fired?"

"No. I'll tell you this. Mr. Rommel will probably be the new owner of Carlotta's. I'd suggest you start looking for a new job right away."

"But, he said you'd still be here."

"He was wrong. Unlike some people, I can't be bought. Oh, don't think you're getting off easy because I'm not going to fire you. I'll bet most businesses around here will be skeptical about hiring you. I guess you didn't look any further than the money. Rommel likes loyalty. You sold me out and he's going to know that for the right price you'll do the same to him."

Trisha returned to her office. Minutes later Julie knocked on the door and handed a hastily jotted resignation and the keys to the front door. Trisha looked around her office. How many others would be ruined just because Rommel wanted this place?

Guy had warned her of Rommel's infatuation but Trisha had ignored it. She'd given up the most precious offer a woman could get, a man's heart, for Carlotta's, so why did Rommel think he could win now?

Trisha ran her hand through her hair. How many ways had Rommel tried to take the inn away from her? He had the papers Guy had signed requesting a loan. He'd gotten Julie to refuse reservations or contact people and cancel them.

She was deep in thought over her next move when Guy burst in the door.

"I think I found a way to get the money," he said. "I can get us out of this mess."

"Guy, we're not going to borrow from our friends."

"No. I have another way. I'm going to try it tonight and tomorrow we'll know."

She didn't want to dampen his enthusiasm so she simply nodded.

"Where's Julie?"

"She resigned. It seems that she'd been telling people that Carlotta's is under renovation and that's why we haven't had guests for awhile."

"The little . . ."

"Now, now, don't get bent out of shape. I told her Rommel would not appreciate disloyalty and she decided to leave."

"Why didn't you just kick her out?"

"I didn't have the energy."

"Well, she's lucky I wasn't here. Don't worry, we can hire someone else. I promise you in a couple of days we'll have enough money to pay off all our debts."

"I'm still going to New York. Jesslyn and I have a monthly shopping trip that I'm not going to give up."

"That's right. I forgot you were going this weekend. I'll see you when you get back."

So now, here she was. The shopping trip had been canceled and she'd poured out her soul to Jesslyn. She just hoped that Guy wouldn't do anything foolish and get them into any more trouble. She tried not to think about the past but it kept sneaking into her thoughts. What would have happened if she'd gone to Wyoming?

Kaliq Faulkner sat on the mountain. He held Namid on his arm. The falcon was still hooded. He'd learned this in a falconry school he'd attended. First he was just going to write an article but then he became so interested he stayed a few more days. The course began with just identifying the types of birds of prey. It was an all day course and he never imagined how it would change his life.

He wanted the same things for inner-city boys. Too many of the young, Black brothers were ending up in jail or dead. He had to find a way to show them other options.

The camp started with ten boys and now he was expanding. He really wanted to see thirty to fifty boys attending during the summer. Maybe there would be other types of camps that would get more of them out of the city and into a new way of thinking.

He took the hood off Namid and cast him in the air just by lifting his arm. It amazed him how the eyes could be so sharp from such heights. The bird would fly into the clouds, or so it seemed, then spot its quarry, swoop down from the sky to the ground, and grab a grouse or partridge or duck. Then it would swoop back to the sky making that strange sound called kakking.

This was a contribution he had to make. He wanted to build a place for inner city boys. One he promised to do if he ever got out of that Mideastern prison. When Palladin showed up he knew his prayers had been answered, but he also knew that he had to make good on his promise to do something for someone else. Something for kids so they knew there was a life outside of tall buildings and concrete sidewalks.

He was almost there when Trisha Terrence entered his life. She was a special woman but he'd made a promise to a higher power. Now he had fulfilled that promise and would continue to do so; but if Trisha Terrence was available, as that call from Palladin had led him to believe, then maybe he could have the best of both worlds.

CHAPTER THREE

At eight in the morning Guy woke up and pulled himself into a cold shower. As the water beat down on him, he remembered what Rommel had done. It was a simple quirk. Most people wouldn't even notice something unusual about what he did. However, for Guy and Trisha it might be the answer they needed to make Rommel get out of their lives forever. He wrapped a towel around him and went to the bedroom. He dressed in jeans and a bulky sweater. He didn't want to look too different from the rest of the people who would be at the restaurant. He wanted to blend in and the lunch crowd wasn't driven by fashion or expecting to be caught by some paparazzi style photographer. Casual wear was the way the crowd dressed; it wouldn't make him stand out. He went to the kitchen and scrambled two eggs, made some toast and a pot of coffee. He wished he could sit out on the terrace but the temperature wouldn't allow it. They were going to have an early winter for sure. He read the paper from the first page to the last as he killed time, waiting for Rommel to be wide awake when he made his call.

He finished breakfast and dropped the dishes into the dishwasher.

It was a quarter after ten when he finally made the call. Rommel's secretary put him through the third degree before transferring him.

"So, what's up?" Rommel asked.

"I just wanted you to know that Trisha decided not to cancel her shopping trip to New York. I won't have a chance to talk to her."

"So?"

"Since we don't have any guests, she might decide to stay longer."

"That's not good. I want this over quickly."

"So do I. I need you to help me get her back."

"And what am I supposed to do?"

"Call your real estate agent and tell her you don't want the inn."

"Are you still drunk or is the hangover frying your brain?"

"No, listen," Guy said desperately. "If she thinks you aren't going to buy it, she'll come back fast so she can see if you'll let her pay off my loan."

"Okay. So I get her back here, what then?"

"I talk her into working for you."

"Can you guarantee that?"

"Yes. I can guarantee it."

"Well, I'll just make that call. But if you're lying and trying to pull a fast one, I'll . . ."

"You don't have to say it. Believe me I've got a plan that's foolproof."

Guy hung up and breathed a sigh of relief. He was going to lead Rommel into a trap. He knew the man would be out on the town, hitting some after hours places in Pennsylvania and New Jersey. While he was having fun, Guy would use the time to put together a crushing defeat. It was another chess game. Only this time, Guy was a pawn who had been used to capture the queen. Since the best laid plans can go astray, Guy saw it as the pawn capturing the king and beating Rommel at his own game.

Trisha selected a couple of nightgowns, underwear, a sweater, and a pair of slacks. She couldn't believe that she and Jesslyn still ended up on a shopping trip. She'd felt so down when she told her friend about her problems and now she felt as if a weight had been lifted from her shoulders.

Maybe what she really needed to do was just tell the whole story to someone. Once it was released to the universe, she could go on with her life.

She watched as Jesslyn picked up something for the twins and a couple of dress shirts for Palladin. Trisha felt a twinge of envy that Jesslyn seemed to have everything she wanted. That feeling evaporated as she remembered it had not come easy for her either. There was actually a time when it seemed that the two would never get together. But they had chosen each other over their careers and found a middle ground that worked. She and Kaliq had chosen their careers and now hers was a shambles. She didn't have a career or a man and she didn't know which hurt the most.

"Do you want to take a bus man's holiday and eat in a restaurant?" Jesslyn asked.

"No. I'd rather just go back to your place and see if you can think of a way to sort out this mess I've gotten myself into."

It was shortly after seven when they returned and, after putting away their purchases, sat in the den with large cups of hot chocolate that Trisha whipped up.

"You always seem to come up with a different recipe for cocoa."

"I don't know why. I think it's just fun to do something with chocolate. When I go to restaurants, I just look around to see what I'd do differently, even with burgers and fries. I noticed you bought some very fancy shirts for Palladin; anything important coming up for you guys?"

"No. It's not really a big event. We have to attend a couple of political fund raisers. No matter how we try to avoid them, something always comes up and we have to show our support for one candidate or another."

"I remember that's how we met."

"Right. Kaliq convinced you to come to New York and then I got amnesia."

"Do you know he never told me right away? He just said you'd been in an accident and didn't want to see anyone. I could understand that."

"Remember that awful scene I made when I thought Palladin was going to end everything?"

"You didn't make a scene. We just got a little tipsy and spouted some strange statements."

"Have you added any more chess sets to your collection?"

"No. The last one I did was for Carlotta's. The pieces are all five feet tall and the patio is designed as a chess board. I'm not sure if I should tear it all up before the new owners take over and probably make it the main attraction. Guy gave me this." She indicated the bishop hanging from a chain around her neck. "It was supposed to be a good luck charm to celebrate the success of Carlotta's Inn."

"How much trouble are you in?"

Trisha felt the tears rise as she thought about their plans. "I don't know what to do next. It's not the money. I could probably come up with the money. It's just that Rommel wants to humiliate us. Oh great. I didn't check my phone messages."

She went into the closet and pulled out her phone from her tote bag. She pressed the button to retrieve the messages. The first three were from Guy, each sounding more frantic, asking her to call him right away. The next message was from Rommel. He apologized for the change in plans.

"What does he mean?" Jesslyn asked.

"I can't imagine." Trisha frowned as she pressed the button to automatically dial Guy's number. He picked up on the first ring.

"Guy. It's me. What's going on?"

A fuzzy voice muttered several swear words and then came in clear as crystal. "Rommel isn't going to buy Carlotta's."

"What? Why not?"

"Because I can't guarantee that you'll be part of the package."

"That's crazy. He knew that all along."

"Yeah, but what he did was scare off all the other buyers."

"He wants us to go bankrupt!"

"Exactly."

"Well, we'll just have to think of something. We can't let him do this."

"I'm going to talk to him. I'll let you know what happens."

"Don't make any deals with him. I'd rather lose everything than work for him."

Trisha cut the connection. "Rommel is trying to ruin us. First he's the buyer with the best offer and now that he's scared the other buyers off. He's saying he doesn't want to complete the deal."

"So maybe you should try to save Carlotta's on your own."

"No way. I'm not going to let you and Palladin bail me out of this one. Actually, I think that's what Rommel wants."

"I don't get it."

"If he can't buy on his terms he wants us to borrow the money and he's probably got a hundred other ways to ruin our business."

"That sounds like a vendetta, but why?"

"He's carried on a campaign to get me to work for him," Trisha explained. "If he can't have that he'll ruin my business. I would rather sell to anyone else. I put out a few feelers with a real estate agent when I needed to come up with the money to pay off Guy's gambling debt."

"Any offers?" Jesslyn asked.

"I thought I had a few. Three agents were so high on the place I thought one of them would buy it.

Several seemed to be interested, two made an offer then withdrew it.''

"You think Rommel had something to do with that?''

"Absolutely.''

"Any proof?'

"Not yet. It's not only that he wants me to work for him he's mad at Guy for beating him at chess. The man is simply a nut case.''

"Guy bought me the chess piece necklace after he won a match from Rommel. High stakes and a lot of pride were on the line, and Rommel is not a good loser.''

"Are you telling me that there is a vendetta over a chess match? Trisha, that sounds too crazy.''

"I know, but the man is crazy. It's too late for me to leave now but I'm going back early tomorrow. Guy's been trying to keep me out of this showdown but I think I need to be there.''

"Let Palladin go with you.''

"No, I don't want to get you involved.''

"We're your friends and we were involved the minute this person tried to ruin you, whether we knew about it or not. Palladin's definitely going with you.''

Despite her bravado, Trisha was glad that Jesslyn insisted that Palladin go with her. They had been good friends and she trusted him to look into this. If she was mistaken about Rommel then maybe he could see that. Or if this was a "guy thing" Palladin could convince the man to back down and leave her alone. Whatever happened, she would have some help making her next step. She just wouldn't accept financial help from them.

*   *   *

"Where is she, Guy?"

"She went to New York to see a friend."

"Oh, really. Maybe this friend has enough money to bail you out?"

They stood in the two-story foyer that once welcomed their guests. The inn had been closed for two weeks. The truth was that since Rommel decided he wanted Carlotta's, only four couples had kept their reservations, and Trisha and Guy needed to regroup.

"No. I called her about you pulling out of the deal and she said she was coming back. She probably will just spend the night."

"You said she would run back. New York is only ninety minutes away. So why isn't she here, Guy?"

Rommel ran his fingers down the lapels of his navy pinstripe Armani suit. His dark brown skin was flawless and he prided himself on how good he looked. He'd come a long way from the streets of Chicago to reinvent himself in the style of the Prohibition Age gangsters whom he watched on movie screens. He wasn't a tall man, but neither was the actor James Cagney, as he often said, but the man demanded respect. He knew it was movie magic but he wanted to be a part of it and he knew the men with the money in his neighborhood were on the other side of the law. It didn't bother him.

He'd taken great pains to dress for this auspicious occasion and the person he wanted to impress the most wasn't even there. He glanced over at the two men who accompanied him everywhere. He referred to them as business associates but most people knew they were simply hired muscle who enforced Rommel's will on many other business owners. They rarely spoke but were menacing enough without talking.

"Think she's putting together a deal there?"

"No. She wouldn't do that. She said she's not going to fight you."

"So why did she go to New York?"

"She does this once a month. She and her friend spend the day shopping and then she comes home."

"What time do you expect her?"

"I don't know. Really, man, she does this all the time."

"I thought you said my phone call would shake her up. What's going on here?"

"Her friends probably encouraged her to spend the night."

"Don't play with me, Guy. I don't want to have to get ugly."

"You won't. My plan will work; just wait."

Rommel watched as beads of sweat formed on Guy's forehead. He loved to see fear in his opponents. His whole reason for being here was to see Trisha's reaction to defeat. She'd spoiled it. He'd just have to wait a little while longer.

"You do understand that she is part of this package?"

"I'm not the one to make that decision."

"I think you can be most influential over the lady."

"You took her dream; she wanted a place like this since she was a kid."

"Then you make sure she stays around for a while or . . ."

"You can't blame me if she doesn't want to stay. I'm just trying to ease her into working for someone.

It's hard when you've only been working for your-self."

"Did you ever wonder who took that money, when you worked for me?"

"Lots of times, but it wasn't me."

"You bought the inn."

"I didn't take it. Trisha had money from her par-ents. She was a respected chef. She still gets offers from restaurants all over the world. She might take one of those jobs."

"She won't be able to get another job as a chef anywhere. I'll see to that. If you don't persuade the lady to hang around, it might not be healthy for you. I'll stop by tomorrow to see Trisha. So throw a scare into the lady or whatever you have to do."

"Let's go," he said to his men.

As soon as they left, Guy made another call to Trisha. She was so angry and she blamed him for what had happened. He told her not to worry, that he'd fix it, but he didn't think she was convinced. He knew that would get her back fast. Once he could talk to her face to face, he was sure he could convince her that Rommel would never let go and that the best thing for them to do would be to find a hiding place.

There was one more thing that Guy knew would hurt Rommel. He had to take something very pre-cious from him and he knew just how to do it. Trisha wouldn't approve so he just wouldn't tell her. This would probably make the man lose it. He'd blame one of his bodyguards. Yeah. The more Guy thought about his little plan the more he knew he was going to do it. Even if he could never tell anyone. He was going to steal Rommel's little nest egg.

Guy went to the safe hidden behind the bar and pulled out his passport and a bankbook. The fifty thousand dollars he had skimmed from Rommel was still drawing interest, and he still had the bearer bonds. This seemed to be the time to take the money and run, but not before he secured the inn for Trisha.

He drove back to the hotel Rommel used as a command center. He parked a few blocks away and then slipped in with a group heading for a party at the hotel. He'd picked up Rommel's schedule while mingling with the lunch crowd. He knew Rommel would go home and change his clothes before coming back to the office and he'd pick up his latest girlfriend. He'd seen the man do this so many times he knew he couldn't fail.

Guy waited near the door to the restaurant and when he saw the lobby was clear he dashed upstairs and slipped into Rommel's office. His secretary had gone home, of course. Guy spent a few minutes fumbling around the secretary's desk before he found the key to the office. He went to the desk and pulled out the leaf that would usually support a computer, but Rommel didn't have one. It was there. Rommel always had trouble remembering numbers and when he opened the flap before he opened the safe it finally clicked in Guy's brain that that was where he put the combination to the safe.

He tapped on the frame of the picture and it snapped open. He had a feeling the ex-wife would approve of what he was doing. He opened the safe. His eyes widened at the contents and found the tray of beautiful little diamonds. Something better than loan notes and markers. He emptied them into his pocket and closed the safe.

As he locked up and put the key back at the secretary's desk he heard someone coming up the stairs. He rushed back in front of the door and knocked loudly. "I need to see you, Rommel." He banged on the door again.

"Hey, what's the matter with you?" one of Rommel's bodyguards called. "He's not here. Get off that door."

"But I've got to see him. I've got to tell him that I can take care of my part." He slurred his speech and staggered around.

Another guard appeared. "Get him out of here," he told the other man.

The man grabbed Guy by his coat and rushed him down the stairs and out to the street. He put him in a cab and gave the driver fifty dollars. "Tell him where you live buddy," the guard said.

Guy mumbled his address. When they were two blocks from the restaurant, Guy told the driver he'd changed his mind. He gave him another address that was walking distance to his car.

The phone rang and Jesslyn grabbed it. She was startled to hear the voice and even more surprised when he asked to speak to Trisha.

"It's for you," she said as she handed Trisha the phone.

She said hello and then her eyes widened. "Kaliq! How did you know I was here?"

"A little bird told me. He seemed to think that you needed help."

"I'm in a little trouble, but nothing I can't handle."

"I just want to say if I can help, give me a call."

"No. Don't worry. I'll be fine."

He insisted she take his number and she did. She hung up and looked at Jesslyn.

"Palladin called him."

"I knew it the minute I heard his voice. Men haven't a clue on being subtle."

"He didn't sound angry with me."

"Are you angry with him?"

"No, of course I'm not angry with him. We couldn't have made it four years ago. We have the worst timing."

"What about now?"

"No. It's still bad timing. How can I think about having him in my life now? Not even as a friend."

"You've got to learn that's what friends are for. If they're only friends when you're successful then why do you need them?"

"I know, I'm independent . . ."

"There's independent and then there's having too much pride."

Trisha shook her head. "You aren't going to start throwing those old lines at me about pride going before a fall."

"Those old lines have been around so long because they're true."

"So what do you think I should do?"

"Let's talk to Palladin and see what he thinks. If you lose Carlotta's you might want to try someplace new."

"I know what he thinks. He'll say I should give Wyoming a try."

"He might be right. I'm sure it took Kaliq a lot of soul-searching before he called you. He's not the kind of man you want to lose twice."

* * *

Palladin came in after nine with two sleeping children hanging around his neck. He played the part of errant father to keep from telling the women he'd been on the phone calling in favors and grilling contacts until he learned exactly what Trisha was facing.

"Where have you been so long?"

"After the show we came back to coach's place and started talking . . ."

"And you forgot the children."

"Well, not exactly. We just didn't realize how late it was."

"Trisha, you see how men are."

Once he and Jesslyn got the kids washed up and in bed they could concentrate on the problem Trisha was facing. The three sat in the living room in front of the fireplace to discuss the day's events.

"Why did you call Kaliq?" Jesslyn asked.

"How do you know I called him?"

"Because he called here and spoke to Trisha."

"Good. Did you listen to him?"

"I know you mean well but . . ."

"I'm not going to tip toe around the facts. You and Kaliq never gave yourselves a chance. You're both stubborn and once he went back to Wyoming you let a little geography keep you apart. If you'd come here just once in the last four years and mentioned there was someone in your life other than your partner I wouldn't have called him."

"What can he do?"

"You may need a place to regroup and Wyoming seems like as good a place as any."

"Sometimes you are so autocratic, and it makes me crazy." Jesslyn said.

"It only makes you crazy when I'm right."

"Okay, I may need some place to think things out. It may or may not be Wyoming." Trisha surrendered. "What should we do right now?"

"Let's see what we're up against."

He waited until Trisha told him all the details of meeting Rommel and how the man had followed her, tried to date her, and then tried to hire her. When she told him about the most recent move of trying to ruin her, Palladin shook his head.

"The man is stalking you. It's not the usual kind of stalking but it has the same results. He's controlling you."

"I didn't see it as stalking but I know that if I let anyone bail me out of this he'll find another way to get at me. I'm afraid of someone getting hurt."

"Maybe I should have a little talk with him."

"No. Absolutely not. You have a family to take care of and I'm not going to put them in danger."

"Then the only thing to do is to talk to your partner and see what he has to say, Trisha. Palladin will go with you," Jesslyn insisted.

"I'll go, but if it looks dangerous to me I want you to promise that you'll come back here with me."

"I promise. I know you're trying to help but I just think it's too late."

"Well, that all depends on what happens. You never know. This may all be over with tomorrow."

Trisha felt some relief and wanted to get off the subject. "How's Lena?"

Palladin and Jesslyn both groaned.

"I don't know how my sister-in-law can find the

most trifling men but she manages." Palladin spoke first.

Trisha had met Lena just before Palladin and Jesslyn got married and she seemed a little wild; sometimes a leopard doesn't change its spots.

"She's doing great with GiftBaskets and we are still doing hang up business but Lena keeps finding these men who are . . . are . . ."

"Looking for a sponsor?" Trisha supplied.

"Exactly. My parents have given up. They're starting to wonder about her sanity."

"Come on. She's going to surprise you one day. She'll find someone and settle down."

"I don't think so."

"I agree with Jesslyn," Palladin said. "Lena's always going to be a wild one. If she ever does find a man who can deal with her whims, she'll run him away."

"We just keep hoping that she's happy and safe."

Rommel spent the night hopping from one bar scene to another, his lady plastered to his side and his bodyguards close behind. He couldn't seem to find a group he enjoyed. His mind kept hopping back to Trisha. He wondered if something happened in New York that changed her mind about working for him and that was what Guy was talking about. Maybe she'd found out that when it came to big money, no matter how much your friends have they won't always share it with you. Maybe she was seeing him as the lesser of two evils now. The greater evil meaning she'd lose Carlotta's.

"What a name for the place," he said aloud.

"What place, honey?" his girlfriend asked.

"Nothing. Just thinking out loud."

"About what?"

"None of your business." He turned to his men. "Let's get out of here. I can have more fun at my own place."

After the women had gone to bed, Palladin sat in his den and waited. His cell phone rang at 3:00 A.M. "Yeah."

"How much trouble do you think she's in?" Kaliq asked.

"A lot, if my contacts are right. She's playing with a loose cannon in Rommel. He's been known to hunt a woman down until she surrenders."

"Then I guess we'd better have a couple of plans together."

"Kaliq, how do you feel about letting her stay with you until I get something?"

"You think she needs to get out of town that badly?"

"I think she should have gotten out yesterday. The only thing I can do now is try to watch her."

"Until I take over that job."

"This isn't going to be too difficult . . ."

"Don't worry, man. I always wondered if she'd come with me when I asked would she still be here. I guess I'm going to get the answer."

"Once I talk to her partner I'll know where she stands. I'll know if he's in as much danger from this man as Trisha is."

"You don't think he is?"

"No. I told Trisha I thought this was a case of the man stalking her. It's not the usual case though. It seems he loses interest once the woman is in his grasps.''

"Can we prove stalking?''

"Not yet. I learned from a contact this isn't the first time he's gone after a woman with this much tenacity. He was married once and I understand he was determined to get her. There was one other case but the woman married someone else and he lost interest.''

"Sounds as if the man has a real problem.''

"We just may have to take care of him so that he can't do this to another woman.''

"How?''

"Put him out of business. Humiliate him. Anything that will make him fight or run. If he fights, we get enough evidence to put him away. If he runs we make sure others know how to handle him. I don't know what will happen if we get the inn back for her.''

"Take care of yourself. If she decides to stay, there isn't much I can do. I just called to tell her she had an alternative. Watch your back.''

"I will, and until you two get together I'll look out for your lady too.''

Trisha slept fitfully. Her dreams seemed jumbled and she struggled to make sense of them or wake up. She saw Rommel chasing her but she got away. Kaliq was there calling her but she couldn't see him. She knew she would be safe if she could just find him but his voice sounded as if it were coming from a different area each time he called. Rommel was catching up with her and she couldn't find Kaliq! She sat upright in the bed and fumbled for the lamp on the night table. She looked around the room, making sure that it was just a dream. Making sure that she was still safe in New York. She laughed to herself. Most people didn't think New York was safe but she considered it a haven.

She pulled the covers up around her and closed her eyes. For the first time since she was very young, she was afraid to turn the light off. She drifted back to sleep.

CHAPTER FOUR

The next day Palladin and Trisha drove to Pennsylvania. She'd called Guy that morning and he said he'd meet them at Carlotta's. Late September and the weather was turning cold. The east coast had enjoyed several years of Indian summers and late snowfalls and Trisha suspected it was time for a change.

Maybe it was time for a change of lifestyle for her. She didn't want to make it seem like she was running away but she needed peace and solitude as she made some important decisions about the next phase of her life. She hated to think this had to happen before she considered trying for another chance with Kaliq but maybe that's why all this was falling apart.

"Do you believe in fate?" she asked Palladin.

"Sometimes. I don't think you should wait around

for fate to make decisions for you but it happens. I guess fate played a role with Jesslyn and me."

"How?"

"I think of fate as a force that pushes you in a certain direction but your decisions make or break you. With all the evidence against her, I chose to believe Jesslyn."

"And you were right."

"I think you and Kaliq were right when you ended your relationship."

"I see." Trisha grew quiet. She'd never imagined that Palladin thought she and Kaliq were wrong for each other.

"At the time you both had promises to keep. Well, now you've kept them. You've done what you wanted and it might be time to give that relationship another chance."

"Because my inn failed?"

"It didn't fail. You had it for two years. You were successful. You proved your point, that you could do it. Maybe that's all fate had in store for this part of your life. Now it's time to move on."

"Go back to Kaliq because I failed?"

"You are going to have to lose that word. How long did you think you could run the inn?"

Trisha had never thought about Carlotta's in any other terms but forever. Palladin's prodding made her see that she hadn't thought about anything but owning a place. She hadn't thought about it over the long haul.

"I didn't think about it."

"Suppose you said I want to have my own business for one year? Did you do it?"

"Yes."

"So if you had said a year you'd consider yourself a success but because you didn't put any time limit on it, you think you failed."

Trisha laughed. "I think you and Kaliq are the only men I know who can change how people look at things."

"It's the viewpoint that gives the answer."

They chatted a little more as they drove and Palladin called Jesslyn twice before they reached Carlotta's.

When they took the turn that led to the winding driveway, Trisha's heart sank. A frisson of frigid air seemed to sweep over her body as they neared the front door. They went inside and looked for Guy. He wasn't there and, while they waited for him, Palladin took a walk around the property.

Trisha Terrence stood in the middle of the living room to the Bed & Breakfast inn she and her partner were selling. She'd already cried enough tears to fill several big city reservoirs. Still seeing the place devoid of people brought more tears to her eyes. Now she had lost her dream. It wasn't fair, she thought. *I gave up so much to make this all happen and now less than two years after I open the doors I have to give it up.*

Kaliq hadn't sounded angry, just concerned, but was he concerned because he cared about her as a friend or was there still some hope that they could try again? She hated coming back to him as a failure. She knew Rommel wanted her to stay and run the inn. What if she took Kaliq up on his offer? Rommel would have failed also. Trisha wouldn't have the inn but she wouldn't be working for Rommel. It made her think about going to Wyoming, but if she did, she'd tell Kaliq just why she was there. If he couldn't handle it she'd go someplace else. Trisha knew that Kaliq could handle anything. He'd lost the use of his legs and he'd come back. He'd lost his wife and alienated his son and he'd turned that around. Jesslyn had mentioned how Brett had decided to stay with his father and help run the ranch. He'd use the winter to take some classes and he was close to his degree in business. Things hadn't always gone well for Kaliq but he'd never considered himself a failure.

Trisha vowed she wouldn't let this problem with Rommel make her give up. She would find a way. She would not worry about Rommel any longer. If Guy was right and he no longer wanted to buy Carlotta's she'd find a way to keep it or find a buyer and walk away.

She remembered reading about an actress who'd lived in the same place for fifty years. When she decided to move she said she went through all her things and only took the items that reminded her of family. Then she walked out of the house and never looked back.

Trisha wondered if maybe it was time for her to do the same thing.

Maybe it didn't matter how she ended up with a second chance with Kaliq. If they could have met when the inn was a success, she could gladly walk away for another chance. Unfortunately Rommel had made that impossible. But what if fate was pointing her in the direction of a second chance? Would she let pride take it away from her?

The phone rang and snapped her back to the reality of the day. She walked to the reception desk and picked it up. It was her friendly real estate salesperson. The woman had another client and wanted to come over immediately. Trisha agreed to stay for an hour to meet the prospective buyer. She hung up and did a quick survey of the room. Some of the furniture she'd put in storage, so the place looked a little bare to her. She hoped the buyer wouldn't notice it too much.

Palladin came in. "You've got a pretty terrific place here."

"I guess someone thinks so. I've had another offer. The agent is going to bring someone out to see it."

"That's good. I think the best thing would be to get rid of the place and start over again."

Twenty minutes later the agent called back to say that her clients had changed their minds. Trisha knew what that meant.

"Rommel got to them. The agent just canceled."

"I don't think so. I think this guy is playing with your head. He had someone call and get your hopes up and then call back and stomp on them. I don't think there was really another buyer."

"I think you're right."

They turned to the man who made the statement. "You must be Guy," Palladin said, not telling the man he'd seen him park his car and use his key to open the front door. He'd let the man think he'd surprised them.

"Right. We haven't had a chance to meet but Trisha's talked about you. So I feel I know you."

"Same here. So what do we do about this mess?"

Guy explained he'd been checking the outside to see if it was being kept up. Things seemed to be in good shape.

"I can't believe he did this to us," Guy said. "He

said he wanted to buy the place and then he backed out of the deal."

Trisha shrugged. He'd been in denial since Rommel had pulled out of the deal. "Why not? Now that all our creditors know we're in bad shape. He can wait us out and pick up the hotel for next to nothing."

"I think he's going to make another offer. A very low one, but given our circumstances, one we'll have to take."

"You could use the money to start over somewhere else. Maybe it's the location he wants."

"Actually," Guy said, "he wants Trisha. Since she's refused his advances, he'll be satisfied if she's his executive chef."

"That's so crazy," Trisha said. She folded her arms across her chest.

"I know, darling, but he just has to have his own way," Guy said. He turned to Palladin. "I went over to see him last night . . ."

"Guy. I told you not to talk to him."

"I know, but don't worry, he wasn't there. I think it's best if we just end this whole thing. Let's take his money and walk away. I bet that would convince him that he couldn't control you."

"I don't want anyone to get hurt." Trisha turned to Palladin. "I'm going to let him have the place. I don't even want it anymore."

Guy took off the little bishop he wore around his neck that matched Trisha's. "We'll exchange these for good luck in future ventures."

Trisha wasn't even thinking as Guy slipped the chain over her neck and replaced it with his.

She noticed his rattled a little. "What's in this?"

"A few tiny rocks. Believe me. They will keep you safe one day."

"This is all your fault. You and your stupid gambling."

"Trisha, come on. It's not the end of the world."

"It's not the end of your world. Don't try to answer for me."

"We can try it again."

"No. I don't want a partner that isn't honest with me. If you'd told me about the gambling, I would have helped."

"I know. Sometimes you can't tell the person you care for about your foibles. Don't throw away the bishop. He may still bring you luck."

"Guy, how can you be so cavalier about this?"

"It may be for the best. You love to plan meals and that's what you could be doing now."

"I can't believe you. This is all your fault and you just want to take what little money is left over and run. Is that it? Did he get to you too?"

"Trisha!" Guy's face paled under his tanned skin. "How could you even think such a thing?"

"Oh, Guy, I just can't take your attitude now. You've never let anything get you down and I guess losing Carlotta's isn't going to be any different."

"You're wrong. It's different. I think we can handle this."

"I think I need a new partner."

"Just wear the bishop for a few days and things will be just fine." He kissed the bishop that he'd put around Trisha's neck and left.

Palladin found the gesture strange but so was the man. He didn't even seem disturbed by what was happening.

Guy said he could be reached at home. Palladin and Trisha decided to stay at the inn.

Once settled in his room, Palladin picked up the phone and used his calling card to reach Jesslyn.

"I don't know what else to tell her. If she tries to fight this in court, she'll be alone. Her partner's too flaky to he an asset. I think she should just forget about it and get out of this business venture. Next time I'm going to check out her business partner."

"But he was her friend."

"The road to purgatory is paved with people who let their friends be their partners."

"I think she should stay with us for a few weeks. Just until she decides what to do next."

"I agree. I'll run that by her in the morning."

They said good-bye and Palladin stripped, showered, and climbed into bed. Still tired from his outing with the twins and the drive to Pennsylvania, he was asleep as soon as his head hit the pillow.

Rommel slammed the hammer down on another of the man's fingers. He groaned but the gag wouldn't let him scream out.

"Someone got in here last night, Frank. Someone got into that safe. Someone cleaned it out completely. They took everything."

The man shook his head and made a muffled plea. Rommel was sure it was the same one he'd made before they stuffed the handkerchief in his mouth. He didn't see anyone. He'd only left his post for five minutes.

Rommel turned to the other guard. He was being

held by four of Rommel's most trusted men. "What have you got to say?"

The man's lips trembled. "Boss, I came on duty at my usual time. I always check the downstairs first. Everything was locked up. I came upstairs to relieve Frank and I found him tied up right in this room."

"What do you think happened?"

"I don't know, sir. None of us would steal from you. It had to be someone a little crazy."

"Crazy?"

"Yes, sir. We all know the consequences of ripping you off." He glanced at Frank who seemed grateful for the lapse of attention. "It had to be someone who's pretty desperate." The man babbled.

"You know," Rommel said. "I think he's right. Now who do we know that would be desperate enough to risk looting the safe?"

One of the henchman looked up. "Why would they take everything out of the safe?"

"So I wouldn't know who did it. If they only took the stuff that incriminated them, we'd know in a heartbeat."

"What do you think they'll do with all that stuff?"

"It could cause me a lot of trouble. We'd better find them before that happens."

"Where do we start looking?"

"My last big deal was taking over Carlotta's. Let's go have a talk with Guy Marshall."

Guy was on his second bourbon when his doorbell rang. He peered through the slender window and was shocked to see Rommel and four of his men. The lights were on and he knew if he didn't open it, they'd break it down.

He opened the door and watched them stroll in. "Rommel, what are you doing here?"

"Trying to plug up a leak."

"A leak?"

"Yeah. Someone paid me a visit last night. They cleaned out my safe."

"They took your money?"

"Money, Bearer Bonds, di . . . , never mind, but you know what?"

"What?"

"I don't think that's what they were really after. I think someone was more interested in the papers I had in there."

"Papers?"

"Yeah. Like promissory notes, loan agreements, things like that."

"Hey, I hope you don't think I had anything to do with it?"

"I thought we'd have a little talk. The last time you worked for me I had a similar situation."

"Yeah, but you caught that guy. It was all over town that he disappeared. We just assumed you took care of him."

"Really? That's so strange." Rommel stepped toward Guy.

Guy backed up and stood next to the staircase. Rommel took another step and Guy ran upstairs and locked himself in his bedroom.

Rommel shook his head. "Get him."

The men rushed upstairs and a shot rang out. Rommel ran after them. "Hey, I didn't want you to kill him!"

He found the men standing over Guy's body. "What's the matter with you?"

"Boss, we never touched him. He grabbed the gun and shot himself before we could get to him."

Rommel walked to the window and saw a light go on in a neighbor's house. "Damn! Let's get out of here."

They ran down the stairs and got into the car and drove off.

The pounding seemed far away as he was pulled from sleep. Then he heard Trisha's voice calling him.

"Yeah. Okay. I'm awake."

"Come downstairs. Please hurry."

He dragged himself from the bed and threw some water on his face. He washed up quickly and got dressed.

When he joined her in the living room section, she was frantic.

"What happened?"

"I got a call from Guy. He said that he'd found a way to fix Rommel. I don't know what he's going to do. He says that he'll never be able to do to anyone what he's done to us. Now he's not answering the phone."

"He wouldn't try to challenge the man alone, would he?"

"I don't know."

"Come on, let's go."

Guy's place was an hour away and Palladin made it in record time. After knocking on the door and ringing the bell, Trisha remembered where he kept his spare key.

They went in, turned on the lights and called. There was no answer. Palladin asked Trisha to stay downstairs. He checked the first bedroom and found nothing. Then he went down to the second one. When he opened the door, he was glad he'd asked Trisha to stay downstairs.

Guy was dead and it wasn't a pretty sight. The flashy way he talked earlier was just a facade. It appeared that the pressure had been too much and he'd used a gun to take his own life.

"Trisha, I have something sad to tell you," Palladin said.

She started for the stairs that led to the bedroom but he blocked her way. "You don't need to see this. He shot himself."

"No!" she screamed and tried to run up the stairs.

Palladin held on until she crumpled on the living room sofa and sobbed.

They spent some time with the police, but Palladin had cautioned Trisha not to make any accusations against Rommel.

"It's really his fault, you know," she said. "We can't prove it so I can't say it without opening myself up for a lawsuit, but we both know he caused it."

The police canvassed the neighborhood and found the neighbor who heard the shot. He was an elderly man and explained that by the time he got to the window he saw a dark car pull off. He couldn't give them any more description than it was big and black.

Trisha didn't want to stay in Pennsylvania but she was all Guy had. She was sorry that she'd screamed at him about being the cause of their troubles. I guess that's always the case. If you don't have a chance to make up, you feel bad but if you had the chance you wouldn't be sorry for telling the truth.

As soon as the police let them go back to the inn, Palladin made two phone calls. The first was to Jesslyn who said she'd get a babysitter and be there as soon as she could.

Brett answered the phone and was shocked at the turn of events. Maybe Trisha Terrence was in real trouble. Palladin explained about the partner's suicide. "She's losing everything and everyone around her. I don't know how she's holding up."

"I'm sure you and Dad will work something out. I just don't want him to be caught up in this and end up a basketcase like the last time."

"Don't worry. He won't."

"I wish I could be as sure as you are."

"That will come in time."

Trisha wandered aimlessly around Carlotta's. She saw everything in a different light. This place had been important to her and Guy was just along for the ride. Now he was gone. If she paid Rommel off and he left her alone would she really ever feel safe or secure here again?

Jesslyn arrived a few hours later to be at her friend's side. The more the police checked into Guy's past, the more they found to unsettle Trisha. First there was Rommel's claim that Guy had never been to see him that night. He backed it up with testimony from his bodyguards and other witnesses that he'd been gambling in Atlantic City when Guy supposedly paid him the visit and hadn't returned until after the newspapers reported Guy's suicide.

He even came by Carlotta's and tried to explain to Palladin that he didn't know the man was so upset about losing the inn. Trisha, of course, refused to see him.

The biggest surprise was when the police discovered Guy's bank book containing $50,000 and a safe with $50,000 in Bearer Bonds. It meant that Guy could pay off his debts at any time.

So why didn't he? Trisha wondered at his funeral. He didn't have any family left and it fell to Trisha to make all the arrangements. She somehow got through everything.

When the Will was read, it was no surprise that he'd left everything to Trisha. She closed up the inn and cashed in the bonds, even though it cost a healthy fee, and put the money in a Trust Fund so it couldn't be touched until she was sixty-five.

"Guy and I always worried that we wouldn't have money to take care of ourselves when we got old. I think that's why he held onto it instead of bailing us out," Trisha told Jesslyn.

Her friends were about to leave when Palladin decided to drive up to his Pennsylvania house and check on things.

Trisha was packing up her books from the library when she heard the door open. She turned and saw Rommel.

"You and your partner are very cute. You say he came to see me before he killed himself and now everyone is wondering if I had something to do with his death."

"You already convinced the police that you weren't here. What do you want?"

"Just what is mine. You see, I think your partner

did come to see me and I think he may have stolen something."

"If you're talking about the bonds . . ."

"I've never been interested in paper. Did he give you anything else?"

"No. I want you to leave."

"I'm not convinced that you don't know what I'm talking about. I would hate to think you needed to be persuaded by one of my associates."

"And I would hate to think that one of your associates made the mistake of trying to persuade anyone in this house."

The men turned to find Kaliq behind them.

He sat in his wheelchair with his overcoat thrown across his lap. No one could tell what was under the coat.

"This is just a friendly business meeting," Rommel said.

"It doesn't sound friendly and I think it's over."

Before Rommel or his men could move they heard a car pulling up and decided to leave.

Rommel turned to Trisha. "I hope we can work things out."

Then he and his men left. They passed Palladin quickly, got in their cars, and drove off.

"What was that all about?" Palladin asked Kaliq.

"It seems that they think there's some unfinished business." He turned to Trisha. "Do you know what he was talking about?"

"I haven't a clue."

Trisha and Jesslyn were lounging on the glass-enclosed patio later that afternoon. They'd taken a dip in the indoor heated pool and Trisha had hoped it would relax her enough to deal with Kaliq's arrival.

Palladin called Jesslyn into the house. Trisha wondered if he'd found out something that he wanted to share with Jesslyn before he told her. She wondered if it had to do with Kaliq or Guy.

Jesslyn threw on a wrap over her bathing suit and hurried inside. Trisha wondered if she'd ever trust a man enough to run to him the way Jesslyn ran to Palladin. She closed her eyes and tried to will her body to be calm. The laps in the pool hadn't worked completely but if she could just close her eyes and forget the past few days she'd be fine.

She shifted around, unable to find a comfortable position. Then she felt more than heard someone near her. She knew Kaliq had joined her but she was afraid of what he would say. She took a deep breath and opened her eyes.

He sat inches away, practically devouring her with his gaze. He'd been for a swim also. His wide chest and narrow waist were athletically formed. His dark skin glowed against the cream colored swimming trunks. It was only when she looked down at his legs that she thought about his inability to walk. Then she remembered reading that paraplegics should use swimming to build upper body strength to supplement the lack of strength in the lower body.

There was something in his eyes that made him appear immovable. There was a strength that she could only wish for.

"I thought you were asleep for a moment. I didn't want to disturb you."

"Was there something you wanted to tell me?"

"Yes. I'm leaving tomorrow morning. Brett and Nia

have to give a speech and demonstration in a couple
of days and I need to get back to the ranch.''

"So did you come all the way just to chase a couple
of bullies and take a swim?''

"Actually I came to make you an offer I don't think
you should refuse.''

"And that is?''

"Come to Wyoming.''

It was almost the same thing he'd said just before
they broke up. Trisha felt that this was his way of
telling her she had another chance, that they could
start over again.

As he continued to speak, that hope died.

"I don't think it's safe here and you need a place
to reorganize your life.''

She tried to control her emotions. Yes, she wanted
to go to Wyoming, but not like this. Not as someone
he was helping out just as he would a stranger. Then
she realized why Jesslyn had hurried away. She didn't
want to say anything that might influence Trisha.

"I don't know how I could do that.''

"It's going to take a lot of work but I think we
should give it a shot.''

He was so cool and reserved with the offer. She
mulled it over in her mind. He'd added *we*. Did that
mean he thought they had a chance?

"We?''

"Yes, we. The police will take God knows how long
to clear up this mess and as long as you're here, the
press is going to be hounding you. You still have the
inn at least. All this publicity made Rommel back
off. You're still front page news and that could get
depressing.''

He was right about that. Jesslyn had been turning

down interviews for her with all the local papers and
a few national ones. If she stayed, it would be twice
as hard.

"So you think I'll be better off in the wilds of Wyoming?"

"I know you will. So what do you say? Should I
book two seats for tomorrow?"

"No . . ."

"Don't be stubborn. Your life may be in danger."

"I'm not being stubborn. I said no for tomorrow.
I need to do a few things here before I can leave."

He let out an audible sigh of relief. "I'm glad you
accepted my offer. I have to admit that it's a different
world in Wyoming and one you may not like. I still
feel it's the best place to take a look at your life and
decide what you want to do next."

"Well, now that it's settled I'm sure you want to go
tell Palladin and Jesslyn."

"There's just one thing."

"And that is?"

"Our friends are trying to play matchmaker. If they
know that you're just coming down to regroup they
might try to continue to play cupid."

"So what do you suggest?"

"Let them think their plan worked and when you
come back you can just say we gave it the old college
try, to no avail."

"How do we fool them?"

"Like this," he said.

He leaned over and placed a kiss on her lips. It was
light but Trisha felt the lightning bolts streak through
her body.

Before she could respond, he'd lifted his head and
pushed away.

"Would you like me to handle your reservations?" he asked.

"Sure," she answered. Why not? He seemed to have already made up his mind about how things were going.

"I'll tell Palladin and get things started. But I think I'll take another few laps in that pool. In fact, Trisha, maybe you could look at my place and see if I can get the same setup. Who knows, we might become partners?"

Seconds after Kaliq went inside, Jesslyn was back.

"So what do you think?"

Trisha hated not being truthful with her friends, but it was for the best. "I don't know. I've always thought of Wyoming as one of those states you have to be born in to enjoy."

"Well, get over that. I'll bet in a couple of months you'll be wondering why you ever doubted you could live there."

Kaliq flew back to Wyoming knowing he had a lot of explaining to do to Brett. His son understood why he had to see for himself what the situation was but he wouldn't understand him forcing Trisha to live in Wyoming.

"Dad, I only see this as being worse for you if it doesn't work out. I remember how you were when you came back four years ago."

"You were only sixteen . . ."

"I had eyes and I had ears. That's all I needed to know you were miserable. You always took me out when you were going to cast Namid. Except then.

You kept going away by yourself and I knew what she'd done to you.''

"It's only going to be for a couple of months. The police are working on the case and Palladin will keep me informed. I'd do this for any friend."

"I just hope you feel the same way when she goes back to her life."

They drove the rest of the way in silence. So much of what Brett said was true. He'd hurt a lot when he and Trisha had parted. He didn't want to hurt again, but she needed him and who knew what would happen once she lived on the ranch? This was a perfect time since the boys were all back in school and only Kaliq, Brett, and the men building the new bunkhouse were around.

Once back at the ranch, Brett called his partner Nia Sebastian to bring her up to date on his father's plans and to see how their lecture offers were coming in.

"I only have a couple lined up but when we give the demonstration maybe we can get some newspaper coverage."

"Fine. I'll meet you tomorrow at the Elks Nest and then we'll go to the hotel. After the lecture I'll pick up Trisha Terrence."

CHAPTER FIVE

Rommel stared at the pretty college student across from him. "Julie, I don't see the problem. I asked you to just go by and apologize to Trisha and get your job back."

"She won't give it to me. I tried, Mr. Rommel. She says she's going out of town for at least a couple of months."

"Where did she say she was going?"

"She wouldn't tell me that either."

"I thought you wanted to earn more money for college?"

"I do sir. But . . . I can't. She doesn't trust me anymore."

"I understand. I'll tell you what, if you get any more information, please call me." He handed her a business card.

"Yes, sir. Thank you, sir."

The young woman left the office. Once she was gone, one of the men turned to Rommel. "Boss, I thought you'd given up on this broad."

"She's not a broad. She's someone I have unfinished business with and I intend to find her."

At the airport in New York, Jesslyn waited with Trisha. "I'm so happy that you and Kaliq are going to give it another try."

"Jesslyn, don't get upset if this doesn't work."

"It will work."

"You are really being a pollyanna over this. I'm going to feel terrible when Kaliq and I see that this is still wrong."

"You're going to feel great when it works."

They laughed and then Jesslyn walked with Trisha to the ramp. "I'll call you as often as I can."

"I feel silly taking Carlotta's off the market and then closing it up for the fall and winter. There are some couples who want to get away before it snows. Are you sure Lena will be all right living there?"

"Please. She'll be fine. She just broke up with someone and needs to be alone for a while. I have enough people to run the shop."

"But I feel like I'm running away."

"Look, you said that if you lost the inn you couldn't go to Kaliq and find out if you two had anything left. Once Guy's suicide hit the papers, Rommel backed off. You used the insurance money to pay your debts. So you aren't begging for protection. You are just taking some time after losing a friend to get yourself back together."

"Jesslyn, I think I should tell you something."

Trisha was tired of hiding the fact that she and Kaliq were not going to try to patch things up.

"Hey, I've got to get back to the twins. I'll call you tomorrow." She gave Trisha a quick hug and was gone.

Trisha went down the ramp to wait for her plane. She'd make a change in Georgia and be on her way to Wyoming.

Jesslyn got to the car and slid in beside her husband. "She's on the way."

"Do you really think we should have let her go?"

"Why not?"

"Come on, she and Kaliq think they put on that show for us, pretending they were finding each other again."

"They think we believe them."

"So what's all this going to prove?"

"That sometimes when you pretend, it's really a wish."

"What if it doesn't work out?"

"Then it's too bad for both of them. They are so right for each other and so stubborn."

"Come on, let's get home. We have to fix another love life."

"Who's?"

Palladin winked at his wife. "Ours."

Trisha found herself looking over her shoulder and scrutinizing anyone she thought was staring at her. She was still in shock over Guy's death and learning of the little nest egg he kept. That money could have

gotten them out of debt but Guy wanted to play the
odds that he could keep the inn, get Trisha to work
for Rommel, and never tell anyone about the money
he'd saved. He actually let Trisha believe that he'd
lost the money. Pure greed had cost him their friendship and his life.

She was starting to get worried when she saw a
familiar face. It wasn't Kaliq, but his son. She'd never
met Brett but she spotted him immediately.

He was tall and solidly built just like his father. His
coat was open and her eyes traveled down his frame
from the denim shirt and jeans to the dusty brown
boots.

His broad, bronze face was smooth, despite the fact
that he worked outside most of the time. His hair was
pulled back into a thick braid that hung just past his
shoulders, a tribute to his Cheyenne heritage.

"Ms. Terrence, I'm Brett Faulkner."

She nodded and shook his hand. Just before land-
ing, Trisha had slipped on an extra sweater. While
the weather in Pennsylvania was chilly, she'd checked
the weather channel and learned that the weather in
Wyoming was about ten degrees colder.

Her gray slacks had a lining so she was sure she
was dressed warmly enough. She was surprised that
Brett didn't have an overcoat or heavy jacket but since
he'd been born here, he probably adjusted to the
cold better than she did.

In fact, there were some nights when Trisha stayed
at the inn rather than go to her house if it started
snowing badly.

Please Lord, she prayed silently. Don't let the winter
be too bad while I'm here. The weather channel was
fond of showing states hit with the most snow during

winter and Wyoming was right up there with Colorado and Wisconsin.

"Thank you for meeting me."

"If you'll give me your ticket, I'll pick up your luggage."

"This is all I brought," she said as she indicated the one carry-on piece of luggage at her side.

Brett frowned. "I thought you were planning an extended stay with us?"

"I thought it would be easier to travel light. Jesslyn is shipping more things to me."

"I see." Brett was surprised she wasn't like most women who always seem to pack more things than they needed. He'd had a couple of girlfriends from his college days who arrived for Christmas break with enough luggage to take them through summer.

He led her out to the airport parking lot and pointed out his green pickup truck with a white cap.

"I guess you were prepared to pick up a lot of luggage."

"Well," he grinned, "I thought it was better to be safe than sorry."

He put her suitcase in the back seat of the truck's cab section and helped her climb into the front seat.

"Do we have a long way to go?"

"I'm afraid so."

Trisha took out the ticket and the phony driver's license that listed her as Ellie Jarvis. Palladin felt that it would be easier if no one could track her to Wyoming. He'd made sure they hadn't been followed to the airport and New York reporters weren't interested in the Trisha Terrence story so there wouldn't be a fear of them tracking her down. Palladin was still not satisfied with Rommel's story. Something about the man said he was still trouble and whatever had happened with Guy, Rommel, and Trisha wasn't over.

When she got off the plane in Casper, Trisha was a little surprised. No matter how she told herself that it was a large city, not a western town, she was still shocked to see skyscrapers and evidence of modern technology. She chided herself for being so foolish.

She tried to strike up a conversation with Brett but he seemed to be long on one-word answers and short on keeping up a conversation.

Finally she decided that she didn't care what Kaliq thought. Brett needed to know where they stood.

"Did your father tell you why I'm here?"

"Just that you wanted to see if you could live in Wyoming."

"Well, that's not quite the truth. I was the victim of a stalker and your father is just offering me a place to stay until he forgets about me."

"A stalker?"

"Oh, not the run-of-the-mill kind who thinks he's in love and refuses to accept no. This man tried to destroy my business so I could come to work for him."

"That seems quite drastic. I know about your partner; I'm sorry."

"Guy was just too fragile when it came to losing the business. I'd like to think we would have been okay if he hadn't killed himself but I really don't know."

"What's with this stalker person?"

"He grew up on the tough side of Chicago and learned to get his way by being a bully. He even changed his name to Rommel."

"Do you mean like the German soldier during WWII?"

"Yes. Now, for a Black man to do that, you know he isn't playing with a full deck."

"I agree with that."

"Well your father is letting me stay with him until I can get myself back together. I have the money. My business is okay. I just need the privacy."

"I thought . . ."

"I know. You thought that your father and I might get back together and then I wouldn't like Wyoming and I'd leave him."

"Something like that."

"I don't think that's going to happen. We still like different things and I'm not sure I'll like the isolation."

"You didn't have to tell me all this."

"I know, but Brett, I'm going to need your help. If your father wants to pretend this is a second chance at love for us I need you to convince him you believe it."

"I understand."

They drove for a few more miles and Brett started telling her about falcons—how long it took to train them and how glad he was in a state where they were protected.

"I always think of knights and warriors using falcons as weapons."

"Most people do. I think once you walk around the ranch you'll get a much different view."

Then he dropped into silence again and she realized that he hadn't been ignoring her before, he just didn't talk much unless it was on a subject he loved. He seemed to love falcons more than Kaliq. Well, at least that was a relief, even though she felt the need to tell everything. She would start out on the right foot with Kaliq's son.

When they reached the ranch he turned to her and said, "My father and I have a lot in common, but one of them is that we both like honest women. If this isn't working for you, I know you'll tell him; but if you're meant to be together you will see that."

Trisha and Brett shook hands. She liked his quiet strength, something else that he shared with his father.

Kaliq was working out in a little cabin not far from the ranch. Brett pointed it out as he drove toward the house. Once at the house, you couldn't see it.

"Dad works out there every day he can."

"Does he think . . ."

"No. He doesn't think it's going to help him walk again. That's not going to happen. He has to keep his upper body strong to compensate."

He took her into the house and she looked around at the open layout. She could tell that the doors were just a little wider than normal and the furniture was arranged so that a wheelchair could have easy access.

Brett led her down the hall to a large bedroom. The walls were painted a soft cream and the large brass bed sat in the middle of the room, facing a huge bay window. There was something feminine about the room. A tiny candle burned, giving off the smell of potpourri.

"The bath's through that door." Brett pointed to the right side of the bed.

"It's . . . beautiful."

"Yeah. My partner Nia Sebastian decorated it. She said you'd like it."

"She was right. I do like it."

"Well, I'll go tell dad you're here and I hope it's a pleasant stay."

"So do I, Brett."

Later in the quiet of her bedroom, Trisha thought back to the scene with Brett and wondered if he'd really mind if his father married her. He was like his father in more ways than he realized. She was sorry he saw her as a threat to Kaliq's happiness. Trisha was beginning to believe this might be the second chance she had prayed for.

When they arrived at the ranch, Brett had introduced her to his lecture partner Nia Sebastian. He'd mentioned briefly that she'd worked in California and had come home to work with him on the lecture circuit.

He put Trisha in the hands of their housekeeper, Linda Martinez. The older woman had worked for the Faulkners since Brett was fourteen and immediately took Trisha under her wing.

She explained that the first breakfast would be around 5:00 A.M. but Trisha was not expected to attend. There would be a later breakfast for her.

"Mr. Faulkner says you need rest and I must see that you get it."

Trisha didn't dare tell her that getting rest was all that anyone had allowed her to do since Guy's funeral.

She showed Trisha the library and waited while Trisha found a couple of mysteries she had been dying to buy but the inn hadn't allowed her time to read for pleasure.

Trisha snuggled down in the big bed and drifted

off to sleep before she finished the third page of the first book she opened. When Kaliq came in to check on her, she was still too sleepy to think about food.

"Okay. We'll let you sleep today but tomorrow you'll have to get out for a little while. I don't want you withering away."

Shaking her head in amusement, Trisha pulled the covers over her and went back to sleep. Since she'd never been one to sleep too much, she paid for the nap by awaking at three in the morning. She couldn't even force herself to go back to sleep. So she picked up the book again and began to read.

She found something decadent about reading when everyone else was fast asleep. Of course, the time she spent reading wouldn't be too long. Running a Bed & Breakfast was something like running a ranch. You had to be up early and have breakfast prepared for your guests. Her days at the inn were sometimes from five in the morning until ten at night. She'd done that so much she didn't realize how tired she was until she stopped and had nothing to do. She surprised herself by thinking of Rommel as a blessing in disguise for her well-being. But not for Guy's. Whenever she thought about him, she wondered how he could have left still convinced that they could get the inn back and then several hours later commit suicide. What had happened that made him change his mind. Was it Rommel?

The more questions she asked, the fewer answers she found. At four she laid the book down and let her body relax enough for sleep to come.

*   *   *

Kaliq rose early and showered and dressed. He stopped at Trisha's door and smiled when he heard a low snore. She was probably like Brett. The only time he snored was when he was overtired.

He went out to check on his falcons. Two of them were just learning how to sit on his arm and not try to fly away until he took the hoods off. They were beautiful and, by the time summer rolled around, they would be fully trained. He took a hooded Namid and drove the truck up the mountain. He got Namid to sit on his arm and then carefully removed the hood. The falcon paused to gain his bearings, after being in the dark for awhile. Then it left the gloved fist and flew up to the sky. He turned as if he was flying a distinct program then plunged to earth and swooped down on a rabbit. He grabbed it with his talons and took it away. The rabbit was now breakfast. Kaliq waited and then the falcon headed for the sky again then back to perch on Kaliq's gloved hand. He put the hood on, put him back in the cage, and drove home.

The housekeeper had prepared a large breakfast for Kaliq and the men who were working on the new bunkhouse. None of the people who worked for him actually stayed on the ranch. They lived in neighboring towns and just worked on the ranch.

Trisha woke up at nine and hurriedly showered and dressed. She didn't find anyone in the kitchen and assumed she'd missed breakfast. The pantry and refrigerator were well supplied so she made herself an omelet and toast and drank orange juice. She was just about to clean up when Linda found her.

"No. No. I'll take care of that. The señorita must rest and those orders came from Mr. Faulkner."

"I think Mr. Faulkner is being a little overprotective. I need something to do besides sit around." She explained that if she sat around she'd just fall asleep again and that was becoming tiresome.

Try as she would to help, Ms. Martinez wouldn't hear of it. Finally Trisha gave up and went back to her room and grabbed a jacket. She wanted to see what a real ranch looked like.

It wasn't as western as she thought it would be. She'd seen too many cowboy movies and expected to walk out the door and see a whole little town. But Kaliq's place seemed to be the only one in miles. She wondered if it was too far off the beaten path. What if they needed help? Then she laughed. Rommel prided himself on changing clothes constantly and that wouldn't work out here. If he didn't know where she was he wouldn't try to follow her.

As she surveyed the area, she walked down to the section that housed the falcons. She didn't see any birds around, just Brett sitting on a horse watching the sky. She walked over and just before she called him, she saw a rabbit. It looked so out of place she started toward it. Then she heard a shrieking noise. She looked up and saw this bird with its wings spread coming toward her.

She started to back up but tripped over the rabbit. The bird came closer and she covered her face and screamed. Then she felt strong hands grab her shoulders and pull her to safety.

"What happened? Where is that thing?" she cried.

"It's okay. She's gone."

Trisha was about to cry when she saw Kaliq pushing hard to get to her.

"What happened?" he said as he pulled Trisha onto his lap.

Trisha wrapped her arms around him and took several deep breaths.

Brett started to say something and then burst into laughter. "I'm sorry Trisha, Dad. I didn't see her until she tried to pick up the rabbit."

"Oh no, Honey, you didn't?"

"What was wrong with that? It looked lost."

"I'm afraid you tried to take a falcon's dinner."

Trisha put her hands over her face. She'd read about falcons when she first met Kaliq. They were birds of prey, and even though they were on the endangered species list, they were animals that attacked. She felt so stupid.

"Come on, let's go back to the house. I think I need to go over some things with you."

Back at the house, everyone seemed to take the blame for Trisha's scare. Linda fussed over her like a mother hen. Kaliq apologized. Brett apologized. Finally Trisha called a halt to all the attention.

"I should have taken Kaliq up on his offer to show me around but I was so sure that this was just an average ranch that raised falcons instead of horses. It's my fault and I promise I'll accept a guide from now on."

Later Trisha talked Linda into letting her cook dessert for everyone. She found the ingredients in the pantry and fixed a pumpkin caramel pudding cake. She was pleased with their reaction.

That night she sneaked into the kitchen and made her favorite sandwich, peanut butter and grape jam.

On her way back to her bedroom she met Kaliq in the hall.

"Are you okay?" he asked. "You aren't having nightmares about what happened today are you?"

"No. I just felt a little hungry for some junk food and made myself a sandwich."

"Good. Tomorrow I will take you on a real tour of the place."

"All right. I guess I acted like a real city slicker today."

"Don't worry about it. We're just glad nothing happened. The talons are weapons and when I think of how close you came . . ."

"I goofed up but it won't happen again."

"One question. Why did you tell Brett about our arrangement?"

"I couldn't let him live with a lie. If this doesn't work, I don't want him to think that I came back into your life to hurt you."

Kaliq took her hand and brought it to his lips. "As the saying goes, 'If it's meant to be, it's up to me.' Or in this case, it's up to you and me."

They said good night and returned to their bedrooms.

The next day Kaliq was true to his word. Right after breakfast he took Trisha on a tour. He told her about how falcons are trained and that if you don't know what you're doing you can ruin a bird.

"Last year I finally got around to naming the place. It's now the Taharqa Ranch."

"How did you pick that name?"

"Taharqa was a soldier who won his first battle at sixteen. He controlled the largest empire in ancient Africa for twenty-five years."

"Sounds as if you plan to give a little history lesson along with falconry?"

"I don't want to get on a soap box, but our young people know so little of their real history. Now to get off my soap box I'm going to let you pick a name for that falcon. The only clue I'll give you is that it's female."

"Okay. Let me think about it for a while."

She loved to hear some of the stories and had to admit, since she'd grown up in Paris, she had less knowledge of her own people than most. Her days and nights had been filled learning how to cook. However, when she returned she found a new way to study history. She bought a book that listed thousands of names for African-American babies. Some names carried a little portion of history. Then when she went to the library, she looked for longer books on these people. It had given her a great start.

The last place he showed her was a little cabin a hundred or so yards away from the main house. It was dusty, tiny, and cramped. It consisted of two rooms, one upstairs and one down. There was an old wheelchair in the corner.

"This was where I lived while the main house was being built. I did a lot of healing here also. I went through a typical 'why me' process until I got involved with counseling at the Veteran's Hospital. Last year I used it as an isolation project."

"What's that?"

"Any boy who acted up was given a choice. Go home or clean the cabin. Most of them would rather clean than leave the falcons. This year they were much better behaved so the place didn't get too many cleanings."

Trisha couldn't wait to call Jesslyn and tell her about the falcon and the rabbit.

Jesslyn roared with laughter. "I'm only laughing because if you can talk about it then you're okay."

"I can't believe that after all I read about training falcons, I didn't even think when I saw Brett on the horse."

They talked a few more minutes about the twins and how Jesslyn would love to come for a visit, but not during the cold months. As Trisha hung up, she knew that from Jesslyn's remarks everyone hoped she and Kaliq could make it. But she wondered if her being such a greenhorn would affect Kaliq's opinion of her ability to live in his world.

Brett met Nia to talk about a series of lectures and demonstrations they were putting together. He told her about Trisha's mishap.

"I want you to come over more and talk to her."

"Why me?"

"You've lived a corporate life and so has she. I think she'll probably open up more. Dad says that my Aunt Jesslyn and Trisha used to meet once a month to go shopping. I think that's a woman thing, so I want you to see if she needs a buddy."

"This is very strange," Nia said. "A week ago you were angry that your father was considering inviting her down. Now you want to get her a best buddy."

"Don't say it. You told me to wait until I met her to judge her."

"So, now I take it that she's not a bad person after all?"

"Right. She's up front and that's what I like about her. I was expecting one of those hot house flower types. I thought she'd be kinda fragile with twenty pieces of luggage. She comes in with just one small carry-on bag. She's having her friend ship some other stuff to her."

Nia laughed. "So you had that big pickup ready and all you needed was the jeep?"

"Hey, I've had girlfriends come for the weekend and the truck wasn't enough."

"I remember. I thought you'd gotten married one time. The girl had so many suitcases even Kaliq started putting you through the third degree."

"He thought I was renting rooms during spring break. I told him that wasn't a bad idea."

"Okay, I'll stop by and keep Trisha company when I can. Maybe she'd like to go on the lecture circuit with us?"

"I don't think my dad's going to let her out of his sight too much. Except for a few shopping trips."

Nia never had too many close female friends. She'd been so set on getting out of Wyoming and finding a job in New York or California. Maybe if she'd known how to have women friends she would have lasted a little longer. She tried being friendly, but she'd been hired for a job one of the other women thought she was getting and the battle lines were drawn. Since she was new to the entire company, she didn't have any allies. She didn't have anything but her natural instinct to survive. She'd almost made it. Until her boss decided that she was the perfect representative for the company's multicultural look.

He'd made no secret that he found her attractive. At least not when they were alone. She'd heard others talking about his messy divorce and how he was inches from a sexual harassment suit until the powers that be made him clean up his act.

Nia hadn't even come close to the top and she was so lonely she just gave up and quit. It was the first time in her life that she'd ever quit anything. Her family was just glad to see her but she still had nagging doubts about what she could have done. She was simple suits and they were designer's specials. She was plain language and their words were covered with dual meanings. But she still thought about going back and doing things her way.

Maybe talking with Trisha would help her understand how companies function and how to handle those cutthroats who wanted to succeed no matter who they stabbed in the back.

Nia had had two letters from her old company asking her to come back. She wanted to go back, be successful, and quit again on her terms, but if the lecture and demonstration series she and Brett put together took off, she wouldn't have the chance to return to the world of business.

Just before supper, Brett talked to Kaliq and confirmed that he wanted Trisha to feel comfortable but safety was the real issue.

"I'm more afraid of her hurting herself right now but from what I saw of Rommel he's not just going to go away."

"Are we really prepared if he comes here?"

"I don't know. I loaded the gun above the fireplace in the living room and if he's sighted heading this way we'll contact the sheriff's division. This guy's such a loose cannon."

"That's not good."

"I will have one thing going for me at all times: the Wyoming weather. He could be in for a real shock."

"That's true. If he comes during the fall or winter

he's in for a pretty rough time. I put a cell phone charger in the cabin and I'm going to have someone clean it out. We'll make it a little more presentable."

Rommel sat next to one of his bodyguards who knew about computers. He punched in the names of the people who had come to Trisha's rescue and whisked her away. They didn't seem to care about the inn. They only wanted the woman safe.

"I want to know how they got her out of town and where she might be."

He punched in Palladin Rush, then let out a low whistle as the information began to fill the screen.

"I don't think you want to take this guy on. He's former Secret Service and has some pretty powerful connections."

"What about the other one?"

The man put in Kaliq's name and was just as surprised at the information that appeared.

"He was a reporter covering a worldwide beat. He was caught behind enemy lines and rescued by Palladin Rush. These are some bad guys to tangle with."

"The true test of my ability is to do just that. Where do they live?"

"Rush lives in New York. A real fancy condo on the east side. Faulkner lives in Wyoming. Now that's weird."

"Wyoming. That would be the perfect place for Trisha. Wide open spaces would give her a real feeling of safety. I see that she has some men who are worthy adversaries. No wonder they could whisk her out of here without a trace."

"You can't just run to Wyoming and think they're going to let you near her."

"Oh, I'll find a way. But you're right. This needs real planning. So I'll let them have false hope that they've beaten me. Then I'll just show up and teach them all a lesson."

The men looked at each other. This was what they were afraid of. Whenever Rommel thought anyone had gotten the best of him he became surly and vindictive. The money he paid them was good but there was the fear of having him turn on them the way he'd done with the other guard.

The man had gone to the hospital and claimed he was mugged but he didn't see his assailant's face. Rommel had arrived and paid all his medical expenses making the people at the hospital think he was a good guy. But the men knew the truth. The man was as close to insane as he could get without being put in a straitjacket.

CHAPTER SIX

Three weeks later Trisha was still fascinated by all that went into running a ranch. She felt good about her decision to come here and even better that she'd talked to Brett. Now if she could just keep her promise to herself.

Besides the grounds, Kaliq told Trisha about the alarm system for the house. Like most of the ranchers in the area, the system was tied into the sheriff's department.

"The problem of course is manpower, especially during a bad winter or in case of forest fires. That's the reason I try to keep the house in a barren area and some specially treated lumber so it doesn't spread as easily."

"Didn't anyone complain when you cut so many trees down to do this?"

"Oh, we have some very vocal ecologists but since

the ranch is promoting the preservation of an endangered species, we got by.''

The wind blew stronger because they were so open. Trisha never realized how much tall buildings protected her. Even though her Bed & Breakfast was somewhat rural, it was nothing compared to this. She couldn't even see the next ranch. That didn't matter. She could see the road and part of the highway.

The nights weren't as bad. She'd rarely had a bad dream and she even felt safe enough to turn the light off some nights. There was one little thing that she wanted to overcome. She wanted to know how it was to be a falconer.

''Am I going to get a lesson in falconry?''

''If you really want one after your first experience.'' Kaliq tried to keep the laughter inside but couldn't. ''I can't tell you how you looked on the ground screaming. I know it's not funny but . . .''

''Do you realize that is a problem with humor? It's not funny to the victim but hilarious to the spectators.''

''Okay, let's get you reintroduced to the world of falcons.''

Every time she left the house she'd known that the ranch hands and the builders were watching to see if she went near the falcons again. She wasn't sure if they were concerned about her safety or just wanted to see her make another dumb mistake.

What they didn't know was that she'd changed her nighttime reading. Instead of mysteries, she'd begun reading about falcons. Kaliq had a treasure trove of books on the subject and she'd even read about the school in Europe where he'd trained. She found that one of the schools was run by a woman and another by a husband and wife team.

The more she read, the better she understood Kaliq and Brett. Falcons were an interesting breed. They mated for life but if one died they would find a new mate. Most species that mated for life didn't do that. They continued being alone until they died.

Brett was sitting on his horse with another falcon perched on his gloved fist.

"This is the first step in training a falcon. You spend hours with the bird sitting on your hand until he feels safe and comfortable with you. You feed him and that promise of food is what makes him come back. Tiring is something we teach them to nibble on. Once a falcon is trained, you can hold up a piece of tiring and it will swoop down, perch on your hand, and eat it."

"Is this how all falcons are trained?"

"Different people have different methods, so training can vary a little."

"See the one Brett has? That's a female and we haven't named her yet. You name her."

"How about Galiana?"

"What's its meaning?"

"Supposedly she was a Moorish princess and the man who loved her built a castle to show how much."

Out of the corner of her eye she saw Kaliq and Brett look at each other. She hoped they didn't think she wanted Kaliq to build her a castle. The name came so fast because she'd been reading a book on names and their meanings that she'd found near the books on falcons. She assumed that's how they named the birds.

"Would you like to try it?" Kaliq asked.

"I don't think so."

"Come on, first we'll get you used to the glove. Hey Brett, Trisha's going to learn how to be a falconer. Give me a glove."

Brett reached in his saddlebag and threw a glove to his father.

"This is a gauntlet. It is worn on the left hand. Falcons are always trained to sit on the left hand."

Kaliq gave it to her and she couldn't believe how heavy it was. She groaned a little as she tried to hold her arm up as if a falcon was sitting on her fist. The glove was too heavy for her to hold for any length of time.

"I'm gaining new respect for men who hunt this way," she said, as she pulled the glove off and handed it back to Kaliq.

"No. It's yours. Practice with it. Once you master it, you can learn how to feed a falcon."

"So you train them to hunt rabbits."

"They hunt rabbits, grouse, pheasants. Some people have dogs they train to scare the quarry from the bushes so the falcon can swoop down and grab it. Ferrets are also trained to do this."

"Ferrets? Those things that look like a long rat?"

"Don't say that. Ferrets are bred here in Wyoming to take the place of dogs when you're hunting."

"Do you have any?"

"No. I'm afraid to have one with the kids who will be here. They've been known to bite."

"I didn't realize there were falconers in the United States. I thought they were all in the U.K."

"Wyoming has a lot to offer."

"I see that, but my profession seems to require a

large city that people want to escape from for a few days."

Kaliq nodded. The opposite worlds they lived in were once again highlighted by what he loved to do and what she loved to do.

Later that afternoon Kaliq and Trisha went into the den to call Palladin.

"Any word?"

"Just that Rommel seems to be gathering his forces. He's recruiting muscle so I guess he thinks he's got a fight on his hands."

Trisha was not shocked to hear this. She knew that Rommel wanted something more of her. She wasn't sure he'd be satisfied that she'd gotten away especially since she still had Carlotta's.

"Does he know where I am?"

There was a long pause, and then Palladin said yes.

"What do you think I should do?"

"Stay there. Even if he knows where you are, he'd have to get by Brett and Kaliq, and my money's on them anytime."

The men talked about strategy for a few minutes and then gave the phones to the women. Kaliq went to check on supper.

"Thanks for adding that camel top coat with your last shipment."

"You're welcome. I guess it will be a little while before we have our shopping day."

"I know. I really miss them."

"How are things going with Kaliq?"

"We're still trying."

"Why don't you force the issue?"

"I'd rather wait until this is all over. I don't want to be still in hiding when we decide our future."

Jesslyn changed the subject and regaled Trisha with stories of the twins and how much trouble they were getting into. She talked about Lena.

"She called me one night and said she was going stir crazy from all the silence."

"It took me a while to get used to it. Do you think she'll be able to stay?"

"Oh, she hasn't given up. It's just so funny to hear about some of her projects to keep busy."

"Like?"

"She tried her hand at canning fruit. She found one of your books and I guess she had too much time on her hands. I'm not sure we should taste it when she finishes, but that's so different from the things she used to do."

Trisha could picture Lena in all her Versace finery pouring fruit into jars. She agreed with Jesslyn about tasting anything from this batch, but who could tell? For once in her life, Lena may have found something to occupy her time rather than looking for men. Lena had truly looked in all the wrong places.

Linda had put together one of her special TexMex meals of chicken fajitas, black beans, and rice. She and Trisha compared recipes. Linda preferred to cook for a small number of people, while Trisha liked crowds.

As Kaliq watched Trisha, he waffled again about wanting her to stay. He would have fifteen or twenty boys to cook for in the summer. Couldn't that be enough of a challenge for her?

He and Trisha had developed a routine like an old married couple. They had supper and then watched

TV or listened to the radio. He noticed Trisha had started tapping her feet to country music—something she swore she didn't like or understand when she first came to the ranch.

They talked about things that didn't matter and rarely did Kaliq find a way to bring the subject back to them. They were living under the same roof and, except for the time Kaliq worked out in the little cabin, they were together almost twenty-four hours a day.

Once Kaliq had even taken her to the cabin. He could tell that Trisha didn't find it the best place to be.

"What's the matter with it?"

"It's a little small. Only one room downstairs and one upstairs."

"It serves its purpose."

"Oh, I'm sure it does. It's okay."

The next day he didn't ask her to accompany him. He told her that Nia Sebastian was coming over and they should talk.

Nia had lived in California and she and Trisha compared city stories.

"How could you leave Paris?"

"Easy. I was such an American. I wasn't disrespectful to the French. I just considered myself a visitor and then later a student."

"Don't you ever think about going back?"

"I used to. I guess when you've grown up in a place, there are times you miss it. Is that why you came back to Wyoming?"

"Not really. I . . ."

Trisha realized her error. Something had happened to Nia and it wasn't pleasant. "I'm sorry. I wasn't trying to get into your business."

"It's okay. I got involved with a man. His name is Kent Hollander. I thought he loved me but he dropped me. He was on the fast track and one of the executive's daughters had a crush on him. Before I knew anything he was saying that we should see other people. Two weeks later I got the wedding invitation."

"So you know he wasn't being truthful with you about the other woman."

"It takes months to put together a wedding like that. She wasn't even a woman. She was nineteen."

"Did it get him what he wanted?"

"No. The executive was strictly business. He didn't think Kent was the right man for the job. He offered it to someone else. Of course, Kent still has access to the company jet and several other perks. He just can't get any further in the company."

"Did the other guy work out?"

"What other guy?"

"The one who got the job offer."

Nia laughed. "That was true irony. He offered it to me."

"You didn't take it."

"No. I wanted to lick my wounds, so I took a leave of absence and came home."

"Can you go back?"

"Oh, I have another couple of months to make that decision. I know they want me but I don't know if I can handle that cutthroat world. What about you?"

"Me?"

"Yes. Are you warming up to Wyoming?"

Trisha laughed. "I have to admit I do like it. I guess

that's why you don't miss California, but you know what?"

"I'm sure you're going to tell me."

"I had to come to Wyoming to settle unfinished business. It's still unfinished but when and if I leave here, it will be."

"So you're saying sooner or later I should go to California because it's unfinished business."

"Exactly."

Trisha liked Nia. In some ways they were kindred spirits. They seemed to like the same kind of life. Trisha knew she was beginning to fall in love with Wyoming.

The women got together whenever Kaliq was exercising and Brett was checking on the builders. Nia was also good with falcons. Trisha went to a school meeting where Brett and Nia gave a talk about falcons and why it's so important to think about endangered species.

Trisha drove home with Kaliq while Brett took the truck so he could drop Nia off before he came home. Somehow she was beginning to fall into the routine of the ranch.

There was still one part of her that she couldn't share. Trisha didn't tell anyone that she slept with the light on because she was afraid to be in a darkened room—afraid that Rommel would find her in the night and she wouldn't be able to escape him.

She covered up by always getting a book from the library and then reading herself to sleep. If she woke in the middle of the night for any reason, she would be able to focus quickly. She would never tell Kaliq. That would be admitting that he couldn't protect her.

The last thing she remembered was reading a section where the female detective was about to reveal the murderer. She must have slept only a few minutes. She didn't know what awakened her. She opened her eyes and everything was pitch black. She sat up and looked around. She thought she saw movement on the right, then on the left. She only knew she had to get away. She leaped off the bed and ran for the door. The knob slipped in her hand several times before she got the door open.

She didn't remember screaming but she must have, because as she came running down the hall she saw a flashlight and heard Kaliq's voice.

"Trisha, it's okay. We just blew a fuse."

"Where's the fuse box? Do you have breakers?"

"Honey, calm down. The fuse box is in the mud room." He handed her the flashlight.

She tried but she couldn't breathe. She ran to the kitchen and into the mud room. She found the box, opened it, and pushed the breaker switch. Nothing happened.

Kaliq rolled over to her and took the flashlight. He reached up on the wall by the back door and flipped the switch. The room was suddenly flooded with light.

"What happened? You were screaming so loud I thought you must have hurt yourself."

"I woke . . . up and it was . . . dark and I . . ."

"Calm down. It's okay. We just had some kind of overload and the breaker kicked off."

She folded her arms over her body and took several deep breaths. Finally she regained control. "I'm so sorry. I must have been having a bad dream and when I woke up I was still under the spell of the dream."

"Do you know what the dream was about?"

"No. I can't remember," she lied.

"Does this happen often?" He knew she wasn't telling the truth. She'd been in a panic without the lights. It was much more than bad dreams. She was terrified.

"No! I am not subject to nightmares."

"So why don't we go in the kitchen and make some warm milk."

She smiled. "You know that's an old wives' tale, that milk calms you down."

"Well, what do you suggest?"

"I think I should make some hot chocolate."

"And you think that will make you feel better?"

"Anything with chocolate in it will make you feel better. It's the true miracle drug."

She turned on the light in the kitchen and then Kaliq turned the one in the mud room off.

"I'm just going to run to my room and get a robe and my slippers."

"I'd better do the same."

It was that moment she realized that when he heard her scream he hadn't bothered getting a robe or anything else. The man slept in the nude. She felt the heat rising to her cheeks. How could she not have noticed? The fear had taken her reasoning but she didn't think it interfered with her sight until now.

She was back in seconds. She got the ingredients and began to make the hot chocolate. Kaliq came in just as the milk was heating up. He now wore a robe that covered him completely.

They sipped the hot chocolate and talked about falcons for a while before Trisha was confident enough to return to her bedroom. They put the dishes in the dishwasher.

"I wonder what Linda thinks when she finds stuff in here when she knows she left the kitchen spotless."

"She doesn't think anything of it. I do it all the time."

"Well, I'm going to get some rest."

"But not in your room. You're coming with me."

"I don't think that's a good idea tonight."

"I think it's the best idea I've had in a very long time." He took her hand. "Come on, I'm talking about getting some real sleep."

She followed him down the hall. She automatically shortened her stride when she walked next to him just as when they were going around the ranch. She didn't pay much attention to his room. She was grateful to see when he removed the robe he was wearing briefs. She just got into bed with him and let him hold her as she drifted off to sleep. Kaliq was right— this wasn't about anything but getting some real sleep.

In Pennsylvania, Rommel was just getting home from a party. He'd thrown several in the past few weeks, each at a different restaurant. He was becoming quite a showman. His parties were coverups for his meetings with snitches. The more he knew about his enemy the better. He'd built dossiers on all the men that surrounded Trisha.

Each dossier had a plan to isolate them and move in on Trisha before they knew what happened. She and her worthless partner would not steal from him and get away with it. He would use Trisha as an example of what happened when you crossed Rommel.

He wondered how Faulkner fit into the plan. He hadn't been around during the robbery. Maybe Guy and Trisha had planned to go stay at his ranch after they sold the Bed & Breakfast. Now Carlotta's was no longer for sale. It was boarded up, for the most part. A woman was staying there. She was a caretaker of sorts.

Rommel wanted his plan to be a surprise attack and to go smoothly. He would find ways to make Trisha Terrence regret she stole from him. His men didn't know about the diamonds. That might have been too great a temptation. All they needed to do was follow his orders when the time came.

The next morning Brett couldn't wait to tell his father the news. They'd finally gotten a group interested in the lectures and demonstrations of falconry. The man on the phone had talked about a series of lectures. He'd hinted that there could be other organizations once he told his colleagues. The twenty-five hundred per lecture was another incentive. Brett drove over and rushed through the mud room door. He found Linda preparing breakfast.

"Good morning," he said. "I know it's early but I've got some great news."

He passed Linda and headed down the hall.

"No, señor, you mustn't," Linda said.

But it was too late; without knocking, Brett opened the door to his father's room.

"Dad, guess what I . . ."

Brett had not been that embarrassed since he got caught skinny dipping by the Sunday School class when he was fifteen. He closed the door and started for the kitchen, but not before he heard his father's rich laughter.

"I tried to stop you, señor Brett," Linda scolded.

"I know. Has this been going on for a long time?"

"Who knows? But when a man and woman are left alone at night, well it's just nature."

Linda continued rolling the dough for her biscuits and Brett made himself a cup of very strong coffee.

Brett didn't agree with her. This was not nature. His father had just told him days before that there had been no intimacy and now he found them in bed together. He'd noticed Trisha taking more of an interest in the ranch and practicing diligently with the metal glove for the falcon.

In the bedroom, Trisha was having a little problem dealing with the situation. "What's he going to think?"

"That we're sleeping together."

"But he's going to get the wrong idea."

"Maybe it'll teach him some manners. He should have knocked."

"Will you explain it to him?"

"No, and you shouldn't either. The more innocent you try to make it, the more it will sound as if we're having orgies as soon as the hands go home."

"I'd better get dressed."

"Okay. Meet you at the breakfast table."

She was still feeling shy. "Check the hall."

"Do what?"

"Check the hall to see if anyone's there. I want to go to my room."

Kaliq did as she asked. "Okay, the coast is clear."

Trisha peeped out just to make sure, then scurried to her room. She normally didn't have breakfast this early so she could take her time. She just wondered how she was going to face Brett.

He'd think they were back together and then after Rommel was out of the picture, she'd go back to Pennsylvania and Brett would think she used his father.

She showered and dressed but decided to wait until the men were gone before going to the kitchen. *I wonder if Linda knows about us,* she thought. She didn't want the older woman to think anything bad about her.

People in big cities wouldn't give it a second thought but out here there were different rules. People lived a certain way and she didn't want to insult them. She'd been so afraid the night before, she hadn't thought of the consequences of wanting to be near Kaliq.

In the kitchen, the table was full of ranch hands and builders. Brett didn't say anything more than a good morning to the men as they arrived. However, Linda seemed to be dancing as she welcomed Kaliq to the table. When they finished and headed out for the day's assignment, Brett and his father were still sitting at the table.

"Dad, I'm sorry . . ."

"Next time, knock." Kaliq had managed to live so his son knew what to expect. When he was with Daphne, it was almost a given they would be sleeping together. Trisha was another story. He didn't deny that he'd wanted the night to be more intimate. Maybe he should have made love to her. That was not an option. She was so frightened, he was afraid to leave her alone. And if his son hadn't barged in, they might have made love that morning. Kaliq sighed. He'd never get her into his bed again.

"Sure, but I can't tell you what a shock it was to find you two together. Not that there's anything wrong. I'm just shocked." Brett kept his eyes on his empty plate all the time he was talking to his father.

"I know you've told me several times. Why is it that you kids never think your parents have sex?"

Brett laughed. "I guess we don't think of our parents as knowing how to have fun."

"Well, for your information, it wasn't what you thought anyway. She had a nightmare and I thought she'd feel safer with me."

Although he'd told Trisha not to try to explain it, he felt the need to ease Brett's pain. But Brett didn't seem to be in any pain. He seemed to be laughing about something Kaliq considered intimate and special.

"Are you saying you think she's safer in your bed than hers? You really believe that? That's a joke, right?"

Kaliq gave up. He'd been right the first time. They shouldn't try to explain anything. "Don't be smart. But the next time, it might not be as innocent. So knock on my door, please."

"I just hope you practice what you preach."

"On what?"

"Safe sex."

So much for easing his son's pain. Now it was becoming a joke.

"What did you want to tell me that was so important?"

"Oh, I almost forgot. Nia and I were contacted by

BUSINESS REPLY MAIL

FIRST-CLASS MAIL   PERMIT NO. 272   RED OAK, IA

POSTAGE WILL BE PAID BY ADDRESSEE

heart&soul

P O BOX 7423
RED OAK IA 51591-2423

a group of librarians who might be interested in having us do several lectures and demonstrations. They're going to contact us later and set up a meeting."

"Did you check them out thoroughly?"

"Dad, they're librarians. We checked the organization and they are members of the Friends of the library in Casper."

"Be careful. They seem too good."

"Don't worry dad, Hank and Millie Court are in their sixties and have lived in Casper all their lives."

"And they just got around to doing something about the falcon's plight?"

"I don't know. Maybe they were always interested. Maybe they just never had the time or resources to put something like this together."

"I'm not trying to diminish your work, but this Rommel person is not your average lunatic."

"I know. Trisha told me about him. You know, maybe it is a good thing you're sleeping together. This means that you can protect her better. Maybe you'll want a couple of the hands to stay around the ranch."

"No. I don't want to cause a panic. He might not even show up."

"Well, make sure you're prepared. Maybe you'd better put a gun in your little cabin."

"Maybe. I'll think about it."

Kaliq didn't want guns all over the ranch. You never know when a kid is going to be doing a little exploring and find it. There had been too many accidents. There had been too many kids killing kids with a gun they'd found.

They finished eating and, while Brett went to work

with the falcons, Kaliq retired to his den to take care of some paperwork.

Trisha marched into the kitchen and said a cheery hello to Linda. She poured her a glass of orange juice and put a couple of biscuits on a small plate. She sat at the table, drenching the biscuits in butter and honey.

"Linda did you hear about . . . did Brett say anything about . . ."

"Don't worry, señorita Trisha, your secret is safe with me."

"But Linda, nothing really happened. I had a nightmare and I slept with . . . I mean, we were in the same bed, but it wasn't what you think."

"I don't know why you are so upset. Señor Kaliq is an honorable man and you almost got married before. Maybe this is a sign for you."

Trisha stopped trying. She just hoped it wasn't all over the ranch by the end of the day, but somehow she knew that was wishful thinking. She was right. While no one said anything outright, she suddenly felt like she was being treated as the lady of the house. A couple of hands had stumbled over their words as they addressed her as Ms. Faulkner.

She was just glad that Jesslyn couldn't hear them. It was what she wanted to happen. Trisha just felt badly that they were all wrong. Yet, in her explaining she found she liked the sound of being called Ms. Faulkner.

Kaliq made the call to the Pennsylvania police department. He and the detective working on Guy's case had talked several times but nothing ever came of the man's efforts.

"Sorry. I don't have anything new to tell you. We

know he's putting together something big and talking about moving back to Paris.''

''I think he'll be paying me a visit before he goes back.''

''Maybe. I hear he's still steamed that Guy and Trisha ripped him off and he's going to get even.''

''Well, thanks for the information. Take care of yourself.''

''Watch your back and the lady's.''

''I will.''

That night when Kaliq and Trisha were alone, he asked her about the reports that she and Guy had stolen something from Rommel. Trisha denied it and Kaliq believed her. Still, he knew that Rommel thought Trisha had something to do with it.

''It must be something Guy took when he said he was going to Rommel's.''

''But Rommel was in Atlantic City gambling.''

''Or maybe he wasn't. Maybe there's a span of time when he doubled back to Pennsylvania and found out that he'd been robbed. He never did bring those papers with Guy's signature.'' Trisha looked at Kaliq. She wanted him to agree with her that the stalking was over. She didn't find the answer in his face. She found more questions that needed to be answered. Unfortunately, only Rommel could answer them.

''I thought he was too embarrassed or afraid to bring them out with the way the papers were reporting Guy's death.''

''I think there's more to this.''

The more she thought about it, the more she agreed with Kaliq. Rommel usually lost interest in a woman if she were out of range or with someone else. He had to know that she was living with Kaliq, so whatever he felt for her should have been over. He was still saying that she owed him something.

"I know this is going to be a strange request, but maybe you should sleep with me."

"That could lead to more trouble."

"Well, maybe not every night. Brett and Nia are going on a lecture tour for a few days and I think . . . well, I don't want you to get the wrong idea."

"Kaliq, I understand and I thank you. But we'll have to cross that bridge when we come to it. I'll have to see how I feel in the night."

"Fine. Just remember that if you get scared, come on down the hall."

place to stay while I deal with Guy's death? Why? Why suicide?

She picked up her necklace from the table. It was the chess piece Guy had given her. He said it had little rocks in it but they would be the way to help them and then he went home and took his own life.

It should have been simple, but Trisha knew that if Kaliq said he was still acting as a friend she would be crushed. He was the ex-journalist; why wasn't he asking her questions about how she felt about him? Maybe he didn't want to tell her that there was no future. She fell asleep running different scenarios through her mind.

Kaliq also tossed and turned. He'd had the misfortune of falling in love with another city girl. Casper, Wyoming was a couple of hours away and it was a city in so many ways, but for Trisha, could it equal New York? Other women might be happy to spend a few days in Casper. For all his globe-trotting, Kaliq knew he was most comfortable at the ranch working with the falcons and the children. That was another thing that bothered him about Trisha. She didn't seem to hear her biological clock ticking. She still wanted a career as an innkeeper. How would she handle fifteen little concrete cowboys for the entire summer? It had to be her decision. He'd given her an option and she'd refused. He'd been through this with Brett's mother. She wanted to be part of the movers and shakers in Washington, D.C. When he'd decided to do fewer stories and wanted to pursue his old dream of a ranch, she'd been his staunchest supporter. Once back in the area she grew up in, she remembered why she'd left.

It hadn't been a good marriage, and after Brett was born she was so melancholy. Back then there weren't that many articles on post partum depression. He thought she was just sulking. Perhaps she thought the same and didn't know her little cold was pneumonia. By the time he realized she was really sick it was too late to save their marriage. She told him if he couldn't pay attention to his family instead of his career, then he should keep his career.

Trisha was made of different stock. It was time to fish or cut bait. Tomorrow he would find out just where they stood. Then he would know what the future would be.

Just after three in the morning, the phone rang. It was Palladin and he had news for Trisha.

"Let me wake her up . . ."

"I thought we'd discuss this before you talk to her."

"I'd rather she hear it first hand from you. Why don't I call you back when we're ready."

After he hung up the phone he wondered if he was doing the right thing. This could change everything. What if she felt stronger about going back to her world?

He knocked gently on her door and was a little surprised at how quickly she answered. Moments later she opened the door. She clutched a thin robe to her body that did little to hide her curves. Her auburn curls fell over her face and she brushed them back as her sleepy eyes focused on Kaliq.

"Palladin has something he wants to talk to us about. Can you meet me in the den in ten minutes?"

Trisha turned and looked at the clock by her bedside. It was twenty after three. What could he possibly want? If it couldn't wait until a decent hour it meant trouble. She knew she had to be clear-headed when she talked to him.

"Make it fifteen," she said.

After a quick sponge bath, she'd splashed cold water on her face to make her alert, then followed her usual morning ablutions before slipping into a cranberry jogging suit. Trisha reached the den first. She thought about it for a moment and realized she'd never really looked at Kaliq's office. She'd been so fascinated at what was going on outside the house that she hadn't given the inside more than a cursory glance.

The white walls and black furniture gave the room a stark appearance at first. The arrangement left plenty of space so Kaliq could maneuver his wheel-chair around without bumping into anything. Behind the desk was a huge expanse of windows giving Kaliq a view of the area where the falcons were.

Besides the banker's lamp on his desk, there were only two other objects: a coffee machine and a bronze statue of a man sitting on a horse. It was about thirty inches high. The design made it appear that the horse was about to rear up. The man held the horse's reins in one hand and perched on the other hand was a falcon. The gold plate said the piece was named "Falconer on Horse" by someone named Mene.

One of the walls had prints of different kinds of birds of prey. They were all limited editions. Another wall represented the falcons Kaliq and Brett had trained. Peregrines were as beautiful as they were deadly. The brown and beige feathers were striking when they were in full wing spread, but at the same time gave a clear view of the sharp talons they used to tear their prey apart.

"That's sort of the history of the ranch on that wall," Kaliq said.

Trisha jumped a little since she hadn't heard him come in. "What happened to them?"

"We sold some. We spoiled some and had to set them free."

"Spoiled?"

Kaliq wheeled over to Trisha's side and pointed to the first pichure. "When you are training a falcon you must practice with it every day. The usual season is from September to February. Since they are birds of prey, you don't get a second chance with them. If they aren't trained properly they will revert to their naturally wild instincts. Then you have only one choice and that's to release them. Let's find out what Palladin has to say."

Minutes later they were going over the new events involving Carlotta's.

"Rommel's bid is back on the table," Palladin told them over the speaker phone.

"I don't know why. He got his money." Trisha looked at Kaliq.

"You know what I think, buddy? He's after something else."

"What?" Trisha and Kaliq asked in unison.

"It has something to do with Guy."

For Trisha that didn't make any sense. Guy was dead and Rommel had been paid for the so-called loan.

"How do you know it's Guy?" Kaliq asked.

"My contacts say Rommel feels he has some unfinished business with Guy. Since Trisha was the sole heir to Guy's estate, he may feel that she should finish the deal."

"So he makes an offer for my place, thinking I'll hop on the next plane and sell it to him?"

"He might think that since you might decide to stay in Wyoming," Palladin offered.

A nervous shudder went through Trisha's body. She didn't realize how visible it had been until she saw a dark shadow fall over Kaliq's face. He must think that I don't like it here, she thought. How could she explain that it was the thought of still having to deal with Rommel that had caused her reaction?

"Tell him the place is not for sale," Kaliq instructed. "But let him know that Trisha won't be returning until March or April. If this matter is important it might force his hand." What Kaliq didn't say was that he wanted Trisha with him for as long as possible. If she stayed through the winter, they'd both know if she could live in the isolated world Kaliq had set up for himself and his family.

"I don't know if that's safe."

"We're surrounded by people here and you'll be watching his movements from there. What could happen?"

A lot, Trisha thought. Maybe he would just wait for her to return and then how safe would she be? Then she understood. If it was important, Rommel wouldn't wait until spring to try to settle the matter.

"Palladin, we have to force his hand. We can't sit by passively and wait until he decides his next step."

"I'll make sure he gets the word."

After Palladin rang off, Kaliq and Trisha stayed in

the den. Although they couldn't hear her, they knew that Linda was in the kitchen preparing for the first meal of the day.

"How do you really get to be a falconer? It can't be just taking a few classes."

"When I got started it was just a little magazine article and a chance for an all-expense-paid trip to Scotland. I did a little research before I left but it wasn't until I actually held a falcon on my glove that I began to appreciate it."

"Does it take a long time?"

"Yes. Here, in some states, you have to have a Master Falconer to sponsor you. You have to take a Falconry test with the Department of Fish and Game and you spend two years with your sponsor learning the sport."

"That's so weird. I mean you really have to devote a good part of your life to falconry."

"Exactly. It's not for the faint of heart or people with an attention span problem."

Trisha stifled a yawn. "I'd love to hear more but I think I'm going to crawl back in bed. Let's talk later. I think Palladin's right. We should be alarmed by Rommel saying he and Guy have unfinished business."

"I agree. It means the man still plans to be in your life since you're Guy's heir. I'll see you later."

After she left, Kaliq went to the coffee maker and brewed a pot. He thought about what she'd said about having to devote a good deal of your life to something. For her it had been the Bed & Breakfast and for him, it had been falconry. He hadn't mentioned that the reason he'd gotten interested in falcons was partly due to his ex-wife. She was from Wyoming and falcons were well protected in her state. He found that interesting and pitched the idea to a men's fashion magazine. They jumped at the chance to do something so different from the usual milieu of contact sports.

Kaliq remembered his first trip into the world of falconry. It had started out as a magazine article for a men's magazine but it had quickly become an avocation for him. He'd continued his research while flying out of New York. The long trip gave him plenty of time. He remembered the time vividly. He could walk, then. . . .

He was met at the airport by a representative from the British School of Falconry and whisked to the estate.

Kaliq walked around the grounds and got a feel for the aura surrounding him. He felt the presence of men from the ancient world who'd perfected hunting with falcons long before there were rules, regulations, or even books to guide them.

"Your first day will just be to watch since we've already scheduled a hunt," his host told him. "Tomorrow we'll get you started."

The man made it seem so easy. He removed the hood from the falcon's head. The bird, whom he'd learned was female, shook its feathers and gained its bearings. Then with the slightest gesture the man cast the bird in the air. Kaliq watched as the bird climbed. Once the falcon was at the right altitude, the dogs were then given their signal and they ran to the brush forcing grouse into the open.

Incredibly, at the speed of 120 miles per hour, the falcon swooped downward. She grabbed the fleeing grouse with her strong talons and flew back into the sky and on to the heathers. The bird dropped the game and plucked at it until the hunters arrived and retrieved it.

When Kaliq got back to the States he couldn't let go of the idea of falcons and falconry. He first mentioned it at a Washington dinner party. It was so out of the norm for a Black person to be so well informed about a subject like falconry, they were soon on the A-list for political parties.

It annoyed Kaliq that people considered him an oddity. If his white counterpart had written the article, would it be so unique? All any group of people needed was a little information and a place to learn more about a subject. That was when he decided that he would give young Blacks a chance to be different and maybe it would open up other doors for them.

He used his contacts in Washington to further the project and then Palladin pointed him to some churches in New York that would be interested in a summer camp for young Black boys.

"Now don't do this just because you're angry," Palladin warned him.

He'd faced the same kind of prejudice when he'd started his hockey league for young Black boys. So he'd learned early that you had to be willing to dedicate a portion of your life to them.

"I know what you mean," Kaliq answered. "I'm going to be a falconer and I've already contacted a Master Falconer. I think my name must have been an omen."

"Faulkner? What kind of career would you have gone for if it had been Baker or Forrester?"

The men laughed and Kaliq continued telling Palladin of his plans. He'd filled a diskette with information and ideas. He just had to write this last article on some trouble brewing in the Middle East and he was going ahead with his plans.

Five days later he was in a prison with several other journalists. Their guide had led them off the path and into the arms of the rebel army. They tried to drive out but their jeep turned over, pinning Kaliq beneath it. Both legs were broken and they must have injured his spine when his captors roughly pulled him from the wreckage. He drifted in and out of consciousness for days. The makeshift splints and the few painkillers they managed to keep from their first aid kit didn't do much good.

He remembered a story from World War II. A soldier, who was a carpenter before being drafted, kept his sanity by constructing a house in his mind and using the wall of his cell to visualize it.

Kaliq did the same thing. He built Taharqa, named for a sixteen-year-old Nubian soldier who defended Israel against the Assyrians. To fight the pain, Kaliq, too, used the wall of his prison to see how it would look in Wyoming. To fight the fear that they would never leave this place, he created a world full of peace and lots of children enjoying fishing, falcons, running free in wide, open spaces.

By the time Palladin rescued him, it was too late to save his mobility. He was cursed to spend the rest of his life confined to a wheelchair.

When he first found out he'd never walk again, he grew sullen and no one could get to him. He'd been estranged from Brett after the divorce and couldn't seem to make a connection with the sullen teenager.

His friends had rallied around him and dragged

him to meet with others who were wheelchair-bound. The journalistic instinct in him sparked and he became almost obsessed in finding out how people lived after they were confined to wheelchairs.

The more he learned, the less he felt sorry for himself. Just as he was pulling this part of his life together, another part collapsed. His ex-wife died and he was forced to become a father to a fifteen-year-old who seemed to take pleasure in rebelling against everything Kaliq suggested. It hadn't been easy. They fought constantly. Whatever he wanted Brett to do was the last thing the stubborn boy would do. Therapy had helped some, but the wounds of an absentee father were deep in Brett's psyche.

Somehow they had found a common ground with the falcons. Brett shared his fathers' fascination for them, but Brett was more attracted to the wild side of them rather than the bond between man and animal. Kaliq used that to grow closer to his son. By the time Brett was sixteen, they were a family. Then Kaliq had met Trisha Terrence.

Thinking of Trisha brought Kaliq back to the present. He was sitting at his desk and the cup of coffee he held was now ice cold. He sat it on the desk. Trisha's problem was Rommel. While she was a beautiful woman, he didn't think that it was about Rommel wanting her so desperately. He wanted something else. Something that he felt Trisha could give him. He'd tried everything to get her to talk to him. If he felt there was an unsettled debt then why didn't he tell her what it was rather than play this cat and mouse game with Carlotta's. What was it? How could they find out without Rommel knowing?

Rommel had been very careful in not talking about the theft from his safe. His men thought that Guy had been after the loan form. They thought once Guy was dead and the debt paid that everything was back to normal. How could he let them believe anything else? The surest way to a downfall was to trust too many people with the truth about you and your operation.

The world knew him as a hotelier with four- or five-star restaurants in each of them. They didn't know he'd turned his ill-gotten gains from his loan shark business into diamonds that could be sold for clean money so he could make other business deals. Trisha Terrence had his diamonds and he wanted them back. He also wanted to bring the haughty woman down a few pegs. She'd always thought she was too good for him and he wanted to teach her a lesson. Maybe he'd manage to do both. If he went to Wyoming and surprised her and her man, what would she do to save Kaliq Faulkner? Pictures of her begging and promising him anything ran through Rommel's mind. He couldn't just walk away. He had to bring her down and get his diamonds.

He watched a young woman of about twenty-five as she found reasons to stroll by his table in her figure-hugging gold outfit. There was a time when he would have been delighted to single her out and charm her into his bed. But now he saw women like that as too greedy and needy. He now preferred sophisticated women who understood the rules. They would be his ornaments in public, his chattel in private, and when it was over, they would simply go away.

He thought when he dangled his money in front of Trisha like a carrot, she would be grateful that he could pull her from the brink of bankruptcy. He thought she'd at least make some attempt to seduce him. That had not been forthcoming. She simply found another way to hold on, just as she'd done since he first met her. Rommel had watched her take small jobs and work at hotels until she built her reputation. Surely that would have made another woman at least call him and try to work out a deal? Trisha was not the kind, nor did she want to be.

Her partner had been easy to trap. His gambling was only one of his weaknesses. His other was fear. The man was so afraid of pain that he'd taken that option away. Only a coward would kill himself.

The biggest problem Rommel had with Trisha had been her choice of men. Here he was with all his body parts in superb order and she would rather be with a man who had wheels for legs.

When Kaliq Faulkner was a journalist, Rommel had read most of his work. Now he was off in a God forsaken place like Wyoming. He was playing "Mr. Give Back to the Community" with this camp he had for inner city kids. The camp was closed now for the winter and wouldn't be open again until June. So Kaliq had all that time to be with Trisha.

Rommel directed his attention to the dancers again and another one caught his eye. She was a tall redhead wearing a navy suit with a very short skirt. He liked her long legs. He sent a drink to her table and she smiled and waved to him. Her friends patted her on the back but he could see in each of their faces that they were jealous he hadn't picked her.

He wished that Trisha had just once looked at him the way these women did. He'd forgive her if she returned his property. He wished that she wanted him the way these women did. It was foolish. He should give up the thought of the woman ever becoming his but he couldn't. He'd overcome so much to be successful and he wouldn't stop until she was his. He knew he was right for her. They could be such a dynamic team. He'd buy the hotels and she'd turn the restaurants in those hotels into five-star eating arenas.

He'd known from the moment he met her that she was special. He even remembered what she'd been wearing: a navy colored dress with white specks through it. Perhaps that's why the woman at the other table caught his eye. She reminded him of Trisha but she wasn't as cultivated.

When he first saw Trisha he'd circled the floor twice in his usual manner of scanning the tiny Parisian club. Then he was just Ernie Roman from Chicago and she thought he was part of security. She was sitting with a man probably just a couple of years older than she. He'd seen the man in the club before but they'd never been introduced. He strolled over to their table.

"I'm Ernie Roman."

"I'm Guy Marshall and this is my partner, Trisha Terrence." The men shook hands and Guy motioned for him to join them. Ernie slid into the chair, nearer to Trisha than Guy.

"What are you partners in?"

"Nothing yet."

"We're future partners," Trisha had added. "We're attending cooking school and we've decided that one day we will be partners."

"I started that way. Now I'm interested in small hotels." He leaned forward and could smell the lemon-based scent of her cologne. Soon after, she and Guy left.

The next time he saw them it was another club and this time he had a woman with him. They talked for a few minutes and then the show started.

The master of ceremonies introduced several people in the audience and one was a Grand Master. Rommel learned that chess was a game that Trisha loved but didn't play very well. She was still fascinated by the game and had started collecting chess sets.

After the show, they brought out a chess set and allowed anyone to challenge the Grand Master. Several brave souls did and were quickly dispersed. Then he'd stepped up. They began to play and soon the Grand Master was in trouble. Another few moves and he was on the losing end.

People raved about the game for months. He saw Trisha and Guy a few more times during his stay in Paris. When he reemerged several years later, he'd changed his name.

Rommel decided to end the suspense and sent one of his men to get the young lady and bring her to his table. Once she was there he knew he'd made a mistake. She was obviously younger than he had suspected and all of her sentences began with "Like" or "You know." He was bored in fifteen minutes. He had someone escort her back to her table and satisfied himself by picking up the tab for the young women. He could see the frustration of defeat on the face of

the young woman he'd singled out and the looks of
joy from her friends that she'd failed to keep his
attention. He was suddenly tired and, in an unusual
move, opted to leave by himself and let his entourage
continue enjoying the night.

Trisha awoke five hours later. She was slightly angry
with herself for being too sleepy to have that little
talk with Kaliq. She loved this land and the more she
saw of the falcons the more she wanted to stay. Maybe
she'd ask Kaliq's advice on selling Carlotta's. If he
understood she was willing to part with it, then maybe
he'd see that she was ready to try a new life. Trisha
headed for the bathroom wishing she'd let her first
reaction to him stay in her mind and not allowed
him to get too close. She stripped and wrapped her
head in a towel.

She stepped into the warm bath she'd drawn earlier. She'd overdone it slightly on the bubble bath so
the tub was blanketed with the rich lather.

Trisha heard Linda and Brett talking in the hallway
and knew the woman had directed him to Kaliq's
den. They'd probably be there for hours since Nia
had mentioned that they were spending long hours
trying to get the bunkhouse ready for his little concrete cowboys.

Kaliq and Brett were huddled in the den working
out something for the ranch.

It had been a week since she'd moved into Kaliq's
bedroom. Sometimes it felt great, other times she
wondered if she was letting her heart rule her head
too often. They didn't only make love but they talked
about everything. She'd been practicing with the

gauntlet and had managed to wear it for fifteen minutes. She didn't understand how those original falconers could do it for the whole day.

She climbed out of the tub and wrapped herself in a bath sheet. This was true luxury. She had lots of extra large towels but the bath sheet seemed to give her a cocoon. She made a mental note to buy some.

She slipped into her beige panties and matching bra and then threw the navy dress over her head.

Trisha padded to the closet and got her comfortable slippers. She had a lot to do to figure out what her next move would be. She worried about how the foreclosure would look on her credit file but she was resigned to start over once they used it as a lure and the powers that be had promised her it wouldn't hurt.

Trisha also made a mental note to revamp her closet. She had only shopped sporadically. Now was a good time to throw everything out and start again. She might even change her brown and beige color scheme to something livelier. Trisha settled herself on the bed and picked up the special package that Kaliq had ordered for her. He called it easy reading. When she tore the paper off her eyes welled up. There were ten *Country Inns* magazines. She wasn't sure if this was good or bad.

Kaliq knocked on her door and she invited him in. He seemed slightly nervous.

"We . . . haven't talked about us . . ." he stammered.

Trisha was amused. She'd never known him to stumble over his words. She also understood that he was about to make a suggestion about their next step.

"I know we haven't talked about it, but I need to tell you so much," she said.

"Me first. I've got to get this off my chest."

"Okay." She dangled her legs off the side of the bed and stared at him.

He moved his chair so he could look into her eyes.

"I'm not sure if this is the right thing to do or to even ask. I want us to try again. I want you to tell me if we have a chance or if you're planning to walk away from me again."

"I didn't want to have to walk away the first time but I had made a promise," she began. "Oh, the heck with this. I want you to stop comparing me to Brett's mother or that other woman I've heard tried to live here. I think I'm stronger than both of them. I could live here very easily and who said I couldn't own Carlotta's and live somewhere else?"

"No one."

"Right! I . . ." She looked at Kaliq and they began to laugh. They were arguing about something they both had come to agree upon.

"I'm going to make another request, Trisha. If you don't feel comfortable about it, please don't hesitate." He paused and then continued. "I want you to move into the master bedroom." He hadn't meant to be so blunt but he was so afraid of her answer he just wanted to hear her decision and go on from there. If she said no, he wasn't going to give up on them. He'd just give her more time to adjust.

"Okay."

"Okay?" He took several deep breaths. "You just made me the happiest man in Wyoming with one small word."

"I don't think there was much more I could say."

"I think we'll say it tonight."

"That sounds like a promise."

"It is."

The promise was fulfilled all through the night.

Kaliq joined Trisha and they sat on the bed. She poured over her special gift for which she had thanked him.

He leaned over and kissed her. It was meant to be a soft, playful kiss, but before she could say anything she was being engulfed by another kiss and another.

Kaliq wanted to spend as much time making love to her as possible so he would have memories if she couldn't stay. Even as they planned their future, something in the back of his mind prepared for a disaster.

Trisha wanted to make love because she thought each time would be an imprint on his brain and he could never let her go.

His mouth moved across hers and she returned the kiss with just as much intensity. It was like liquid fire shooting though her.

He removed her dress and eased it over her head. He loved just looking at her warm, inviting body. She had never responded to anyone else this way. They teased each other. Seconds later he'd removed all his clothes and they stretched out on the bed. They lay there just holding on, when Linda knocked on their door.

Kaliq answered and told her, "We'll be right there."

They showered, changed into something casual, and went to supper.

Kaliq and Brett poured over the plans and figures for their new venture. Kaliq wanted to find someone to act as manager and to groom him. He and Brett agreed that one of them should always be there.

It would take a while to make it operational. During that time Trisha might agree to stay while the changes were being implemented. The fireplace in the den should be off limits since it was in very good shape. All those other projects slowed them down.

"Have you heard from that couple who want you to do the lecture series?"

"Yes, they keep postponing the meeting."

"Maybe they aren't for you?"

"Maybe, but they sure would have put us on the map as speakers."

"What does Nia say?"

"That we'll wait, but if we get another opportunity, it's too bad."

"Good for her. Now what's the story with you two?"

"It's still the same."

"Why?"

"Because we're just friends."

"Why?"

"What do you mean by that?"

"Your business partner is one of the most beautiful women in the state and you seem to be dragging your feet."

Brett looked up from his numbers. "Can't a man and woman just be good friends?"

"Sure, but you and Nia need to be more."

"Stop playing matchmaker until we make our first million. Besides, I plan to travel a little before I take the big step."

Kaliq had noticed that Brett wasn't seeing anyone in particular and thought it might be a good idea to nudge him in the right direction.

"What kind of traveling are you talking about?"

"Oh, take a flight to Rome and then on to Paris, with a trip to London for a nightcap."

"Why don't you do that for the honeymoon?"

"I'm going to take Namid and Galiana out today."

"You can run but you can't hide, and one of these days you and Nia will find out."

CHAPTER EIGHT

Brett had gone home and once again Trisha and Kaliq were alone in the main house. Trisha enjoyed this time with Kaliq, when the house was quiet and they could talk about the future. She could feel his uncertainty that it wouldn't last but they both were going to give it the best try in the world. Somehow there was a nagging doubt that Rommel would ever be out of her life. The man didn't understand why she didn't want him. How could she explain he wasn't Kaliq.

He was such a gallant gentleman, a role he played with everyone he came in contact with. He'd made no effort to hide his affection for Trisha. In fact he treated her as if she was his wife. She'd have to check the laws in Wyoming to see if a common-law marriage was recognized. She smiled at her little joke. Trisha knew that if she wasn't legally married, for her it didn't count. She didn't really care what the courts said.

If Rommel knew that she was being treated in such a courtly manner he would be green with envy. He always tried to be a gentleman but people learned early that it was just an act.

The weather was growing colder as September faded and October moved in. During all this time Trisha and Kaliq lived, worked, ate, and slept in the same house—most of the time the same bed. They were a couple in every sense of the word. Still, she felt he was holding something back.

As time passed, Kaliq was polite, gentle, and the most considerate man she'd ever known. He told her a lot about himself, but nothing of any true importance. She'd learned about his schooling, his career as a journalist, and even his love of falconry; but he'd held back things of real importance. He never talked about Brett's mother or what it was like raising a child. He never talked about the things closest to him.

Yet in bed he was the most considerate lover she could have hoped for. It was as if when his clothes were on, they were a shield against anyone invading his space; but when his clothes were off and they were locked in an embrace, he was on fire.

Although there were days when Trisha thought it was futile to try to get him to talk, at night when he came to bed she could no more refuse him as stop breathing. Pennsylvania had a different type of cold weather. She wondered if the fact that there were no other houses for several miles had something to do with the way the chill invaded her bones.

She had to wear one more sweater than Nia to keep warm. It wasn't unpleasant having to do that, just unusual. Sometimes she wanted to burst into tears and tell him what she was feeling. Truthfully, she was afraid of him sending her away if she did that. Trisha walked the tight rope of showing just enough but not too much emotion.

Kaliq loved the fact that Trisha was beginning to show so much interest in the falcons. She'd told him she was tired of wearing the glove and wanted to move to the next step. He'd explained that she needed to watch a little more before they added anything.

"Remember it takes two years of working with an appropriate bird and we haven't decided that Galiana is the right one for you."

"She seems to like me."

"Falcons are unpredictable. You don't bond to them the way you do with a dog or cat."

"So where are we going?"

"To watch Brett and Nia. They're practicing for this library lecture series."

Trisha noticed that Kaliq didn't seem as enthusiastic about the lectures as Brett did. "What's bothering you about that picture?"

"I guess it's timing. They've been trying to get this thing off the ground for months and now these people call and offer everything but a promise to make it a PBS special. Call me cynical."

"Don't let Brett or Nia hear you say that. If you're

right they're going to need your support even more. They won't need to hear 'I told you so' from the people they love.''

"You are right, of course.''

"Have you heard from Palladin?''

"No, and I feel that's good. Maybe Rommel has finally gone on with his own life.''

Trisha hoped he had. She knew that she would have to return to Carlotta's and reopen it but she didn't want to think about it now. By spring she probably would hire a nice couple to run it and divide her time between Wyoming and Pennsylvania. She would have to throw in a few trips to New York for a shopping spree with Jesslyn. She thought about those changes and she giggled.

"What's so funny?''

"I was just thinking about how most people who have two houses have one they stay in during the winter in a nice warm climate so they can avoid the cold weather. Do you realize that Wyoming and Pennsylvania have pretty much the same weather cycle?''

"Well, maybe we need another house for a getaway place.''

"Then when would we work?''

"We wouldn't. We would have someone else do the work and just hop from place to place checking up on them.''

"When is the best season for the falcons?''

"September to February, but they can handle the heat much better than the cold.''

They reached the place where Brett and Nia had

parked and got out. Trisha still had to caution herself not to rush to help Kaliq with his wheelchair. She just couldn't help being a little nervous on the rocky terrain.

"Come on over," Nia called to Trisha. "We brought Galiana and your glove. It's time you started working with her a little."

Trisha turned to Kaliq and saw the slow grin cross his face. "You wretch, you knew about this."

"I thought you needed a surprise for today."

Trisha ran over to where Nia and Brett were standing and took the glove. She put it on her hand and made a fist. Brett put the bird on Trisha's hand and backed away.

"Now gently take off the hood," he instructed.

Trisha could hear her heart pounding as she lifted the small sheath. On Brett's silent signal she lifted her hand and the falcon flew away. Nia gave Trisha a piece of tiring, a thin strip of food, to hold up so the bird would see it and return.

As much as she'd worn the glove, when the falcon returned and nibbled on the tiring, Trisha's arm dropped noticeably. She quickly recovered and she spent the morning practicing to 'cast' as they called signaling the falcon to leave and getting her to return for the food.

"That's how you train a falcon," Nia explained. "They don't feel the need to please nor will they take any scolding. Some people have ruined falcons by thinking they can force the bird to do anything they want it to do."

"It's really not us training the falcon. It's learning to show total respect to the bird," Brett added.

When they got back to the ranch Trisha was practically dancing. Kaliq had to make some phone calls and Trisha decided to walk over and see how the bunkhouse was coming along. She thought it looked a little small to be able to hold up to fifteen boys.

The foreman was kind enough to provide her with a hard hat and show her around a little.

"It's not as if they're going to be doing anything more than sleeping," he said as he pointed out the way the double deck beds would be situated. "The days' activities should be so draining that they'll fall asleep as soon as their heads hit the pillows."

Trisha had her doubts. If the energy and adrenalin is flowing they may not need sleep. She wondered how she'd feel cooking for fifteen boys, six permanent ranch hands, Brett, and Kaliq. Linda would certainly welcome her help in the kitchen.

As she thought about that she decided to ask Linda about the type of food she prepared for the camp.

"Thanks for the tour," she told the foreman as she handed him the hard hat. "I'll see you later."

She turned and started for the main house when she head a swishing sound and a man's voice scream for her to watch out. It was too late. Something hit the side of her head and she fell to the ground.

Trisha opened her eyes, saw the ceiling spinning around, and quickly closed them. She made a slight groaning noise and felt someone grab her hand.

"Trisha, Trisha, can you hear me?"

It was Kaliq's voice but it sounded so far away. She struggled to open her eyes again. The spinning was still there, but not as jarring.

"What happened?"

"You're a very lucky young woman," a man said.

Trisha didn't recognize his voice and turned to looked at him. His face was like a montage and she closed her eyes again.

"This is Doc Williams," Kaliq said.

This time his voice seemed closer. "What happened?"

"You stepped in the way of a two by four that was being thrown from the roof."

"Fortunately," the doctor said, "it only grazed you. I hate to think what could have happened if you'd been a couple of inches to your right."

"It would have been even better if I'd been a couple of inches to my left."

The doctor laughed. "That's right. It would have missed you all together."

"Do we need to take her to the hospital?" Nia asked.

"No. It's just a mild concussion. As long as someone will be with her all night and check on her every hour, she'll be fine."

The doctor and Kaliq left the room. Trisha lay back on the pillow and talked without opening her eyes. "I feel so stupid."

"Don't; it could happen to anyone. Just stay away from anything under construction or you'll give my father a heart attack."

"Was he . . . upset?"

"Upset!" Nia said, then laughed. "I don't think that's the word when the man wanted to call the emergency team in with a helicopter and fly you to a hospital."

"Oh, that doesn't make me feel any better. I'm so sorry."

"It was an accident. We can't help it if Kaliq considered it a national emergency. Don't worry. Once he saw that you weren't hurt as badly as it looked, he was fine." Nia patted her hand and left the room.

"We'll let you get some sleep. See you in the morning." Brett leaned down and kissed her forehead.

Trisha's eyes were closed but she couldn't keep the tears from welling up and slipping down her cheeks. Brett, who had been so distant, even though he'd been polite, had never said anything to her about their conversation in the truck when he brought her to the ranch and the new arrangements with Kaliq. He was not the kind of man who showed the tender side of his personality and now he'd accepted her.

She was still crying when Kaliq came back into their bedroom.

"What's wrong?"

"Nothing. I'm okay. I just . . . I'm happy that it's not serious."

That night, Kaliq seemed to hold her just a little bit closer. It had been a scare for all of them and in a way it brought them closer.

"That fool! What did he think I sent him out there for?" Rommel screamed. "He was supposed to watch her, not try to kill her."

"Boss, I'm sure he didn't mean for her to get hurt.

He just wanted to scare her. He thought she'd want to come back east.''

"I don't pay him to think. I pay him to take orders. I want to know what's going on so I can know what to do next.''

"They all think it was just an accident . . .''

"That's the only thing that's saving his life. Tell him I just want information. I don't want trouble. I don't want them to be on their guard when I show up.''

His bodyguard had been with him for a while and felt he could make a suggestion. "Boss, do you really need to go there? I'm sure she'll be back in the spring.''

"I can't wait that long. I'm going to have to move soon.''

The man knew he couldn't push Rommel. He liked his job, since he got to travel around the world and eat at great places. The worse part about the job had been the incident with Guy Marshall. The man was such a fool. They weren't going to kill him—maybe knock him around a little. Why did he have to kill himself? Well, it wasn't their fault. Now they were going to have to go to Wyoming since the boss didn't want to wait for Trisha Terrence to come back.

The next day Trisha woke up with a pounding headache. She pulled herself to the bathroom and showered. She added a T-shirt and a sweatshirt under her jogging suit top. She put on leggings under the jogging suit pants. Then she headed for the dining room.

Four pairs of eyes stared at her as she sat down at

the table: Kaliq, Linda, Nia, and Brett. She'd already begun to fill her plate when Kaliq spoke.

"Why are you up?"

"I have to go with Brett and Nia to train Galiana."

"No way," Brett said.

"I don't think so," Nia added.

Linda made a strange clicking sound and hurried off to the kitchen.

"You said that if you don't train the falcon every day you can lose her."

"If that's true, then I'll get you another one. But you aren't leaving this house." Kaliq hadn't raised his voice but it had the effect of a loudspeaker.

"I don't want another one. I want Galiana."

"You need rest for the next forty-eight hours. So you'll just have to take your chances with the falcon."

"Kaliq, really, I'm okay. It's just a little bump on the head." She got up from the table and started for the door. Kaliq rolled his chair in front of her to block her way. "This is not going to happen. The doctor says forty-eight hours and that's how it is."

Trisha took one step backward. "You are such a bully. Do you know that?" She turned and walked back to the bedroom.

"Wow," Nia said. "I haven't seen you give anyone that look in a long time."

"It's reserved for recalcitrant brats. I can't believe that she would even try to work with a falcon today. I have to save her from herself."

"Dad, I don't know how to break this to you, but I think you're going to have a real hard time convincing her you were saving her."

"Oh? What will she think?"

"That you pulled a power play. She knew that there

was no way Nia or I would take her on the mountain after you were so adamant. I don't think she's going to be too forgiving on this one."

"It was for her own good."

"Brett's right. You see it as protecting her. She sees it as you making decisions for her. She's going to wonder if you won't be the same way when she needs to make a business decision."

Kaliq knew they were right. What else could he do? If she wasn't up to par she couldn't handle a falcon. She probably couldn't even handle the glove. He just couldn't think of another way to handle the situation.

Trisha lay on the bed filled with anger. She was angry with herself because she should have known better than to avoid the doctor's orders. Her anger was directed at Kaliq because he'd been so difficult. If she'd gone around him, it would have appeared that she did it because he was in a wheelchair and she didn't think he could stop her. Brett and Nia would certainly have taken his side and she would have defied Kaliq for nothing.

She'd never thought about having to handle arguments differently when the person was in a wheelchair. She never wanted him to feel that he wasn't man enough to make his point.

How could she have been so foolish? She picked up the phone and turned it on. Kaliq always turned it off at night so the answering machine would pick up calls.

She was relieved to have her friend answer.

"Jesslyn, I've made a complete fool of myself." Trisha sobbed.

"What happened?"

Trisha explained and could not believe the reaction. Jesslyn was laughing.

"I'm sorry, Trisha, but that's so typical of a new relationship. You think because you had a fight it's all over."

"I'm not the type to back down the way I did today. I'm wondering if he wasn't . . ."

"I know. You think if he wasn't in that wheelchair you could really give him a piece of your mind. Or you think you'd just walk out the door and too bad if he didn't like it."

"Exactly."

"Well, think about this. I'm barely five feet. I'm married to a man well over six feet. I've had friends tell me, if they were my height, they would be afraid to talk back to him."

"Well, he is pretty big."

"That's not the point. We don't even think about size when we disagree. The only time I back down quickly is when I know I'm wrong."

"Mea Culpa."

"You certainly are guilty. You did something stupid and then you got angry with him because he stopped you. Believe me, if you were right, it wouldn't have mattered and you too would still make up."

"Any advice on how to get out of this?"

"Accept his apology and then tell him how glad you are that he cared enough to protect you."

"What if he doesn't apologize?"

"Trust me."

When she hung up she was feeling a lot better. She knew that Kaliq would probably be in his office. She also knew she couldn't let him be the first to apologize. She went in the bathroom and washed her face. She did need a little courage and stopped by the kitchen and got a cola.

"Soda pop? Isn't it too early?" Linda asked.

"I need the caffeine," she said. After taking four or five sips she headed to the den. She knocked once and didn't open the door until he said she could. They stared at each other for a moment.

"I'm so . . ." Kaliq began.

"Don't say it," Trisha interrupted. "I'm the one who caused the scene. I'm sorry."

Kaliq laughed. "I can't believe you were so stubborn. If I hadn't blocked your way I think you would have gone by yourself."

"No. I think I would have gotten to the jeep and realized that I can't do it all by myself."

"I had this picture of walking into my bedroom and finding that you'd moved back to the guest room."

"That would have been so childish." Trisha smiled. "Although I guess not any more childish than what I actually did."

"Man, I'm glad that's over. Now go get some sleep and you can start training again in a couple of days."

She didn't move and he knew that it sounded like an order. "Go get some sleep, please?"

She turned and walked back to the bedroom. She did feel a little lightheaded and was glad no one took her seriously about going out with the falcon today. She'd have to find something else to keep her busy.

The next day she felt stronger and began to reread all the *Country Inns* magazines that Kaliq had given her. She turned to the recipe section and studied it.

She kept changing the recipes in the magazine. *Maybe I need to write a cookbook,* she thought. That was it. She would write a cookbook for country inns and incorporate things she'd learned during her training in Paris. This would give her something to do besides wait until Kaliq finished working in his office. She just needed a computer set-up like the one she had at Carlotta's.

Kaliq was right about her health. Two days later they were all on the mountain as she practiced casting. The falcons made strange noises. Nia told her it was called Kakking. They watched as Namid and Galiana seemed to become a couple in the air. They flew together, swooped together, and protected each other from other birds that might be nearby. She learned that they weren't the wild, tough creatures they appeared to be. Falcons were actually afraid of some raptors and it was up to the falconer to guide them to the best opportunities for them to attack.

When she first mentioned the idea to Kaliq he wasn't sure she should try it. There were so many cookbooks out there. Trisha explained that if she didn't sell it to a publisher it would just become the stock for Carlotta's. If she was going to have someone manage it, she wanted them to work from her guide. He relented and said he'd make arrangements about getting her computer moved.

Trisha had come a long way since her Cordon Bleu days and she'd never let those instructors embarrass her. She'd treat Kaliq almost the same way—show respect but don't let them destroy you. If he wasn't going to open up then neither was she.

Trisha found another outlet for her energy. She started creating recipes for large crowds like a full complement of young city dwellers.

She'd gone shopping with Linda only to come back with several spiral notebooks. She would use these to work on the dinners that served four to six to dinners that serve twenty until she could get her computer.

Now she had two things to keep her busy. Her guidebook and her falcon.

The work was satisfying and simply a means of escape whenever she was left alone.

Her hobby began to pay off. She'd sent some of the expandable recipes to a magazine and they wanted her to do a column called "Feed the Crowd." She told them she'd think about it and let them know.

Despite the cold, Trisha found herself falling in love with the wide open spaces. She liked seeing the stars at night and she didn't mind having to dress warmly to do it.

Each time she left the ranch for any reason, when she returned she felt a sense of home coming, to the man and to the land.

Since it was apparent she'd be there at Thanksgiving, she and Linda began to work out a menu—something that was traditional and yet trendy. Something that everyone enjoyed, even if they were tasting it for the first time. There were some special ingredients she needed and she asked Nia when she was going into Casper. They set a day and Nia and Trisha spent the day shopping and having lunch.

Kaliq accompanied her on the next shopping trip. He helped her find obscure little stores that weren't on the map but had dynamic spices that would tickle the taste buds. By the time they got back to the ranch she needed a whole shelf.

The day her computer arrived, she was out with Galiana and they'd completed another exercise that led her to believe that she was coming along as a falconer.

They set up the computer in the guest room and Nia had been thoughtful enough to order one hundred diskettes.

"I remember when I worked in an office, we were always running out of diskettes. I started keeping my own private stash."

"Are you ever going back there?"

"I don't know. I loved the projects I was assigned but I couldn't believe all the corporate backstabbing. I know it goes with the territory but I can't believe you can stay in that environment and not be seduced into that world."

"Wouldn't that depend on how badly you wanted to get ahead?"

"Not really. People would actually refer to you as a friend and then go to the boss behind your back and say that you were difficult to work with."

"What did your boss say?"

"That I shouldn't worry about it and just do my job."

"Maybe that's the best advice. Somehow I don't think you've closed the door on that part of your life."

"Sometimes I think I just need to go back and complete a project, faster than it's been done, better than it's been done, and then walk out."

"I think that's a dream you share with everyone who works for someone else."

"I think you're right. If you have any trouble with the computer, give me a call."

After Nia left, Trisha began reviewing some of the programs she'd learned. She was having so much fun she didn't realize the time, until Kaliq knocked on the door and asked her if she was coming to bed.

CHAPTER NINE

Trisha had never really liked ranch houses, but when she first arrived she understood Kaliq's need for one. Now she knew that there were a lot of advantages to a ranch. True, Kaliq could get around easily, but she thought about how many times she'd run up and down the stairs at the inn.

As Trisha took over the evening meals it gave her more confidence. She felt useful and needed. Everyone who worked at the ranch was a guinea pig. She thought nothing of baking a batch of cookies and then asking anyone in range for an opinion. The men working on the bunkhouse were the most appreciative. After the accident, they all had been walking on eggshells with Trisha. They would even stop work if they saw her come out of the house. There had been more hits than misses once she learned they preferred plain food rather than anything too fancy.

Everything she did now made her feel more and more like she was part of a family. It had been so long.

She remembered growing up as an only child could sometimes be lonely. Once a bigger girl had tried to bully Trisha at school and one of the older girls had come over and made her stop. That made Trisha wish she had an older sister around all the time. Some of her friends had older sisters that they hated. They would tell Trisha all the problems that came up when you had an older sister. They always told Trisha how lucky she was.

Until Jesslyn, Trisha didn't even have a best friend. It was difficult keeping in touch with her old schoolmates, some of whom were a continent away. Then she'd met Jesslyn. How appropriate it seemed to be that Kaliq's best friend's wife was Trisha's best friend.

Things were so good in her life now she was afraid to pinch herself. She might wake up and find that all this was just a dream. Trisha was beginning to blend in and she had such a sense of belonging. She hadn't even known she needed it until it happened.

Nia came by and sat in the kitchen while Trisha worked. She munched on cinnamon rolls and drank a rich cup of coffee.

"I wanted to ask you something," Nia began. "Is the world of a professional chef as cutthroat as the business world?"

"Of course. Any time there's a hint of competition you get people who are willing to do anything to win."

"How did you survive?"

"Survive? That's an interesting way to put it. Have you had a bad experience in California?"

"Uh-huh. I got out of college and thought I could take on California. I had a fresh new degree in computer science and I thought that was my ticket."

Trisha came over and sat at the table. "There's no easy way to put this. You're involved in a war the minute you're hired by a company. There's always someone who thinks you got the job that they deserved and they would rather die than help you succeed."

"Whew! That's a lot to take on," Nia said.

"But sometimes it's worth it when you pull it off."

"How do you pull it off?"

"There are lots of ways. Take my friend Jesslyn. She was accused of industrial espionage and forced to resign. They later found out that she didn't do it, but by that time she'd founded a terrific company she named GiftBasket and her business is doing so well they couldn't get her back."

"But what if you want to stay with the company?"

"Then find out who the players are and get a mentor. Find someone who believes in you."

"You make it sound easy."

"It isn't. So then you are planning to go back."

"I've been thinking about it. I was so green that I gave away all my secrets. If someone asked me how to do something, I showed them."

Trisha laughed. "I know exactly what you mean. I once gave someone a recipe and they used it in a contest and beat me."

Kaliq came in while they were laughing. "Is this a private joke or can I hear the punch line?"

"Sorry, it's a girl thing."

Nia finished her coffee and mumbled about a project she had to work on and left.

"You ran her off," Trisha said.

"Good. I tried to have my most menacing look. I wanted to ask you to go to a movie with me tonight. I know that you probably went twice a week back home . . ."

"I'd love to go. Only, find a comedy. I can't stand anything too dramatic right now."

"Great, we have to leave at six to get into Casper before the movie starts."

At six on the dot, after carefully applying makeup, Trisha was dressed and ready to leave. She wore a brown and beige long sleeved sweater with a matching fringed scarf wrapped around her neck. She opted for army green ankle-length skirt rather than the leggings she'd been using as a uniform. She topped it with a gold, beige, and brown crocheted cap.

She knew she was tempting fate by wearing stockings and pumps but Kaliq had made the invitation sound like a date and she wanted to dress up a little. She grabbed a heavy camel-haired jacket that Jesslyn had added when she sent Trisha's other clothes.

Kaliq issued a low whistle when she walked into the living room.

"I second that, Dad," Brett said.

"Thank you, gentlemen." Trisha felt feminine and pretty as they walked out to the car. Kaliq surprised her with a bright blue Lincoln. It was a specially built one that used hand controls.

"Where have you been hiding this?"

"Brett's house. He borrowed it for a date about a year ago and I haven't seen it sense."

She'd only been to Brett's house once since she came to Wyoming. Nia had forgotten a report and she needed it that night. They hadn't stayed long, but Trisha thought of it as the ultimate bachelor pad with nice clean lines, sparse furniture, and beautiful paintings. He said they were from a friend. Later Nia told her they were done by an ex-girlfriend. She hadn't even noticed the car then.

Kaliq was an excellent driver and when they hit the highway it was a straight shot into Casper. They put the car in a parking garage and Kaliq got his wheelchair from the back seat. He was so adept at changing between modes of transportation, it always amazed her.

Unfortunately the first movie house they tried wasn't equipped for a wheelchair. They had to walk another six blocks to a theater that was.

Suddenly Trisha found herself thinking about the changes one had to make because of a wheelchair. She'd become so accustomed to seeing the disability logo on places she went that she thought every place was equipped. She knew it had been true at the inn where she was working when she first met Kaliq, and, of course, her own Bed & Breakfast.

The movie was more slapstick humor than jokes or double entendres and for Trisha it was just what the doctor ordered. She laughed so much she wasted her popcorn. On the way back to the ranch, she was still giggling over some of the antics.

Kaliq had not seen this side of Trisha. When they were dating he usually picked upscale events and clubs. He didn't know she could let herself go this way. He'd have to find more movies of this type for her.

The main house was deserted by the time they got back. The alarm system was in place and Trisha waited while Kaliq punched in the code and opened the door. He flipped a switch and the room was bathed in a soft pink light.

There was more of a chill in the air and Trisha felt it even though it was a few steps from the car to the house. She felt as if she was being watched.

Trisha knew there were people watching Rommel and if he headed their way they would know. Although Kaliq didn't actually tell her he'd beefed up security, Trisha had noticed several men watching her.

Every time she thought about Guy she asked herself why he'd be so desperate that he felt the only way out was to take his own life. She still wore the chess piece he'd given her. Why didn't he trust her enough to talk to her? Sure she was angry with him, but it wasn't the first time they'd clashed. She ran her fingers along the chain that held the last thing he gave her. The chess piece. Now she wore Guy's rather than her own.

"Care for a night cap?" Kaliq asked.

"I'd love one."

Kaliq selected a brandy bottle from the bar in the little alcove off the dining room. He poured some in a glass and swished it around to release the bouquet. Then he rolled the glass in his hands hoping the heat from his hands would pass through the glass and release more flavor. He handed the glass to Trisha and she waited while he prepared his own drink in the same manner.

"To more movies that make you laugh," he said, as he touched his glass to hers.

One sip of the fiery liquid and she quickly felt its warmth spreading through her body. She sat on the sofa and he pulled his chair next to her.

"Do you use brandy in your cooking?"

"Sometimes, but never this."

"Why not?"

"This is not to cook with. This is to savor on your taste buds and remember." She let the tip of her tongue slide across her lips.

"Of course you would recognize it. I keep forgetting you learned to cook in Paris. Do you ever wish you were back there?"

"Sometimes. When the cake sags or the oven is off by degrees and I burn something. Then I wish I was back in school with those perfect chefs that seemed to do everything right. Once they delivered the wrong cut of meat and my instructor simply invented a recipe and a new class to go with it."

"Do you ever watch those cooking shows on cable TV?"

"Oh yes, I was hoping to do something like that from Carlotta's."

"Directly from the inn?"

"Yes. We were going to call it 'Carlotta's Cuisine' and we would have a celebrity and a guest from the inn watch us prepare the food."

Kaliq hoped his voice sounded stronger to Trisha than it did to him as he said, "Sounds like a good idea."

She had plans. What hurt the most was that she deserved to have a chance to do that cooking show. She'd studied and worked hard and he knew from his days as a journalist that that was the key to success. How could he deny her that? Perhaps that could be arranged. He still had some friends with connections in the media. Maybe he'd call a few of them and see. There was a whole cable channel dedicated to food;

it might be nice to have Carlotta's kitchen as one of the shows.

While his head told him that he had to let her fly, his heart told him that he couldn't replace her and his body told him that he could at least have beautiful memories of her in his bed. If only they could spend time in all the places they loved.

"Let's get some sleep." He took her hand and stared into her eyes. His meaning was clear. She smiled and nodded.

They put the brandy away and slipped the glasses into the dishwasher. She followed him down the hall to his bedroom.

She took off her boots and pulled herself on the bed so she was sitting next to him. Her head was lowered. The best cure for that was to give her something else to think about. Kaliq leaned over, put his finger under her chin, and gently raised her head so he could look at her.

"You are beautiful," he said, as his lips came down on hers.

He continued with little tiny kisses as they undressed each other. Then he lay motionless as her warm breath tickled his shoulder.

He smiled and shifted so she was lying across his chest. He was just enjoying the closeness, the intimacy. He held her in his arms until the demands of his hardened body couldn't take it anymore. He pulled her on top of him. She lifted her head and placed little biting kisses on his face and neck. As always, he kept a thin silver foil with him. He'd never failed to protect her, not even from himself. She moved against him and he almost lost control. Tiny explosions burst inside his body as he sought her mouth. She was not a passive lover, he thought, as he felt her tongue thrusting inside his mouth. She created a bonfire inside him that would almost detonate the fires of passion but each time he grew close she retreated.

It was a game lovers played—each testing the other's ability to control the body while giving the other person pleasure. His mouth slipped to her nipple and he grinned in the darkness he heard her gasp.

She whispered a few French words and his travels had taken him to enough French-speaking countries that he fully understood. Her lips traveled down and across his chest and then returned to his mouth.

Flickering darts of desire charged through them. Now he took control. He mimicked her trail of kisses, down her body, across her breasts. He felt the ripples and when she tried to move and bring the craving to a halt he held her firm and listened to her pleas and cries of satisfaction as she slipped over the edge of passion.

A shudder tore through him and he held Trisha closer to him despite her body's urging for more. Finally he allowed her to fit herself on his throbbing manhood. He moved inside her. It was like hot, wet silk and he didn't want to continue, but his body began a natural rhythmic movement that increased as his longing did and grew faster until they shattered the night.

He awoke first and got dressed and tidied up his room. When he'd first had the house built he'd put an extra strength washer and dryer in the laundry room and a smaller washer and dryer in his room. There were times he changed clothes during the day and he liked the convenience of doing as much for himself as he could. The one thing he liked about

Trisha is that she slept so soundly he could use the machines and not wake her. If he tried to use the laundry room, Linda or Brett or whoever was in the house would be there offering to help. Having this little unit in the bedroom gave him a chance to do things himself. Just like in the little cabin where he'd worked out each day until his upper body was strong enough to make up for his withered legs.

Trisha hadn't liked the cabin. He didn't try to take her back there once he'd given her the tour. But, it was time for him to start using the gym again. He'd spent so much time around the house eating Trisha's cookies and Linda's dinners that he was putting on weight. He'd go over the next day and see what needed to be done. Then he'd get back to his fighting weight.

He took a deep breath. "Damn. Admit it," he said aloud. "You love her." Of course he'd told her he did. In many ways he believed it, but this bolt of lightning he felt for her now was nothing compared to anything he'd ever felt before. By taking that step and confessing he didn't feel the relief he'd hoped for. He felt as if he'd made things worse. He looked up at the ceiling. How could he ever let go now? He'd find a way to make all her dreams happen. Only if he couldn't would he let her go.

Trisha lay there with her face hidden under the covers as she smiled. Kaliq obviously thought she was asleep or he wouldn't have spoken the words out loud. She could tell that he was a little surprised himself. It felt good.

As they began to build this new life together, Trisha thought about the four years they'd been apart. She knew that if she'd come here four years ago it wouldn't have worked. Then she didn't love anyone enough to give up her dream, and if she'd done so, she would have come to hate this place.

She wasn't ready for Kaliq's love then. Now she felt they could handle any problem. It was ironic that she owed this second chance to a man who had stalked her from Paris to Pennsylvania. When Guy said he'd found a way out, she'd been so happy. Then when he'd committed suicide she'd been torn apart. There were so many times something would happen, or she would see something and want to share it with him. He would always be in her heart.

The next morning it seemed a great day to work with the falcons. They took them up to the ridge. Kaliq had some business to take care of but said he'd join them later.

As Trisha pulled the hood from Galiana's face, the bird suddenly fluttered. Trisha held up the tiring but instead of nibbling on it the bird suddenly spread her wings and flew off.

"You cast her too soon," Brett called.

"I didn't cast her at all. She just took off by herself."

"Uh oh." Brett quickly cast Namid. The falcon began to soar and as he spread his wings and turned, they saw Galiana join him.

"Maybe something scared her. If they fly together for a little while she may calm down."

"What happens if she doesn't?" Trisha looked at Brett and then at Nia.

"She may not come back, Trisha," Nia told her. "Not all falcons can be trained. Truthfully, none of them can. They do what they want to do."

"If I spoiled this falcon, Kaliq is going to be really upset."

"No he isn't. Dad and I haven't had success with every bird. It happens. Just because you grow close to them, don't ever forget that they aren't pets. They can turn any time."

They watched as Namid and Galiana swooped down toward the earth. Namid found a rabbit and Brett had to go to him to keep him from tearing it to shreds. Galiana only pretended to grab at the rabbit and then flew off.

Trisha watched until she disappeared. Then she stood on the mountain next to Nia and cried. She was still crying when Brett returned with Kaliq.

"I don't know what happened," she told him.

He took her hand. "Come on, let's go home."

She sat next to him and fought the tears as they drove back to the ranch. Galiana was gone. Like everything and everyone she loved, she'd lost again.

Kaliq had Linda make some hot chocolate, while he helped Trisha out of her clothes and into bed. Linda brought the drink in on a tray and added a couple of cookies Trisha had baked a few days earlier.

He stayed with her until she fell asleep. Then he talked to Brett and Nia. They were all in agreement. Sometimes falcons had minds of their own.

"I think I could have handled it if it had been Namid," Brett said. "I know falcons. Trisha thought that if you passed the initial state where the bird was coming back then it always would."

"Please talk to her, Kaliq. If she gives up now she'll never be a falconer. I personally think she could be a good one."

"So do I. We'll see how she feels tomorrow."

When he went in the house he could tell that Trisha still wasn't dealing with the loss. She even mentioned going to the little cabin where he exercised, to get away for a few days.

That was surprising, because he knew she didn't particularly care for the little cabin. He'd even thought of tearing it down once the bunkhouse was complete but he had deep memories of putting his life back together in that very cabin. He just held her close and waited until she fell asleep.

The next day Trisha was almost in mourning. It was as if her falcon had died. Each time Kaliq tried to talk about it, she refused. Finally after they were in bed she opened up a little. She'd never had a pet. There was never a way to care for them properly and her mother wouldn't get her one. As she grew older and moved around herself she realized it wouldn't be fair to a pet.

"First," Kaliq said, "You have to stop thinking about them as pets. Think of them the way they did in the twelfth century. They are weapons. If you were going hunting and you lost your gun would you be sitting here crying like this?"

"No. It's not alive."

"Maybe not but you could probably depend on the gun more than on a falcon. No one knows why they go back to the wild."

"Maybe I spoiled it somehow."

"Brett and Nia were with you. If they thought you were doing something wrong, they would have stopped you."

"I really wanted that falcon."

"They don't care about you. So don't think of them as pets. You can get another falcon."

"It's not the same."

"But that's how you have to think about it. Falcons

don't have feelings. They perform a service. They aren't hunting because you need food. Sure we eat what they catch, but they aren't doing it for you. They do it because they are raptors. It's their nature."

What he didn't tell her was that sometimes falcons return. He didn't want her living on false hope.

It took a while for all that to sink into Trisha's brain but once she accepted the facts, she felt better. She would get another falcon and try again.

CHAPTER TEN

Today was a big day for Trisha. Once she decided to accept the fact that Galiana wasn't meant to be the kind of falcon she needed, Trisha could look at another falcon and try again. She'd been so hurt when Galiana hadn't returned. Brett and Nia said there was nothing you could do about it. After her talk with Kaliq she understood that she had to get away from the mentality that a falcon was a pet and accept it as a predator.

When it first happened she was so devastated that she'd actually cried herself to sleep. Kaliq just held her and murmured sweet sounds.

She thought about the practice while she showered and dressed. She slipped on pantyhose, a bra, and then white straight leg jeans. She selected a teal and white striped sweater.

She sat down at the bathroom dressing table and

carefully applied her makeup. She'd been pretty casual around the ranch but today she followed her usual workday routine. It made her feel better and the eye drops she put in helped rid her eyes of some of the redness.

Kaliq had entered the room to see how she was doing. He was stunned when she walked out. Her auburn hair was piled high on her head. She'd carefully constructed delicate wisps of curls to dangle along her cheekbones.

It was those very cheekbones that had first attracted Kaliq to Trisha. Her high cheekbones had just a touch of blush and made her look healthy and happy. The jeans hugged her curves and Kaliq wondered for a moment if he should allow her to walk around the building crew.

"We're not leaving the grounds. We're just going to look at a couple of other birds."

"I know that. I just . . . I feel better."

"I certainly agree with that. It's sort of a trip to the city look."

"I guess."

The look was a far cry from the crumpled woman who had arrived weeks earlier. Then she wasn't concerned about her makeup or her outfits. For days she'd been seen in oversized shirts and leggings. There was a variety, but she just seemed aimless as she went through the motions of the ranch activities.

Now this was the woman he'd fallen in love with. Now it was up to him to make it easy for her to decide to stay. He wondered if this was something to make her feel better or a wish that she was going into the city, New York City, maybe. He knew they needed to talk and once that happened he'd know exactly where he stood, but right now she needed to learn to deal with all that had happened to her. Losing a falcon had made some people give up completely. He just hoped it wouldn't happen again. If it did, there would be no consoling her.

"Good morning," she said shyly.

"Good morning." Kaliq was moved by the shyness. It meant that she wasn't accustomed to letting a man see her cry the way she had the night before. He was sure there had been other men in her life since they'd parted, just as there had been other women in his. Neither of them had found a match. Maybe they were fated to be together. He liked that idea.

"You could have stayed in bed longer," he said. "No one's around except the builders and they don't come in the main house."

Trisha had considered that but quickly discarded that option. It was time to face life again. She wanted a new falcon and she wanted to go back to Pennsylvania and get Carlotta's ready.

"I know that Brett is waiting for me and I don't want to disappoint him."

"I don't think Brett would ask for an explanation."

She laughed. "I guess not. I just didn't want to be in your bed, alone."

The statement sent a piercing dart to Kaliq's very soul. He shook off the emotions that followed.

"I got up early to see if your packages had arrived."

"Have they?"

"Yes. You can set up a real gourmet kitchen now."

"I know you don't believe me but what you cook in has a bearing on its presentation."

"Whatever you say."

"What's on the agenda for me today?"

"Nia will take you shopping. Now that you have all the equipment you need, I guess it's time you stocked the pantry. When you come back we'll see about a new companion for you. Are you warm enough?"

"I'd better get my other coat."

She turned and Kaliq watched the smooth strides she took. She had a dancer's body and the fact that she sampled everything she cooked was a testament to her exercise program.

Kaliq went out to wait with Nia. She'd pulled the jeep around to the front door and was checking her shopping list.

"I want you to be careful."

"I know, I'm to be part shopping buddy and part bodyguard."

"Don't let her know we're worried."

"I think she's going to know anyway. She's not a hothouse flower."

Trisha joined them and climbed into the passenger's seat.

"Drive carefully," Kaliq said as he waved them off. "We'll check out the falcons when you come back. We might try a red-tail hawk or an American Kestrel this time."

"Not a Kestrel," Nia said. "They look like parakeets. I think a hawk is better."

They'd been driving for a few moments when Trisha asked, "So are you carrying a gun in case we're attacked?"

Nia laughed. "Yes, I have a gun, but it's in case we run into the creatures of the four feet or no feet variety."

"Four feet or no feet?"

"Mountain cats and snakes."

"Uh, why did you tell me that?"

"I just want you to know that I'm a very good shot. I can even butcher a sheep."

"How did you learn that?"

"It's what little girls are taught on reservations. We go back to the old ways of doing things. I wanted something of my Native American heritage to be with me when I went off to California."

When they got to Casper, Nia loved showing Trisha around. There was something about a large city, whether it was in New York, Pennsylvania, France, or Wyoming. They had similar set-ups. People dressed a little differently and talked a little differently but a city was still a city. Maybe that was why she was so fascinated with Taharqa. It was different. It was almost a little town in itself. She regretted the fear that had kept her away. She wanted to learn more about the state.

When they were at the supermarket, Trisha picked up a couple of magazines about Wyoming life. Nia took her to a newsstand with out-of-town papers and she found one from Pennsylvania. It wasn't one that she normally read but she was hungry for news that Rommel had married and was off to Europe for his honeymoon, anything to get him out of her life. Until he was taken care of, she wouldn't be sure if she was adapting to the state or she was too afraid to live in the city again.

They spent three hours shopping and then headed home.

"You can tell me to mind my own business," Trisha

began. "But I'd like to know if you and Brett ever were or wanted to be more than friends."

Nia laughed. "You're not the only one. Would you believe our dads are the same way? I think every time we go on a business trip our fathers are crossing their fingers that we'll elope."

"So come on, answer my question."

"Okay, but don't tell Kaliq or Brett. Once I thought we might have a romance, but I'm five years older and I don't want to spoil a really good friendship."

"Five years isn't a big deal these days."

"I know, but I guess I've treated him like a kid brother so long I don't think we could be anything else."

Trisha understood that. She and Guy had the same relationship. She wondered if Kaliq hadn't come along, if she would have drifted into a marriage of convenience with Guy. Now she would never know. Rommel had seen to that.

Rommel and his new date sat in the private screening room watching a new release. She was the same age of her predecessor, but she'd gotten a degree in business and could actually discuss business news with him.

The old girlfriend still called and tried to get back together with him, but to no avail. He tried to avoid the press. He knew the police were following him from time to time and he knew he'd have to lose them before he went after Trisha.

* * *

Palladin and Kaliq were also very interested in Rommel's movements. So far he had been keeping a low profile. But the two men kept in touch.

"How are things going?"

"None of your business," Kaliq said and laughed.

"That means I'll tell Jesslyn to get ready for a wedding."

"Maybe."

By the time he hung up, Kaliq was laughing to himself. He'd run through so many possibilities for them now. Kaliq had even debated dual city living for himself. He could let Brett run the ranch in the winter and he'd come back each summer. That way he could live wherever Trisha did. He just hadn't found an appropriate moment to bring up the subject.

what made them more like brother and sister than anything else.

"This is the last chance we can do this. The next step is to put the falcons up for the winter."

Kaliq joined them. "Are you sure you should take this job? I really don't like the weather report."

"Dad, we just went over this with Trisha. If the weather gets bad, we'll be back tomorrow morning. Besides, the money is too good to turn down."

"Don't forget they talked about a lecture circuit," Nia added. "That could mean we could have a full schedule of lectures and demonstrations ahead of us."

"It just sounded a little too good to be true," Kaliq said.

"Now don't start dredging up your old reporter days or paying too much attention to those mysteries Trisha likes to read," Nia scolded.

"Don't worry, Dad. Namid and the others are just fine. Tommy will check on them and we'll be back with the clients in a couple of days."

Trisha listened to the banter of a family. She'd almost begun to feel as if she were a part of it. Kaliq said over and over no matter what her feelings were now they would wait to make a decision when the danger was over. She'd called Jesslyn but no one had seen the illusive Rommel.

After saying goodbye to Brett and Nia, Trisha had gone back to the main house. She felt one of those marathon cooking moods coming on. She decided on some nice soup or maybe one of her chili variations. Of course, she'd also make a large batch of cookies. Visions of double rich chocolate chip danced in her head.

Kaliq joined her in the kitchen but his mind was still on Brett's sudden windfall. "It's crazy, but I can't shake this feeling."

"I know what you mean but I think you're getting a little too suspicious. Who would make that offer?"

"How about Rommel?"

"He's not after Brett and Nia. He's looking for me."

"What if he's already found you and he just needs all able-bodied people out of the way?"

"Why would you say that?"

"Linda had an emergency and won't be here today. There was a mixup at the lumber company so our shipment is late and that means there won't be any workers here today."

A cold chill ran down Trisha's spine. "I never thought of it that way."

"I may be wrong, but it's just too many coincidences."

"What are we going to do?"

"Prepare for the worst and hope for the best. If nothing happens, I'd rather it just be between you and me. I'm going to charge up the cell phone and I need you to look over the cabin."

"The cabin? I thought you said that it wasn't used anymore."

"It isn't, but you never know."

Trisha thought he was being a little paranoid and she would just humor him. She trudged off in the snow to the little cabin that sat on a hill overlooking Taharqa.

She'd seen the place once when Kaliq gave her a tour but she wasn't really familiar with it. She opened the door and glanced around.

"Ahhh. What this place needs is to be torn down," she said aloud. She surveyed the downstairs, which consisted of one large room and a bathroom and then she climbed the stairs. The room on top was exactly the same size as downstairs and it too had a bathroom. The place hadn't been cleaned in some time but the linens and quilts where neatly folded and packed in plastic bags so they were nice and clean. She was amazed at how many there were. Then she came downstairs and inspected the pantry. She found a pencil and pad on the door and jotted down some things they needed to add. She stuffed the note in her coat pocket and continued looking around. The place was too small for one person, she thought. Then she returned to the house and started cooking.

Kaliq came in to check on her. "How did it go?"

"Fine. You really need to clean that place more."

"It usually gets a pretty good going over during the summer. If one of the boys gives me trouble, that's his assignment."

"What if he refuses?"

"He can get put on a plane home the next day."

She knew how dedicated he was to his boys. "Have you ever sent a boy home?"

"No. By the time we hit the highway, they've changed their minds about cleaning."

"Do you have a gun?"

"Just the one over the fireplace. Brett took the rifle. I try not to keep too many firearms around. The last thing I want is to have one of the kids find it. You know how accidents happen. I have a handgun in my bedroom."

This was the first time they'd been the only two people at the place since she'd arrived. One minute she felt like a wife, and then when Rommel crossed her mind, she felt like a fugitive looking over her shoulder, afraid to get too comfortable in case she had to move quickly.

"I'm going to bake some cookies," she said. "The chili is almost finished."

They lived in the same house and for the most part slept in the same bed and still she felt there was a part of Kaliq that he held back, as if he was preparing himself for a time when she wouldn't be there.

"I thought you baked cookies a couple of days ago?"

"They're all gone. Brett and Nia took the last of them."

"So what's the flavor of choice today?"

"I think I'll try double chocolate chip."

"Sounds good to me."

While Kaliq busied himself with chores around the house, Trisha concentrated on her cookies. As she kneaded the dough, she decided that she'd waited long enough to ask Kaliq where they stood.

She didn't want to do it when they were in bed. Passion had a way of making a person say anything to please even if it was a lie. She wanted them to just talk to each other.

She was cutting circles in the dough when he returned. He got a cup of coffee and sat at the table watching her.

"When this is all over," she began, "what happens to us?"

"That's up to you."

"Why me?"

"I was selfish before and you were right. You needed to fulfill your dream as much as I needed to complete mine. We both were successful. If you hadn't learned that you could run a Bed & Breakfast it would have always been in the back of your mind."

"I was so scared. We hadn't known each other that long and you were asking me to move to Wyoming and live on a ranch, for God's sake. I knew how to at least get a job in the tri-state area. I wouldn't even know how to begin in Casper."

"I know. I would have taken care of you. If it didn't work, I would have called in a few favors and you'd be set to try again."

"I know that. It was part of the problem. I didn't want anyone taking care of me. I wanted to be an equal partner in any relationship."

"So what do you think now? Could you really live here?"

She walked over to him. Her hands were covered with flour so she bent over and kissed him. "I think I've proven that I'm not afraid of falcons."

"Umm?"

"Well, not like the first day. I'm learning more about them and I think I want to be a falconer."

He was happy she wanted to stay, but her life as a falconer meant she'd have to be able to handle the hunt. He wasn't too sure about that.

"Well, maybe you're right," she said, answering the silence. "I can just watch them fly and not watch them hunt."

"Now that I can believe."

She returned to her cookies and he sat in the kitchen with her, talking sometimes, but mostly enjoying the silence. For Trisha that was a true sign that she was finally at home.

* * *

Brett and Nia drove along feeling good about the job. The light dusting of snow in the past two days wouldn't impede them, but any more and demonstrations were out.

"Suppose we continue the lecture series and just postpone the demonstrations," Nia suggested.

"I don't know. These people were more interested in the demonstrations than the lectures."

"But they aren't the experts. We are and I think they should appreciate that."

"I thought in that big corporate world you used to work in the customer was always right."

"Yeah. That's why I didn't fit in. I have a tendency to be pretty blunt about things."

"So you're saying we should just reschedule?"

"Reschedule or cancel. I don't want to deal with people who aren't aware of the endangered species list and you know that." She punched him in the arm.

"I like to hear you get on that soap box."

"Well, those corporate suits didn't like it."

"None of them?"

Nia bit her lip. "There was one, but he was on the fast track and he certainly didn't need an outspoken administrative assistant."

"You miss it sometimes?"

"Once in a while. I look at the fifteen-inch snowfall and wish for the days of my California lifestyle."

"You should think about going back and trying again."

"I don't know. There are times when I want to and then I just say forget it."

"You ran away. Until you go back and face it, you won't be satisfied."

"How did you grow up to be so smart?"

"It's from trailing around behind you when you were my first crush."

"I thought Candy Evans was your first crush."

"No, I mean my first real crush. Candy was just the first girl I tried to kiss."

"Tried?"

"Yeah, I threw my arms around her and she kicked me in the shins."

"So, she's the girl that got away."

"That was when we were six. She didn't get away when we were older. In fact, she liked my kisses then."

"How old were you?"

"Nine."

Nia and Brett burst into laughter. She wondered how he'd gone from the kid she babysat to her friend and partner. She just remembered coming home from college that first semester and seeing that he was a man instead of a scrawny kid.

Trisha had asked why they were only friends and Nia's only answer was that it just worked out that way. There were times when she, too, wondered if they could cross that line between friends and lovers. Shaking that thought from her head she concentrated on their business. For weeks they'd been on a precipice. Their small business had a few repeat customers but nothing like this offer. They were going to give the lecture and the demonstration to a couple who hinted that this could just be the beginning of lectures and demonstrations across the state. If that happened, she wouldn't have to go back to that nine to five life that almost destroyed her.

When she came back home, Brett was the one that told her she should only lecture on what she really knew. That was falcons. She loved what she was doing. She didn't tell Brett about the letter from I.G. asking her to come back to her old administrative assistant job. There would be a pay raise and she would be allowed to voice her opinion as long as it wasn't on national TV.

"What did our mailbox look like?" Brett asked. As usual he hadn't realized how much time had elapsed since they'd said anything.

"I got another request for the lecture series."

"When?"

"Three days ago."

"This is great. Why didn't you tell me?"

"The request came from I.G. with strings attached."

"What kind of strings? Was it from someone in particular at I.G.?"

"My old boss."

Brett remembered the strained look on her face when she first returned to Wyoming. She talked about her experience in spurts and he never got a full account of what happened. He just sensed she felt she'd been used and that she ran rather than walked away from the lucrative position. He never tried to force her to tell him. He'd just been there as a good friend.

"So why do you think you want to explore that avenue again?"

"Because it will give us enough money so we don't jump at every offer."

"So why didn't you tell me about it?"

"We got this offer and I don't know if I can deal with office politics again."

Brett glanced at her. "Maybe it's time you did go back."

"If this lecture thing falls through, I'll give them a call."

"Having an alternative sounds good."

They arrived in Casper and checked into the hotel. They'd selected adjoining rooms so they could work easier. After showering and changing clothes, Nia knocked on the door.

Brett opened it and stared at her. "Don't laugh."

She smothered a giggle as he stood there in his bathrobe. His thick black hair was still soaking wet.

"Having a little trouble with the hair dryer?"

"Make that a lot of trouble. At home when I wash it, in the summer I just sit in the sun, and in the winter I sit by the fireplace. I thought this thing was supposed to be better than either of those options."

She took the dryer from him and directed him to a straight back chair by the desk. "Your hair is so thick it's hard to dry."

Nia separated the hair through her fingers as she dried it. It took another ten minutes. They listened to the weather report and learned that a storm was moving toward them.

"I hope that doesn't mean we won't be able to get back."

"We'll keep listening and if it gets worse we'll drive back tonight."

"Now get moving; we have clients to meet."

Hank and Millie Court were waiting for them when they got to the dining room. The older couple seemed unfamiliar with this sort of meeting and Brett suspected that they were volunteers who would just listen, write a report, and maybe someone would pay attention to it. His hopes dimmed for this being a successful venture.

He tried to hide his feelings but now his instincts told him his father was right. This was a set up. Something to lure him away from the ranch. They were paying for Brett and Nia's rooms and this dinner.

After dinner, Brett suggested they meet in the older couple's room for a drink. He told them he and Nia had to make a couple of business calls before joining them.

Once he and Nia were back in his room, he told her his theory.

"I agree and I don't think they're pros. Let's go talk to them."

They took the elevator to the Presidential suite and knocked on the door. Hank opened it and invited them inside.

"Hank, let's get to the point," Brett said. "Who are you and why did you contact us?"

"I don't know . . ."

"Don't lie anymore. You don't know anything about falcons. So what's the story?"

Flustered, the man stepped away from Brett but stayed in the living room. "I don't know what's going on."

"Let's start with who hired you."

"What?"

"I want an answer, not another question. What game are you playing?"

Millie came out of the bedroom. Her gray hair was thin and scraggly as it hung around her shoulders. She wore a thin, well-worn cotton robe.

"What's going on out here?"

"That's what we want to know," Nia said.

"Millie, these young people seem to think we haven't been up front with them."

Millie pulled her robe tighter. "Get out. We'll call the manager."

"Oh, we'll go one better," Brett said. "We'll call the police."

"NO!" Hank shouted. "Don't get them involved."

"Then you'd better start talking."

Hank shrugged his shoulders. "Millie and me been married a lot of years. I got hurt on my job and had to retire early. We lived okay for a while. I bought a little newsstand and with Millie's salary we've managed to hang on. Then Millie's company folded before she had enough years to get vested. It's been tough."

"So you pretended you were interested in falcons and someone picked up the tab."

"Yeah. I met the man only once. He gave me your phone number."

"How much did he pay you?"

"$20,000."

Nia gasped, "$20,000!"

"I know we should have asked more questions but he said all we had to do was to take you out to dinner and let you tell us about falcons."

Brett turned to Nia. "We've got to get home."

Before they left, Millie gave them an envelope. "I was supposed to give you this tomorrow, but under the circumstances . . ."

Brett opened it and found more money.

They reassured the older couple that they wouldn't

call the police and went back to their rooms and packed.

They called the sheriff's office and told them Kaliq might be in danger. The sheriff promised to drive to Taharqa. Brett also called his father but now a light but steady rain was falling and the connection wasn't good.

"Dad, we're on the way back," he said. "You were right."

"Sorry, son, I can't hear you. I was right about what?"

"The sheriff's going to stop by. We'll be there in . . ."

Kaliq put the phone down. "That was Brett. Something changed. He's on the way back. I think he said he'd be here in a little while. He said the sheriff might stop by."

"Well, that's a relief. He probably heard about the snow storm moving toward us and wants to be here by nightfall."

"Okay, let's get out of here," Brett said. "The sheriff's department is going to be spread pretty thin trying to answer calls."

"I just hope we aren't too late."

Rommel sat on the mountain and stared down at the ranch. He'd made sure that Kaliq and Trisha were alone. He'd paid dearly to get Brett and Nia out of the way. They would be busy while he got his revenge on Trisha. No woman had ever walked away from him and no one had ever stolen from him and gotten away. He could have given Trisha so much more than this ranch on a desolate mountain. She had chosen

Wyoming over all the capitals of the world. She had chosen a cripple over him. And she had thought she could make everything happen by using the diamonds she'd stolen to finance that life with another man. He could forgive her for her choices but the theft was the only one of her vices that sealed her death.

He ordered his men to drive the camper near the bunkhouse and they would walk from there. When they got to the front door he signaled his men to step back while he rapped loudly on the door.

Before Kaliq or Trisha could answer, the largest of the men with Rommel pushed against the unlocked door and shoved it open.

Rommel walked in. "Well, at last we all meet."

"What are you doing here?" Trisha's tone was laced with anger.

"I expected you to be more hospitable to the man who helped your career so much." Rommel fiddled with the chess piece hanging from the chain around his neck. "We even have the same taste in jewelry."

Trisha's eyebrow arched in a silent question. She slid her hand down to grasp the bishop that Guy had given her. "I don't know what you're talking about."

"I doubt that. I understand your late partner explained everything he'd done for the good of the inn. I always suspected you two were more than just friends and partners."

She looked at Kaliq. His face was passive as if he was just a spectator but his eyes told another story. She knew that survival was the main goal at this point.

"I don't know what you're talking about," she said.

"If you didn't then why did you run?"

"I ran because I didn't want to get involved with

anything that had your fingerprints on it. Guy was my friend and you preyed on his weakness.''

''Whatever, let's get on with the business at hand. You have something that belongs to me and I want it back.''

''I still don't know what you're talking about.''

''Silly girl. Don't be like Guy. He held out a long time before he finally told us he gave the diamonds to you.''

''Diamonds! You must be crazy. Guy never gave me any diamonds.''

''Don't force my hand. My associate enjoys his work.''

Trisha turned to the man who had been standing by the door. He must have been a professional wrestler in another life. His arms were practically bursting out of his ill-fitting jacket. He grinned at her. It was a menacing, threatening grin. Her heart skipped a beat as she realized that what he was saying was that Guy didn't kill himself.

''What makes you think that Guy told you the truth? Maybe he lied so you would put him out of his misery.''

The sound of a truck halted the conversation. Rommel signaled for Kaliq and Trisha to go into the bedroom.

''Don't make a sound or I'll have to make your visitor a victim,'' Rommel said as he closed the bedroom door.

''Did Guy ever say anything about diamonds?''

''Never. But this means that Guy didn't kill himself. Palladin wouldn't let me see the body because the gunshot was to the face. Rommel killed him.''

"Don't let on that you know. We have to find a way to hold them off until Brett gets here."

Kaliq heard Tom talking to Rommel and his men. He was trying to explain that one of the falcons had gotten loose and flew away. Tom said he'd keep looking and return the next day. Rommel offered him a shot of whiskey and he took it.

All concept of time had deserted Trisha. Although it seemed she and Kaliq had been locked in the bedroom for days she knew it had only been hours. Where were Brett and Nia? They should have been back by now.

Kaliq was sitting quietly next to the bed and she knew he was working out a plan. They couldn't just sit around and wait for the cavalry. Her cell phone was so weak she was afraid to drain it any more. The charger was in the room with the enemy.

Trisha sat with her back against the door. There was a loud bang, followed by someone jumping against the door. She was startled for a moment.

"Don't worry, they can't get in."

"Good, but I know those goons of his will find something else to do."

She hoped her voice wasn't trembling as much as her body. She closed her eyes as a storm of angry voices came from the other room.

"Damn you. Why don't you just come out of there? I'll win and you'll lose."

Keeping her eyes closed, Trisha concentrated on her breathing and keeping herself calm.

"When it gets a little darker, we're out of here."

"How?"

"When I first brought the kids out here, I put the older ones in this room. There was a window behind that chest of drawers. But they kept climbing out of the window and hot wiring my truck so they could go into Casper and hang out. I finally put the chest in front of the window and boarded up the outside."

"So we just have to move the chest and we can get out?"

"It's a little more complicated than that. We may need to make some noise to cover our handiwork.

"See that armoire?" Kaliq asked. "It's on wheels. Roll it over against the door."

Trisha didn't ask why; she just did it. Then she saw the window. This one wasn't boarded up. Once the armoire was positioned, he leaned over and smashed the wheels. It didn't make much noise but without the wheels it became an inmoveable object.

"Tell Mr. Faulkner to be careful. Snow's moving in fast and before you know it you're stuck."

"I'll be sure to give him the message," Rommel said. "But hadn't you better be on your way before the storm comes?"

"Yes, sir. I'll see you guys later."

As soon as Tom left, Rommel signaled his men to make sure he was off the property. When they returned, he nodded. "Now let's deal with our other friends. I've had enough of the hunt. Now it's time for the kill."

Kaliq breathed an audible sigh of relief when he knew that Tom was gone. He didn't need his neighbor in any trouble. He opened the closet and got out two heavy duty parkas. He tossed one to Trisha.

"Put this on quickly."

"You're not going to try to get out of here. It's too dangerous."

"Is it more dangerous than staying here and waiting to see what Rommel has in store for us?"

"You have a point there." She slipped into the parka.

Kaliq picked up the phone but all he got was static. The bad weather was knocking out lines and making it hard to travel.

"We'll keep trying."

Trisha nodded. That was the one bad thing about cell phones and living in such wide open space. The weather could interfere easily. She was sure that the sheriff's department was also strained. Bad weather led to accidents and tough times getting the victims in. She didn't have any hope of the deputies getting to them before Brett.

"What are we going to do?"

"Try to hide in here. That door is solid."

They heard the doornob twist. Then someone tried to batter the door in.

"They're getting restless and I think we'd better leave."

"Where will we go?"

"To the cabin. It's small but we can hide there all night if necessary. Brett will be back soon."

"What's the plan?"

"We crawl out of the window and get to the cabin. They don't know the area well enough to find it in the dark."

Another crash against the door and Trisha knew that this was their only chance. She grabbed a scarf and wrapped it around her neck.

"Are you going to be able to crawl that far?" Trisha asked. She knew they'd have to leave his wheelchair behind.

"Don't worry. I have a very good incentive."

Kaliq picked up a hammer and two nails. He slipped out of the window first, wiggling to the ground and using his upper body strength to make up for his lifeless legs. Trisha followed. Kaliq lowered the window and nailed it shut. His hammering was masked by Rommel's pounding on the door. They crawled toward a tree and hid behind it.

The darkness was really becoming their friend.

"Why are we stopping?"

"To give them a chance to come around and check the window. Once they see it's nailed from the outside we can move toward the cabin."

Just as he suspected, the henchmen came around the side and checked the window. They tried to open it, then they looked around for another way out. The wind had already covered their path.

"They think we're inside."

"Every moment we can delay them is a chance that puts Brett closer to home."

Kaliq felt the wind picking up. They had to retreat until they came up with a plan. They waited a few minutes and then saw the two men run to the front of the house.

Rommel waited inside and he was not pleased with their report.

"They have to still be in there. The window is nailed shut from the outside. Do you want us to break the door down?"

"No, I have a much better way. I want you to burn this place to the ground. If my diamonds mean that much, let them die with them."

"What about the cops?"

"We'll just be city slickers who got caught in the

storm and ended up here. Too bad we couldn't help anyone." He walked over to the door and yelled. "Do you hear me? I'm going to burn this place."

When there was no answer he turned to his men. "Get the camper. I want to see to this personally."

Rommel took great pleasure in crumpling newspapers near the bedroom door. He added magazines and then put cooking oil all around them. He turned on the stove and lit several strips of papers. He started the fire by the door.

"So long, lovebirds." He strolled out of the house and climbed into the camper.

Despite Kaliq's telling Trisha not to look back, like Lot's wife she couldn't help herself. She saw the flames and uttered a whimper. "Fire. They set your house on fire."

Kaliq looked back and cringed for a moment. So many irreplaceable things would be lost in a fire. Pictures, keepsakes, notebooks. Fortunately the important papers were in his safe deposit box.

It was only the main house that was on fire. As long as the wind didn't change, it wouldn't reach the bunkhouse. But Rommel didn't care about that. He just wanted Kaliq and Trisha dead.

He tugged at Trisha's parka. "Come on. We just need to survive the night."

Trisha knew he was right. She turned and crawled behind him. She was afraid if she stood up, someone might catch a glimpse of her. They had to survive. She had to see that Rommel was punished for Guy. She had to see he was punished for destroying Kaliq's dream. She also vowed to build him a new one. She was a Cordon Bleu graduate. Why didn't she put those skills to use in Kaliq's summer camp? If he was going to introduce them to the wide open spaces, she was going to cultivate their palates. If . . . no, when, they survived this, she'd show him what kind of future they could build together.

The wind picked up even more and Trisha felt the snow and sleet on her face.

From the camper, Rommel and his men watched the fire and then saw the snow and rain putting most of it out.

"Think they're dead, boss?"

"I don't know. We'll wait until morning and check. I'm not leaving until I'm sure."

"What diamonds did Guy have?"

"Some items from my safe. I don't care if I lose them if it means I've gotten over on Trisha Terrence."

"The fire's dying down but it looks as if it cremated anyone inside the house."

Rommel had them bring some sandbags from the bunkhouse and put out the fire.

"I'm going to get some shut-eye, boss. We'll check in the morning."

Rommel watched the snow swirl around. It alternated between snow and very fine rain. If the police came, they'd just show how they put the fire out but not in time to save the occupants. He hadn't even gotten the satisfaction of hearing them scream as they died.

CHAPTER TWELVE

The new fallen snow made the trek even more hazardous. She crawled along what had been a path before the winds blew the snow over it. Trisha's fingers throbbed from the cold. At this distance, she could see the smoldering fire destroying both their dreams. The bunkhouse that had seemed so sturdy was now charred and the bitter fumes were still in her throat. She followed closely behind Kaliq as he crawled up the hill. His legs would not feel the cold but she knew his upper body was gradually succumbing to the chill and the strain.

She never knew how badly Rommel wanted her. Not for her beauty, not even for the cooking skills he marveled over. He was possessive and tying her to the debt of the inn was just another way of him exercising his control. Since he'd learned he couldn't control her, then he wanted her dead.

The cabin was several hundred yards away and she prayed they would make it. Her foot slipped and she made a small yelp.

"What is it?" Kaliq called. "Are you okay?"

"Fine. Keep going," she gasped.

"Don't look back," he warned her.

Trisha almost told him that she had already seen what was left of Taharqa. She almost told him that she wasn't tough enough to live out here. She almost said that she was cold and hungry and she wished she'd never come to Wyoming. She bit back the remarks. She knew it was fear, not anything else, that was causing her to lose it. Kaliq was the one who should be complaining. His upper arms and upper body strength had to bear all of his weight but he was still edging toward the cabin. She had to find a way to keep her mind off the cold and pain. She could only think of . . . recipes. Mentally she began to reconstruct her cookbook. She started with dessert. Something she'd planned to make for the children Kaliq had invited to the ranch for the upcoming summer. She began assembling the ingredients for her favorite chocolate chip cookies with extra dark, rich chocolate and lots of nuts. She preferred chopped Brazil nuts and pecans. In her mind she could see herself performing each step. She was just about to put them in the oven when Kaliq's voice snapped her back to reality.

"Trish, honey, we made it."

She looked up and they were at the door of the cabin. She'd crawled up the ramp and she hadn't even realized it. She stood up quickly and got the key. She opened the door and almost reached for the light switch. She caught herself in time. Instead she picked up the flashlight Kaliq kept by the door. She held it low to the floor as they made their way inside. Then she pulled the heavy drapes over the windows before she walked back and turned on the light.

Kaliq used the rails he'd had specially built around the walls to get to his other wheelchair and hoisted himself in it. "We're safe for now. I just need to contact Brett and the police. I'm going to put the phone on the charger. By morning we should be able to get a call through."

But would it be in time? Trisha thought. She remembered how she disliked the cabin the first time she'd seen it. How things had changed. Now it was a haven. She also remembered one other thing. She reached in her pocket and pulled out the list she'd made the day before. She scanned it and shook her head. They could have used every item on it.

Kaliq turned on the stove and they knew it would only be minutes before the little house would be warm. The rustic furniture was as welcome as any Park Avenue penthouse. The best thing was that Kaliq and Brett still had clothes in the cabin.

After warming themselves in the shower and slipping into some of those jogging suits and sweatshirts, they found themselves in the main room.

As she hung up their wet clothes, Trisha realized she'd lost the scarf Kaliq had bought for her at the flea market.

"How long do you think we have?" she asked.

"The wind is blowing pretty hard. It should cover our tracks and he'll think we died when the house fell down."

"He won't be satisfied until he sees bodies."

"Then we have until morning and if Brett's on target he'll be here with the cavalry. What's the real reason he wants you dead?"

"Control. He can't control me so he wants me dead."

"Don't get me wrong, you're a beautiful woman," Kaliq said. "I just don't buy the idea that it's as simple as him wanting to control you."

"I can't think of anything else."

"What about the inn?"

"The inn was part of it. He was building an empire, or so he thought. He and his partner bought the land surrounding the inn and they wanted to make it a corporate retreat. The inn would stay as the dining area and the employees' living quarters. He could have that without me."

Kaliq shook his head. The story she told when she arrived never really made sense to him. There had to be more to what happened than she was telling or more than she knew.

"So, they played on your partner's weakness for gambling?"

"He lost everything and I was so angry." Tears welled in her eyes and trickled down her cheeks. She wiped them away with the back of her hand. "I told Guy to get away from me. I screamed at him that he'd ruined my dream. I was awful to him."

"You were understandably angry. You said things that you didn't mean. We all do that at times."

"But I didn't get a chance to take them back. Two days later he killed himself."

"Are you sure he was the type to commit suicide?"

"People do strange things when they're under pressure. What else could it be?"

"Murder?"

Trisha gasped. "Why?"

"Guy may have chosen the lesser of two evils. Rommel scared him so much he killed himself rather than let Rommel do it."

Kaliq's journalist background always led him to keep asking questions until he got the right answers. Until Rommel actually appeared he'd written off Trisha's problems as just another matchmaking device by Jesslyn and Palladin. Someone really wanted her dead. The thought sent chills through his body. He would never allow that to happen.

"Think. Did Guy say anything the last time you saw him?"

"He said he had a way out but he didn't tell me anything else. He just gave me his lucky bishop." She held up the chess piece that hung around her neck.

"What's so important about it?"

"Rommel thinks of himself as a chess Grand Master without the title . . ."

Trisha dropped her face in her hands. "My God . . ."

"What is it?"

She dropped her hands and walked over to Kaliq. She didn't say anything until she sat down on the sofa next to his chair. "Remember I told you that Guy and I met Rommel in Paris at a party?"

"Yeah."

"He was a chess player who fancied himself a genius. At the party he played a true Grand Master and won. He sacrificed his queen and won with his bishop."

"The one he wears around his neck like yours?"

"When I first saw him I thought he was mocking

me. I thought he knew Guy gave it to me but now I think it's something else."

"Like what?"

"Guy said I should hold onto this until he got our inn back. He said it had little rocks in it and every time he shook it, he was that closer to winning." Trisha stood up and began to pace.

"Puzzles and more puzzles. Brett's hunting party should be over. Oh, no!"

"What is it?"

"You know what they say about things that are too good to be true?"

"They're usually a scam."

"We should have looked closely into that deal with the hunting party seminars that Brett and Nia were invited to host."

"Just something to keep them out of the way."

"We'd better start thinking of a little surprise for your friends. Once they find out we're not dead they're going to be looking for us."

Kaliq was right. That job came just at the right time. Taharqa was closed for the winter so that left just the four adults at the ranch. Brett and Nia were young and strong. So Rommel had reduced the odds by taking them away on business. That left only a man who did not have use of his legs and a woman who was a fish out of water when it came to surviving a Wyoming winter.

"So what do we do without weapons?"

"No such thing." He waved his hand indicating she should look around the cabin.

Trisha had no idea what she was looking for. "I see a wine rack with a few bottles, a kerosene drum, candles." She shrugged. "What am I supposed to see?"

"With a few strips of cloth, like those napkins, and a book of matches, I see a pretty good way of making Molotov cocktails."

"Not much good against guns."

"That depends on what else we have available. We aren't going to make this easy for them."

Trisha remembered her training in Paris. Often her instructors warned the class about how dangerous a kitchen could be. She looked through the cabinets and found a cast iron skillet. Then she opened the refrigerator door and searched its freezer section until she found two packages of bacon. They didn't have to be fresh. No one was going to eat it. She lit the stove and put the skillet on. It would give them something to munch on while they prepared their fortress.

The silverware was minimal but held some sharp knives and forks. She bundled them together in a napkin and put them on the coffee table.

"Trisha, honey, go upstairs and bring all the bedding down."

She nodded and walked up the ramp to the bedroom. It took her three trips to clear out the linen closet. The thick comforters, quilts and blankets would guard against winter but she needed them to guard against bullets. All of this preparation was just a futile attempt to keep her sanity.

When she returned for her final trip she saw that Kaliq had been just as busy. He'd assembled candles, flares, rubbing alcohol, napkins, and matches.

"We might be able to make them think there are

more people in here than just the two of us. They wouldn't know if someone else is staying here.''

"There are five of them.''

"I know, but only one is on a mission.''

"Rommel.''

"Exactly. We find a way to take him out and dollars to donuts, the others will split.''

"What if he just sends them in to . . . take care of us?''

"He won't. His ego won't let him.''

Trisha returned to the kitchen and put the bacon on plates. She poured most of the oil into a large pot and left it on the stove. It would only take seconds to heat up. For a moment she wondered if she could really throw hot oil on another human being. She'd seen the results of an accidental spill in the kitchen on her first job. It wasn't a pretty sight. Then she looked over at Kaliq. This was a matter of life or death. Yes! She could throw the oil to protect him.

They were ready. She scrambled a few eggs and put them on the plate with the bacon and brought it over to him. It was odd eating breakfast food at this time of night but she knew that neither of them wanted anything heavy. As they ate, Trisha avoided discussing their situation.

"When the boys come in the summer, how many extra people do you need?''

"Ten or twenty. I try to match up two boys per hand.''

"Why did you choose Wyoming?''

"I did an article on falcons a few years before I retired and learned this is one of the states that protect them.''

"It must have been nice roaming the country and doing stories that interested you."

Kaliq shook his head. "You don't always get a choice of stories. I didn't want to cover that Middle East skirmish." He shrugged his shoulders. "Things happen."

"I never explained why I was so adamant about having a career," she said.

"You didn't have to. I knew what it took to be successful. I was wrong in trying to change your dream."

"It wasn't just my dream. When my dad passed away, my mother saw it as a chance to do something she couldn't have done being a wife. She'd always wanted to see Paris."

"I remember you telling me that."

"It was great. I had a chance to go through an exclusive and intensive training program and I loved to cook so it was the best thing for me. She wanted so much for me to have my dream so she kept telling me over and over not to let anyone stand in the way. What she didn't tell me was that she was dying."

"What happened to her?"

"Cancer. She knew before we left New York but she was so determined to get us to France. The last thing I said to her was that I'd buy a little Bed & Breakfast type of business."

"So when I met you . . ."

"I was months away from fulfilling that promise. I knew that if it was a success I would be locked into it and I couldn't fit in your world out here."

"You could have done the same thing here."

"Not really. I was on the brink in Pennsylvania. I

would have had to start all over again and I knew nothing of Wyoming."

"Well you know a little bit about it now. What do you think?"

"About what?"

"About trying a business out here."

"I've been thinking of it. We could build a couple of cottages and have a select clientele. Only people interested in learning about falconry need apply."

"That might not be a bad idea to have adults around at the same time as the kids and then adults in the off season. Who says they have to live in the cabins? Maybe some will live in the bunkhouse."

They spread the bedclothes out on the cabin floor and wrapped themselves in them until they felt snug and secure.

"Was Brett's mother interested in falcons?"

"No. She was impressed by my career. She wanted to travel and she thought with me she could see the world. She found out too late that my assignments meant leaving her at home more than taking her with me. We met in D.C. She was part of a tour from Wyoming and I was on an assignment covering a breaking story about a State Department official involved in a scandal about using his office to make deals with foreign governments. When I did a story in Wyoming we met again. I fell in love with her world and she fell in love with mine. I think I'm doomed to get involved with women who are completely opposite. When I went off to cover another story she wanted to come along, but she was pregnant. In a way it was good. Brett arrived a little ahead of schedule. She hated to live outside the hustle and bustle of D.C., but every time I went off on an assignment she'd get more restless."

"So you wouldn't take her with you and your marriage broke up."

"I would've taken her if I could. She didn't understand that it wasn't feasible. After Brett was born we didn't see much of each other and just drifted apart. We went back to D.C. for a visit and she found her friends had moved on. She felt left out so she chose to stay in Wyoming as a way of punishing me."

"How?"

"I made her give up her chance to be with the 'in crowd.' "

"Then she died."

"Brett was fifteen. I got caught behind enemy lines and Palladin came in and got me. I bought the ranch soon after that. Brett loved falcons as much as I did and that brought us together."

When Kaliq talked of Brett there was so much love in his voice. Trisha hoped that Brett would somehow know they were in trouble and get home. If he didn't, she wasn't sure if she and Kaliq would survive. They were outnumbered. They snuggled closer and fell asleep.

Rommel and his men waited until there was enough light to search the rubble. He'd prided himself on his bulldozing technique to tear the house apart but wanted to see for himself his nemeses were indeed consumed by the fire. He'd kept the fire under control, for as much as he wanted to burn everything, he knew that anything that appeared out of control would bring more attention than he could handle. All he wanted was the diamonds.

"They aren't here," one of his men shouted. They'd spent the night in the camper but it had a clear view of Kaliq's vehicles.

"They've gotta be. Where could they go?"

"We don't see any signs of them. Could they have escaped?"

"No," Rommel said as his face contorted into a sneer. "How far can a cripple and a scared woman go?" His eyes narrowed as he scanned the horizon. They had to be close. The nearest neighbor was ten miles. They couldn't have made it in the dark. "They can't be far. Fan out and look around. One of you take the jeep and drive down the road."

Fifteen minutes later the men returned.

"Hey boss, check this out." He held the scarf Trisha had worn.

Rommel grinned. Soon he'd take care of Faulkner and keep Trisha alive long enough for her to tell him where Guy hid the diamonds. He hadn't told his men about them. They assumed that he just wanted revenge on his woman running off with another man. Revenge they understood. Diamonds they would want to share.

Once they showed him where they found the scarf, he took out his binoculars and looked around until he spotted the little cabin.

"We don't know if someone was living there or not, so let's be careful," Rommel warned.

Trisha felt someone shaking her. She didn't want to open her eyes. She was so comfortable, warm, and happy. Slowly she was pulled from her peaceful sleep back into the world of the present.

"Trish. Wake up. They're here."

Kaliq's whisper finally reached her brain and she awoke fully.

"Did you see them?"

"I saw movement by the trees more than actually seeing them. They can't wait because there's a chance that Brett and Nia will be here soon."

"If they can get here."

"Oh, they aren't going to do anything to them. They need them for witnesses."

"Witnesses to what?"

"A tragic accident happened last night. While Brett Faulkner was away on business his father and father's companion were killed by persons unknown. Get dressed."

She got up and ran to the bathroom. She splashed cold water on her face and on her wrists as a way of making her body stay awake when what she really wanted to do was crawl back under the covers. She dressed in another pair of Brett's old jeans and Kaliq's football jersey.

"I'm lucky I'm tall or I'd be in real trouble with these clothes. Did you keep everything he outgrew?"

"Most of the stuff. I thought about this place for kids for a long time and I knew some of the kids probably would need some old clothes to play in."

"What do we do next?"

"We level the playing field. They don't know who's in here or whether or not we have weapons. My bet is they'll send a scout. I want you to put on your coat and clear as much snow off the porch as possible. Push it toward the ramp."

"Why?"

"No time to explain now. Just do it. Don't worry, you're safe. Rommel wants something from you and he won't shoot. If you see someone come back inside."

He hated sending her out but there was no way he could clear the deck area in time for his plan. He had to find a way to hold them off until the phone was charged and they got help.

Within minutes Trisha found herself cleaning the porch, but as Kaliq told her, blocking the ramp entrance.

She walked over to the stove and turned on the pot holding the now congealed grease. She shivered as again she thought about using it as a weapon.

"Well, as one of my favorite chefs likes to say, 'let's kick it up a notch.' "

"Meaning?"

"Meaning they're going to know that it was a fight not a massacre."

She turned and saw Kaliq putting on his coat.

"Where are you going?"

"Outside. I see one of the men coming up to the cabin. He probably is just scouting to make sure we're the only ones here."

"Are you crazy? He'll kill you."

"No. Not until he's sure he can and not until Rommel gives the order."

"Please don't do this . . ."

"I'll be fine. See if the battery charged enough to call for some help."

She knew how determined he could be and there was no sense in fighting him. Four years ago when he decided that it couldn't work he walked away. A month ago when he decided that they could make it work he'd knocked down all her defenses. She wondered if Rommel had ever come up against someone like Kaliq Faulkner.

Kaliq rolled his chair onto the deck and picked up the shovel they left at the edge of the ramp. He pushed the chair into a corner and using the specially designed rails, he stood up and leaned against the house. He shoveled snow but watched as the man came closer.

"Hey buddy," he called, when he reached the end of the ramp. "I had a little car trouble. Could I use your phone?"

"Sure thing," Kaliq said. The visitor was obviously from a warm climate; his teeth chattered noticeably as he came up the ramp.

He saw the man turn away and reach into his jacket pocket. Kaliq turned and swung the shovel with all his strength. The sharp edge of the shovel caught the man across both shins and he screamed. Kaliq swung the shovel back in a higher arc and caught the man on the side of the head. The man fell to the deck, unconscious. Kaliq easily removed the gun from his hand. "Thanks, buddy, I needed this." He used the rails to pull himself back to his chair and rolled over and opened the door.

"Trish." He waited until she turned to show her the gun. "He's out for the count. The shovel did the trick. One down, four to go. Stay inside." He closed the door.

Somehow he made the odds seem as if they were in their favor. The cabin didn't have a back door but it had a window on the rear wall. She walked over to it and stood to the side as she peered out of the glass.

A slight movement caught her eye. Two men were coming to the back of the cabin. They probably thought their cohort was keeping Kaliq occupied.

She picked up the cell phone and hit the fast dial to Brett. The phone rang and she almost burst into tears as a static-filled voice answered.

"Dad, what's going on?"

"Brett, thank God. They're trying to kill us." Trisha knew she was rambling but she couldn't stop herself. "It's Rommel."

"Okay, okay. Calm down. Where's my father?"

"We're at the cabin. They burned the house down. Kaliq's outside. In front. He knocked one of the men unconscious but there are four more."

"We'll be there in fifteen minutes. Hold on."

Trisha hung up the phone and put it in her pocket. She opened the door and Kaliq came in. "Some circuits freed up. I talked to Brett," she paused and sighed. "It'll take him less time to get here than the sheriff."

"Great! Now if we can only hold these guys off."

She walked to the rear of the cabin and stood against the wall by the window. Trisha gently pulled the curtain to the side just enough to glance out. "Two are out back."

"Well, let's give them a little welcome." He pulled his chair near Trisha and peered out. The men were making their way toward the cabin, slowly, cautiously. Kaliq couldn't see Rommel or his other henchman.

"Trish, my darling," Rommel called from the front of the house. "Why don't you stop this nonsense. You'll only get your friend hurt. Come out and talk to me. Surely we can settle this matter."

Kaliq motioned Trisha to go to the door. "Talk to

him, but don't stand in front of the door and don't open it under any circumstances.''

She followed his instructions. ''What do you want?''

''Come on, don't play coy at this stage of the game. I want the diamonds and I'll get them. It's up to you whether you die for them. Think they're worth it?''

''I don't know what you're talking about.''

''Guy told me. Just before he died he told me he gave them to you. They were his last gift for unrequited love.'' Rommel laughed then continued. ''Did you know that he was in love with you? Sure you did. You like having men fall in love with you so you can walk out on them. You did it to me. You did it to Guy. I'll bet you even did it to your new friend.''

Trisha shook her head. Her voice was barely above a whisper. ''Guy wasn't in love with me,'' she told Kaliq. ''We were only partners, and don't even entertain the thought that I could be with a man like Rommel.''

''What did Guy give you?''

''I told you, just this.'' Trisha indicated the chess piece she wore around her neck. She touched it and it rattled.

''What's in it?''

''I don't know. Guy said it was tiny rocks.''

''Rocks? Like the nickname for diamonds?''

Her eyes widened and she shook her head. Guy had said to use the rocks to build a new dream. She hadn't understood what he meant.

She went to the tool chest and picked up a hammer. Quickly she slipped the chain over her neck and put the chess piece on the floor. She struck it twice with the hammer before it shattered and she saw a key and a piece of paper that had been folded several times. Her fingers trembled as she opened the paper. It was the location of a lockbox registered under her name and Guy's. She looked up at Kaliq. There was no doubt that the lockbox contained the diamonds that Rommel wanted. She put the key and paper in her pocket.

"Rommel's not going to be too thrilled to learn that you're the only one who can get the diamonds," Kaliq told her.

"He's going to be more angry that Guy beat him after all."

"So we have to stall some more. Rommel doesn't know that Brett's on the way."

"I have an idea but you have to let me do this my way."

"I don't like the sound of that."

"Don't worry. He won't kill me until he has the diamonds, and he won't kill you because he knows that I won't give them to him if he does."

Outside, Rommel became impatient. Once his men knew that there was little chance to escape from the rear of the house they had returned to his side.

"Should we just kick the door down and see what they've got?" one suggested.

"No. The man lives here year round. Something tells me that he knows very well how to take care of himself. I want to get a better look." He started up the ramp only to be distracted by a weak moan. He looked in the corner of the narrow porch and his face turned into a sneer.

"Get him up," he said to the men.

They rushed over to the man Kaliq had subdued.

The knots Kaliq tied were with rawhide and the
leather had tightened from the snow's moisture. They
had to cut them apart and it was obvious the man
was of no use. He was still groggy from the blow to
the head and probably had a concussion.

"I'll take him back to the trailer, boss."

Rommel nodded.

He and the other men approached the cabin door.
The largest one threw himself against the door and
jumped to the side and waited. If Kaliq had a gun,
surely he would have used it. The man repeated the
motion of throwing his shoulder against the door
and, when there was no response, he felt comfortable
that the two people they were after were trapped
inside. Again he used his weight against the door and
this time it gave way. They found Trisha and Kaliq
near the stove and Rommel pulled his gun and leveled
it at Trisha.

Brett turned the jeep into the driveway and saw the
unfamiliar camper parked in front of the charred
frame of his home. Even though Trisha had warned
him of the destruction, he'd not been prepared for
it. Nia was silent but he saw her eyes brim with tears.
Then he saw the two men heading toward the camper.
He got out of the jeep. One of the men was clearly
injured. Brett hid on the other side of the camper.

Nia stepped out and waved at the men. "Need any
help?"

"Yeah, lady. I need to get me and my buddy outta
here."

"I can drive you to the hospital."

The men were standing in front of her. "That won't

be necessary. We can drive ourselves. In your jeep, of course."

As the man reached for his gun, Brett stepped behind him and slashed down with his right hand. He connected with just enough force to knock the man to his knees. His friend was still not in control of his body and fell on top of him.

At that time the sheriff's division arrived and took control. Minutes later, the men were in handcuffs in the backseat of the patrol car, but Brett wondered how costly those minutes might be.

"My father and his friend are in trouble," Brett explained. "But if we all go charging up there we could get them killed."

"You really should let us handle this, Faulkner."

"If these other men see uniforms, they're going to start shooting. We can't take that chance."

"So what's your plan?"

"Stay out of the open until we know what's going on in that cabin."

"Well, you used to be a deputy so I'll just call you out of retirement for now." The sheriff turned to Nia. "Stay here. I'm not risking civilians."

Nia nodded and prayed that they would be in time to save Kaliq and Trisha.

Rommel sniffed the air. "Preparing a little breakfast, my dear?"

"Too late. We've already eaten."

"Pity. I did so enjoy your breakfasts at the inn. We could have worked things out, you know."

"I doubt it."

"Why are you so stubborn?"

"Why won't you take no for an answer?"

Trisha enjoyed the verbal sparring with Rommel. She knew it was really to get Kaliq in position.

As Kaliq turned to face his adversary he slipped his hand in his pocket and got the gun.

"All of this could have been avoided if you didn't have such a greedy partner, my love."

"I told you Guy didn't give me anything of value." Trisha stood by the stove and glanced down. The hot oil was just beginning to bubble.

"I know what you told me. I also know what he took from my safe. One way or another I'm going to get it back."

Brett handed Nia a rifle and they ignored the sheriff's orders as they followed him up toward the cabin. Each of them took a position behind a tree and waited.

Kaliq heard the other men on the ramp as they stomped through the snow. If they came in, he and Trisha didn't have a chance. He nodded to her. Without taking the gun from his pocket, he fired, catching Rommel in the leg. He fell to the floor and Kaliq leaped out of the wheelchair on top of him. Shots from outside could only mean one thing . . . the cavalry had arrived.

One of Rommel's men charged at Trisha. She tilted the pot and let hot oil spill on his leg and hand. His screams were loud and piercing as he fell to the floor. Trisha ran to the door in time to see the other men being held at gunpoint by the sheriff, Brett, and Nia.

"Brett, quick," she called.

"Go ahead," Nia urged him. "The sheriff and I

can herd this group up." They signaled for the men to keep walking.

Inside, Rommel had gotten the gun, and when Brett and Trisha came in, he pointed it at them.

"Don't try anything," he warned them. "Get in the chair."

Rommel backed away as Kaliq got in his wheelchair. He was going to have a very vulnerable hostage. The police wouldn't dare try to take him.

"Rommel, wait, don't take him," Trisha cried.

"How touching."

"Okay, take him and kiss those little diamonds goodbye." She picked up a piece of tiring she used to train Galiana.

"Trisha, no, don't," Kaliq pleaded.

"So my pretty, you do know where they are."

"Of course. I'm the only one who can get them for you."

"I knew it. You're right. I should take you rather than him."

Rommel stepped behind Trisha and placed the gun near her head. "She used you. Did you think she wanted half a man? Let's go."

"I can't walk," said his associate. He was in tears as he studied the blisters on his hand. "The pain . . ."

"Stop whining over a little pain. Get up or I'll leave you."

Rommel nudged Trisha toward the door. His friend managed to pull himself up and hobble after them.

Nia and the sheriff had moved the other men from the path so Rommel didn't know they'd been caught. "We're going to get in the camper and get out of here."

Trisha looked back and saw Kaliq coming down

the ramp. She knew he'd never let Rommel take her away but she didn't want him to die trying to save her.

Then she heard it. Kakking. That sound that falcons make when they're excited. The eyesight of a falcon was incredible. She watched Namid and his mate Galiana soar and then begin to dive. Trisha still had the tiring in her hand. Pretending she was trying to keep her balance on the snow, Trisha held her hand out.

Kaliq watched in horror. If she continued holding her arm out like that, the falcon would try to land on her arm and tear her to pieces.

They were almost at the camper when Galiana made her final swoop. She headed straight for Trisha. Rommel raised his gun to shoot the bird but Trisha pushed him and at the same time put her arm under his, forcing his arm to be used as her mesh glove.

The talons of the falcon gripped his arm and he screamed. Trisha slipped away from his grip and fell to the snow. Galiana released him and soared once again. Rommel was still screaming when the sheriff's reinforcements arrived.

Later that week Trisha was still not sure how her relationship with Kaliq would change, now that the danger was past. Would he feel that she should have let him call the shots or would he be happy that she'd come up with a plan?

Once Rommel had been arrested it gave the authorities a chance to look through his safe, and what they found would probably put him away for fifty or sixty years. All the loan-sharking records, plus papers that indicated he had a motive for killing his wife were in there. Their prenuptial agreement would have bank-rupted him if she'd divorced him.

At last Trisha and Kaliq could sit down and discuss their future.

"At least Rommel's pressure got you to come to Wyoming."

EPILOGUE

The January temperature had risen to what Trisha now considered a comfortable thirty degrees by the time they returned from their honeymoon. It was two weeks after she'd testified in court. The men who trashed Taharqa had been sent away for more years than they had left. It seems that once Trisha had been bold enough to come forth, there were other business owners who had been terrorized ready to tell their stories.

She and Kaliq had married in a small ceremony at Brett's place. Neither of them wanted to wait until Taharqa had been restored. The four years they'd already been apart were quite enough.

Palladin and Jesslyn had flown in with the twins. Trisha couldn't believe how much they'd grown in the few months since she'd seen them. They were

almost as wild as the falcons. They loved the ranch
and wanted to explore everything.

For the ceremony, Trisha had selected an Armani
silver silk gown overlaid with beading and chiffon.
Jesslyn, as her matron of honor, had worn a deep
pink dress with sliver strands through it, and Nia wore
a matte silver sheath. The men were in black Armani
suits. Brett served as best man while Palladin gave the
bride away.

The next day, Kaliq and Trisha flew into New Jersey
and rented a car to drive to Carlotta's. He'd been
afraid for her to find it less than perfect and Kaliq
had hired a team to clean it up and try to recapture
the cozy atmosphere of its brochure.

A couple would be running the place most of the
time since Trisha would be living in Wyoming.

Trisha, Kaliq, Brett, and Nia had developed plans
for Taharqa to be turned into a year-round facility.
In the spring, fall, and winter it would be a lodge.
The summer would be reserved for the young people
Kaliq cared so much about. It would give them the
best of both worlds. There were so many more plans
and Trisha was grateful they had someone to turn
Carlotta's over to.

They flew on to England for Trisha's choice of a
honeymoon and returned to Wyoming a month later.

The publicity of the trial had brought a couple of
offers for the cookbook Trisha had been working on.
Even though she would need at least six months to
complete it, now recipes danced in her head. She
watched the sky and waited for the falcons to return.

* * *

Kaliq looked at the remarkable woman who had become his wife. He studied her tight jeans, long legs, and the way she'd pulled her hair back into a ponytail. She was a far cry from the person who'd arrived three months before. Then she'd been beaten down and defeated. All of her dreams had crashed and burned. Now she'd just replaced them with new ones. She was a vibrant woman who embraced life in the same manner he did.

Now she stood with a hooded falcon gripping the mesh glove on her hand just as Namid sat on his arm.

How many women would have spent their honeymoon in England at a falconry school? A grin spread across his face and Trisha turned and caught him.

"What's so funny?"

"Nothing."

"Nothing?"

"Well, I was just thinking about a woman who was afraid of birds . . ."

"I wasn't afraid of birds. I was afraid of falcons. Those talons still give me shivers sometimes."

"It's all in knowing how to handle them."

"That's true of a lot of things and people."

She slipped her other hand through his and closed it tightly. They had only a few months before the camp would open and the ranch would be a place for kids accustomed to concrete to see how people lived in wide open spaces.

He knew she was a little apprehensive about the camp. Having fifteen boys running about was enough to make anyone nervous, but Kaliq knew she was capable of handling anything after the way they'd survived Rommel's attack. He also was sure that the boys would be impressed with a woman who could control falcons. She laughed when she thought that Jesslyn had to be a magician to take care of twins. Now she would have fifteen boys, even if just for the summer.

"When I taught you about taking care of falcons I didn't expect you to become my competition."

"It's so exhilarating to watch her soar," Trisha admitted.

"I could have taught you more but you insisted on going to England to study more."

"Honey, there are some things a man can't teach his wife, like how to drive," Trisha explained. "Falconry is best left to someone else. Besides, you would never have told me that I have the only bird that can truly be called a falcon."

She referred to the classic Medieval definition of a falcon as being a female Peregrine, although now any long-winged bird of prey was called a falcon.

Trisha cast the bird from her hand and watched it climb into the heavens. The falcon soared and searched for grouse. Galiana waited patiently for Rusty to flush them out. The dog hadn't found anything and Trisha watched as Galiana gained altitude for another stoop. The bird was as incredible as the Moorish princess she was named for. No matter how many times Trisha saw the bird reach breathtaking heights and then spiral down to the ground, there was still something magical about it.

After a few minutes of failed attempts to find game, Trisha held out her hand and waited for her falcon to return. The Peregrine swooped up again and then headed straight for Trisha's outstretched arm. Once her falcon was back, she quickly hooded her.

"Beautiful," Kaliq said.

"Yes. The way she soars . . ." She turned and realized he was not talking about the falcon. He was looking directly at his wife.

She smiled and then slowly walked over to where he sat with Namid still on his arm. "Aren't you going to cast him?"

"Nope. I decided to let the ladies have the day."

"Chicken. I plan to be an expert by the time the children arrive."

"Our children?"

"Not yet. Let's get the place cleaned up and running again before we decide to bring little ones into the world."

"I just want to catch up with Palladin."

"Umm, sounds like a race. But they already have two and they have a head start on us."

"We could catch them?"

"Maybe, but right now I want us to have a little time and a little fun before we take on that responsibility."

"Ever the clear thinker, but can't you hear your biological clock ticking?"

"Not as loud as you seem to, but I guess we need to do something about that."

"I guess we do."

With the falcon perched on her arm, Trisha walked behind her husband's wheelchair as they headed home. She thought of how much she had in common with the Peregrine. Galiana had flown away once but she'd returned. Trisha had run away once. She'd hidden behind cookbooks and big plans for a Bed & Breakfast when she'd really wanted a home.

Falcons mate for life, she thought, as she saw the sprawling ranch ahead of her and knew that she, also, had mated for life. For Galiana and Trisha, love had returned to enfold them into a greater joy.

ABOUT THE AUTHOR

Viveca Carlysle was born Marsha-Anne Tanksley in Detroit, Michigan. She grew up in New York City. Her love for reading is a gift from her mother, who started reading to her from the day they came home from the hospital. She is Vice-President of Romance Writers of America's NYC chapter. She belongs to Women Writers of Color. Currently she is a customer service supervisor with New York City Transit.

Dear Reader:

I hope you enjoyed Trisha and Kaliq's story. Too often we forget that someone with a disability has the same need and capacity for love. When I created Kaliq Faulkner he was only to be the best friend of my hero. I gave him a rare pet, a falcon, named Namid because it seemed to fit his personality. Trisha was someone that appeared on page before I realized she had a story to tell.

Then readers and friends said they wanted to know what happened to Trisha and Kaliq and they wanted me to write their story. Since there was no way to bring Kaliq and his falcon to Trisha I had to find a way to get her to Wyoming. Once they were in the same place I could let nature take it's course.

Sometimes the characters a writer creates become like old friends. I admit that I also enjoyed revisiting Jesslyn and Palladin from my first book, *Sweet Lies*.

I love to hear from readers and you can contact me at the following address:

Viveca Carlysle
POB 340027
Rochdale Village, NY 11434-0027

COMING IN OCTOBER . . .

FOOLS RUSH IN   (1-58314-037-9, $4.99US/$6.99CAN)
by Gwynne Forster
When Justine Montgomery discovers that her long-lost daughter has been adopted by journalist Duncan Banks—and that he's looking for a nanny—she enters into a web of deceit and divided loyalties with her new employer. Their fragile trust and unexpected passion force them to risk everything to claim a love they never thought possible.

SECRET PASSION   (1-58314-042-5, $4.99US/$6.99CAN)
by Layle Giusto
Stalking-victim Julia Smalls moves to Chicago to start a new life—one without terror. Her boss is suspicious of her secrecy but no one can deny their sizzling attraction. When strange accidents start happening, Julia believes her past has come back to haunt her and must make the choice between her life . . . and the love of her life.

FALSE IMPRESSIONS   (1-58314-038-7, $4.99US/$6.99CAN)
by Marilyn Tyner
After Zoe Johnson stumbles onto a plot to steal high-tech software, she unwittingly becomes the inventor's hostage. He thinks she's a thief . . . but she thinks he's stunningly attractive. As the weeks go by, both the truth and an unexpected desire unfurl as the couple are thrown into a perilous game that could rob them of their lives—and their love.

A SURE THING   (1-58314-048-4, $4.99US/$6.99CAN)
by Courtni Wright
ER physician Katherine Winters finds she must compete bitterly with Thomas Baker for the chief of staff position at her hospital. Yet she can't help being fiercely drawn to the attractive doctor. For his part, Thomas finds Katherine irresistible. Can their desire melt bitter rivalry into sweet love?

Available wherever paperbacks are sold, or order direct from the publisher. Send cover price plus 2.50 for the first book and $.50 per each additional book for shipping and handling to BET Books, c/o Kensington Publishing Corp., Consumer Orders, or call (toll free) 888-345-BOOK, to place your order using Mastercard or Visa. Residents of New York, Washington D.C., and Tennessee must include sales tax. DO NOT SEND CASH.

NEW ARABESQUE ROMANCES . . .

ONE LOVE by Lynn Emery
1-58314-046-8 $4.99US/$6.99CAN

When recovering alcoholic Lanessa Thomas is reunited with the only man she ever loved, and the man she hurt the most, Alexander St. Romain, she is determined to ignore her passionate temptations. But when Lanessa's hard-won stability is threatened, both she and Alex must battle unresolved pain and anger in order to salvage their second chance at love.

DESTINED by Adrienne Ellis Reeves
1-58314-047-6 $4.99US/$6.99CAN

Teenage newlywed Leah Givens was shocked when her father tore her away from bridal bliss and accused her husband Bill Johnson of statutory rape. His schemes kept them apart for thirteen years, but now Bill's long search for his lost love is over and the couple must decide if they are strong enough to heal the scars of their past and surrender to their shared destiny.

IMPETUOUS by Dianne Mayhew
1-58314-043-3 $4.99US/$6.50CAN

Four years ago, Liberty Sutton made the worst mistake of her life by granting custody of her newborn to her married lover. But just as handsome executive Jarrett Irving enters her life, she's given the chance to reclaim a life with her child. Trying to reconcile a troubled past with a future that promises happiness will take luck and the love of a good man.

UNDER A BLUE MOON by Shirley Harrison
1-58314-049-2 $4.99US/$6.99CAN

After being attacked at sea, Angie Manchester awakens on an exotic island with amnesia—and Dr. Matthew Sinclair at her side. Thrown together by chance, but drawn by desire, the puzzle of Angie's identity and Matt's own haunted past keeps a wall between the two until the vicious thugs return. Forced to hide in the lush forest, their uncontrollable passion finally ignites.

Please Use Coupon on Next Page to Order

BERLITZ

DUTCH
FOR TRAVELLERS

By the staff of Berlitz Guides

Berlitz Trademark Reg. U.S. Patent Office
and other countries—Marca Registrada

Berlitz Guides
Avenue d'Ouchy 61
1000 Lausanne 6, Switzerland

Tipping recommendations

The figures below are shown either as a percentage of the bill or in local currency. They indicate a suggested tip for the service described. Even where service is included, additional gratuities are expected by some employees; it's also customary to round off a bill or payment, and leave the change.

Obviously, tipping is an individual matter, and the correct amount to leave varies enormously with category of hotel or restaurant, size of city and so on. The sums we suggest represent normal tips for average middle-grade establishments in big cities.

	Holland	Belgium
HOTEL		
Service charge, bill	incl.	incl.
Porter, per bag	f 1–2	30 F
Bellboy, errand	f 2–5	40 F
Maid	optional	20–50 F
Doorman, hails cab	f 1–2	20–50 F
RESTAURANT		
Service charge, bill	incl.	incl.
Waiter	optional	optional
Hat check	f 1–2	50 F
Lavatory attendant	50 cents	10 F
Canal-boat guide	optional	–
Taxi driver	optional	optional
Tourist guide	5–10%	10%
Barber/Women's hairdresser	incl.	10–15%
Cinema/Theater usher	50 cents–f 1	20 F

Preface

In preparing this complete revision of *Dutch for Travellers*, we took into consideration a wealth of suggestions and criticisms received from phrase book readers around the world. As a result, this edition features:

- all the phrases and vocabulary you will need on your trip
- a wide variety of tourist and travel facts, tips and useful information
- a complete phonetic transcription throughout indicating the pronunciation of all the words and phrases
- a logical system of presentation so that you can find the right phrase for the immediate situation
- special sections showing the replies your listener might give to you. Just hand him the book and let him point to the appropriate phrase. This is especially practical in certain difficult situations (doctor, car mechanic, etc.)
- quick reference through colour coding. The major features of the contents are on the back cover and a complete index is provided on pages 190–191
- tipping recommendations and a comprehensive reference section in the back of the book

These are just a few of the practical advantages. In addition, the book will prove a valuable introduction to life in Holland as well as help you should you be travelling to the northern part of Belgium where approximately 5 million people speak a version of Dutch called Flemish. Life styles and patterns vary, however, between Holland and Belgium and thus the observations included on the Dutch way of life are not necessarily reflective of the Belgian scene.

There is a comprehensive section on eating out, with translations and explanations for virtually anything likely to be found on a Dutch menu. Belgian (Flemish) dishes have also been included. There is a complete shopping guide that will enable you to obtain virtually anything you could possibly want. Trouble with the car? Turn to the mechanic's manual with its dual-language instructions. Feeling ill? Our medical section provides the surest communication possible between you and the doctor.

To make the most of *Dutch for Travellers*, we suggest that you start with the "Guide to Pronunciation". Then go on to "Some Basic Expressions". This not only gives you a minimum vocabulary but also helps you to learn to pronounce the language.

We are particularly grateful to Mrs. T.E. Anderson for her help in the preparation of this book and to Dr. T.J.A. Bennett who devised the phonetic transcription. We also wish to thank the Netherlands National Tourist Office for its assistance.

We shall be very pleased to receive any comments, criticisms and suggestions that you think may help us in preparing future editions.

Thank you. And have a good trip.

Throughout this book, the symbols illustrated here indicate small sections where phrases have been compiled of what your foreign listener might like to say to *you*. If you don't understand him, give him the book and let him point to the phrase in his language. The English translation is just beside it.

Basic grammar

Dutch is a Germanic language spoken throughout Holland and, under the name of Flemish, by about 5 million Belgians. The following concise outline of some essential features of Dutch grammar will be of help to you in understanding and speaking the language.

Articles

Dutch nouns are either common gender (originally separate masculine and feminine) or neuter.

1) **Definite article (the)**

   The definite article in Dutch is either **de** or **het. De** is used with roughly two thirds of all common-gender singular nouns as well as with all plural nouns, while **het** is mainly used with neuter singular nouns and all diminutives:

de straat the street **het huis** the house **het katje** the kitten

2) **Indefinite article (a; an)**

   The indefinite article is **een** for both genders, always unstressed and pronounced like *an* in the English word "another". As in English there is no plural. When it bears accent marks (**één**) it means "one" and is pronounced rather like the vowel in "lane", but a pure vowel, not a diphthong.

een man	a man	**een vrouw**	a woman	**een kind**	a child
mannen	men	**vrouwen**	women	**kinderen**	children

Plural

The most common sign of the plural in Dutch is an **-en** ending:

krant	newspaper	**woord**	word	**dag**	day
kranten	newspapers	**woorden**	words	**dagen**	days

a) In nouns with a double vowel, one vowel is dropped when **-en** is added:

uur	hour	**boot**	boat	**jaar**	year
uren	hours	**boten**	boats	**jaren**	years

b) most nouns ending in **-s** or **-f** change this letter into **-z** and **-v,** when **-en** is added:

prijs	the price	**brief**	letter
prijzen	prices	**brieven**	letters

Another common plural ending in Dutch is **-s**. Nouns ending in an unstressed **-el**, **-em**, **-en**, **-aar** as well as **-je** (diminutives) take an **-s** in the plural:

tafel/		**winnaar/**	winner(s)
tafels	table(s)	**winnaars**	
deken/		**kwartje/**	
dekens	blanket(s)	**kwartjes**	25-cent piece(s)

Some exceptions:

stad/steden	town(s)	**auto/auto's**	car(s)
schip/schepen	ship(s)	**paraplu/**	umbrella(s)
kind/kinderen	child(ren)	**paraplu's**	
ei/eieren	egg(s)	**foto/foto's**	photo(s)
		musicus/musici	musician(s)

Adjectives

When the adjective stands immediately before the noun, it usually takes the ending **-e**:

de jonge vrouw	the young woman
een prettige reis	a pleasant trip
aardige mensen	nice people

However, no ending is added to the adjective in the following cases:

1) When the adjective follows the noun:

De stad is groot.	The city is big.
De zon is heet.	The sun is hot.

2) When the noun is neuter singular and preceded by **een**
(a/an), or when the words **elk/ieder** (each), **veel** (much),
zulk (such) and **geen** (no) precede the adjective:

een wit huis	a white house
elk goed boek	each good book
zulk mooi weer	such good weather
geen warm water	no hot water

Demonstrative adjectives (this/that):

this	**deze**	(with nouns of common gender)
	dit	(with nouns of neuter gender)
that	**die**	(with nouns of common gender)
	dat	(with nouns of neuter gender)
these	**deze**	(with all plural nouns)
those	**die**	(with all plural nouns)

Deze stad is groot.	This city is big.
Dat huis is wit.	That house is white.

Personal pronouns

Subject			Object		
I	ik		me	mij	
you	jij or je (fam.)*		you	jou or je (fam.)*	
you	u (pol.)**		you	u (pol.)**	
he	hij		him	hem	
she	zij		her	haar	
it	het		it	het	
we	wij		us	ons	
you	jullie (fam.)*		you	jullie (fam.)*	
they	zij or ze		them	hen	

---

* The familiar **jij** or **je** (singular) and **jullie** (plural) and their associated forms are
used only when talking to familiars, close friends and children.

** When addressing people you don't know well, use **u** (and its associated form **uw**)
in both singular and plural.

10

Possessive adjectives

my	mijn
your	jouw (fam.)*
your	uw (pol.)**
his	zijn
her	haar
its	zijn
our	ons (with singular neuter nouns)
	onze (with singular and plural nouns of common gender)
your	jullie (fam.)*
their	hun

Verbs

First a few handy irregular verbs. If you learn only these, or even only the "I" and polite "you" forms of them, you'll have made a useful start.

1) The indispensible verbs **hebben** (to have) and **zijn** (to be) in the present:

I have	ik heb	I am	ik ben
you have	jij hebt*	you are	jij bent*
you have	u hebt**	you are	u bent*
he/she/it has	hij/zij/het heeft	he/she/it is	hij/zij/het is
we have	wij hebben	we are	wij zijn
you have	jullie hebben*	you are	jullie zijn*
they have	zij hebben	they are	zij zijn

2) Some more useful irregular verbs (in the present):

Infinitive		willen (to want)	kunnen (can)	gaan (to go)	doen (to do)	weten (to know)
I	ik	wil	kan	ga	doe	weet
you	jij*	wilt	kunt	gaat	doet	weet
you	u**	wilt	kunt	gaat	doet	weet
he	hij	wil	kan	gaat	doet	weet
she	zij	wil	kan	gaat	doet	weet
it	het	wil	kan	gaat	doet	weet
we	wij	willen	kunnen	gaan	doen	weten
you	jullie*	willen	kunnen	gaan	doen	weten
they	zij	willen	kunnen	gaan	doen	weten

GRAMMAR

3) Infinitive and verb stem:

In Dutch verbs, the infinitive generally ends in **-en**: **noemen** (to name).

As the verb stem is usually the base for forming tenses, you need to know how to obtain it. The general rule is: the infinitive less **-en**:

infinitive: **noemen**   stem: **noem**

4) Present and past tenses:

First find the stem of the verb (see under 3 above).

Then add the appropriate endings, where applicable, according to the models given below for present and past tenses.

Note: in forming the past tense, the **-de/-den** endings shown in our example are added after most verb stems. However if the stem ends in **p**, **t**, **k**, **f**, **s**, or **ch**, add **-te/-ten** instead.

Present tense		Past tense	
ik noem	I name	ik noemde	I named
jij noemt*	you name	jij noemde*	you named
u noemt**	you name	u noemde**	you named
hij/zij/het noemt	he/she/it names	hij/zij/het noemde	he/she/it named
wij noemen	we name	wij noemden	we named
jullie noemen*	you name	jullie noemden*	you named
zij noemen	they name	zij noemden	they named

5) Past perfect (e.g.: "I have built"):

This tense is generally formed, as in English, by the verb "to have" **(hebben)** (see page 10) + the past participle.

To form the past participle, start with the verb stem, and add **ge-** to the front of it and **-d** or **-t** to the end:

*/** See footnote, page 9

infinitive:	**bouwen** (to build)
verb stem:	**bouw**
past participle:	**gebouwd**

The past participle must be placed *after* the object of the sentence:

Ik heb een huis gebouwd.   I have built a house.

Note: Verbs prefixed by **be-**, **er-**, **her-**, **ont-** and **ver-** do not take **ge-** in the past participle.

Instead of **hebben**, the verb **zijn** (to be) is used with verbs expressing motion (if the destination is specified or implied) or a change of state:

Wij zijn naar Parijs gevlogen.	We have flown to Paris.
Hij is rijk geworden.	He has become rich.

Negatives

To put a verb into the negative, place **niet** (not) after the verb, or after the direct object if there is one:

Ik rook.	I smoke.	**Ik heb de kaartjes.**	I have the tickets.
Ik rook niet.	I don't smoke.	**Ik heb de kaartjes niet.**	I don't have the tickets.

Questions

In Dutch, questions are formed by placing the subject after the verb:

Hij reist.	He travels.	**Ik betaal.**	I pay.
Reist hij?	Does he travel?	**Betaal ik?**	Do I pay?

Questions are also introduced by the following **interrogative pronouns:**

Wie (who)	Who says so?	**Wie zegt dat?**
	Whose house is that?	**Van wie is dat huis?**
Wat (what)	What does he do?	**Wat doet hij?**
Waar (where)	Where is the hotel?	**Waar is het hotel?**
Hoe (how)	How are you?	**Hoe gaat het met u?**

Guide to pronunciation

This and the following chapter are intended to make you familiar with the phonetic transcription we have devised, which is based on Standard British pronunciation, and to help you get used to the sounds of Dutch.

As a minimum vocabulary for your trip, we've selected a number of basic words and phrases under the title "Some basic expressions" (pages 17–21).

An outline of the spelling and sounds of Dutch

The bold letters in the transcriptions should be read with more stress than the others. In the more unusual diphthongs, we print the weaker element in a raised position, e.g. **oa**^{ee} means that the **oa** element is the more prominent sound in the diphthong and the **ee** sound is short and fleeting.

The imitated pronunciation should be read as if it were English except for any special rules set out below. Of course, the sounds of any two languages are never exactly the same; but if you follow carefully the indications supplied here, you'll have no difficulty in reading our transcriptions in such a way as to make yourself understood.

Consonants

Letter	Approximate pronunciation	Symbol	Example	
f, h, k, l, m, n, p, q, t, y, z	as in English			
b	as in English but, when at the end of a word, like **p** in cup	b p	ben heb	behn hehp
c	1) before a consonant and a, o, u, like **k** in keen	k	inclusief	inklewseef
	2) before e and i, always like **s** in sit	s	ceintuur	sehntewr

ch	1) generally like ch in Scottish loch	kh	**nacht**	nahkht
	2) in words of French origin like sh in shut	sh	**cheque**	shehk
chtj	like Dutch ch followed by Dutch j	khy	**nichtje**	nikhyer
d	as in English, but, when at the end of a word, like t in hit	d / t	**doe** / **avond**	doo / aavont
g	1) generally like ch in Scottish loch, but often slightly softer and voiced	gh	**zagen**	zaaghern*
	2) in a few words of French origin, like s in pleasure	zh	**genie**	zhernee
	3) like ch in Scottish loch when at the end of a word (and quite often at the beginning)	kh	**deeg**	daykh
j	1) like y in yes	y	**ja**	yaa
	2) in certain words borrowed from French, like s in leisure	zh	**lits-jumeaux**	lee-zhewmoo^ow
ng	ng is pronounced as in English sing	ng	**toagang**	tooghang
nj	like ñ in Spanish señor or like ni in onion	ñ	**oranje**	oarahñer
r	always trilled, either in the front or the back of the mouth	r	**warm**	Vahrm
s	like s in sit or ss in pass	s or ss	**ross**	roass
sj, stj	like sh in shut	sh	**meisje**	maiysher
sch	like s followed by a Dutch ch	skh	**schrijven**	skhraiyvern
th	like t in tea	t	**thee**	tay
tj	like ty in hit you	ty	**katje**	kahtyer
v	pronounced basically as in English, but is often harder and not voiced, so that, to an English or American ear,	v	**hoeveel** / **van**	houvayl / van

* The final n of a word is not usually heard during a fast conversation; it is heard, however, when words are spoken slowly.

	it sounds more like **f**, especially at the beginning or end of a word			
w	quite like English **v**, but with the bottom lip raised a little higher	V̸	**water**	V̸aaterr
x	always like **ks** in kna**cks**	ks	**taxi**	**tah**ksee

Vowels

Dutch vowels are long when at the end of a word, or when followed by a single consonant followed by a vowel, or when written double.

a	1) when short, between **a** in **cat** and **u** in **cut**	ah	**kat**	kaht
	2) when long, like **a** in **cart**	aa	**vader**	**vaa**derr
e	1) when short, like **e** in **bed**	eh	**bed**	beht
	2) when long, like **a** in **late**, but a pure vowel, not a diphthong	ay	**zee**	zay
	3) in unstressed syllables, like **er** in oth**er**	er*	**zitten**	**zit**tern
eu	approximately like **ur** in **fur**, said with rounded lips and with no **r** round	ur*	**deur**	durr
i	1) when short, like **i** in **bit**	i	**kind**	kint
	2) when long (also spelt **ie**), like **ee** in b**ee**	ee	**bier**	beer
	3) sometimes, in unstressed syllables, like **er** in oth**er**	er*	**monnik**	**mon**nerk
ij	sometimes, in unstressed syllables, like **er** in oth**er**; see also under "Diphthongs"	er*	**lelijk**	**lay**lerk
o	1) when short, like a very short version of **aw** in l**aw**n	o	**pot**	pot
	2) when long, something like **oa** in r**oa**d, but a pure vowel, with rounded lips	oa	**boot**	boat
oe	(long) like **oo** in m**oo**n and well rounded	oo	**hoe**	hoo

* The **r** should not be pronounced when reading this transcription.

PRONUNCIATION

| u | 1) when short, something like **ur** in **hurt**, but with rounded lips | ur* | **bus** | burss |
| | 2) when long, like **u** in French **sur** or **ü** in German **für**; say **ee**, and without moving your tongue, round your lips. | ew | **nu** | new |

Diphthongs

ai	like **igh** in **sigh**	igh	**ai**	igh
ei, ij	between **a** in **late** and **igh** in **sigh**	aiy	**reis**	raiyss
au, ou	Dutch short **o** followed by a weak short **u**-sound; can sound very much like **ow** in **now**	o^{ow}	**koud**	ko^{ow}t
aai	like **a** in **cart** followed by a short **ee** sound	aa^{ee}	**draai**	draa^{ee}
eeuw	like **a** in **late** (but a pure vowel), followed by a short **oo** sound	ay^{oo}	**leeuw**	lay^{oo}
ieuw	like **ee** in **free**, followed by a short **oo** sound	ee^{oo}	**nieuw**	nee^{oo}
ooi	like **oa** in **wrote** (but a pure vowel) followed by a short **ee** sound	oa^{ee}	**nooit**	noa^{ee}t
oei	like **oo** in **soon**, followed by a short **ee** sound	oo^{ee}	**roeit**	roo^{ee}t
ui	like **ear** in **learn** followed by a short Dutch **u** sound, as described in **u** 2)	ur^{ew}*	**huis**	hur^{ew}ss
uw	like the sound described for **u** 2), followed by a weak **oo** sound	ew^{oo}	**duw**	dew^{oo}

* The **r** should not be pronounced when reading this transcription.

Note: When two consonants stand next to each other, one will often influence the other even if it is not in the same word, e.g. *ziens* is pronounced *zeenss*, but in the phrase *tot ziens*, it is pronounced *seenss* under the influence of the t before it.

PRONUNCIATION

Some basic expressions

Yes.	**Ja.**	yaa
No.	**Nee.**	nay
Please.	**Alstublieft.***	ahlstew**bleeft**
Thank you.	**Dank u.**	dahnk ew
Thank you very much.	**Hartelijk dank.**	**hahr**terlerk dahnk
That's all right.	**Niets te danken.**	neets ter **dahnk**er

Greetings

Good morning.	**Goedemorgen.**	ghooder**morgher**
Good afternoon.	**Goedemiddag.**	ghooder**middahgh**
Good evening.	**Goedenavond.**	ghooder**aavont**
Good night.	**Goedenacht.**	ghooder**nahkht**
Good-bye.	**Tot ziens.**	tot seenss
See you later.	**Tot straks.**	tot strahks
This is Mr ...	**Dit is Mijnheer ...**	dit iss mer**nayr**
This is Mrs ...	**Dit is Mevrouw ...**	dit iss mer**vro**ow
This is Miss ...	**Dit is Juffrouw ...**	dit iss **yurfro**ow
I'm very pleased to meet you.	**Aangenaam kennis te maken.**	**aan**ghernaam **keh**niss ter **maa**kern
How are you?	**Hoe gaat het?**	hoo ghaat heht
Very well, thank you.	**Heel goed, dank u.**	hayl ghoot dahnk ew
And you?	**En u?**	ehn ew
Fine.	**Uitstekend.**	ur**ew**t**stay**kernt
Excuse me.	**Neemt u me niet kwalijk.**	naymt ew mer neet k**vaa**lerk

---

* In Dutch, *alstublieft* is a courtesy word often added to the end of a sentence. It has no real English equivalent.

Questions

Where?	**Waar?**	√aar
Where is ...?	**Waar is ...?**	√aar iss
Where are ...?	**Waar zijn ...?**	√aar zaiyn
When?	**Wanneer?**	√ahnayr
What?	**Wat?**	√aht
How?	**Hoe?**	hoo
How much?	**Hoeveel?**	hoovayl
How many?	**Hoeveel?**	hoovayl
Who?	**Wie?**	√ee
Why?	**Waarom?**	√aarom
Which?	**Welk/Welke?**	√ehlk/√ehlker
What do you call this?	**Hoe noemt u dit?**	hoo noomt ew dit
What do you call that?	**Hoe noemt u dat?**	hoo noomt ew daht
What does this mean?	**Wat betekent dit?**	√aht bertaykernt dit
What does that mean?	**Wat betekent dat?**	√aht bertaykernt daht

Do you speak...?

Do you speak English?	**Spreekt u Engels?**	spraykt ew ehngerlss
Do you speak German?	**Spreekt u Duits?**	spraykt ew dur^{ew}ts
Do you speak French?	**Spreekt u Frans?**	spraykt ew frahnss
Do you speak Spanish?	**Spreekt u Spaans?**	spraykt ew spaanss
Do you speak Italian?	**Spreekt u Italiaans?**	spraykt ew itahliaanss
Could you speak more slowly, please?	**Kunt u wat lang-zamer spreken, alstublieft?**	kurnt ew √aht lahngzaamerr spraykern ahlstewbleeft
Please point to the phrase in the book.	**Wijs me de zin aan in het boek, alstublieft.**	√aiyss mer der zin aan in heht book ahlstewbleeft
Just a minute. I'll see if I can find it in this book.	**Een ogenblik. Ik zal proberen het in dit boek op te zoeken.**	ayn oagherblik. ik zahl proabayrern heht in dit book op ter zookern

| I understand. | **Ik begrijp het.** | ik berghraiyp heht |
| I don't understand. | **Ik begrijp het niet.** | ik berghaiyp heht neet |

Can...?

Can I have ...?	**Mag ik ... hebben?**	mahkh ik ... hehbern
Can we have ...?	**Mogen wij ... hebben?**	moaghern ✓aiy ... hehbern
Can you show me ...?	**Kunt u me ... tonen?**	kurnt ew mer ... toanern
Can you tell me ...?	**Kunt u mij zeggen ...?**	kurnt ew maiy zehghern
Can you help me, please?	**Kunt u mij helpen, alstublieft?**	kurnt ew maiy hehlpern ahlstewbleeft

Wanting

I'd like ...	**Ik wil graag ... hebben.**	ik wil ghraakh ... hehbern
We'd like ...	**Wij willen graag ... hebben.**	✓aiy ✓illern ghraakh ... hehbern
Please give me...	**Geeft u me ..., alstublieft.**	ghayft ew mer ... ahlstewbleeft
Give it to me, please.	**Geeft u het me, alstublieft.**	ghayft ew heht mer ahlstewbleeft
Please bring me...	**Brengt u me ... alstublieft.**	brehngt ew mer ... ahlstewbleeft
Bring it to me, please.	**Brengt u het me, alstublieft.**	brehngt ew heht mer ahlstewbleeft
I'm hungry.	**Ik heb honger.**	ik hehp hongerr
I'm thirsty.	**Ik heb dorst.**	ik hehp dorst
I'm tired.	**Ik ben moe.**	ik behn moo
I'm lost.	**Ik ben verdwaald.**	ik behn verrd✓aalt
It's important.	**Het is belangrijk.**	heht iss berlahngraiyk
It's urgent.	**Het is dringend.**	heht iss dringernt
Hurry up!	**Vlug!**	vlurkh

It is/There is...

It is/It's...	**Het is...**	heht iss
Is it...?	**Is het...?**	iss heht
It isn't...	**Het is niet...**	heht iss neet
There is/There are...	**Er is/Er zijn...**	ehr iss/ehr zaiyn
Is there/Are there...?	**Is er/Zijn er...?**	iss ehr/zaiyn ehr
There isn't any/There aren't any...	**Er is geen/Er zijn geen...**	ehr iss ghayn/ehr zaiyn ghayn
There isn't any/There aren't any.	**Er is er geen/Er zijn er geen.**	ehr iss ehr ghayn/ehr zaiyn ehr ghayn

A few common words

big/small	**groot/klein**	ghroat/klaiyn
quick/slow	**snel/langzaam**	snehl/**lahng**zaam
early/late	**vroeg/laat**	vrookh/laat
cheap/expensive	**goedkoop/duur**	**ghoot**koap/dewr
near/far	**dichtbij/ver**	dikhtbai/vehr
hot/cold	**warm/koud**	ᴠahrm/ko°°t
full/empty	**vol/leeg**	vol/laykh
easy/difficult	**gemakkelijk/moeilijk**	ghermahkerlerk/moo••lerk
heavy/light	**zwaar/licht**	zᴠaar/likht
open/shut	**open/dicht**	oapern/dikht
right/wrong	**juist/verkeerd**	yurᵉᵂst/verr**kayrt**
old/new	**oud/nieuw**	o°ᵂt/nee°°
old/young	**oud/jong**	o°ᵂt/yong
beautiful/ugly	**mooi/lelijk**	moaᵉᵉ/**lay**lerk
good/bad	**goed/slecht**	ghoot/slehkht
better/worse	**beter/slecht**	**bay**teer/slehkht

Some prepositions and a few more useful words

at	**te**	ter
on	**op**	op
in	**in**	in
to	**naar**	naar
from	**van**	vahn
inside	**binnen**	binnern
outside	**buiten**	bur⁰ʷtern
up	**op**	op
down	**neer**	nayr
before	**voor**	voar
after	**na**	naa
with	**met**	meht
without	**zonder**	zonderr
through	**door**	doar
towards	**naar**	naar
until	**tot**	tot
during	**tijdens**	taiydernss
and	**en**	ehn
or	**of**	off
not	**niet**	neet
nothing	**niets**	neets
none	**geen**	ghayn
very	**zeer**	zayr
also	**ook**	oak
soon	**spoedig**	spooderkh
perhaps	**misschien**	mersskheen
here	**hier**	heer
there	**daar**	daar
now	**nu**	new
then	**dan**	dahn

Arrival

Passport control

Here is my passport.	**Hier is mijn paspoort.**	heer iss maiyn **pahs**poart
I'll be staying...	**Ik blijf hier...**	ik blaiyf heer
a few days	**een paar dagen**	ayn paar **daag**hern
a week	**een week**	ayn ✓ayk
several weeks	**enkele weken**	**ehn**kerler ✓**ay**kern
I don't know yet.	**Ik weet het nog niet.**	ik ✓ayt heht nokh neet
I'm here on holiday.	**Ik ben hier met vakantie.**	ik behn heer meht vaa**kahn**see
I'm just passing through.	**Ik ben op doorreis.**	ik behn op **doar**raiyss
I'm sorry, I don't understand.	**Neemt u mij niet kwalijk, ik begrijp u niet.**	naymt ew maiy neet k✓**aa**lerk ik ber**ghraiyp** ew neet
Is there anyone here who speaks English?	**Is er iemand hier die Engels spreekt?**	iss ehr **ee**mahnt heer dee **ehng**erlss spraykt

Customs

As at almost all major airports in Europe, an honour system for clearing customs has been adopted at Amsterdam's Schiphol airport. Baggage is often not even opened, although spot checks are a possibility. After collecting your baggage, you've a choice: follow the green arrow if you have nothing to declare. Or leave via a doorway marked with a red arrow if you have items to declare (in excess of those allowed).

niets aan te geven	**aangifte goederen**
nothing to declare	goods to declare

CAR/BORDER FORMALITIES, see page 146

The chart below shows what you can take in duty-free.*

	Cigarettes		Cigars		Tobacco	Spirits	Wine
European residents: bought outside EEC or inside EEC tax-free	200	or	50	or	250 g.	1 l.	and 2 l.
bought inside EEC countries not tax-free (Eur. residents)	300	or	75	or	400 g.	1½ l.	and 5 l.
for visitors from outside Europe	400	or	100	or	500 g.	1 l.	and 2 l.

Dutch customs may inquire about tea or coffee, since only a limited quantity of either is admitted duty-free.

I've nothing to declare.	Ik heb niets aan te geven.	ik hehp neets aan ter ghayvern
I've a...	Ik heb een...	ik hehp ayn
bottle of whisky/wine carton of cigarettes	fles whisky/wijn slof sigaretten	flehss viskee/vaiyn sloff seeghaarehtern
It's for my personal use.	Dit is voor mijn persoonlijk gebruik.	dit iss voar maiyn pehrsoanlerk gherbrur^{ew}k
It's a present.	Het is een cadeau.	heht iss ayn kaadoa

Uw paspoort, alstublieft.	Your passport, please.
Hebt u iets aan te geven?	Have you anything to declare?
Wilt u deze tas even open maken?	Please open this bag.
U moet hiervoor invoerrechten betalen.	You'll have to pay duty on this.
Hebt u nog meer bagage?	Do you have any more luggage?

ARRIVAL

* All allowances are subject to change without notice.

Baggage—Porters

These days porters are only available at airports or the railway stations of large cities such as Amsterdam, Rotterdam, Utrecht and Antwerp. Where no porters are available, you'll find luggage trolleys for the use of passengers.

Porter!	**Kruier!**	krur^{ew}yerr
Please take these bags.	**Wilt u deze koffers meenemen, alstublieft.**	ʋilt ew dayzer kofferss maynaymern ahlstewbleeft
That's mine.	**Die is van mij.**	dee iss vahn maiy
That's my suitcase.	**Dat is mijn koffer.**	daht iss maiyn kofferr
That ... one.	**Die...**	dee
big/small black/check blue/brown	**grote/kleine zwarte/geruite blauwe/bruine**	ghroater/klaiyner zʋahrter/gherrur^{ew}ter blo^{ow}ʋer/brur^{ew}ner
There's one ... missing.	**Er ontbreekt een...**	ehr ontbraykt ayn
bag suitcase	**reistas koffer**	raiysstahss kofferr
Take these bags to...	**Breng deze reistassen naar...**	brehng dayzer raiysstahssern naar
the bus the luggage lockers the taxi	**de bus de bagagekluizen de taxi**	der burss der baaghaazherklur^{ew}zern der tahksee
How much is that?	**Hoeveel is het?**	hoovayl iss heht
Where can I find a luggage trolley?	**Waar kan ik een bagagewagentje vinden?**	ʋaar kahn ik ayn baaghaazherʋaagherntyer vindern

Changing money

At all airports and railway stations, you'll find a bank or *wisselkantoor* (currency-exchange office). Most of them stay open in the evening. In case you have trouble changing money late at night, your hotel might be able to help you.

See pages 134–136 for details of money and currency exchange and banking hours.

Where's the nearest currency exchange?	**Waar is het dichtst-bijzijnde wissel-kantoor?**	√aar iss heht dikhtst-baiyzaiynder √isserl-kahntoar
Can you change these traveller's cheques (checks)?	**Kunt u deze reis-cheques inwisse-len?**	kurnt ew dayzer raiys-shehks in√isserlern
I want to change some ...	**Ik wil enige ... inwisselen.**	iik √il aynergher ... in√isserlern
dollars	**dollars**	dollahrss
pounds	**ponden**	pondern
Can you change this into...?	**Kunt u dit tegen ... inwisselen?**	kurnt ew dit tayghern... in√isserlern
guilders	**guldens**	ghurldernss
Belgian francs	**Belgische franken**	behlgheesser frahnkern
What's the exchange rate?	**Wat is de wissel-koers?**	√aht iss der √isserlkoorss

Where?

All airports and most railway stations have information offices, and some even have a hotel reservation bureau.

Could you book a hotel room/room in a boarding house, please?	**Kunt u een hotel-kamer/kamer in een pension voor mij reserveren?**	kurnt ew ayn hoatehl-kaamerr/kaamerr in ayn pehnsyon voar maiy rayzehrvayrern
in the centre	**in het centrum**	in heht sehntrurm
near the station	**bij het station**	baiy heht stahtsyon
for one person/ two people	**voor één person/ twee personen**	voar ayn pehrsoan/ t√ay pehrsoanern
not too expensive	**niet te duur**	neet ter dewr
Where is the hotel/ boarding house?	**Waar is het hotel/ het pension?**	√aar iss heht hoatehl/ heht pehnsyon
Do you have a city map?	**Hebt u een stads-plan?**	hehpt ew ayn stahtsplahn
How do I get to...?	**Hoe kom ik naar...?**	hoo kom ik naar

FOR NUMBERS, see page 175

Is there a bus into town?	**Gaat er een bus naar de stad?**	ghaat ehr ayn burss naar der staht
Where can I get a taxi?	**Waar kan ik een taxi vinden?**	₩aar kahn ik ayn **tahksee** vindern
Where can I hire a car?	**Waar kan ik een auto huren?**	₩aar kahn ik ayn **oᵒʷtoa hewrern**

Car hire

There are car hire firms at most airports and terminals. There will most likely be someone who speaks English. But if this is not the case, try the following:

I'd like a...	**Ik wil graag een... huren.**	ik ᐯil ghraakh ayn ... hewrern
car	**auto**	oᵒʷtoa
small/large car	**kleine/grote auto**	klaiyner/ghroater oᵒʷtoa
I'd like it for...	**Ik wil het graag voor...**	ik ᐯil heht ghraakh voar
a day/4 days	**één dag/4 dagen**	ayn dahkh/veer **daa**ghern
a week/2 weeks	**één week/2 weken**	ayn ᐯayk/tᐯay ᐯaykern
What's the charge per day/week?	**Wat is het tarief per dag/week?**	ᐯaht iss heht taa**reef** pehr dahkh/ᐯayk
Does that include mileage?	**Is het aantal kilometers hierbij inbegrepen?**	iss heht **aantahl** keeloamayterrs **heer**baiy inberghraypern
What's the charge per kilometre?	**Wat is het tarief per kilometer?**	ᐯaht iss heht taa**reef** pehr keeloamayterr
Is petrol (gasoline) included?	**Is dat inclusief benzine?**	iss daht inklewseef behnzeener
I want full insurance.	**Ik wil een all-risk verzekering, alstublieft.**	ik ᐯil ayn "all-risk" vehrzaykerring ahlstewbleeft
What's the deposit?	**Hoeveel bedraagt de waarborgsom?**	hoovayl berdraakht der ᐯaarborkhsom
I've a credit card.	**Ik heb een betaalpas.**	ik hehp ayn bertaalpahss
Here's my driving licence.	**Hier is mijn rijbewijs.**	heer iss maiyn raiyberᐯaiyss

FOR SIGHTSEEING, see page 75

Taxi

In Holland, hailing a cab in the street is not a very common practice. You'll find taxi ranks at airports, railway stations and at various points in the cities. Meters are usually fitted to the dashboard of the taxi, showing the fare inclusive of tip. There is no extra charge for luggage or night trips. Rates may differ from place to place, it's usually best to ask the approximate fare beforehand.

Where can I get a taxi?	**Waar kan ik een taxi vinden?**	ⱽaar kahn ik ayn **tahk**see vindern
Please get me a taxi.	**Wilt u een taxi voor mij bestellen?**	ⱽilt ew ayn **tahk**see voar maiy ber**stehl**ern
What's the fare to…?	**Wat kost het naar…?**	ⱽaht kost heht naar
How far is it to…?	**Hoever is het naar…?**	**hoo**vehr iss heht naar
Take me to…	**Brengt u mij naar…**	brehngt ew maiy naar
this address	**dit adres**	dit aa**drehss**
the airport	**het vliegveld**	heht **vleegh**vehlt
the … Hotel	**het … Hotel**	heht … hoa**tehl**
the station	**het station**	heht **stahtsyon**
the town centre	**het stadscentrum**	heht **stahts**sehntrum
Turn left/right at the next corner.	**Bij de volgende hoek linksaf/rechtsaf.**	baiy der **vol**ghernder hook **links**ahf/**rehkhts**ahf
Go straight ahead.	**Rechtuit, alstublieft.**	rehkhturᵉwt ahlstew**bleeft**
To the right/left at the traffic lights.	**Bij de stoplichten rechtsaf/linksaf.**	baiy der **stop**lightern **rehkhts**ahf/**links**ahf
Please stop here.	**Wilt u hier stoppen, alstublieft.**	ⱽilt ew heer **stop**pern ahlstew**bleeft**
I'm in a hurry.	**Ik heb haast.**	ik hehp haast
I'm not in a hurry.	**Ik heb geen haast.**	ik hehp ghayn haast
Could you drive more slowly?	**Kunt u wat langzamer rijden, alstublieft?**	kurnt ew ⱽaht **lahng**zaamerr **raiy**dern ahlstew**bleeft**
Would you help me carry my bags?	**Wilt u mij met mijn koffers helpen, alstublieft?**	ⱽilt ew maiy meht maiyn **koffer**ss **hehl**pern ahlstew**bleeft**

FOR TIPPING, see page 1

ARRIVAL

Hotel—Other accommodation

Particularly during the summer tourist season (April–September) it is highly advisable to reserve rooms well in advance. You may be asked to pay a deposit which could be claimed as compensation if the reservation is cancelled. Bookings can be made direct with the hotel of your choice, via a travel agency or airline, or through the National Reservation Centre (NCR). Most towns and arrival points have a tourist information office (VVV—*Vereniging voor Vreemdelingen Verkeer*), and that's the place to go if you're stuck without a room.

Hotel
(hoatehl)

Hotels in Holland are classified, first, according to category, from 1 (highest) to 5 (lowest), and secondly by a number of red stars. The categories concern the number of rooms, amenities, etc. (e.g. lifts, baths), whereas the red stars reflect the quality and comfort of a hotel (e.g. the location and the services offered). Thus a hotel shown as C1 (Class 1) with five stars would be a big hotel with maximum comfort and service in a beautiful location, while a hotel shown as C5 with no red stars would mean a small hotel with accommodation of the simplest type and virtually no service. Both category and number of stars may appear on a sign outside the hotel. Prices do not necessarily relate to this two-faceted classification.

Motel
(moatehl)

Motels are increasingly found near superhighways and other major roads.

Pension
(pehnsyon)

Many boarding houses are of a family nature. They normally offer *vol pension* (full board) or *half pension* (bed and breakfast plus one other meal). The local VVV office will supply you with addresses.

Zomerhuisje
(zoamerrhur^ewsher)

Bungalows can be rented in many tourist resorts, but you must book far in advance.

Jeugdherberg	Youth hostels are open all year round to young
(**yurkht**hehrbehrkh)	people who are members of a youth hostel
	organization in their own country or hold an
	international youth hostel card.

In this section, we're mainly concerned with the smaller and medium-priced hotels and boarding houses. You'll have no language difficulties in the luxury and first-class hotels, where most of the staff speak English.

In the next few pages we consider your requirements—step by step—from arrival to departure.

Checking in—Reception

My name is ...	**Mijn naam is ...**	maiyn naam iss
I've a reservation.	**Ik heb gereserveerd.**	ik hehp gherrayzerrvayrt
We've reserved two rooms, a single and a double.	**Wij hebben twee kamers gereserveerd; een éénpersoonskamer en een tweepersoonskamer.**	ѵaiy hehbern tѵay kaamerrss gherrayzehrvayrt ayn aynpehrsoanskaamerr ehn ayn tѵaypehrsoanskaamerr
I wrote to you last month.	**Ik heb u vorige maand geschreven.**	ik hehp ew voarergher maant gherskhrayvern
Here's the confirmation.	**Hier is de bevestiging.**	heer iss der bervehsterghing
I'd like a ... room.	**Ik zou graag een ... kamer willen hebben.**	ik zoo^{ow} ghraakh ayn ... kaamerr ѵi̬llern hehbern
single	**éénpersoons**	aynpehrsoanss
double	**tweepersoons**	tѵaypehrsoanss
with twin beds	**met lits-jumeaux**	meht lee-zhewmo^{ow}
with a bath	**met badkamer**	meht bahtkaamerr
with a shower	**met douche**	meht doosh
with a balcony	**met balkon**	meht bahlkon
with a view	**met uitzicht**	meht ur^{ew}tzikht
We'd like a room ...	**Wij willen graag een kamer ...**	ѵaiy ѵillern ghraakh ayn kaamerr
in the front	**aan de voorkant**	aan der voarkahnt
at the back	**aan de achterkant**	aan der ahkhterrkahnt
facing the sea	**met uitzicht op de zee**	meht ur^{ew}tzikht op der zay

HOTEL

It must be quiet.	**Het moet er rustig zijn.**	heht moot ehr **rur**sterkh zaiyn
Is there ...?	**Is er ...?**	iss ehr
air conditioning	**air-conditioning**	ehrkondisherning
heating	**verwarming**	verr√ahrming
hot water	**warm water**	√ahrm √aaterr
a laundry service	**een wasserij**	ayn √ahsserraiy
a radio	**een radio**	ayn **raa**deeyoa
running water	**stromend water**	**stroa**mernt √aaterr
a television in the room	**een televisie op de kamer**	ayn taylerveezee op der **kaa**merr
a private toilet	**een eigen toilet**	ayn **aiy**ghern t√aaleht

How much?

What's the price ...?	**Hoeveel kost het ...?**	**hoo**vayl kost heht
per night	**per nacht**	pehr **nahkht**
per week	**per week**	pehr √ayk
for bed and breakfast	**voor overnachting met ontbijt**	voar oaverr**nahkh**ting meht ont**baiyt**
excluding meals	**zonder maaltijden**	**zon**derr **maal**taiydern
for full board	**voor vol pension**	voar vol pehn**syon**
for half board	**voor half pension**	voar hahlf pehn**syon**
Does that include ...?	**Is dat inclusief ...?**	iss daht inkle**wseef**
breakfast	**ontbijt**	ont**baiyt**
service	**bediening**	berdeening
value-added tax (VAT)*	**B.T.W.**	bay-tay-√ay
Is there any reduction for children?	**Is er een reductie voor kinderen?**	iss ehr ayn rerdurksee voar **kin**derrern
Do you charge for the baby?	**Berekent u iets voor de baby?**	berraykernt ew eets voar der **bay**bee
That's too expensive.	**Dat is te duur.**	daht iss ter dewr
Haven't you anything cheaper?	**Hebt u niets goedkopers?**	hehpt ew neets ghoot**koa**perrss

---

* Americans note: a type of sales tax, called *B.T.W.* in Holland and Belgium. It's nearly always included in purchases, rentals, meals, etc.

FOR NUMBERS, see page 175

HOTEL

How long?

We'll be staying ...	Wij blijven ...	√aiy blaiyvern
overnight only	alleen vannacht	ahlayn vahnnahkht
a few days	een paar dagen	ayn paar daaghern
a week (at least)	(minstens) een week	(minsternss) ayn √ayk
I don't know yet.	Ik weet het nog niet.	ik √ayt heht nokh neet

Decision

May I see the room?	Mag ik de kamer zien?	mahkh ik der kaamerr zeen
No. I don't like it.	Nee, die bevalt me niet.	nay dee bervahlt mer neet
It's too ...	Hij is te ...	heht iss ter
dark/small	donker/klein	donkerr/klaiyn
noisy	lawaaierig	laawaa•°yerrerkh
I asked for a room with a bath.	Ik heb om een kamer met bad gevraagd.	ik hehp om ayn kaamerr meht baht ghervraakht
Do you have any-thing ...?	Hebt u iets ...?	hehpt ew eets
better	beters	bayterrss
bigger	groters	ghroaterrss
cheaper	goedkopers	ghootkoaperrss
quieter	rustigers	rursterkherrss
Do you have a room with a better view?	Hebt u een kamer met een beter uit-zicht?	hehpt ew ayn kaamerr meht ayn bayterr ur•°t-zikht
That's fine. I'll take it.	Deze is prima. Die neem ik.	dayzer iss preemah. dee naym ik

The bill (check)

Usually, bills have to be paid weekly and of course upon departure if you stay less than a week. Some hotels might give a reduction for children under six. Find out about it when you make reservations.

FOR DAYS OF THE WEEK, see page 181

HOTEL

Service charges and tax (VAT) are normally included in the bill, but you can ask:

| Is service included? | **Is het inclusief bediening?** | iss heht inklew**seef** berdee**ning** |

Tip the porter when he brings the bags to your room; tip the bellboy if he does any errands for you. So you should keep some small change at hand. (See also inside back-cover.)

Registration

Upon arrival at a hotel or boarding house you'll be asked to fill in a registration form (*aanmeldingsformulier—***aan**mehldingsformewleer). It asks your name, home address, passport number and further destination. It's almost certain to carry an English translation. If it doesn't, ask the desk-clerk (*de receptionist—*rerssehpseeyo**nist**):

| What does this mean? | **Wat betekent dit?** | ∨aht bertay**kernt** dit |

The desk-clerk will also ask you for your passport. If you don't understand what he is saying, show him the section below:

☞	☜
Mag ik uw paspoort even zien?	May I see your passport, please?
Zoudt u zo vriendelijk willen zijn dit formulier in te vullen?	Would you mind filling in this registration form?
Hier tekenen, alstublieft.	Please sign here.
Hoelang bent u van plan te blijven?	How long will you be staying?

| What's my room number? | **Wat is mijn kamernummer?** | ∨aht iss maiyn **kaamerr**-nurmerr |
| Will you have my/our bags sent up? | **Wilt u mijn/onze bagage naar boven laten brengen?** | ∨ilt ew maiyn/onzer baag**haa**zher naar **boa**vern laatern **brehng**ern |

Service, please

Now that you are safely installed, meet the other members of
the hotel staff:

bellboy	de piccolo	der peekoaloa
maid	het kamermeisje	heht kaamerrmaiysher
manager	de direkteur	der deerehkturr
switchboard operator	de telefoniste	der taylerfoanister
waiter	de kelner	der kehlnerr
waitress	de serveerster	der sehrvayrsterr

Call the members of the staff *Juffrouw* (**yur**fro^{ow})—Miss, or
Mevrouw (mer**vro**^{ow})—Madam, and *Mijnheer* (mer**nayr**)—
Sir. Address the waiter as *Ober* (**oa**berr) when calling for
service.

General requirements

Please ask the maid to come up.	Wilt u het kamermeisje vragen boven te komen?	vilt ew heht kaamerrmaiysher vraaghern boavern ter koamern
Just a minute.	Een ogenblikje.	ayn oaghernblikyer
Come in!	Binnen!	binnern
Is there a bath on this floor?	Is er een badkamer op deze verdieping?	iss ehr ayn bahtkaamerr op dayzer verrdeeping
Could you send up ..., please?	Kunt u ... boven laten brengen, alstublieft?	kurnt ew ... boavern laatern brehngern ahlstewbleeft
two cups of coffee	twee kopjes koffie	tvay kopyerss koffee
a sandwich	een sandwich	ayn "sandwich"
Can we have breakfast in our room?	Kunnen we in onze kamer ontbijten?	kurnnern ver in onzer kaamerr ontbaiytern
I'd like to leave these in your safe.	Ik wil dit graag in de hotel-kluis deponeren.	ik vil dit ghraakh in der hoatehl-klur^{ew}ss daypoanayrern
Can you get me a babysitter?	Kunt u een babysitter voor mij krijgen?	kurnt ew ayn "babysitter" voar maiy kraiyghern

HOTEL SERVICE

May I have a/an ...?	Kan ik ... krijgen?	kahn ik ... kraiyghern
ashtray	een asbak	ayn ahsbahk
bath towel	een badhanddoek	ayn bahthahndook
extra blanket	een extra deken	ayn ehkstraa daykern
envelopes	enveloppen	ehnverloppern
(more) hangers	(nog) een paar kleerhangers	(nokh) ayn paar klayrhahngerrss
hot-water bottle	een kruik	ayn krurᵉwk
ice cubes	ijsblokjes	aiysblokyerss
needle and thread	naald en draad	naalt ehn draat
reading-lamp	een bedlampje	ayn behtlampyer
soap	zeep	zayp
writing-paper	schrijfpapier	skhraiyfpaapeer

Where's the ...?	Waar is ...?	√aar iss
bathroom	de badkamer	der bahtkaamerr
cocktail lounge	de bar	der bahr
dining-room	de eetzaal	der aytzaal
hairdresser's	de kapper	der kahperr
restaurant	het restaurant	heht rehstoarahnt
telephone	de telefoon	der taylerfoan
television room	de televisiekamer	der taylerveezeekaamerr
toilet	het toilet	heht t√aaleht

Breakfast

The Dutch breakfast, or *ontbijt*, consists of coffee or tea, three or four types of bread or rolls (*broodjes*—**broa**tyerss), thin slices of cheese or ham, preserves and sometimes a boiled egg. Most of the larger hotels, however, are now used to providing an English or American breakfast.

I'll have some ...	Ik wil graag ... hebben.	ik √il ghraakh ... hehbern
cocoa	cacao	kaakoᵒʷ
coffee	koffie	koffee
black	zwarte	z√ahrter
with cream	met room	meht roam
with milk	met melk	meht mehlk
decaffeinated	cafeïnevrije	kahfayeenervraiyyer
juice	sap	sahp
grapefruit	grapefruit	"grapefruit"
orange	sinaasappel	seenaasahperl
tomato	tomaten	toamaatern

FOR EATING OUT, see pages 38–64

HOTEL SERVICE

milk	**melk**	mehlk
hot/cold	**warme/koude**	✓ahrmer/ko^{ow}der
skimmed	**taptemelk**	tahptermehlk
tea	**thee**	tay
with milk	**met melk**	meht mehlk
with lemon	**met citroen**	meht seetroon
May I have a/an some ...?	**Mag ik ... hebben?**	mahkh ik ... hehbern
bacon and eggs	**spiegeleieren met ontbijtspek**	speegherlaiyererrn meht ontbaiytspehk
boiled egg	**een gekookt ei**	ayn gherkoakt aiy
hard	**hard**	hahrt
medium	**medium**	meedeeyurm
soft	**zacht**	zahkht
bread	**wat broot**	✓aht broat
butter	**wat boter**	✓aht boaterr
cereals	**wat cornflakes**	✓aht kornflayks
cheese	**wat kaas**	✓aht kaass
crispbread	**wat beschuit**	✓aht berskhur^{ew}t
honey	**wat honing**	✓aht hoaning
marmalade	**wat marmelade**	✓aht mahrmaerlaader
rolls	**een paar broodjes**	ayn paar broatyerss
toast	**wat toast**	✓aht toast
yoghurt	**wat joghurt**	✓aht yokhurrt
Could you bring me a/some ...?	**Kunt u mij ... brengen?**	kurnt ew maiy ... brehngen
cream	**wat room**	✓aht roam
lemon	**wat citroen**	✓aht seetroon
pepper	**wat peper**	✓aht payperr
saccharin	**wat saccharine**	✓aht sahkhaareener
salt	**wat zout**	✓aht zo^{ow}t
sugar	**wat suiker**	✓aht sur^{ew}ker
glass of water	**een glas water**	ayn glahss ✓aaterr
hot water	**wat warm water**	✓aht ✓ahrm ✓aaterr

Difficulties

The ... doesn't work.	**... werkt niet.**	... ✓ehrkt neet
fan	**de ventilator**	der vehnteelaator
heating	**de verwarming**	der verr✓ahrming
light	**het licht**	heht likht
radiator	**de radiateur**	der raadeeyaaturr
radio	**de radio**	der raadeeyoa

shower	**de douche**	der doosh
tap	**de kraan**	der kraan
television set	**de televisie**	der taylerveezee
toilet	**het toilet**	heht tⱽaaleht
ventilator	**de ventilatie**	der vehnteelaatsee

The wash-basin is clogged.	**De wastafel is verstopt.**	der ⱽahstaaferl iss verrstopt
The window is jammed.	**Het raam klemt.**	heht raam klehmt
The blind is stuck.	**De jaloezie zit vast.**	der yaaloozee zit vahst
These aren't my shoes.	**Dit zijn mijn schoenen niet.**	dit zaiyn maiyn skhoonern neet
This isn't my laundry.	**Dit is mijn wasgoed niet.**	dit iss maiyn ⱽahsghoot neet
There's no hot water.	**Er is geen warm water.**	ehr iss ghayn ⱽahrm ⱽaaterr
I've lost my watch.	**Ik heb mijn horloge verloren.**	ik hehp maiyn horloazher verrloarern
I've left my key in my room.	**Ik heb mijn sleutel in mijn kamer laten liggen.**	ik hehp maiyn slurterl in maiyn kaamerr laatern lighern
The bulb is burnt out.	**De lamp is gesprongen.**	der lamp iss ghersprongern
The … is broken.	**… is kapot.**	… iss kaapot
lamp	**het licht**	heht likht
plug	**het stopkontakt**	heht stopkontahkt
shutter	**het luik**	heht lurᵂk
switch	**de schakelaar**	der skhaakerlaar
venetian blind	**de store**	der stoar
window shade	**het zonnescherm**	heht zonnerskhehrm
Can you get it repaired?	**Kunt u het laten repareren?**	kurnt ew heht laatern raypaarayrern

Telephone—Mail

| Can you get me Amsterdam 311-34-67? | **Kunt u me met Amsterdam 311-34-67 verbinden?** | kurnt ew mer meht ahmsterrdahm 311-34-67 verrbindern |
| Are there any messages for me? | **Zijn er boodschappen voor mij?** | zaiyn ehr boatshahpern voar maiy |

FOR POST OFFICE AND TELEPHONE, see pages 137–141

Have you received any mail for me?	**Hebt u post voor mij ontvangen?**	hehpt ew post voar maiy ontvahngern
Do you have stamps?	**Hebt u postzegels?**	hehpt ew postzaygherlss
Would you please mail this for me?	**Wilt u dit voor mij posten, alstublieft?**	vilt ew dit voar maiy postern ahlstewbleeft

Checking out

May I please have my bill?	**Mag ik mijn rekening, alstublieft?**	mahkh ik maiyn raykerning ahlstewbleeft
I'm leaving early tomorrow. Please have my bill ready.	**Ik vertrek morgenochtend vroeg. Wilt u mijn rekening klaarmaken, alstublieft?**	ik verrtrehk morghernokhternt vrookh. vilt ew maiyn raykerning klaarmaakern ahlstewbleeft
We'll be checking out around noon/soon.	**Wij vertrekken omstreeks 12 uur/ spoedig.**	vaiy verrtrehkern omstrayks tvaalf ewr/spooderkh
I must leave at once.	**Ik moet onmiddellijk vertrekken.**	ik moet onmidderlerk verrtrehkern
Is everything included?	**Is alles inbegrepen?**	iss ahlerss inberghraypern
You've made a mistake in this bill, I think.	**Ik geloof, dat u een vergissing in de rekening gemaakt hebt.**	ik gherloaf daht ew ayn verghissing in der raykerning ghermaakt hehpt
Can you get us a taxi?	**Kunt u een taxi voor ons bestellen?**	kurnt ew ayn tahksee voar onss berstehlern
When's the next ... to Brussels?	**Wanneer vertrekt de/het volgende ... naar Brussel?**	vahnayr verrtrehkt der/ het volghender ... naar brursserl
bus/plain/train	**bus/vliegtuig/trein**	burss/vleeghturewkh/traiyn
Would you send someone to bring down our baggage?	**Wilt u onze bagage naar beneden laten brengen?**	vilt ew onzer baaghaazher naar bernaydern laatern brehngern
We're in a great hurry.	**Wij hebben erge haast.**	vaiy hehbern ehrgher haast
Here's my forwarding address. You have my home address.	**Hier is mijn volgende adres. Mijn huisadres hebt u al.**	heer iss maiyn volghender aadrehss. maiyn hurewssaadrehss hehpt ew ahl

FOR TIPPING, see page 1

HOTEL SERVICE

Eating out

There are many different types of eating and drinking places in Holland and the restaurants, especially in Amsterdam, are as varied in atmosphere as in menu.

Bar (bahr)	A sophisticated drinking place, where all sorts of drinks are served.
Bistro (beestroa)	A cosy place to eat, where special, tasty meals are served.
Broodjeswinkel (broatyersvinkerl)	A sandwich shop; serves a great variety of sandwiches made of *broodjes* (rolls) with different types of meat, fish and cheese. This is one of the Dutchman's favourite places for lunch or a quick snack.
Café (kahfay)	This is the place where the Dutch go to have a drink and to play billiards.
Cafetaria (kahfertayreeyaa)	Serves hot meals and is often self-service.
Hotel (hoatehl)	Most hotel restaurants are open to the public.
Koffieshop (koffeeshop)	A coffee-house where the Dutch go for their *kopje koffie* (cup of coffee) and *gebak* (pastries) in the morning.
Motel or Weg-restaurant (moatehl vehghrehstoarahnt)	Eating places along the major highways; international choice of food.
Nachtclub (nahkhtklurp)	A nightclub, generally with a floor show and strip-tease.
Pannekoekhuisje (pahnerkookhur^{ew}sher)	A pancake-house serving a wide variety of *flensjes* (a thin type of pancake) and *pannekoeken* (pancakes). You could also try *poffertjes* (a kind of small round pancake) which are served with butter and powder sugar.
Proeflokaal (proofloakaal)	A bar/shop where you can sample (but not free!) various local drinks. Here you can try *jenever* (Dutch gin). There are also lemon-, redcurrant- and blackberry-flavoured jenevers. Just ask for a *borreltje* (glass of jenever).

Restaurant (rehstoa**rahnt**)	Many restaurants in Holland specialize in French, Italian, Indonesian, Greek, Japanese, Indian and Turkish cooking. A few of them even advertise *Dutch restaurant,* in English, on the door.
Snackbar	Useful for a bite on the run. For snacks, see page 62.
Tea-room	These serve tea and coffee. The Dutch like to take their tea between 3 and 5 p. m. with *koekjes* (biscuits) or *gebak* (pastry).

Meal times

Breakfast (*ontbijt*—ont**baiyt**) is generally served between 7 and 10 a. m. See page 34 for a breakfast menu.

Lunch is generally served from noon until 2 p. m. The *koffietafel* (**ko**ffeetaaferl) is a sandwich lunch (including coffee, milk or tea), consisting of various types of bread, cold meats, cheese and possibly a warm dish, and preceded by a bowl of soup or a salad.

Dinner (*diner*—dee**nay**) is usually served between 6 and 8 p. m.

BTW en bediening inbegrepen. These words simplify your life as a tourist in Holland. They mean: Value Added Tax and service charge included. But it's customary to round off payment or give an extra guilder or two if service has been particularly good.

Eating habits

Most restaurants display a menu in the window. Look for the *dagschotel*—**dahkh**skhoaterl (daily special), which is usually a simple but tasty dish at a reasonable price. Some 750 restaurants throughout Holland offer a tourist menu, consisting of an appetizer, a main course and a dessert, for quite a modest sum. These restaurants can be recognized by the emblem shown here.

Hungry

I'm hungry/I'm thirsty.	**Ik heb honger/Ik heb dorst.**	ik hehp **hong**err/ik hehp dorst
Can you recommend a good restaurant?	**Kunt u een goed restaurant aanbevelen?**	kurnt ew ayn ghoot rehstoa**rahnt** aanbervaylern
Are there any inexpensive restaurants around here?	**Zijn er hier goedkope restaurants in de buurt?**	zaiyn ehr heer ghoot**koaper** rehstoa**rahnts** in der bewrt

To be sure of getting a table in a well-known restaurant, it's advisable to telephone in advance.

I'd like to reserve a table for 4. We'll come at 8.	**Ik wil graag een tafel voor 4 personen reserveren. Wij komen om 8 uur.**	ik √il ghraakh ayn **taafer**l voar 4 pehr**soa**nern rayzehr**vay**rern. √aiy **koa**mern om 8 ewr

Wat wenst u?	What would you like?
Ik kan u dit aanbevelen.	I recommend this.
Wat wilt u drinken?	What would you like to drink?
Wij hebben geen ...	We haven't got ...
Wilt u ...?	Do you want ...

Asking and ordering

Good evening. I'd like a table for 2.	**Goedenavond. Ik wil graag een tafel voor 2 personen.**	ghoodern**aa**vont. ik √il ghraakh ayn **taafer**l voar 2 pehr**soa**nern
Could we have a table ...?	**Kunnen wij een tafel ... krijgen?**	**kurn**nern √aiy ayn **taafer**l ... **kraiy**ghern
in the corner	**in de hoek**	in der hook
by the window	**bij het raam**	baiy heht raam
outside	**buiten**	bur**ᵉʷ**tern
on the terrace	**op het terras**	op heht teh**rahss**

Are these places taken?	**Zijn deze plaatsen bezet?**	zaiyn dayzer **plaats**ern berzeht
Waiter/Waitress!	**Ober/Juffrouw!**	oaberr/yurfro^{ow}
We'd like something to eat/drink.	**We willen graag iets eten/drinken.**	ver villern ghraakh eets aytern/drinkern
Could I have the menu/wine list?	**Mag ik de spijs-kaart/wijnkaart hebben?**	mahkh ik der spaiysskaart/vaiynkaart hehbern
What's this?	**Wat is dit?**	vaht iss dit
Do you have ...?	**Hebt u ...?**	hehpt ew
a set menu	**een menu**	ayn mernew
local dishes	**speciale gerechten van deze streek**	spaysyaaler gherrehkhtern vahn dayzer strayk
Is service included?	**Is het inclusief bediening?**	iss heht inklewseef berdeening
Could you serve me straight away, please? I'm in a hurry.	**Kunt u me meteen bedienen, alstu-blieft? Ik heb haast.**	kurnt ew mer mertayn berdeenern ahlstewbleeft ik hehp haast
Could I have an extra plate for the child?	**Mag ik een extra bord voor dit kind hebben?**	mahkh ik ayn ehkstraa bort voar dit kint hehbern
Could we have a/an/some ..., please?	**Kunnen we een ... krijgen?**	kurnern ver ayn ... kraiyghern
ashtray	**asbak**	ahsbahk
another chair	**nog een stoel**	nokh ayn stool
bottle of ...	**fles ...**	flehss
fork	**vork**	vork
glass	**glas**	ghlahss
glass of water	**glas water**	ghlahss vaaterr
knife	**mes**	mehss
matches	**lucifers**	lewsseefehrss
napkin	**servet**	sehrveht
plate	**bord**	bort
serviette	**servet**	sehrveht
spoon	**lepel**	layperl
toothpick	**tandestoker**	tahnderstoakerr
I'd like a/an/some...	**Ik wil graag ... hebben.**	ik vil ghraakh ... hehbern
aperitif	**een aperitief**	ayn aapayreeteef
appetizer	**een voorgerecht**	ayn voargherrehkht

FOR COMPLAINTS, see page 58

EATING OUT

beer	**een biertje**	ayn beertyer
bread	**wat brood**	√aht broat
butter	**boter**	boaterr
cheese	**kaas**	kaass
chips	**patates frites**	paataht freet
coffee	**een kopje koffie**	ayn kopyer koffee
dessert	**een nagerecht**	ayn naagherrehkht
fish	**vis**	viss
french fries	**patates frites**	paataht freet
fruit	**fruit**	frurᵉʷt
fruit-juice	**vruchtesap**	vrurkhternsahp
game	**gevogelte**	ghervoagherlter
ice-cream	**ijs**	aiyss
ketchup	**wat ketchup**	√aht kehtshurp
lemon	**citroen**	seetroon
lettuce	**een kropsla**	ayn kropslaa
meat	**vlees**	vlayss
milk	**een glas melk**	ayn glahss mehlk
mineral water	**mineraalwater**	meenerraal√aaterr
mustard	**mosterd**	mosterrt
oil	**wat olie**	√aht oalee
olive oil	**wat olijfolie**	√aht oalaiyfoalee
pasta	**piment**	peemehnt
pepper	**peper**	payperr
potatoes	**aardappels**	aardahperlss
poultry	**kip**	kip
rice	**rijst**	raiyst
rolls	**een paar broodjes**	ayn paar broatyerss
salad	**sla**	slaa
salt	**zout**	zoᵒʷt
saccharin	**saccharine**	sahkhaareener
sandwich	**een sandwich**	ayn "sandwich"
seafood	**schaal- en schelp-dieren**	skhaal ehn skhehlpdeeren
seasoning	**wat kruiden**	√aht krurᵉʷdern
soft drink	**een frisdrank**	ayn frisdrahnk
soup	**soep**	soop
spaghetti	**spaghetti**	spaakhehtee
starter	**een voorgerecht**	ayn voargherrekht
sugar	**suiker**	surᵉʷkerr
tea	**een kopje thee**	ayn kopyer tay
vegetables	**groenten**	ghroontern
vinegar	**wat azijn**	√aht aazaiyn
(iced) water	**(ijs)water**	(aiys) √aaterr
wine	**wijn**	√aiyn

What's on the menu?

Our menu is presented according to courses. Under the headings below you'll find alphabetical lists of dishes likely to be offered on a Dutch menu, with their English equivalents. You can also show the book to the waiter. If you want some fruit, for instance, show him the appropriate list and let him point to what's available. Use pages 40–42 for ordering in general.

Typical Dutch cooking can "stick your ribs together": the Dutch like hearty meals, especially when the weather is cold. In most restaurants you'll find a choice of international dishes. Centuries of Dutch colonial presence in what is now Indonesia have added another dimension to the cuisine of the Netherlands. Rice-based, sometimes spicy Indonesian and Chinese-influenced food is found in many specialized restaurants throughout the country, in towns and sometimes even villages as well as in the large cities.

Here, then is our guide to good eating and drinking. Turn to the section you want.

	Page
Appetizers	44
Salads	45
Eggs and omelets	45
Soup	46
Fish and seafood	47
Meat	49
Game and fowl	51
Vegetables	52
Sauces	54
Cheese	55
Fruit	56
Dessert	57
Drinks	59
Eating light – Snacks	62
Indonesian dishes	63
Belgian (Flemish) specialities	64

EATING OUT

Appetizers

I'd like an appetizer.	Ik wil graag een voorgerecht hebben.	ik vil ghraakh ayn voargherrekht hehbern
What do you recommend?	Wat beveelt u mij/ons aan?	vaht bervaylt ew maiy/onss aan
aspergepunten	ahspehrzherpurntern	asparagus tips
bitterballen	bitterrbahlern	small round breaded meatballs
champignons op toast	shahmpeeñonss op toast	mushrooms on toast
croquetten (ham, kaas, kip, vlees, garnalen)	kroakehtern (hahm kaass kip vlayss ghahrnaalern)	croquettes (ham, cheese, chicken, meat, shrimps)
eieren	aiyyerrern	eggs
gevulde	ghervurlder	stuffed
Russische	rursseesser	Russian
garnalen	ghahrnaalern	shrimps
garnalencocktail	ghahrnaalernkoktayl	shrimp cocktail
gevarieerde hors d'œuvre	ghervaareeyayrder hor dervr	assorted appetizers
haring	haaring	herring
nieuwe/gerookte	nee°°ver/gherroakter	raw/smoked
kaasbroodje	kaassbroatyer	Welsh rarebit
kaviaar	kaaveeyaar	caviar
kievitseieren	keeveetsaiyyerrern	plover's eggs
krabcoctail	krahpkoktayl	crabmeat cocktail
kreeft	krayft	lobster
kreeftecocktail	krayfterkoktayl	lobster cocktail
makreel (gemarineerd)	maakrayl (ghermaareenayrt)	mackerel (soused)
meloen	merloon	melon
mosselen	mosserlern	mussels
oesters	oosterrss	oysters
paling	paaling	eel
gerookte	gherroakter	smoked
gesmoorde	ghersmoarder	stewed
pastei	pahstaiy	pâté
pasteitje	pahstaiytyer	pastry shell filled with sweetbreads, chicken or veal
schelvislever	skhehlvislayverr	haddock liver
soufflé	sooflay	soufflé
asperge	ahspehrzher	asparagus
ham	hahm	ham
kaas	kaass	cheese

tomaten	toamaatern	tomatoes
gevulde	ghervurlder	stuffed
zalm	zahlm	salmon
gerookte	gherroakter	smoked

The Dutch make a lot of their snacks, or *borrelhapjes* (**bor**-rerlhahpyerss), when inviting guests for drinks: small portions of toast surmounted with various garnishes; small pieces of vegetables with dips; *zebras*—layers of rye bread alternating with cream-cheese, cut in small sections, etc.

Salads

The Dutch sometimes take these salads as part of their *koffietafel* (see p. 39).

What salads do you have?	**Welke soorten salade hebt u?**	**V**ehlker **s**oartern saalaader hehpt ew
aspergesalade	ahspehrzhersaalaader	asparagus, egg, pickles, ham, radishes
haringsalade	haaringsaalaader	herring, beetroot, apple, potato, pickles and mayonnaise
huzarensalade	hewzaarernsaalaader	potato, hard-boiled egg, mayonnaise and pickles
Italiaanse salade	eetaalyaanser saalaader	mixed salad with tomato, olives and tunny fish

Eggs and omelets

omelet	ommerleht	omelet
boerenomelet	boorernommerleht	with diced vegetables and bacon
fines herbes	feen zehrb	with herbs
met champignons	meht shahmpeeñonss	with mushrooms
met ham	meht hahm	with ham
met kaas	meht kaass	with cheese
met kippelevertjes	meht kipperlayverrtyerss	with chicken livers
roerei	rooraiy	scrambled eggs
spiegeleieren met ham	speegherlaiyerrern meht hahm	ham and eggs

EATING OUT

Soup

Soups are an important part of Dutch cooking. They are either served as a hot dish with the traditional Dutch *koffietafel* (see p. 39) or as the first course of the main meal. Two types of soup can be found on menus: *heldere soep* consommé or clear soup), and *gebonden soep* (cream). Sometimes the French word *potage* is used.

aardappelsoep	aardahperlsoop	potato soup
aspergesoep	ahspehrzhersoop	asparagus soup
bisque de homard	beesk der ommaar	lobster chowder
bloemkoolsoep	bloomkoalsoop	cauliflower soup
bouillon	boo⁰ᵒyon	broth
met croutons	meht krootonss	with fried bread cubes
met eiergelei	meht aiyyerrzherlaiy	with an egg (consommé royal)
met groenten	meht ghroontern	with chopped vegetables (consommé julienne)
met omelet	meht ommerleht	with thin shreds of omelet (consommé célestine)
bruine bonensoep	brur⁰ᵂner boanernsoop	bean soup
champignonsoep	shahmpeeñonsoop	mushroom soup
erwtensoep	ehrternsoop	thick pea soup (see specialities)
Franse uiensoep	frahnser ur⁰ᵂyernsoop	French onion soup
groentesoep (met balletjes)	ghroonternsoop (meht bahllertyerss)	vegetable soup (with meat-balls)
kervelsoep	kehrverlsoop	chervil soup
kippesoep	kippersoop	chicken soup
koninginnesoep	koaniyinnersoop	cream of chicken
kreeftesoep	krayftersoop	lobster chowder
Londonderrysoep	londondehrreesoop	Londonderry soup: creamy soup with hot spices
oestersoep	oosterrsoop	oyster soup
ossestaartsoep	osserstaartsoop	oxtail soup
palingsoep	paalingsoop	cream of eel
preisoep	praiysoop	cream of leeks
soep van de dag	soop vahn der dahkh	soup of the day
spinaziesoep	speenaazeesoop	spinach soup
schildpadsoep	skhiltpahtsoop	mock turtle
vermicellisoep	vehrmersehleesoop	clear noodle soup

Fish and seafood

Even though it may sound a little too exotic for your taste at
first hearing, salted raw herring—called "new herring"
(*nieuwe haring* or *Hollandse nieuwe*)—is a treat not to be
missed during the first weeks of May. The Dutch tradition-
ally buy it at street stalls, but it is also served in restaurants.
The big Zeeland oysters and mussels are mainly available
from September to March.

I'd like some fish.	**Ik wil graag vis hebben.**	ik vil ghraakh viss hehbern
What kinds of fish do you have?	**Welke soorten vis hebt u?**	vehlker soarten viss hehpt ew
baars	baarss	perch
bokking	bokking	kipper
bot	bot	flounder
brasem	braazerm	bream
forel	foarehl	trout
garnalen	ghahrnaalern	shrimp
griet	ghreet	brill
haring	haaring	herring
heek	hayk	hake
heilbot	haiylbot	halibut
kabeljouw	kahberlyoᵒʷ	cod
karper	kahrpehr	carp
knorhaan	knorhaan	gurnard
krab	krahp	crab
kreeft	krayft	lobster
maatjesharing	maatyershaaring	matie, maty
makreel	maakrayl	mackerel
mosselen	mosserlern	mussels
oesters	oosterr	oysters
paling	paaling	eel
pelser	pehlzerr	pilchard
poon (grote)	poan (ghroater)	sapphirine gurnard
poon (kleine)	poan (klaiyner)	grey gurnard
rivierkreeft	reeveerkrayft	crayfish
sardines	sahrdeenerss	sardines
schar	skhahr	dab
schelvis	skhehlviss	haddock
schol	skhol	plaice
snoek	snook	pike
snoekbaars	snookbaarss	perch-pike
sprot	sprot	sprats

EATING OUT

tarbot	tahrbot	turbot
tong	tong	sole
tongschar	tongskhahr	lemon sole
tonijn	toanaiyn	tuna
wijting	Vaiyting	whiting
witvis	Vitviss	whitebait
zalm	zahlm	salmon
zeebaars	zaybaarss	bass
zeeforel	zayfoarehl	seatrout
zeehaan	zayhaan	(red) mullet
zeekreeft (kleine)	zaykrayft (klaiyner)	scampi
zeelt	zaylt	tench
zeepaling	zaypaaling	conger eel
zeewolf	zayVolf	catfish

baked	in de oven gebakken	in der oavern ghebahkern
fried	gebakken	gherbahkern
grilled	geroosterd/gegrilleerd	gherroasterrt/gherghreeyayrt
marinated	gemarineerd	ghermaareenayrt
poached	gekookt/gepocheerd	gherkoakt/gherposhayrt
sautéed	snel aangebraden	snehl aangherbraadern
smoked	gerookt	gherroakt
steamed	gestoofd	gherstoaft
stewed	gesmoord	ghersmoart

Fish specialities

Gerookte paling
(gherroakter paaling)
delicately smoked eel, served on toast or with potatoes and salad

Haring, or **Hollandse nieuwe**
(haaring, hollahntser nee°°Ver)
filleted, salted herring. Hold it by the tail, dip it in chopped onions and gobble it down like a true Dutchman—or Dutchwoman!

Mosselen
(mosserlern)
mussels served with a mustard sauce and chips (french fries).

Rolmops
(rolmops)
rolled up fillets of herring marinated in spiced vinegar

Stokvis
(stokviss)
stockfish: dried cod with rice, fried potatoes and onions, mustard sauce

Zure haring
(zewrer haaring)
marinated herring, served on bread or toast

Meat

I'd like some...	Ik wil graag ... hebben.	ik vil ghraakh ... hehbern
beef/lamb	rundvlees/lamsvlees	rurntvlayss/lahmsvlayss
pork/veal	varkensvlees/ kalfsvlees	vahrkehnsvlayss/ kahlfsvlayss
biefstuk	beefsturk	fillet of beef
biefstuk tartare	beefsturk	steak tartare
blinde vinken	blinder vinkern	stuffed fillets of veal
borststuk	borststurk	breast
braadworst	braatvorst	frying sausage
contre-filet	kontr-feeleh	sirloin steak
Duitse biefstuk	durewtser beefsturk	hamburger steak
entrecôte	ahntrerkoat	rib-steak
gehakt	gherhahkt	minced meat
gehaktbal	gherhahktbahl	meat-ball
hachee	hahshay	stew served with potatoes
Hollandse biefstuk	hollahntser beefsturk	loin cut of T-bone steak
kalfsborst	kahlfsborst	breast of veal
kalfshaas	kahlfshaass	tenderloin of veal
kalfskotelet	kahlfskoaterleht	veal cutlet
kalfsoester	kahlfsoosterrss	thin fillet of veal
karbonade	kahrboanaader	chop
kotelet	koaterleht	cutlet
lamsbout	lahmsbo^{ow}t	leg of lamb
lamskarbonades	lahmskahrboanaader	lamb chops
lever	layverr	liver
niertjes	neertyerss	kidneys
ossestaart	osserstaart	oxtail
rolpens	rolpehnss	tripe
rookworst	roakvorst	smoked sausage
rosbief	rosbeef	roast beef
saucijsjes	soasaiysherss	sausages
schapevlees	skhaapervlayss	mutton
schouderstuk	skho^{ow}derrsturk	shoulder
spek	spehk	bacon
tong	tong	tongue
tournedos	toornerdoa	thick round fillet cut of prime beef
varkenshaas	vahrkernshaass	fillet of pork
varkenskarbonade	vahrkernskahrboanaader	pork chop
worst	vorst	sausage
zwezerik	zvayzerrik	sweetbreads

How do you like your meat?

baked	in de oven gebakken	in der oavern gherbahkern
boiled	gekookt	gherkoakt
braised	gesmoord	ghersmoart
fried	gebraden	gherbraadern
grilled	geroosterd	gherroastert
roasted	gebakken	gherbahkern
sautéed	snel aangebraden	snehl aanngherbraadern
stewed	gestoofd	gherstoaft
underdone (rare)	licht gebakken/rood	likht gherbahkern/roat
medium	net gaar gebakken	neht ghaar gherbahkern
well-done	doorgebakken	doargherbahkern

Meat specialities

Typical Dutch fare is very substantial and consists of a mix (*stamppot*—**stahm**pot) of vegetables and potatoes served with sausages and bacon.

Boerenkool met worst
(boorern**kool** meht ✓orst)

curly kale and potatoes, served with smoked sausage; typical winter dish

Erwtensoep met kluif
(ehrtternsoop meht klurᵉʷf)

thick pea soup with pieces of smoked sausage, cubes of pork fat, pig's knuckle and slices of pumpernickel (black rye bread); often served with brown bread

Hete bliksem
(hayter blikserm)

potatoes, bacon and apple, seasoned with butter, salt and sugar (the name means "hot lightning")

Hutspot met klapstuk
(hurtspot meht klahpsturk)

potatoes, carrots and onions, often served with *klapstuk* (beef)

Jachtschotel
(yahkhtskhoaterl)

a casserole of meat, onions and potatoes, often served with apple sauce

Rolpens met rode kool
(rolpehnss meht roader koal)

fried slices of spiced and pickled minced beef and tripe, topped with a slice of apple and served with red cabbage

Zuurkool
(zewrkoal)

sauerkraut; often served with bacon or tender roast partridge

Game and fowl

Chicken, duck and turkey are served in Dutch restaurants all through the year. For game proper you'll have to go to a special restaurant in the hunting areas (mainly in the east and south Netherlands). The hunting season runs from August/September to January/February. Ask the local tourist office for further details.

I'd like some game.	**Ik wil graag wild hebben.**	ik vil ghraakh vilt hehbern
braadhaantje	**braadhaantje**	braathaantyer	spring chicken
duif	**duif**	dur^{ew}f	pigeon
eend	**eend**	aynt	duck
fazant	**fazant**	fahzahnt	pheasant
gans	**gans**	gahnss	goose
gevogelte	**gevogelte**	ghevoagherlter	fowl
haan	**haan**	haan	cockerel
haas	**haas**	haass	hare
hazepeper	**hazepeper**	haazerpayperr	jugged hare
houtsnip	**houtsnip**	ho^{ow}tsnip	woodcock
kalkoen	**kalkoen**	kahlkoon	turkey
kip	**kip**	kip	chicken
gebraden kip	**gebraden kip**	gherbraadern kip	roast chicken
konijn	**konijn**	koanaiyn	rabbit
korhoen	**korhoen**	korhoon	grouse
kuiken	**kuiken**	kur^{ew}kern	spring chicken
kwartel	**kwartel**	kvahrterl	quail
parelhoen	**parelhoen**	paarerlhoon	guinea fowl
patrijs	**patrijs**	paatraiyss	partridge
reebout, reerug	**reebout, reerug**	raybo^{ow}t	venison
smient	**smient**	smeent	widgeon
speenvarken	**speenvarken**	spaynvahrkern	suckling-pig
taling	**taling**	taaling	teal
watersnip	**watersnip**	vaaterrsnip	snipe
wild	**wild**	vilt	game
wild zwijn	**wild zwijn**	vilt zvaiyn	wild boar

You usually have a choice of accompaniment to go with game:

brussels sprouts	**spruitjes**	spru^{ew}tyerss
chestnut purée	**kastanjepuree**	kahstahnyerpewray
cranberry sauce	**vossebessen**	vosserbehssern
mashed potatoes	**aardappelpuree**	aardahperlpewray

Vegetables

Fresh vegetables are available all year round, thanks to glasshouse cultivation. Large white asparagus, especially, is grown there, and you'll find it on the menu in May and June.

aardappelen	aardahperlern	potatoes
andijvie	ahndaiyvee	endive (Am. chicory)
artisjoken	ahrteeshokkern	artichoke
asperge(punten)	ahspehrzher(purntern)	asparagus (tips)
augurken	o^{ow}ghurrkern	gherkins
bieten	beetern	beetroot
bloemkool	bloomkoal	cauliflower
boerenkool	boorernkoal	kale
bonen	boanern	beans
witte bonen	vitter boanern	white beans
bruine bonen	brur^{ew}nern boanern	kidney beans
Brussels lof	brursserlss lof	chicory (Am. endive)
doperwtjes	dopehrrtyerss	peas
eierplant	aiyyerrplahnt	aubergine (eggplant)
grauwe erwten	ghro^{ow}ver ehrrtern	chick-peas
groenten	ghroontern	vegetables
gemengde groen-	ghermehngder	mixed vegetables
ten	ghroontern	
kappertjes	kahperrtyerss	capers
kapucijners	kahpewsaiynderrss	marrowfat peas
knolselderij	knolsehlderraiy	celeriac
komkommer	komkommerr	cucumber
kool	koal	cabbage
rode kool	roader koal	red cabbage
zuurkool	zewrkoal	sauerkraut
kropsla	kropslaa	lettuce
linzen	linzern	lentils
maïs	mah^{ee}ss	sweet corn
maïskolven	mah^{ee}skolvern	corn on the cob
paddestoelen	pahderstoolern	mushrooms
peultjes	purltyerss	sugar peas
pompoen (kleine)	pompoon (klaiyner)	vegetable marrow (zucchini)
postelein	posterlaiyn	purslane
prei	praiy	leeks
prinsessenbonen	prinsehsernboanern	green beans
radijs	raadaiyss	radishes
selderij	sehlderraiy	celery
sla	slaa	salad
snijbonen	slaaboanern	haricot beans
spinazie	speenaazee	spinach

spruitjes	sprur**e w**tyerss	brussels sprouts
tomaten	toamaatern	tomatoes
tuinbonen	tur**ew**nboanern	broad beans
uien	ur**ew**yern	onions
venkel	vehnkerl	fennel
waterkers	**√**aaterrkehrss	watercress
worteltjes	**√**orterltyerss	carrots

And as a Dutch meal wouldn't be complete without potatoes, here are some ways of preparation:

aardappelpuree	aardahperlpewray	mashed potatoes
aardappelcroquet-ten	aardahperlkroakehtern	croquettes
gebakken	gherbahkern	fried
gekookt	gherkoakt	boiled
in de schil gekookt	in der shkil gher**koakt**	boiled in their jackets
nieuwe aardappel-tjes	nee**oo√**er aardahperltyerss	new potatoes
patates frites	paataht freet	chips (french fries)

Some herbs commonly used in Dutch cooking:

basilicum	baa**zee**leekurm	basil
bieslook	beesloak	chive
bonenkruid	boanernkrur**ew**t	savory
dragon	draaghon	tarragon
kervel	kehrverl	chervil
knoflook	knofloak	garlic
kruiden	krur**ew**dern	herbs
(gemengde)	(ghermehngder)	(mixed)
kruidnagel	krur**ew**tnaagherl	clove
mierikswortel	meeriks**√**orterl	horseradish
marjolijn	mahryolaiyn	origan
nootmuskaat	noatmur**skaat**	nutmeg
peterselie	payterrsaylee	parsley
rozemarijn	roazermaaraiyn	rosemary
tijm	taiym	thyme

You might also want:

mustard	**mosterd**	mosterrt
pepper	**peper**	payperr
salad dressing	**slasaus**	slaas**ow**ss
salt	**zout**	zo**ow**t
sugar	**suiker**	sur**ew**kerr

Sauces and preparations

The Dutch consume huge quantities of gravy (*saus*—so^{ow}ss or *jus*—zhew) and mayonnaise with their food. In the better restaurants you'll be served mainly French sauces. Below are brief descriptions of most sauces and garnishes you are likely to encounter.

Béarnaise saus	a creamy sauce flavoured with vinegar, egg yolks, white wine, shallots and tarragon
Béchamelsaus	a white sauce made of butter, flour and milk
Botersaus	a sauce made of butter, flour and fish stock
Bruine saus	butter, flour, stock, thyme, onions, parsley, cloves and bacon
Chaud-froid	gelatine, thick cream, egg yolks, mushrooms, onions and cloves
Gesmolten boter	melted butter, often served with fish
Hollandse saus (Sauce hollandaise)	egg yolks, butter and cream
Kaassaus	butter, flour, milk or stock and grated cheese
Kappertjessaus	butter, flour, stock, capers and vinegar
Madeirasaus	butter, flour, bacon, stock, cloves, thyme and Madeira
Mayonaise	egg yolks, oil, flavoured with vinegar or lemon juice
Mosselensaus	butter, flour, fish stock and mussels
Mosterdsaus	mustard added to a white sauce
Paprikasaus	butter, flour, stock, onion and paprika
Peterseliesaus	butter, flour, stock and parsley
Pikante saus	butter, flour, onions, vinegar, capers and white wine
Ravigottesaus	tarragon, chervil, chives, with stock and vinegar; served hot or cold
Speksaus	bacon, onions, flour, stock, flavoured with lemon juice
Tomatensaus	Tomatoes, onions, thyme and flour
Vinaigrettesaus	oil, vinegar, onion, parsley, gherkins and hard-boiled egg

Witte wijnsaus	butter, flour, stock, white wine and cream
Zure saus	butter sauce to which vinegar is added

Cheese

Although the round Edam cheese is better known abroad, many connoisseurs prefer Gouda, Leiden or cumin cheese. In Holland 26 different varieties of cheese are produced, including dessert cheeses such as the soft, creamy Kernhem. Generally speaking, it is not customary to eat cheese as a dessert except on rather special occasions. It is served either at breakfast and with a cold lunch, or in cubes together with ginger and pineapple chunks with an aperitif. Here are the names of some of the most popular cheeses:

Delftse kaas (dehlftser kaass) **Leidse kaas** (laiytser kaass)	both these cheeses have the same flattened shape as Gouda cheese but they are made with cumin seeds; they are for this reason called *komijnekaas* (cumin cheese); less fatty than Edam and Gouda cheese.
Edammer kaas (aydahmerr kaass)	a firm round sphere; red on the outside (from Edam)
Friese Nagelkaas (freesser naagherlkaass)	made from skimmed milk and cloves (from Friesland)
Kernhemmer (kehrnhehmerr)	a successful effort to create a Dutch cheese of the soft dessert type; mellow in taste (from Kernhem)
Limburgse kaas (limburrghser kaass)	a creamy cheese with a spicy taste (from Limburg)
Witte meikaas (Vitter maiykaass)	a creamy cheese with a high fat content; made from the first spring milk

Age is very important for Dutch cheeses. Young, fresh cheeses are called *jonge kaas* and the older ones *belegen kaas*. With age the taste becomes stronger and the texture firmer. If you like an aged cheese, ask for *oude* or *belegen kaas* (old cheese).

Fruit

Do you have fresh fruit?	Hebt u vers fruit?	hehpt ew vehrss frur^{ew}t

Do you have fresh fruit?

Hebt u vers fruit?

hehpt ew vehrss frur^{ew}t

I'd like a (fresh) fruit cocktail.

Ik wil graag een (verse) vruchten-salade.

ik vil ghraakh ayn (vehrser) vrurkhtern-saalaader

aardbeien	aartbaiyyern	strawberries
abrikozen	aabreekoazern	apricots
amandelen	aamahnderlern	almonds
ananas	ahnaanahss	pineapple
appel	ahperlss	apple
banaan	baanaan	banana
bosbessen	bosbehsern	blueberries/bilberries
bramen	braamern	blackberries
citroen	seetroon	lemon
dadels	daaderlss	dates
druiven	drur^{ew}vern	grapes
frambozen	frahmboazern	raspberries
grapefruit	"grapefruit"	grapefruit
groene pruimen	ghrooner prur^{ew}mern	greengages
hazelnoten	haazerlnoatern	hazelnuts
kastanjes	kahstahnyerss	chestnuts
kersen	kehrsern	cherries
zwarte kersen	zvahrter kehrsern	black cherries
kokosnoot	koakosnoat	coconut
kruisbessen	krur^{ew}sbehsern	gooseberries
mandarijn	mahndaaraiyn	tangerine
meloen	merloon	melon
noten	noatern	nuts
gemengde noten	ghermehngder noatern	mixed nuts
olijven	oalaiyvern	olives
peer	payr	pear
perzik	pehrzik	peach
pompelmoes	pomperlmooss	grapefruit
pruimen	prur^{ew}mern	plums
pruimedanten	prur^{ew}merdahntern	prunes
rabarber	raabahrberr	rhubarb
rozijnen	roazaiynern	raisins
sinaasappel	seenaasahperlss	orange
vijgen	vaiyghern	figs
walnoten	vahlnoatern	walnuts
watermeloen	vaaterrmerloon	watermelon

Dessert

English	Dutch	Pronunciation
I'd like a dessert, please.	**Ik wil graag een nagerecht, alstublieft.**	ik vil ghraakh ayn naagherrehkht ahlstewbleeft
What do you recommend?	**Wat beveelt u aan?**	vaht bervaylt ew aan
Something light, please.	**Iets lichts, graag.**	eets likhts ghraakh
Just a small portion.	**Een kleine portie, alstublieft.**	ayn klaiyner porsee ahlstewbleeft
Nothing more, thank you.	**Niets meer, dank u.**	neets mayr dahnk ew
appelbeignets	ahperlbehñehss	apple fritters
appelgebak	ahperlgherbank	apple pastry
appeltaart	ahperltaart	apple tart
broodschoteltje	broatskhoaterltyer	kind of bread pudding with apples, currants or raisins
Dame blanche	daam blahnsh	ice-cream with chocolate sauce
flensjes	flehnsyerss	thin pancakes
met ananas	meht ahnaanahss	with pineapple
fruit naar keuze	frurⁱᵗ naar kurzer	a choice of fruit
gember met slagroom	ghehmberr meht slahghroam	lumps of fresh ginger with whipped cream
ijs	aiyss	ice-cream
aardbeien	aartbaiyyern	strawberry
chocolade	shokoalaader	chocolate
pistache	peestahsh	pistachio
vanille	vaaneeyer	vanilla
pannekoeken	pahnerkookern	pancakes
poffertjes	pofferrtyerss	small round fritter with butter and powder sugar
rijstebrijpudding	raiysterbraiypurdding	rice pudding
schuimomelet	skhurⁱᵐmommerleht	fluffy dessert omelet
slagroom	slahghroam	whipped cream
vla	vlaa	custard
vlaai (Limburgse)	vlaaᵉᵉ (limburrghser)	fruit tart
vruchtensla	vrurkhternslaa	fruit salad
wentelteefjes	vehnterltayfyerss	fried slices of bread, dipped in egg batter and fried

EATING OUT

The bill (check)

I'd like to pay.	**Ik wil graag afrekenen.**	ik ∨il ghraakh ahfraykernern
We'd like to pay separately.	**Wij willen graag apart afrekenen.**	∨aiy ∨illern ghraakh aapahrt ahfraykernern
You made a mistake in this bill, I think.	**Ik geloof, dat u een vergissing in de rekening gemaakt hebt.**	ik gherloaf daht ew ayn verrghissing in der raykerning ghermaakt hepht
What is this amount for?	**Voor wat is dit bedrag?**	voar ∨aht iss dit berdrahkh
Is service included?	**Is het inclusief bediening?**	iss heht inklew**seef** berdeening
Is everything included?	**Is alles inclusief?**	iss ahlerss inklew**seef**
Do you accept traveller's cheques?	**Neemt u reis-cheques aan?**	naymt ew raiysshehks aan
Thank you, this is for you.	**Dank u wel, dit is voor u.**	dahnk ew ∨ehl dit iss voar ew
Keep the change.	**Houdt u het wissel-geld maar.**	ho°ʷt ew heht ∨isserlghehlt maar
That was very good.	**Dat was erg lekker.**	daht ∨ahs ehrkh lehkerr
We enjoyed it, thank you.	**Wij hebben genoten, dank u wel.**	∨aiy hehbern ghernoatern dahnk ew ∨ehl

> **INCLUSIEF BEDIENING**
> SERVICE INCLUDED

Complaints

But perhaps you'll have something to complain about:

That is not what I ordered. I asked for ...	**Dat heb ik niet besteld. Ik heb ... gevraagd.**	daht hehp ik neet bersтehlt. ik hehp ... ghervraakht
May I change this?	**Kan ik wat anders krijgen?**	kahn ik ∨aht ahnderrss kraiyghern

The meat is ...	Het vlees is ...	heht vlayss iss
overdone	te gaar	ter ghaar
underdone	te rauw	ter ro^{ow}√
too rare	te rood	ter roat
too tough	te taai	ter taa^{ee}
This is too ...	Dit is te ...	dit iss ter
bitter/salty/sweet	bitter/zout/zoet	bitterr/zo^{ow}t/zoot
The food is cold.	Het eten is koud.	heht aytern iss ko^{ow}t
This isn't fresh.	Dit is niet vers.	dit iss neet vehrss
What's taking you so long?	Waarom duurt het zo lang?	√aarom dewrt heht zoa lahng
Where are our drinks?	Waar blijven onze drankjes?	√aar blaiyvern onzer drahnkyerss
This isn't clean.	Dit is vuil.	dit iss vur^{ewl}
Would you ask the head waiter to come over?	Wilt u de chefkelner vragen even hier te komen?	√ilt ew der shehfkehlnerr vraaghern ayvern heer ter koamern

Drinks

Aperitifs

Of all the alcoholic drinks, beer and jenever are the most favoured by the Dutch. The two best known local beers are *Amstel* and *Heineken.* If you want draught beer, just ask: *"Een pils van het vat, alstublieft"* (ayn pilss vahn heht vaht ahlstew**bleeft**).

There is also a kind of stout with a sweetish taste and a dark-brown colour, called *oud bruin*—o^{ow}t brur^{ew}n (old brown). Dutch jenever is mostly drunk as an aperitif. It is sometimes served with angostura or other bitters, in which case the *borreltje*—**bo**rrerltyer (a glass of jenever) becomes a *bittertje.* In addition to old and young jenever, there are lemon-, red currant- and blackberry-flavoured jenevers.

I'd like a ...	Ik wil graag ... hebben.	ik √il ghraakh ... hehbern
glass of beer	een biertje/een pils	ayn beertyer/ayn pilss
glass of jenever	een borreltje	ayn borrerltyer

I'd like ... of ...	**Ik wil graag ...**	ik vil ghraakh
a carafe	**een karaf**	ayn kaarahf
a bottle	**een fles**	ayn flehss
half a bottle	**een halve fles**	ayn hahlver flehss
a glass	**een glas**	ayn ghlahss
a litre	**een liter**	ayn leeterr
I want a bottle of red/white wine.	**Ik wil een fles rode/witte wijn.**	ik vil ayn flehss roader/vitter vaiyn

If you enjoyed the wine, you may want to say:

| Please bring me another ... | **Wilt u mij nog een ... brengen, alstublieft?** | vilt ew maiy nokh ayn ... brehngern ahlstewbleeft |
| Where does the wine come from? | **Waar komt de wijn vandaan?** | vaar komt der vaiyn vahndaan |

red	**rood**	roat
white	**wit**	vit
rosé	**rosé**	roazay
dry	**droog**	droakh
light	**licht**	likht
full-bodied	**vol**	vol
sparkling	**mousserend**	moossayrernt
very dry	**brut**	brewt
sweet	**zoet**	zoot

Other alcoholic drinks

In most restaurants, but especially in bars, you'll find a wide variety of cocktails or highballs. Names are generally the same as in English.

aperitif	**aperitief**	aapayreeteef
beer	**bier**	beer
brandy	**brandewijn**	brahndervaiyn
gin-fizz	**gin-soda**	zhin soadaa
liqueur	**likeur**	leekurr
Scotch	**Scotch whisky**	skotsh viskee
vodka	**wodka**	votkaa

glass	**een glas**	ayn ghlahss
bottle	**een fles**	ayn flehss
neat (straight)	**zonder water**	zonderr vaaterr
on the rocks	**met ijsblokjes**	meht aiysblokyerss
with water	**met water**	meht vaaterr

Here are some typical Dutch drinks you may come across:

advocaat	ahtvoakaat	a sort of egg-nog (egg liqueur); served with a small spoon
berenburg	bayrernburkh	Frisian gin
bessenjenever	behssernyernayverr	red currant-flavoured Dutch gin
bisschopswijn	bisskhopsvaiyn	mulled claret (warm)
boerenjongens	boorernyongernss	Dutch brandy with raisins
boerenmeisjes	boorernmaiysherss	Dutch brandy with apricots
jenever	yernayverr	Dutch gin
jonge jenever	yonger yernayverr	"young" Dutch gin
oude jenever	o^{ow}der yernayverr	"old" Dutch gin
klare	klaarer	common term for jenever
oranjebitter	oarahñerbitterr	orange-flavoured bitters
pils	pilss	general name for beer

Dutch liqueurs are fairly reasonably priced.

Curaçao	kewraaso^{ow}	orange-flavoured liqueur
half om half	hahlf om hahlf	brownish liqueur with a sweet taste; rather strong
parfait d'amour	pahrfeh daamoor	highly perfumed, amethyst-coloured

I'd like to try a glass of ..., please.	**Ik wil graag een glas ... proberen, alstublieft.**	ik vil ghraakh ayn ghlahss ... proabayrern ahlstewbleeft

PROOST!
(proast)
CHEERS!

EATING OUT

Other beverages

buttermilk	**karnemelk**	kahrnermehlk
(hot) chocolate	**(warme) chocolade-melk**	(√ahrmer) shoakoalaadermehlk
coffee	**koffie**	koffee
cup of coffee	**een kopje koffie**	ayn kopyer koffee
coffee with cream	**koffie met room**	koffee meht roam
coffee with whipped cream	**koffie met slag-room**	koffee meht slahghroam
espresso coffee	**een expresso**	ayn eksprehssoa
fruit juice	**vruchtesap**	vrurkhtersahp
lemonade	**limonade**	leemoanaader
milk	**melk**	mehlk
mineral water	**mineraalwater**	meenerraal√aaterr
squash	**kwast**	k√ahst
tea	**thee**	tay
with milk/lemon	**met melk/citroen**	meht mehlk/seetroon
iced tea	**ijsthee**	aiystay

Eating light—Snacks

bitterballen	bitterrbahlern	small round breaded meatballs
belegde broodjes	berlehghder broatyerss	sandwiches
broodje	broatyer	roll
met ham	meht hahm	with ham
halfom	hahlfom	with liver and salted meat
met paling	meht paaling	with smoked eel
met rookvlees	meht roakvlays	with smoked beef
knakworst	knahkv√orst	hot smoked sausage
loempia	loompeeyaa	spring-roll; with vegetables and soya sprouts
pannekoek	pahnerkook	pancake
poffertjes	pofferrtyerss	small fritters
een zakje patates	ayn zahkyer paataht	portion of chips (french fries)
met/zonder	meht/zonderr	with/without
mayonaise	maayoanehzer	mayonnaise
uitsmijter	ur^{ew}tsmaiyterr	two slices of bread with ham, roast beef or cheese, topped by fried eggs

An excellent place to go for a snack is a *pannekoekhuisje* (pancake house) which may serve more than 50 different sorts of pancakes. Some have apple rings cooked in with them, others include currants, ginger or cheese. The most traditional one is *pannekoek met spek en stroop*—**pah**nerkook meht spehk ehn stroap (pancake with bacon and treacle [molasses]). Large towns sometimes have a *poffertjestent*, a stall which serves the delicious small round fritters called *poffertjes*—**po**fferrtyerss, laced with powder sugar and butter, all day long. Dutch children, especially, love them!

Indonesian dishes

As a result of many centuries of colonial presence in Indonesia (then called the Dutch East Indies), the Dutch have developed a real taste for spicy foods, and now consider Indonesian food part of Dutch cuisine. Here are some of the best known Indonesian specialities, including some adapted from Chinese cuisine, often found on the menu.

Bami goreng (baamee ghoarerng)	Chinese noodles with fried vegetables, diced pork, shrimp and shredded omelet
Kroepoek (kroopook)	a crisp, golden-brown shrimp wafer, often accompanying *rijsttafel*
Nassi goreng (nahssee ghoarerng)	fried rice with onions, meat, chicken, shrimp, ham and varied spices, usually topped with a fried egg
Nassi rames (nahssee raamehss)	a mini *rijsttafel*
Pisang goreng (peesahng ghoarerng)	fried banana, usually served with *rijsttafel*
Sajoer kerrie (saayoor kehree)	spicy cabbage soup; side dish to *rijsttafel*
Sambal goreng kering (sahmbahl ghoarerng kayring)	fried cabbage and ginger in coconut-milk sauce
Sateh babi (saatay baabee)	grilled cubes of pork on skewers; usually dipped in a hot peanut-butter sauce

The most famous Indonesian speciality is *rijsttafel*—(**raiyst-taaferl**) a real banquet of a meal. It consists of white rice served with an amazing number of small and very tasty dishes: stewed vegetables, delicately prepared beef and chicken, meat on skewers with peanut-butter sauce, fruits and spices, to name only a few. The spicy dishes can be extremely hot. Anything containing the word *sambal* will be peppery-hot; especially the tiny portions of *sambal oelek* and *sambal goreng*, that look like a ketchup paste, should be used sparingly.

Belgian (Flemish) specialities

Ballekesoep (**bahlerkersoop**)	a soup made from beef or chicken stock and onions, turnips, leeks and carrots; served with tiny meat-balls
Hochepot (**hoshpot**)	a casserole of beef, pork, mutton, carrots, cabbage, leeks, onions, potatoes and spices; garnished with fried sausages
Vlaamse bloedworst (**vlaamser blootworst**)	black pudding served with apples
Vlaamse karbonade (**vlaamser kahrboa-naader**)	beef slices and onions braised in beer
Vlaamse kool (**vlaamser koal**)	green cabbage prepared with apples and gooseberry jelly
Vlaamse hazepeper (**vlaamser haazerpayperr**)	jugged hare stewed with onions and plums
Waterzooi (**Vaaterrzoa**ee)	chicken poached in white wine and shredded vegetables, cream and egg-yolk
Waterzooi met vis (**Vaaterrzoa**ee **meht viss**)	a delicious fish soup

Two somewhat special Belgian brews of beer you might like to try are *Kriekenlambiek* (**kree**kernlahmbeek), a strong Brussels bitter beer flavoured with morello cherries, and *trappistenbier* (trah**pis**ternbeer), a malt beer brewed originally by Trappist monks.

Travelling around

Plane

Holland is a small country and you are more likely to travel by car or train than by air. However, there are domestic flights between Amsterdam and Groningen, Enschede and Maastricht. In many tourist resorts, pleasure flights are operated all year round. The following expressions may therefore come in handy.

Is there a flight to Enschede?	**Is er een vlucht naar Enschede?**	iss ehr ayn vlurkht naar ehnskherday
When's the next plane to Amsterdam?	**Wanneer gaat het volgende vliegtuig naar Amsterdam?**	√ahnayr ghaat heht volghernder vleeghtur^{ew}kh naar ahmsterrdahm
Can I make a connection to Maastricht?	**Heb ik aansluiting naar Maastricht?**	hehp ik aanslur^{ew}ting naar maastrikht
I'd like a ticket to Brussels.	**Ik wil graag een vliegbiljet naar Brussel.**	ik √il ghraakh ayn vleeghbilyeht naar brursserl
What's the fare to Groningen?	**Hoeveel kost een vlucht naar Groningen?**	hoovayl kost ayn vlurkht naar ghroaningern
single (one-way) return (round trip)	**enkele reis retour**	ehnkeler raiyss rertoor
What time does the plane take off?	**Hoe laat vertrekt het vliegtuig?**	hoo laat verrtrehkt heht vleeghtur^{ew}kh
What time do I have to check in?	**Hoe laat moet ik mij melden?**	hoo laat moot ik maiy mehldern
What's the flight number?	**Wat is het vluchtnummer?**	√aht iss heht vlurkhtnurmerr
What time do we arrive?	**Hoe laat komen wij aan?**	hoo laat koamern √aiy aan
Is there a dutyfree shop?	**Is er een duty-free winkel?**	iss ehr ayn "duty-free" √inkerl

AANKOMST ARRIVAL	**VERTREK** DEPARTURE

Train

Due to its geographical location, a dense rail network and short distances, Holland lends itself very well to sightseeing by train. Season tickets entitle the holder to unlimited travel on the entire Dutch railway system. There are one-day, eight-day, weekend and monthly season tickets. For further information apply to the railway stations or the VVV offices.

TEE-trein (tay ay ay traiyn)	Trans-Europ-Express; a luxury international service with first class only; supplementary fare and advance booking required.
D-trein (day traiyn)	Through train, often connecting with an international train. Seat reservation advisable.
Auto-slaaptrein (o^{ow}toa slaaptraiyn)	Car train. Put your car aboard and take a rest.
Intercity (interrsitee)	Fast train stopping only at a few stations.
Sneltrein (snehltraiyn)	Long-distance express stopping only at main stations.
Stoptrein (stoptraiyn)	Local train stopping at all stations.
Boottrein (boattraiyn)	Boat train connecting with the ferry crossing to England.

ROKEN SMOKERS	**ROKEN VERBODEN** NON SMOKERS

Slaapwagen (slaap√aaghern)	Sleeping-car with individual compartments (single or double) and washing facilities.
Couchette (koosheht)	Berth with blankets and pillows. An ordinary compartment can be transformed into six berths.
Restauratiewagen (rehstoaraatsee- √aaghern)	Dining-car.
Bagagewagen (baaghaazher- √aaghern)	Guard's van (baggage car); normally only registered luggage permitted.

To the railway station

Where's the railway station?	**Waar is het station?**	ʋaar iss heht stahtsyon
Taxi, please!	**Taxi, alstublieft!**	tahksee ahlstewbleeft
Take me to the railway station.	**Naar het station, alstublieft.**	naar heht stahtsyon ahlstewbleeft
What's the fare?	**Hoeveel ben ik u schuldig?**	hoovayl behn ik ew skhurlderkh

INGANG	ENTRANCE
UITGANG	EXIT
NAAR DE PERRONS	PLATFORMS (TRACKS)

Where's the...?

Where is/are the ...?	**Waar is/zijn ...?**	ʋaar iss/zaiyn
accommodation bureau	**het huisvesting-bureau**	heht hur^{ew}svehstingbewroa
booking office	**het plaatsbureau**	heht plaatsbewroa
currency-exchange office	**het wisselkantoor**	heht ʋisserlkahntoar
florist's	**de bloemist**	der bloomist
information	**het inlichtingen-bureau**	heht inlikhtingernbewroa
left luggage office (baggage check)	**het bagagedepot**	heht baaghaazher-dehpoat
letter box	**de brievenbus**	der breevernburss
lost-property (lost and found) office	**het bureau voor gevonden voor-werpen**	heht bewroa voar gher-vondern voarʋehrpern
luggage lockers	**de bagagekluizen**	der baaghaazherklur^{ew}zern
news-stand	**de kiosk**	der keeyosk
platform 7	**perron 7**	pehrron 7
reservations office	**het bespreekbureau**	heht berspraykbewroa
restaurant	**het restaurant**	heht rehstoarahnt
snack bar	**de snackbar**	der "snackbar"
ticket office	**het loket**	heht loakeht
track 7	**spoor 7**	spoar zayvern
waiting-room	**de wachtkamer**	der ʋahkhtkaamerr
Where are the toilets?	**Waar zijn de toi-letten?**	ʋaar zaiyn der tʋaalehtern

FOR TAXI, see page 27

TRAVELING AROUND

Inquiries

In Holland and Belgium $\boxed{\mathbf{i}}$ means information office.

When is the … train to The Hague?	**Wanneer gaat de … trein naar Den Haag?**	√ahnayr ghaat der … traiyn naar dehn haakh
first/last/next	**eerste/laatste/ volgende**	ayrster/laatster/ volghernder
What time does the train for Utrecht leave?	**Hoe laat vertrekt de trein naar Utrecht?**	hoo laat verrtrehkt der traiyn naar ewtrehkht
What's the fare to Haarlem?	**Hoeveel kost een kaartje naar Haarlem?**	hoovayl kost ayn kaartyer naar haarlehm
Is it a through train?	**Is het een doorgaande trein?**	iss heht ayn doarghaander traiyn
Will the train leave on time?	**Vertrekt de trein op tijd?**	verrtrehkt der traiyn op taiyt
What time does the train arrive at Rotterdam?	**Hoe laat komt de trein in Rotterdam aan?**	hoo laat komt der traiyn in rotterrdahm aan
Is there a dining-car on the train?	**Is er een restauratie-wagen in de trein?**	iss ehr ayn rehstoaraatsee-√aaghern in der traiyn
Is there a sleeping-car on the train?	**Is er een slaapwagen in de trein?**	iss ehr ayn slaap√aaghern in der traiyn
Does the train stop at Groningen?	**Stopt de trein in Groningen?**	stopt der traiyn in ghroaningern
What platform does the train from Gouda arrive at?	**Op welk perron komt de trein uit Gouda aan?**	op √ehlk pehrron komt der traiyn ur*ewt gho*ow daa aan
What platform does the train for Brussels leave from?	**Van welk perron vertrekt de trein naar Brussel?**	vahn √ehlk pehrron verr-trehkt der traiyn naar brursserl
I'd like to buy a timetable.	**Ik wil graag een spoorboekje hebben.**	ik √il ghraakh ayn spoarbookyer hehbern

INLICHTINGEN WISSELKANTOOR	INFORMATION CURRENCY EXCHANGE

69

Het is een doorgaande trein.	It's a through train.
U moet overstappen in...	You have to change in...
Stapt u in ... over en neemt u dan een stoptrein.	Change at ... and get a local train.
Perron 7 is...	Platform 7 is...
daar/boven	over there/upstairs
aan uw linkerhand/rechterhand	on the left/right
Om ... is een trein naar ...	There's a train to ... at ...
Uw trein vertrekt van perron 8.	Your train will leave from platform 8.
Er is een vertraging van ... minuten.	There'll be a delay of... minutes.

TRAVELLING AROUND

Tickets

I want a ticket to Alkmaar.	Ik wil graag een ... naar Alkmaar hebben.	ik vil ghraakh ayn ... naar ahlkmaar hehbern
single (one-way)	enkele reis	ehnkerler raiyss
return (roundtrip)	retourtje	rertoortyer
first/second class	kaartje eerste/ tweede klas	kaartyer ayrster/ tvayder klahss
Isn't it half price for the child?*	Betaalt men voor kinderen niet halve prijs?	bertaalt mehn voar kinderrern neet hahlver praiyss
He/She is 8.	Hij/Zij is 8.	haiy/zaiy iss 8

Eerste of tweede klas?	First or second class?
Een enkele reis of een retourtje?	Single or return (one-way or roundtrip)?
Hoe oud is hij/zij?	How old is he/she?

* In Holland children between 4 and 9 years of age travel half fare; in Belgium, between 4 and 12.

FOR NUMBERS, see page 175

All aboard

Is this the right platform for the train to Paris?	**Is dit het goeie perron voor de trein naar Parijs?**	iss dit heht **gooyer** peh**rron** voar der traiyn naar paa**raiyss**
Is this the right train to Antwerp?	**Is dit de trein naar Antwerpen?**	iss dit der traiyn naar ahnt**√ehrpern**
Excuse me. May I get by?	**Neemt u mij niet kwalijk, mag ik er even langs?**	naymt ew maiy neet k**√aa**lerk mahhk ik ehr **ay**vern lahngss
Is this seat taken?	**Is deze plaats bezet?**	iss **day**zer plaats ber**zeht**
I think that's my seat.	**Ik geloof dat dit mijn plaats is.**	ik gher**loaf** daht dit maiyn plaats iss
Would you let me know before we get to Arnhem?	**Wilt u mij waarschuwen voordat wij in Arnhem aankomen?**	√ilt ew maiy **√aars**khew**√ern voar**daht √aiy in **ahrn**hehm **aan**koamern
What station is this?	**Welk station is dit?**	√ehlk stahts**yon** iss dit
How long does the train stop here?	**Hoe lang stopt de trein hier?**	hoo lahng stopt der traiyn heer
When do we get to The Hague?	**Wanneer komen wij in Den Haag aan?**	√ah**nayr** koamern √aiy in dehn haahk aan

Sometime on the journey the ticket collector (*de conduc-teur*—der kondurk**turr**) will come around and say: *Uw kaar-tjes, alstublieft!* (Tickets, please!)

Eating

If you want a full meal in the dining-car, you may have to get a ticket from the attendant who will come round to your compartment. There are usually two sittings each for break-fast, lunch and dinner.

You can get snacks and drinks in the buffet-car and in the dining-car when it's not being used for main meals. On some trains an attendant comes around with snacks, coffee, tea and soft drinks. At the larger stations there are refreshment carts.

First/Second call for dinner!	**Eerste/Tweede bediening!**	ayrster/tᵛayder berdeening
Where's the dining-car?	**Waar is de restauratiewagen?**	ᵛaar iss der rehstoaraatseeᵛaaghern

Sleeping

Are there any free compartments in the sleeping-car?	**Zijn er nog slaap-coupés vrij?**	zaiyn ehr nokh **slaap-**koopayss vraiy
Where's the sleeping-car/couchette-car?	**Waar is de slaap-wagen/de couchette-wagen?**	ᵛaar iss der **slaap-**ᵛaaghern/der **koo**shehterᵛaaghern
Where's my berth?	**Waar is mijn couchette?**	ᵛaar iss maiyn **koo**shehter
Compartments 18 and 19, please.	**Coupé 18 en 19, alstublieft.**	koopay 18 ehn 19 ahlstewbleeft
I'd like a lower berth.	**Ik wil graag een couchette beneden.**	ik ᵛil ghraakh ayn **koo**shehter bernaydern
Would you make up our berths?	**Wilt u onze couchettes gereedmaken?**	ᵛilt ew onzer **koo**shehterss gherraytmaakern
Would you call me at 7 o'clock?	**Wilt u mij om 7 uur wekken?**	ᵛilt ew maiy om 7 ewr ᵛehkern
Would you bring me some coffee in the morning?	**Wilt u mij morgen-ochtend een kopje koffie brengen?**	ᵛilt ew maiy morghern-okhternt ayn **kop**yer koffee brehngern

Baggage—Porters

Porter!	**Kruier, alstublieft!**	krurᵉʷyerr ahlstewbleeft
Can you help me with with my bags?	**Kunt u mij met mijn bagage helpen?**	kurnt ew maiy meht maiyn baaghaazher hehlpern
Can I register these bags?	**Kan ik deze koffers ter verzending aangeven?**	kahn ik dayzer kofferss tehr verzehnding aangayvern

FOR PORTERS, see also page 24

Lost property

Where's the lost-property (lost and found) office?	**Waar is het bureau voor gevonden voorwerpen?**	ʋaar iss heht bewroa voar ghervondern voar-ʋehrpern
I've lost my...	**Ik heb mijn ... verloren.**	ik hehp maiyn... verrloarern
handbag	**handtas**	hahnttahss
passport	**paspoort**	pahspoart
ticket	**biljet**	bilyeht
wallet	**portefeuille**	porterfur^{ew}yer
I lost it in...	**Ik heb het in ... verloren.**	ik hehp heht in ... verrloarern
It's very valuable.	**Het is heel kostbaar.**	heht iss hayl kostbaar

Underground (subway)

The nature of the subsoil in Holland long made the construction of an underground impossible. However, Amsterdam and Rotterdam do now have their subways *(metro)*. The complete underground/overground run will eventually link Amsterdam's Central Station with Schiphol Airport and The Hague.

| Where's the nearest metro station? | **Waar is het dichtst-bijzijnde metro-station?** | ʋaar iss heht dikhtst-baiyzaiynder maytroa-stahtsyon |

Ferry services and tolls

With so much water around, ferries still have a real function in Holland. Many ferry services can be found on secondary roads crossing rivers and canals. Most ferries are equipped to carry motor vehicles and their fares are reasonable. Delays may occur, especially when there is fog. In certain cases tolls are charged for bridges, dams and tunnels.

| What time does the next ferryboat cross? | **Hoe laat vertrekt de volgende veerboot?** | hoo laat verrtrehkt der volghernder vayrboat |
| How much is the toll fee? | **Hoeveel tol moet ik betalen?** | hoovayl tol moot ik bertaalern |

Bus—Tram (streetcar)

Public transport in the cities is provided mainly by buses and trams. Between cities and smaller towns and villages, there are regular bus services. Many bus companies have cheap day tickets for their whole system. VVV offices will supply you with the necessary information on departure times and fares. Some cities have introduced an automatic system of paying the fare, whereby you insert the exact change into a ticket dispenser at the bus stop or have the machine validate your prepaid ticket.

Where's the nearest bus/tram stop?	**Waar is de dichtst- bijzijnde bus-/tram- halte?**	Vaar iss der dikhtst- baiyzaiynder burss-/ trehmhahlter
I'd like a booklet of tickets.	**I wil graag een rit- tenkaart, alstublieft.**	ik Vil ghraakh ayn burssritternkaart ahlstewbleeft
Where can I get a bus/tram to the town centre?	**Waar kan ik een bus/ tram naar het cen- trum nemen?**	Vaar kahn ik ayn burss trehm/naar heht sehntrurm naymern
What bus do I take for the Central Museum?	**Welke bus moet ik naar het Centraal Museum nemen?**	Vehlker burss moot ik naar heht sehntraal mewzayyurm naymern

> **BUSHALTE** REGULAR BUS STOP
> **STOPT OP VERZOEK** STOPS ON REQUEST

When is the ... bus to the Rokin?	**Wanneer gaat de ... bus naar het Rokin?**	Vahnayr ghaat der ... burss naar heht roakin
first/last/next	**eerste/laatste/ volgende**	ayrster/laatster/ volghernder
How often do the buses to the zoo run?	**Hoe vaak gaan de bussen naar de dierentuin?**	hoo vaak ghaan der burssern naar der deererntur^{ew}n
How much is the fare to ...	**Wat kost een kaartje naar...?**	Vaht kost ayn kaartyer naar
Do I have to change buses?	**Moet ik overstappen?**	moot ik oaverrstahpern
How long does the journey take?	**Hoelang duurt de reis?**	hoolahng dewrt der raiyss

Other modes of transport

Bicycles and mopeds are extremely popular in Holland. A well-developed system of cycle tracks and trails throughout the country may encourage many people to tour Holland by bike. Bikes can be hired from bicycle shops or at railway stations. Prices vary and will depend on the duration of the contract and the quality of the bike.

You may find yourself trying any one of these types of vehicles to get around:

barge	**schuit**	skhur^{ew}t
bicycle	**fiets**	feets
boat	**boot**	boat
canoe	**kano**	kaanoa
motorboat	**motorboot**	moaterrboat
rowing-boat	**roeiboot**	roo^{ee}boat
sailing-boat	**zeilboot**	zaiylboat
car	**auto**	o^{ow}toa
hovercraft	**glijboot**	ghlaiyboat
moped	**bromfiets**	bromfeets
motorcycle	**motorfiets**	moaterrfeets
paddle-wheel steamer	**raderstoomboot**	raadehrstoamboat

Or perhaps you prefer:

hitchhiking	**liften**	liftern
horse-riding	**paardrijden**	paartraiydern
walking	**lopen**	loapern

The Dutch are enthusiastic walkers, and all year round walking tours through woodland and heath as well as on the beaches and through the dunes are organized. If you wish to participate in one of these walking events, go to a VVV office for information.

Around and about—Sightseeing

In this section we are more concerned with the cultural aspects of town life. For entertainment see page 80.

Can you recommend a good guide book on Amsterdam?	**Kunt u mij een goede reisgids voor Amsterdam aanbevelen?**	kurnt ew maiy ayn **ghoo**der raiysghits voar ahmsterrdahm **aan**bervaylern
Is there a tourist office?	**Is er een VVV?**	iss ehr heer ayn vayvayvay
Where's the tourist office?	**Waar is de VVV?**	∀aar iss der vayvayvay
What are the main points of interest?	**Wat zijn de belangrijkste bezienswaardigheden?**	∀aht zaiyn der ber**lahng**raiykster berzeenss∀aarderghhaydern
We're here for...	**Wij blijven hier maar...**	∀aiy blaiyvern heer maar
only a few hours	**een paar uur**	ayn paar ewr
a day	**een dag**	ayn dahkh
3 days	**3 dagen**	3 daaghern
a week	**een week**	ayn ∀ayk
Can you recommend a sightseeing tour?	**Kunt u mij een rondleiding aanbevelen?**	kurnt ew maiy ayn **ront**laiyding **aan**bervaylern
Where does the bus start from?	**Van waar vertrekt de bus?**	vahn ∀aar verr**trehkt** der burss
Will it pick us up at the hotel?	**Haalt hij ons van het hotel af?**	haalt haiy onss vahn heht hoa**tehl** af
Where's the nearest point of departure for canal boat trips?	**Waar is het dichtstbijzijnde vertrekpunt voor een rondvaart op de grachten?**	∀aar iss heht dikhtstbaiyzaiynder verr**trehk**purnt voar ayn **ront**vaart op der **ghrahkh**tern
What bus/tram (streetcar) do we take?	**Welke bus/tram moeten we nemen?**	**∀ehl**ker burss/trehm **moo**tern ∀er **nay**mern
How much does the tour cost?	**Wat kost de rondleiding?**	∀aht kost der **ront**laiyding
What time does the tour start?	**Hoe laat begint de rondleiding?**	hoo laat ber**ghint** der **ront**laiyding

FOR TIME OF DAY, see page 178

We'd like to hire a car for the day.	Wij willen graag voor vandaag een auto huren.	√aiy √illern ghraakh voar vahndaakh ayn o^{ow}toa hewrern
Is there an English speaking guide?	Is er een gids die Engels spreekt?	iss ehr ayn ghits dee ehngerlss spraykt
Where is/are the …?	Waar is/zijn …?	√aar iss/zaiyn
abbey	de abdij	der apdaiy
airport	het vliegveld	heht vleeghvehlt
aquarium	het aquarium	heht aak√aareeyurm
art gallery	het museum voor beeldende kunst	heht mewzayurm voar bayldernder kurnst
artists' quarter	de artiestenbuurt	der ahrteesternbewrt
botanical gardens	de botanische tuinen	der boataaneesser tur^{ew}nern
business district	de zakenwijk	der zaakern√aiyk
canal	de gracht	der ghrahkht
castle	het kasteel	heht kahstayl
cathedral	de kathedraal	der kahterdraal
cave	de grot	der ghrot
cemetery	het kerkhof	heht kehrkhof
chapel	de kapel	der kaapehl
church	de kerk	der kehrk
city centre	het stadscentrum	heht stahtssehntrurm
city hall	het stadhuis	heht stahthur^{ew}ss
concert hall	het concertgebouw	heht konsehrtgherbo^{ow}
convent	het klooster	heht kloasterr
docks	de dokhavens	der dokhaaverns
downtown area	het stadscentrum	heht stahtssehntrurm
exhibition	de tentoonstelling	der tehntoanstehling
fortress	het fort	heht fort
fountain	de fontein	der fontaiyn
gardens	het park	heht pahrk
harbour	de haven	der haavern
lake	het meer	heht mayr
market	de markt	der mahrkt
memorial	het gedenkteken	heht gherdehnktaykern
monastery	het klooster	heht kloasterr
monument	het monument	heht moanewmehnt
museum	het museum	heht mewzayyurm
observatory	het observatorium	heht opsehrvaatoareeyurm
old town	het oude stadscentrum	heht o^{ow}der stahtssehntrurm
opera house	de opera	der oaperraa
palace	het paleis	heht paalaiyss
park	het park	heht pahrk

parliament building	**het parlements-gebouw**	heht pahrler**mehnts**-gherbo^{ow}
planetarium	**het planetarium**	heht plaanertaa**ree**yurm
post office	**het postkantoor**	heht **post**kahntoar
ruins	**de ruines**	der rew**Vee**nerss
shopping centre	**de winkelwijk**	der √inkerl√aiyk
stadium	**het stadion**	heht staa**dee**yon
statue	**het standbeeld**	heht **stahnt**baylt
stock exchange	**de beurs**	der burrss
supreme court	**het Hooggerechts-hof**	heht hoaghgher**rehkht**shof
theatre	**de schouwburg**	der **skho**^{ow}burrkh
tomb	**het graf**	heht ghrahf
tower	**de toren**	der **toa**rern
town hall	**het stadhuis**	heht staht**hur**^{ew}ss
windmill	**de windmolen**	der √int**moa**lern
zoo	**de dierentuin**	der deerern**tur**^{ew}n

Admission

Is ... open on Sundays?	**Is ... open op zondag?**	iss ... **oa**pern op **zon**dahkh
When does it open/close?	**Wanneer gaat het open/dicht?**	√ah**nayr** ghaat heht **oa**pern/dikht
How much is the entrance fee?	**Hoeveel is de toe-gangsprijs?**	hoo**vayl** kost der **too**ghahngspraiyss
Is there any reduction for...?	**Is er reduktie voor...?**	iss ehr rer**durk**see voar
children	**kinderen**	**kin**derrern
pensioners	**gepensioneerden**	gherpehnsyoa**nayr**dern
students	**studenten**	stew**dehn**tern
Can I buy a catalogue?	**Mag ik een katalo-gus van u?**	mahgh ik ayn kaataa-**loa**ghurss vahn ew
Have you a guide book in English?	**Hebt u een gids in het Engels?**	hehpt ew ayn ghits in heht **ehng**erlss
Is it all right to take pictures?	**Mag je hier foto's nemen?**	mahgh yer heer **foa**toass **nay**mern

---

VRIJE TOEGANG	ADMISSION FREE
VERBODEN TE FOTOGRAFEREN	NO CAMERAS ALLOWED

Who—What—When?

What's that building?	**Wat is dat voor een gebouw?**	✓aht iss daht voar ayn gherbo**ow**
Who was the...	**Wie was...?**	✓ee ✓ahss
architect	**de architekt**	der ahrkhee**tehkt**
artist	**de artiest**	der ahr**teest**
painter	**de schilder**	der **skhild**err
sculptor	**de beeldhouwer**	der baylt**ho**ow**err**
Who built it?	**Wie heeft het gebouwd?**	✓ee hayft heht gherbo**ow**t
When was it built?	**Wanneer is het gebouwd?**	✓ah**nayr** iss heht gherbo**ow**t
Who painted that picture?	**Wie heeft dat schilderij gemaakt?**	✓ee hayft daht skhilderr**ay** gher**maakt**
When did he live?	**Wanneer leefde hij?**	✓ah**nayr** lay**fder** haiy
Where's the house where ... lived?	**Waar is het huis waar ... gewoond heeft?**	✓aar iss heht hur**ew**ss ✓aar ... gher**woant** hayft
We're/I'm interested in...	**Wij hebben/Ik heb belangstelling voor...**	✓aiy **hehb**ern/ik hehp berlahng**stel**ling voar
antiques	**antiek**	ahn**teek**
applied art	**kunstnijverheid**	**kurnst**naiyverr**haiyt**
archaeology	**archeologie**	ahrkhayoaloa**ghee**
art	**kunst**	kurnst
botany	**plantkunde**	**plahnt**kurnder
ceramics	**ceramiek**	sayraa**meek**
coins	**munten**	**murn**tern
crafts	**ambachten**	**ahm**bahkhtern
fine arts	**beeldende kunst**	**bayl**dernder kurnst
furniture	**meubelen**	**mur**berlern
geology	**geologie**	ghayoaloa**ghee**
medicine	**geneeskunde**	gher**nays**kurnder
music	**muziek**	mew**zeek**
natural history	**natuurlijke historie**	naa**tewr**lerker histo**aree**
ornithology	**vogelkunde**	**voagherl**kurnder
painting	**schilderkunst**	**skhil**derrkurnder
pottery	**pottenbakkerij**	potternbahk**ke**rraiy
sculpture	**beeldhouwkunst**	**bayl**tho**ow**kurnst
zoology	**dierkunde**	**deer**kurnder
Where's the ... department?	**Waar is de ... afdeling?**	✓aar iss der ... **ahf**dayling

Just the adjective you've been looking for ...

It's...	Het is...	heht iss
amazing	**verbazingwekkend**	verrbaazing**v**ehkernt
awful	**afschuwelijk**	ahfskhew**v**erlerk
beautiful	**mooi**	moa^{ee}
gloomy	**somber**	**somb**err
impressive	**indrukwekkend**	indrukr**v**ehkernt
interesting	**interessant**	interrehss**sahnt**
magnificent	**geweldig**	gher**vehl**dikh
overwhelming	**overweldigend**	oaverr**vehl**derghernt
strange	**vreemd**	vraymt
superb	**prachtig**	**prahkh**terkh
terrible	**vreselijk**	**vray**serlerk
terrifying	**angstaanjagend**	ahngstaan**yaa**ghernt
tremendous	**enorm**	**ay**norm
ugly	**lelijk**	**lay**lerk

Religious services

Three-quarters of Holland's population is more or less equally divided into Catholics and Protestants (the remaining one-fourth is non-denominational). A number of other religions are also represented. Most churches are only open during the services. If you want to visit a church, apply to the sexton (*koster*—**kos**terr).

Is there a ... near here?	**Is er een ... in de buurt?**	iss ehr ayn ... in der bewrt
Catholic church	**Katholieke kerk**	kahtoa**lee**ker kehrk
Protestant church	**Protestantse kerk**	proatehs**tahnt**ser kehrk
synagogue	**Synagoge**	seena**ghoa**gher
At what time is...?	**Hoe laat begint de...?**	hoo laat ber**ghint** der
mass/the service	**hoogmis/dienst**	**hoagh**miss/deenst
Where can I find a ... who speaks English?	**Waar kan ik een... vinden die Engels spreekt?**	**v**aar kahn ik ayn **vin**dern dee **ehng**erlss spraykt
minister	**dominee**	**doa**meenay
priest	**priester**	**pree**sterr
rabbi	**rabbi**	**rah**bee

Relaxing

Cinema (movies)—Theatre

Film showings in Holland are seldom continuous. Seats can generally be reserved in advance. The programme usually consists of one feature film, a short documentary or newsreel and numerous advertisements. There is an intermission during the feature. The first performance starts at about 2 p.m., the last at about 10 p.m. Late-night shows on Saturdays are found mainly in the large cities. Cinemas always show films in the original language with subtitles in Dutch.

Dutch theatres close one day a week. You can find out what is playing from newspapers or from the local tourist office (VVV). In the larger places there are publications of the type "This week in…", and the VVV offices there have a theatre booking office. It is advisable to book in advance.

There is an *Informaphone* in the VVV office in front of Amsterdam's Central Station which will tell you (in English) what's on in Amsterdam. The people in the tourist office will tell you how to use the phone.

Have you a copy of "This week in…"?	Mag ik een exemplaar van „Deze week in…" van u?	mahkh ik ayn ehksehmplaar vahn dayzer vayk in … vahn ew
What's showing at the cinema tonight?	Wat draait er van-avond in de bios-coop?	√aht draaᵉᵗ ehr vahn-aavont in der beeyoskoap
Where's that new film by … being shown?	Waar draait die nieuwe film van…?	√aar draaᵉᵗ dee neeᵒᵒ√er film vahn
What's playing at the … Theatre?	Wat wordt er in de … schouwburg gespeeld?	√aht √ort ehr in der … skhoᵒ√burrkh gherspaylt
What sort of play is it?	Wat voor een toneelstuk is het?	√aht voar ayn toanaylsturk iss heht

Who's the playwright?	**Wie is de schrijver?**	vee iss der **skhraiyverr**
Can you recommend a...?	**Kunt u mij ... aanbevelen?**	kurnt ew maiy aanber**vayler**n
comedy	**een blijspel**	ayn **blaiy**spehl
good film	**een goede film**	ayn **ghoo**der film
something light	**iets luchtigs**	eets **lurkh**terkhs
musical	**een musical**	ayn "musical"
play	**een toneelstuk**	ayn to**nayl**sturk
revue	**een revue**	ayn re**rvew**
thriller	**een sensatiestuk**	ayn sehn**saat**seesturk
western	**een western**	ayn **vehs**terrn
At what theatre is that new play by ...being performed?	**In welke schouw-burg speelt dat nieuwe stuk van...?**	in **vehl**ker **skhoo°w**burrkh spaylt daht **nee°°ver** sturk vahn
Who's in it?	**Wie spelen er in?**	vee **spay**lern ehr in
Who's playing the lead?	**Wie speelt de hoofdrol?**	vee spaylt der **hoaf**trol
Who's the director?	**Wie is de regisseur?**	vee iss der ray**ghee**ssurr
What time does it begin?	**Hoe laat begint het?**	hoo laat ber**ghint** heht
What time does the show end?	**Hoe laat is de voor-stelling afgelopen?**	hoo laat iss der **voar**stehling **ahf**gherloapern
Are there any tickets for tonight?	**Zijn er nog plaatsen voor vanavond?**	zaiyn ehr nokh **plaat**sern voar vahn**aa**vont
I want to reserve 2 tickets for the show on Friday evening.	**Ik wil graag 2 plaat-sen bespreken voor de voorstelling van vrijdagavond.**	ik vil ghraakh 2 **plaat**sern ber**spray**kern voar der **voar**stehling vahn **vraiy**dahkhaavont
Can I have a ticket for the matinée on Tuesday?	**Ik wil graag één plaats voor de mid-dagvoorstelling op dinsdag.**	ik vil ghraakh ayn plaats voar der **mid**dahghvoarstehling op **dins**dahkh
I want a seat in the stalls (orchestra)/ circle (mezzanine).	**Ik wil graag een plaats in de stalles/ op het balkon.**	ik vil ghraakh ayn plaats in der **stah**lerss op heht bahl**kon**
How much are the front-row seats?	**Wat kosten de plaatsen op de eerste rij?**	vaht **kos**tern der **plaat**sern op der **ayr**ster raiy
Not too far back.	**Niet te ver naar achteren.**	neet ter vehr naar **ahkh**terrern

RELAXING

| May I please have a programme? | **Mag ik een programma, alstublieft?** | mahkh ik ayn proaghrahmaa ahlstewbleeft |
| Where's the cloak-room? | **Waar is de vestiaire?** | Vaar iss der vehstyehrer |

Het spijt me, alles is uitverkocht.	I'm sorry, we're sold out.
Er zijn alleen nog een paar plaatsen over op het balkon/in de stalles.	There are only a few seats left in the circle (mezzanine)/stalls (orchestra).
Mag ik uw kaartje zien, alstublieft?	May I see your ticket?
Dit is uw plaats.	This is your seat.

Opera—Ballet—Concert

Where's the opera house?	**Waar is het operagebouw?**	Vaar iss heht oaperraagherboow
Where's the concert hall?	**Waar is het concertgebouw?**	Vaar iss heht konsehrtgherboow
What's on at the opera tonight?	**Welke opera is er vanavond?**	Vehlker oaperraa iss ehr vahnaavont
Who's singing?	**Wie zingt er?**	Vee zingt ehr
Who's dancing?	**Wie danst er?**	Vee dahnst ehr
What time does the programme start?	**Hoe laat begint de voorstelling?**	hoo laat berghint der voarstehling
What orchestra is playing?	**Welk orkest speelt er?**	Vehlk orkehst spaylt ehr
What are they playing?	**Wat spelen ze?**	Vaht spaylern zer
Who's the conductor?	**Wie is de dirigent?**	Vee iss der deereeghehnt

FOR TIPPING, see page 1

Night-club—Discotheques

Night-clubs and discotheques are the same the world over, so we'll content ourselves with the following:

Can you recommend a good night-club?	**Kunt u mij een goede nachtclub aanbevelen?**	kurnt ew ayn **ghoo**der **nahkht**klurp **aan**bervaylern
Is there a floor show?	**Is er een floorshow?**	iss ehr ayn "floorshow"
What time does the floor show start?	**Hoe laat begint de floorshow?**	hoo laat ber**ghint** der "floorshow"
Is evening dress necessary?	**Is avondkleding noodzakelijk?**	iss **aa**vontklayding **noat**zaakerlerk

And once inside...

A table for 2, please.	**Een tafel voor 2 personen, alstublieft.**	ayn **taa**ferl voar 2 pehr-**soa**nern ahlstew**bleeft**
My name is ... I reserved a table for 4.	**Mijn naam is ... Ik heb een tafel voor 4 personen gereserveerd.**	maiyn naam iss ... ik hehp ayn **taa**ferl voar 4 pehr**soa**nern gherray-zehr**vayrt**
I telephoned you earlier.	**Ik heb u vooraf gebeld.**	ik hehp ew voar**ahf** gher**behlt**
We haven't got a reservation.	**Wij hebben niet gereserveerd.**	ⱱaiy **hehb**ern neet gherayzehr**vayrt**

Dancing

Where can we go dancing?	**Waar kunnen we gaan dansen?**	ⱱaar **kur**nern ⱱer ghaan **dahn**sern
Is there a disco-theque in town?	**Is er een discotheek in de stad?**	iss ehr ayn disko**atayk** in der staht
Is there an admission charge?	**Moet er toegang betaald worden?**	moot ehr **too**ghahng ber**taalt** ⱱordern
There's a dance at the...	**Er is een dansavond in de...**	ehr iss ayn **dahns**aavont in der
Would you like to dance?	**Wilt u dansen?**	ⱱilt ew **dahn**sern

Do you happen to play...?

Do you happen to play chess?	**Schaakt u misschien?**	skhaakt ew mersskheen
I'm afraid I don't.	**Jammer genoeg niet.**	yahmerr ghernookh neet
No, but I'll give you a game of draughts (checkers).	**Nee, maar ik wil wel met u dammen.**	nay maar ik vil vehl meht ew dahmern

king	**koning**	koaning
queen	**koningin**	koaniyin
castle (rook)	**kasteel**	kahstayl
bishop	**loper**	loaperr
knights	**paard**	paart
pawn	**pion**	peeyon
Checkmate!	**Schaakmat!**	skhaakmaht

Do you play cards?	**Speelt u kaart?**	spaylt ew kaart
bridge	**bridge**	'bridge'
canasta	**canasta**	kaanahstaa
poker	**poker**	poakerr
pontoon (21)	**eenentwintigen**	aynehntvinterghern
whist	**whist**	vist

ace	**aas**	aass
king	**heer**	hayr
queen	**vrouw**	vroow
jack	**boer**	boor
joker	**joker**	yoakerr
hearts	**harten**	hahrtern
diamonds	**ruiten**	rurawtern
clubs	**klaveren**	klaaverrern
spades	**schoppen**	skhoppern

RELAXING

Casino and gambling

There are two casinos in Holland, in Zandvoort on the coast and in Valkenburg in the south of Holland. Mainly roulette and blackjack are played. They are open all year round from 2 p.m. to 2 a.m. In Belgium there are many casinos.

Entry into a casino requires correct dress and an identity card or passport. You must be over 18 and have a clean record in the gambling world. You need have no doubts about the honesty of the game. Casinos are regularly controlled by government inspectors.

Entrance fees are nominal. A ticket (for a day, a week or a month) will be issued to you for admission. English is usually spoken by the croupiers and dealers of the casinos.

SPELEN INZETTEN! PLACE YOUR BETS!	**RIEN NE VA PLUS!** NO MORE BETS!

For the more modest gamblers, there is also a national lottery (*Staatsloterij*—staatsloater**raiy**) as well as a *Sport-toto*—**sport**toatoa, where people bet on football teams.

Horse racing is not uncommon in Holland and betting is permitted, although it is usually done at the race-track.

Sports

I'd like to see a/an...	**Ik wil graag een... zien.**	ik vil ghraakh ayn ... zeen
boxing match	**bokswedstrijd**	boksvehtstraiyt
football (soccer) match	**voetbalwedstrijd**	vootbahlvehststraiyt
ice-hockey match	**ijshockeywedstrijd**	aiyshokkeevehtstraiyt
Can you get me 2 tickets?	**Kunt u 2 kaartjes voor mij krijgen?**	kurnt ew 2 kaartyerss voar maiy kraiyghern
Who's playing?	**Wie speelt er?**	vee spaylern ehr

FOR NUMBERS, see page 175

What's the admission charge?	**Wat is de toegangsprijs?**	✔aht is der **tooghahngs**praiyss
Where's the nearest golf course?	**Waar is het dichtstbijzijnde golferrein?**	✔aar iss heht dikhtstbaiy**zaiy**nder **gholf**tehraiyn
Where are the tennis courts?	**Waar zijn de tennisbanen?**	✔aar zaiyn der **tehniss**baanern
Can I hire rackets?	**Kan ik raketten huren?**	kahn ik raa**keh**ttern **hew**rern
What's the charge per...?	**Wat kost het per...?**	✔aht kost heht pehr
day/hour/round	**dag/uur/spel**	dahkh/ewr/spehl
Do I have to sign up beforehand?	**Moet ik van te voren reserveren?**	moot ik vahn ter **voa**rern rayzehr**vay**rern
Where can I hire a bike?	**Waar kan ik een fiets huren?**	✔aar kahn ik ayn feets **hew**rern
Where's the nearest race course (track)?	**Waar is de dichtstbijzijnde renbaan?**	✔aar iss der dikhtstbaiy**zaiy**nder **rehn**baan
Is there a bowling alley here?	**Is er hier een kegelbaan in de buurt?**	iss ehr heer ayn **kaygher**lbaan in der bewrt
Is there a swimming pool here?	**Is hier een zwembad in de buurt?**	iss heer ayn z✔**ehm**baht in der bewrt
Is it open-air or indoors?	**Is het in de open lucht of overdekt?**	iss heht in der **oa**pern lurkht of oaverr**dehkt**
Is it heated?	**Is het verwarmd?**	iss heht verr✔**ahrmt**
Can one swim in the lake/river?	**Kan men in het meer/in de rivier zwemmen?**	kahn mahn in heht mayr/in der **ree**veer z✔**eh**mern
Is there any good fishing around here?	**Kun je hier in de buurt goed vissen?**	kurn yer heer in der bewrt ghoot **vi**ssern
Do I need a permit?	**Heb ik hiervoor een vergunning nodig?**	hehp ik **heer**voar ayn verr**ghur**ning **noa**derkh
Where can I get one?	**Waar kan ik die krijgen?**	✔aar kahn ik dee **kraiy**ghern

On the beach

With one fifth of its surface covered with lakes, canals and rivers, Holland is an ideal country for all types of water-sports. Boating, fishing, swimming, water-skiing and surfing are possible wherever you go in the lake districts and along the North Sea coast, with its 150 miles of sandy beaches. For information concerning boat hires, fishing restrictions and maps of local waterways, contact the local VVV office.

Is it safe for swimming?	**Kan men hier veilig zwemmen?**	kahn mehn heer **vaiy**lerkh z**v**ehmern
Is there a life-guard?	**Is er hier een reddingsbrigade?**	iss ehr heer ayn rehdingsbreeghaader
Is it safe for children?	**Is het hier veilig voor kinderen?**	iss heht heer **vaiy**lerkh voar kinderrern
The sea is very calm.	**De zee is erg kalm.**	der zay iss ehrkh kahlm
There are some big waves.	**Er zijn grote golven.**	ehr zaiyn **ghroa**ter **ghol**vern
Are there any danger-ous currents?	**Zijn er gevaarlijke stromingen?**	zaiyn ehr gher**vaar**lerker **stroa**mingern
What time is high/low tide?	**Wanneer is het vloed/eb?**	**v**ahnayr iss heht vloot/ehp
What's the temper-ature of the water?	**Hoeveel graden is het water?**	hoo**vayl** ghraadern iss heht **v**aaterr
I want to hire a/an/some…	**Ik wil graag … huren.**	ik **v**il ghraakh … **hew**rern
air mattress	**een luchtbed**	ayn **lurkht**beht
bathing hut	**een badhokje**	ayn **bahd**hokyer
deck-chair	**een badstoel**	ayn **bahd**stool
sunshade	**een parasol**	ayn paaraa**sol**
surfboard	**een surfplank**	ayn **surrf**plahnk
water-skis	**een paar waterski's**	ayn paar **v**aaterrskeess
Where can I hire a …?	**Waar kan ik… huren?**	**v**aar kahn ik … **hew**rern
canoe	**een kano**	ayn **kaa**noa
motorboat	**een motorboot**	ayn **moa**terrboat
rowing-boat	**een roeiboot**	ayn roo**••**boat
sailing-boat	**een zeilboot**	ayn **zaiy**lboat
What's the charge per hour?	**Wat kost het per uur?**	hoo**vayl** kost heht pehr ewr

Before you take a swim, you will want perhaps to ask your neighbour on the beach:

| Could you look after this a moment, please? | **Kunt u hier even op letten, alstublieft?** | kurnt ew heer **ay**vern op **leht**ern ahlstew**bleeft** |

| **PRIVESTRAND** PRIVATE BEACH | **VERBODEN TE ZWEMMEN** NO BATHING |

Other sports

There are many skating rinks in Holland, of which some are indoor. They are generally open from mid-October to March and a few months longer for the indoor rinks.

| Is there a skating rink here? | **Is hier een ijsbaan in de buurt?** | iss heer ayn **ai**yssbaan in der bewrt |
| I want to hire some skates. | **Ik wil graag een paar schaatsen huren.** | ik ¥il ghraakh ayn paar **skhaat**sern **hew**rern |

Gliding *(zweefvliegen)* has become a popular sport in Holland. Many gliding week-ends are organized by clubs scattered all over the country. The minimum age is 14.

RELAXING

Camping—Countryside

There are many excellent camping sites in Holland and Belgium. No special permit is required. Charges vary from place to place, and it might therefore be better to inquire about the fees immediately upon arrival so as to avoid any misunderstanding when settling the bill. The Netherlands National Tourist Office and local VVV offices will provide you with lists of camping sites. Camping is only permitted on specially designated sites.

Can we camp here?	Mogen we hier kamperen?	moaghern ʋer heer kahmpayrern
Is there a camping site near here?	Is hier een kampeerterrein in de buurt?	iss ehr heer ayn kahmpayrtehraiyn in der bewrt
Have you room for a tent/caravan (trailer)?	Hebt u plaats voor een tent/caravan?	hehpt ew plaats voar ayn tehnt/"caravan"
May we camp in your field?	Mogen we onze tent op uw land neerzetten?	moaghern ʋer onzer tehnt op ewᵉᵉ lahnt nayrzehtern
Can we park our caravan here?	Mogen we onze caravan hier neerzetten?	moaghern ʋer onzer "caravan" heer nayrzehtern
Is this an official camping site?	Is dit een officieel kampeerterrein?	iss dit ayn offeesyayl kahmpayrtehraiyn
May we light a fire?	Mogen we een vuurtje maken?	moaghern ʋer ayn vewrtyer maakern
Is there drinking water?	Is er drinkwater?	iss ehr drinkʋaaterr
Are there shopping facilities on the site?	Is er een winkel op het kampeerterrein?	iss ehr ayn ʋinkerl op heht kahmpayrtehraiyn
Are there...?	Zijn er...?	zaiyn ehr
baths	badgelegenheden	bahtgherlayghernhaydern
showers	douches	doosherss
toilets	toiletten	tʋaalehtern

What's the charge…?	Wat kost het…?	ѵaht kost heht
per day	per dag	pehr dahkh
per person	per persoon	pehr perrsoan
per child	per kind	pehr kint
for a car	voor een auto	voar ayn oᵒʷ toa
for a tent	voor een tent	voar ayn tehnt
for a caravan (trailer)	voor een caravan	voar ayn "caravan"

Is the tourist tax included?	Is de belasting er-bij inbegrepen?	iss der berlahsting ehrbaiy inberghraypern
Is there a youth hostel near here?	Is hier een jeugd-herberg in de buurt?	iss hier ayn yurght-hehrbehrgh in der bewrt
Do you know anyone who can put us up for the night?	Kent u iemand die ons vannacht kan herbergen?	kehnt ew eemahnt dee onss vahnnahkht kahn hehrbehrghern

VERBODEN TE KAMPEREN	VERBODEN VOOR CARAVANS
NO CAMPING	NO CARAVANS (TRAILERS)

Landmarks

barn	de schuur	der skhewr
bridge	de brug	der brurkh
brook	het beekje	heht baykyer
building	het gebouw	heht gherboᵒʷ
canal	het kanaal	heht kaanaal
chimney	de schoorsteen	der skhoarstayn
church	de kerk	der kehrk
cliff	de klif	der klif
copse	het hakhout	heht hahkhoᵒʷt
cottage	de hut	der hurt
crossroads	het kruispunt	heht krurᵉʷ spurnt
dike	de dijk	der daiyk
farm	de boerderij	der boorderraiy
ferry	de veer	der vayr
field	het veld	heht vehlt
footpath	het voetpad	heht vootpaht
forest	het bos	heht boss

hamlet	het gehucht	heht gherhurkht
heath	de hei	der haiy
highway	de grote weg	der ghroater √ehkh
hill	de heuvel	der hurverl
house	het huis	heht hur^{ew}ss
inn	de herberg	der hehrbehrkh
lake	het meer	heht mayr
lighthouse	de vuurtoren	der vewrtoarern
marsh	het moeras	heht moorahss
moorland	de heide	der haiyder
ocean	de oceaan	der oaseeyaan
path	het pad	heht paht
pond	de vijver	der vaiyverr
pool	de plas	der plahss
river	de rivier	der reeveer
road	de weg	der √ehkh
road sign	het verkeersbord	heht verrkayrsbort
sea	de zee	der zay
spring	de bron	der bron
stream	de stroom	der stroam
swamp	het moeras	heht moorahss
telegraph pole	de telefoonpaal	der taylerfoanpaal
track	het pad	heht paht
tree	de boom	der boam
village	het dorp	heht dorp
waterfall	de waterval	der √aaterrvahl
well	de put	der purt
wood	het bos	heht bos
What's the name of that river?	Hoe heet die rivier?	hoo hayt dee reeveer
Are we below/above sea level?	Bevinden we ons beneden/boven zeeniveau?	bervindern √er onss bernaydern/boavern zayneevoa
Is there a scenic route to...?	Is er een mooie weg naar...?	iss ehr ayn moa^{ee}yer √ehkh naar

CAMPING — COUNTRYSIDE

... and if you're tired of walking, you can always try hitch-hiking (*liften*—**lif**tern).

Can you give me a lift to...?	Kunt u mij een lift geven naar...?	kurnt ew maiy ayn lift ghayvern naar

FOR ASKING THE WAY, see page 144

Making friends

Introductions

A few phrases to get you started:

May I introduce Miss...?	**Mag ik u juffrouw... even voorstellen?**	mahkh ik ew **yur**froᵒʷ ayvern **voar**stehlern
Glad to know you.	**Aangenaam kennis te maken.**	aangher**naam keh**niss ter **maa**kern
How do you do?	**Hoe maakt u het?**	hoo maakt ew heht
Very well, thank you.	**Uitstekend, dank u.**	urᵉʷᵗ**stay**kernt dahnk ew
Fine, thanks. And you?	**Best, dank u. En u?**	behst dahnk ew√. ehn ew
I'd like you to meet a friend of mine.	**Ik zou u graag aan een vriend van mij willen voorstellen.**	ik zoᵒʷ ew ghraakh aan ayn vreent vahn maiy √illern **voar**stehlern
John, this is...	**John, dit is...**	john dit iss
My name is...	**Ik heet...**	ik hayt
... sends his/her best regards.	**U krijgt heel veel groeten van...**	ew kraight hayl vayl **ghroo**tern vahn

Follow-up

How long have you been here?	**Hoe lang bent u hier al?**	hoo lahng behnt ew heer ahl
We've been here a week.	**Wij zijn hier al een week.**	√aiy zaiyn heer ahl ayn √ayk
Is this your first visit?	**Bent u hier voor de eerste keer?**	behnt ew heer voar der **ayr**ster kayr
No, we came here last year.	**Nee, we zijn hier verleden jaar ook geweest.**	nay √er zaiyn heer veer**lay**dern yaar oak gher**√ayst**

Are you enjoying your stay?	**Bevalt het u hier?**	bervahlt heht ew heer
Yes, I like it very much.	**Ja, het bevalt mij heel goed.**	yaa heht bervahlt maiy hayl ghoot
I like the landscape a lot.	**Ik vind dit landschap erg mooi.**	ik vint dit **lahnt**skhahp ehrkh moo^{ee}
Are you on your own?	**Bent u alleen?**	behnt ew ah**layn**
I'm with...	**Ik ben hier met...**	ik behn heer meht
my children	**mijn kinderen**	maiyn **kinder**rern
my wife	**mijn vrouw**	maiyn vro^{ow}
my husband	**mijn man**	maiyn mahn
my family	**mijn gezin**	maiyn gher**zin**
my parents	**mijn ouders**	maiyn o^{ow}derrss
some friends	**vrienden**	**vreen**dern
Where do you come from?	**Waar komt u vandaan?**	Vaar komt ew vahn**daan**
What part of... do you come from?	**Uit welk gedeelte van ... komt u?**	ur^{ew}t Vehlk gher**dayl**ter vahn ... komt ew
I'm from ...	**Ik kom uit...**	ik kom ur^{ew}t
Where are you staying?	**Waar verblijft u?**	Vaar verr**blaiyft** ew
We're camping.	**Wij kamperen.**	Vaiy kahm**pay**rern
We're here on holiday.	**Wij zijn hier met vakantie.**	Vaiy zaiyn heer meht vaa**kahn**see
I'm a student.	**Ik ben student.**	ik behn stew**dehnt**
What are you studying?	**Wat studeert u?**	Vaht stew**dayrt** ew
I'm here on a business trip.	**Ik ben hier voor zaken.**	ik behn heer voar **zaa**kern
What kind of business are you in?	**Wat voor zaken doet u?**	Vaht voar **zaa**kern doot ew
I hope we'll see you again soon.	**Ik hoop dat we elkaar gauw weerzien.**	ik hoap daht Ver ehl**kaar** gho^{ow} **Vayr**zeen
See you later!	**Tot ziens!**	tot seenss
See you tomorrow!	**Tot morgen!**	tot **morg**hern
We'll certainly see each other again one of these days.	**We zullen elkaar zeker weerzien een dezer dagen.**	Ver **zurl**ern ehl**kaar** **zay**kerr **Vayr**zeen ayn **day**zerr **daag**hern

Weather ... or not

Always a popular subject:

What a lovely day!	**Wat een prachtig weer!**	√aht ayn **prahkh**terkh √ayr
What awful weather!	**Wat een afschuwelijk weer!**	√aht ayn ahf**skhew**√erlerk √ayr
Cold today, isn't it?	**Koud vandaag, vindt u niet?**	ko°°t vahndaakh vint ew neet
Isn't it hot today?	**Wat een hitte vandaag, nietwaar?**	√aht ayn hitter vahndaakh neet√aar
Is it usually as warm as this?	**Is het hier altijd zo warm?**	iss heht heer **ahl**taiyt zoa √ahrm
What's the temperature like outside?	**Wat is de temperatuur buiten?**	√aht iss der tehmperraatewr bur°°tern
The wind's up.	**Het waait.**	heht √aa°°t
What a fog!	**Wat een mist!**	√aht ayn mist
Do you think it'll ... tomorrow?	**Denkt u dat het morgen...?**	dehnkt ew daht heht morghern
clear up	**op zal klaren**	op zahl **klaa**rern
rain	**regent**	**ray**ghernt
snow	**sneeuwt**	snay°°t
be sunny	**zonnig weer is**	**zonn**erkh √ayr iss

Invitations

My wife/My husband and I would like you to to dine with us on Friday.	**Mijn vrouw/Mijn man en ik willen u graag op vrijdag voor een etentje uitnodigen.**	maiyn vro°°/maiyn mahn ehn ik √illern ew ghraakh op √raiydahk voar ayn ayterntyer ur°°tnoaderghern
Can you come to dinner tomorrow night?	**Kunt u morgenavond bij ons komen eten?**	kurnt ew **morghern**aavont baiy onss **koa**mern aytern
Can you come over for cocktails this evening?	**Komt u vanavond een borreltje drinken?**	komt ew vahn**aa**vont ayn **borrerl**tyer **drin**kern
There's a party. Are you coming?	**Er wordt een feestje gehouden. Komt u ook?**	ehr √ort ayn **fays**tyer gherho°°dern. komt ew ook

That's very kind of you.	**Dat is bijzonder vriendelijk van u.**	daht iss beezonderr **vreen**derlenk vahn ew
Great! I'd love to come.	**Ik kom dolgraag!**	ik kom **dolg**hraakh
What time shall we come?	**Hoe laat verwacht u ons?**	hoo laat verr**vahkht** ew onss
May I bring a friend/ girl friend?	**Mag ik een vriend/ vriendin meenemen?**	mahkh ik ayn vreent/ vreendin **may**naymern
I'm afraid we've got to go.	**Helaas moeten we nu weg.**	hay**laass** mootern **v**er new **v**ehkh
Next time you must come to visit us.	**De volgende keer moet u bij ons komen.**	der **volg**hernder kayr moot ew baiy onss **koa**mern
Thanks for the evening. It was great.	**Hartelijk bedankt voor de gezellige avond. Het was fantastisch.**	**hahr**terlerk ber**dahnkt** voar der gher**zehl**lergher **aa**vont. heht **v**ahss fahn**tahs**teess

Dating

Can I get you a drink?	**Wilt u iets drinken?**	**V**ilt ew eets **drink**ern
Would you like a cigarette?	**Wilt u een sigaret?**	**V**ilt ew ayn seeghaa**reht**
Do you have a light, please?	**Hebt u een vuurtje, alstublieft?**	hehpt ew ayn **vewr**tyer ahlstew**bleeft**
Excuse me, could you please help me?	**Neemt u mij niet kwalijk, kunt u mij misschien helpen?**	naymt ew maiy neet **kvaa**lerk kurnt ew maiy merss**kheen hehl**pern
I'm lost. Can you show me the way to…?	**Ik ben de weg kwijt. Kunt u mij de weg naar … wijzen?**	ik behn der **v**ehk k**v**aiyt. kurnt ew maiy der **v**ehk naar … **vaiy**zern
Are you waiting for someone?	**Wacht u op iemand?**	**v**ahkht ew op **ee**mahnt
Leave me alone, please!	**Laat me met rust, alstublieft!**	laat mer mett rurst ahlstew**bleeft**
Are you free this evening?	**Bent u vanavond vrij?**	behnt ew vahn**aa**vont vraiy
Thank you, I've got another engagement this evening.	**Nee, dank u. Ik heb al een andere afspraak voor vanavond.**	nay dahnk ew. ik hehp ahl ayn **ahn**derrer **ahf**spraak voar vahn**aa**vont

Would you like to go out with me tomorrow evening?	**Hebt u zin om morgenavond met mij uit te gaan?**	hehpt ew zin om **morghern**aavont meht maiy ur^{ew}t ter ghaan
Would you like to go dancing?	**Hebt u zin om te gaan dansen?**	hehpt ew zin om ter ghaan **dahnsern**
I know a good discotheque.	**Ik weet een goede discotheek.**	ik √ayt ayn **ghooder** diskoatayk
Shall we go to the cinema (movies)?	**Zullen we naar de bioscoop gaan?**	zurlern √er naar der beeyoskoap ghaan
Where shall we meet?	**Waar zullen we afspreken?**	√aar zurlern √er **ahf**spraykern
I'll pick you up at your hotel.	**Ik kom u in uw hotel afhalen.**	ik kom ew in ew^{oo} hoatehl **ahf**haalern
I'll call for you at 8.	**Ik kom u om 8 uur afhalen.**	ik kom ew om 8 ewr **ahf**haalern
Would you like to go for a drive?	**Hebt u zin om een eindje te gaan rijden?**	hehpt ew zin om ayn aiyntyer ter ghaan **raiy**dern
No, I'm not interested, thank you.	**Nee, ik voel er niet voor, dank u.**	nay ik vool ehr neet voar dahnk ew
May I take you home?	**Mag ik u naar huis brengen?**	mahkh ik ew naar hur^{ew}ss **brehng**ern
Can I see you again tomorrow?	**Zie ik u morgen weer?**	zee ik ew **morghern** √ayr
Thank you, I've enjoyed myself tremendously.	**Dank u wel, ik heb geweldig genoten.**	dahnk ew √ehl ik hehp gher√ehlderkh ghernoatern
What's your telephone number?	**Wat is uw telefoonnummer?**	√aht iss ew^{oo} taylerfoannurmerr
Do you live alone?	**Woont u alleen?**	√oant ew ahlayn
What time is your last bus/train?	**Hoe laat gaat uw laatste bus/trein?**	hoo laat ghaat ew^{oo} **laat**ster burss/traiyn

Shopping guide

This shopping guide is designed to help you find what you want with ease, accuracy and speed. It features:

1. a list of all major shops, stores and services (p. 98)

2. some general expressions required when shopping to allow you to be specific and selective (p. 100)

3. full details of the shops and services most likely to concern you. Here you'll find advice, alphabetical lists of items and conversion charts listed under the headings below.

		Page
Bookshop	books, magazines, newspapers, stationery	104
Camping	camping equipment	106
Chemist's (drugstore)	medicine, first-aid, toilet articles, cosmetics	108 110
Clothing	clothes, shoes, accessories	112
Electrical appliances	radios, tape-recorders, shavers, records	119
Hairdresser	barber, ladies' hairdresser, beauty salon	121
Jeweller– Watchmaker	jewellery, watches, watch repairs	123
Laundry–Dry cleaning	usual facilities	126
Photography	cameras, accessories, films, developing	127
Provisions	this section is confined to basic items required for picnics	129
Souvenirs	souvenirs, gifts, fancy goods	131
Tobacconist	smokers' supplies	132

SHOPPING GUIDE

Shops—Stores—Services

Shops are usually open Monday to Friday from 8.30/9 a.m. to 5.30/6 p.m. and on Saturdays till 4 p.m. (food shops). Most businesses except department stores close during lunch-time. In many towns, shopkeepers have introduced late closing on either Thursday or Friday night. Department stores and many other shops are closed on Monday morning. Food shops, however, close one afternoon a week. In holiday centres and seaside resorts, you'll find shops open in the evening and during the weekend.

Where's the nearest...?	Waar is de/het dichtstbijzijnde...?	Vaar iss der/heht dikhtstbaiyzaiynder
antique shop	de antiekwinkel	der ahnteekvinkerl
baker	de bakker	der bahkerr
barber	de herenkapper	der hayrernkahperr
beauty salon	de schoonheidssalon	der skhoanhaiytssaalon
bookshop	de boekhandel	der bookhahnderl
butcher	de slagerij	der slaagherraiy
chemist's	de apotheek	der ahpoatayk
confectioner	de banketbakkerij	der bahnkehtbahkerraiy
dairy	de melkwinkel, zuivelhandel	der mehlkvinkerl zurᵉʷverlhahnderl
delicatessen	de delicatessenzaak	der dayleekaatehssernzaak
department store	het warenhuis	heht vaarernhurᵉʷss
drugstore	de drogisterij	der droaghisterraiy
dry-cleaner	de stomerij	der stoamerraiy
fishmonger	de vishandel	der visshahnderl
flea market	de vlooienmarkt	der vloayernmahrkt
florist	de bloemist	der bloomist
furrier	de bontzaak	der bontzaak
greengrocer	de groenteboer	der ghroonterboor
grocery	de kruideniers-winkel	der krurᵉʷderneersvinkerl
hairdresser (ladies')	de dameskapper	der daamerskahperr
hairdresser (men's)	de herenkapper	der hayrernkahperr
hardware store	de ijzerhandel	der aiyzerrhahnderl
health-food store	de reformawinkel	der rerformaavinkerl
jeweller	de juwelier	der yewverleer
launderette	de wasserette	der vahsserrehter
laundry	de wasserij	der vahsserraiy
liquor store	de slijterij	der slaiyterraiy

market	de markt	der mahrkt
milliner	de hoedenwinkel	der hoodern√inkerl
newsagent	de krantenverkoper	der krahnternverrkoaperr
news-stand	de krantenkiosk	der krahnternkeeyosk
off-licence	de slijterij	der slaiyterraiy
optician	de opticiën	der opteessyehn
pharmacy	de apotheek	der ahpoatayk
photo shop	de fotozaak	der foatoazaak
shoemaker (repairs)	de schoenmaker	der skhoonmaakerr
shoe shop	de schoenwinkel	der skhoon√inkerl
souvenir shop	de souvenirwinkel	der sooverneerv√inkerl
sporting goods shop	de sportzaak	der sportzaak
stationer	de kantoorboek-handel	der kahntoarbookhahnderl
supermarket	de supermarkt	der sewperrmahrkt
tailor	de kleermaker	der klayrmaakerr
tobacconist	de sigarenwinkel	der seeghaarernv√inkerl
toy shop	de speelgoedwinkel	der spaylghoot√inkerl
watchmaker	de horlogemaker	der horloazhermaakerr
wine merchant	de wijnhandel	der √aiynhahnderl

...and some further useful addresses:

bank	de bank	der bahnk
currency-exchange office	het wisselkantoor	heht √isserlkahntoar
dentist	de tandarts	der tahntahrts
doctor	de dokter	der dokterr
hospital	het ziekenhuis	heht zeekernhur^{ew}ss
lost-property (lost and found) office	het bureau voor gevonden voor-werpen	heht bewroa voar ghervondern voar√ehr-pern
police station	het politiebureau	heht poaleetseebewroa
post office	het postkantoor	heht postkahntoar
tourist office	het VVV-kantoor	heht vayvayvay-kahntoar
travel agent	het reisbureau	heht raiysbewroa

SHOPPING GUIDE

UITVERKOOP	SALE

General expressions

Where?

Where's a good...?	**Waar is een goede...?**	Vaar iss ayn ghooder
Where's the nearest...?	**Waar is de dichtst-bijzijnde...?**	Vaar iss der dikhtst-baiyzaiynder
Where can I find a...?	**Waar kan ik een ... vinden?**	Vaar kahn is ayn ... vindern
Can you recommend a cheap...?	**Kunt u een goed-kope ... aanbevelen?**	kurnt ew ayn ghootkoaper... aanbervaylern
Where's the main shopping centre?	**Waar is het winkel-centrum?**	Vaar iss heht Vinkerl-sehntrurm
How far is it from here?	**Hoe ver is het hier vandaan?**	hoo vehr iss heht heer vandaan
Where's the cashier's?	**Waar is de kassa?**	Vaar iss der kahsaa

Service

Can you help me?	**Kunt u mij helpen?**	kurnt ew maiy hehlpern
I'm just looking around.	**Ik kijk alleen even rond.**	ik kaiyk ahlayn ayvern ront
I want...	**Ik wil ... hebben.**	ik Vil ... hehbern
Can you show me some...?	**Kunt u mij ... laten zien?**	kurnt ew maiy ... laatern zeen
Do you have any...?	**Hebt u...?**	hehpt ew

That one

Can you show me...?	**Kunt u mij ... laten zien?**	kurnt ew maiy ... laatern zeen
this/that	**dit/dat**	dit/daht
the one in the window/in the display case	**die in de etalage/ in de uitstalkast**	dee in der aytaalaazher/ in der ur ᵉʷtstahlkahst
It's over there.	**Daar is het.**	daar iss heht

Defining the article

| I'd like a ... one. | **Ik wil graag een ... hebben** | ik vil ghraakh ayn ... hehbern |

big	**grote**	ghroater
cheap	**goedkope**	ghootkoaper
coloured	**gekleurde**	gherklurrder
dark	**donkere**	donkerrer
large	**grote**	ghroater
light (weight)	**lichte**	likhter
light (colour)	**lichte**	likhter
round	**ronde**	ronder
small	**kleine**	klaiyner
soft	**zachte**	zahkhter
square	**vierkante**	veerkahnter

Preference

Haven't you anything...?	**Hebt u niet iets...?**	hehpt ew neet eets
cheaper/better larger/smaller	**goedkopers/beters groters/kleiners**	ghootkoaperss/bayterrss ghroaterss/klaiynerrss
Can you show me some more?	**Kunt u mij nog wat laten zien?**	kurnt ew maiy nokh vaht laatern zeen

How much?

How much is it?	**Hoeveel kost dit?**	hoovayl kost dit
How much are they?	**Hoeveel kosten ze?**	hoovayl kostern zer
Please write it down.	**Schrijft u het alstublieft even op.**	skhraiyft ew heht ahlstewbleeft ayvern op
I don't want to spend more than .. guilders.	**Ik wil niet meer dan ...gulden uitgeven.**	ik vil neet mayr dahn ...ghurldern ureʷtghayvern

Decision

| That's just what I want. | **Dat is precies wat ik zoek.** | daht iss prerseess vaht ik zook |
| It's not (quite) what I want. | **Dat is niet (precies) wat ik zoek.** | daht iss neet (prerseess) vaht ik zook |

FOR COLOURS, see page 113

No, I don't like it.	**Nee, het bevalt mij niet.**	nay heht bervahlt maiy neet
I'll take this one.	**Ik neem dit.**	ik naym dit

Ordering

Can you order it for me?	**Kunt u het voor mij bestellen?**	kurnt ew heht voar maiy berstehlern
How long will it take?	**Hoe lang duurt het?**	hoo lahng dewrt heht
I'd like it as soon as possible.	**Ik zou het zo gauw mogelijk willen hebben.**	ik zoᵒʷ heht zoa goᵒʷ moagherlerk villern hehbern

Delivery

I'll take it with me.	**Ik neem het mee.**	ik naym heht may
Deliver it to the ... Hotel.	**Stuurt u het naar het ... Hotel.**	stewrt ew heht naar heht ... hoatehl
Please send it to this address.	**Stuurt u het alstublieft naar dit adres.**	stewrt ew heht ahlstewbleeft naar dit aadrehss
Will I have any difficulty with the customs?	**Krijg ik geen moeilijkheden met de douane?**	kraiykh ik ghayn moo••lerkhaydern meht der doovaaner

Paying

How much is it?	**Hoeveel is het?**	hoovayl kost heht
Can I pay by traveller's cheque?	**Kan ik met reischeques betalen?**	kahn ik meht raiysshehks bertaalern
Do you accept credit cards?	**Neemt u kredietkaarten aan?**	naymt ew krerdeetkaartern aan
Haven't you made a mistake in the bill?	**Hebt u geen vergissing in de rekening gemaakt?**	hehpt ew ghayn verrghissing in der raykerning ghermaakt
Could I have a receipt, please?	**Mag ik een kwitantie van u hebben, alstublieft?**	mahkh ik ayn kveetahntsee vahn ew hehbern ahlstewbleeft
Could I have a plastic bag, please?	**Mag ik een plastic zak van u hebben, alstublieft?**	mahkh ik ayn plehsteek zahk vahn ew hehbern ahlstewbleeft

FOR NUMBERS, see page 175

Anything else?

No, thanks, that's all.	**Nee, dank u, dat is alles.**	nay dahnk ew daht iss ahlerss
Yes, I want...	**Ja, ik wil graag...**	yaa ik vil ghraagh
Show me...	**Laat u ... even zien.**	laat ew ... ayvern zeen
Thank you.	**Dank u wel.**	dahnk ew vehl
Good-bye.	**Tot ziens.**	tot seenss

Dissatisfied

Can you please exchange this?	**Kan ik dit ruilen, alstublieft?**	kahn ik dit rur^{ew}lern ahlstewbleeft
I want to return this.	**Ik wil dit teruggeven.**	ik vil dit terrurghghayvern
I'd like a refund.	**Ik wil graag mijn geld terug.**	ik vil ghraagh maiyn ghehlt terrurkh
Here's the receipt.	**Hier is de kwitantie.**	heer iss der kveetahnsee

Kan ik u helpen?	Can I help you?
Welke ... wilt u hebben?	What ... would you like?
kleur/model	colour/shape
kwaliteit/hoeveelheid	quality/quantity
Het spijt mij, maar dat hebben we niet.	I'm sorry, we haven't any.
Zullen wij het voor u bestellen?	Shall we order it for you?
Wilt u het meenemen of zullen wij het u toesturen?	Will you take it with you or shall we send it?
Nog iets?	Anything else?
Dat is dan ... gulden, alstublieft.	That's ... guilders, please.
De kassa is daar.	The cashier's over there.
Wij nemen geen krediet- kaarten/reischeques aan.	We don't accept credit cards/ traveller's cheques.

SHOPPING GUIDE

Bookshop—Stationer's—News-stand

In Holland, bookshops and stationers' are usually separate shops, although the latter will often sell paperbacks. Newspapers and magazines in English and other languages are sold in kiosks and in many bookshops as well as in hotels.

Where's the nearest...?	Waar is de dichtst-bijzijnde...?	Vaar iss der dikhtst-baiyzaiynder
bookshop	boekhandel	bookhahnderl
news-stand	krantenkiosk	krahnternkeeyosk
stationer	kantoorboekhandel	kahntoarbookhahnderl
Where can I buy a newspaper in English?	Waar kan ik een Engelse krant kopen?	Vaar kahn ik ayn ehng-erlsser krahnt koapern
I want to buy a/ an/some...	Ik wil graag ... hebben.	ik vil ghraakh ... hehbern
address book	een adresboekje	ayn aadrehsbookyer
ball-point pen	een ballpoint	ayn "ballpoint"
blotting paper	vloeipapier	vloo••paapeer
book	een boek	ayn book
box of paints	een verfdoos	ayn vehrfdoass
carbon paper	karbonpapier	kahrbonpaapeer
cellophane tape	plakband	plahkbahnt
detective story	een detectiveverhaal	ayn daytehkteeververrhaal
dictionary	een woordenboek	ayn voardernbook
English-Dutch	Engels-Nederlands	ehngerlss/nayderrlahnts
Dutch-English	Nederlands-Engels	nayderrlahnts/ehngerlss
drawing pins	punaises	pewnehserss
envelopes	enveloppen	ehnverloppern
eraser	een gummetje	ayn ghurmertyer
exercise book	een schrift	ayn skhrift
fountain pen	een vulpen	ayn vurlpehn
glue	lijm	laiym
guide book	een reisgids	ayn raiysghits
ink	inkt	inkt
labels	etiketten	ayteekehtern
magazine	een tijdschrift	ayn taiytskhrift
map	een landkaart	ayn lahntkaart
newspaper	een krant	ayn krahnt
American/English	Amerikaanse/ Engelse	aamayreekaansser/ ehngerlsser
notebook	een notitieboekje	ayn noateetseebookyer
paperback	een pocketboek	ayn pokkertboek

paper napkins	papieren servetten	paapeerern sehrvehtern
paste	plaksel	plahkserl
pen	een pen	ayn pehn
pencil	een potlood	ayn potloat
pencil sharpener	een puntenslijper	ayn purnternslaiyperr
picture book	een prentenboek	ayn prehnternbook
playing cards	een kaartspel	ayn kaartspehl
postcards	briefkaarten	breefkaartern
refill (for a pen)	een vulling (voor een pen)	ayn vurling (voar ayn pehn)
road map	een wegenkaart	ayn vayghernkaart
rubber	een gummetje	ayn ghurmertyer
rubber bands	elastiekjes	aylahsteekyerss
ruler	een liniaal	ayn leeneeyaal
stamps	postzegels	postzaygherlss
string	touw	too͏ow
thriller	een detective-verhaal	ayn daytehkteever-haal
thumbtacks	punaises	pewnehserss
tissue paper	zijdepapier	zaiyderpaapeer
town map	een plattegrond	ayn plahterghrond
typewriter ribbon	een schrijfmachine-lint	ayn skhraiyfmaasheener-lint
typing paper	schrijfmachine-papier	skhraiyfmaasheener-paapeer
wrapping paper	pakpapier	pahkpaapeer
writing pad	een bloknoot	ayn bloknoat
Where's the guide book section?	Waar is de afdeling reisgidsen?	Vaar iss der ahfdayling raiysghitsern
Where do you keep the English books?	Waar staan de Engelse boeken?	Vaar staan der ehngerlsser bookern
Have you any of …'s books in English?	Hebt u een boek van … in het Engels?	hehpt ew ayn book vahn… in heht ehngerlss

Here are some contemporary Dutch authors whose books are available in English translation:

Simon Carmiggelt	Anton Koolhaas
Jan Cremer	Jan Mens
Johan Fabricius	Harry Mullisch
Hella Haasse	Maarten Toonder
Jan de Hartog*	Adriaan van der Veen
Willem Frederik Hermans	Jan Wolkers

* Jan de Hartog writes in both Dutch and English.

Camping

Here we're concerned with the equipment you may need.

I'd like a/an/ some...	Ik wil graag ... hebben.	ik vil ghraakh hehbern
aluminium foil	aluminiumfolie	ahlewmeeneeyurmfoalee
axe	een bijl	ayn baiyl
bottle opener	een flesopener	ayn flehssoapernerr
bucket	een emmer	ayn ehmerr
butane gas	butagas	bewtaaghahss
camp bed	een veldbed	ayn vehltbeht
camping equipment	een kampeer-uitrusting	ayn kahmpayr-ur^{ew}trursting
can opener	een blikopener	ayn blikoapernerr
candles	wat kaarsen	vaht kaarsern
chair	een stoel	ayn stool
charcoal	houtskool	ho^{ow}tskoal
clothes-pegs	knijpers	knaiyperrss
compass	een kompas	ayn kompahss
corkscrew	een kurketrekker	ayn kurrkertrehkerr
crockery	eetgerei	aytgherraiy
cutlery	bestek	berstehk
deck-chair	een ligstoel	ayn dehkstool
fishing tackle	visgerei	visgherraiy
folding chair	een vouwstoel	ayn vo^{ow}stool
folding table	een vouwtafel	ayn vo^{ow}taaferl
frying pan	een koekepan	ayn kookerpahn
grill	een braadrooster	ayn braatroasterr
grill spits	braadspitten	braatspitern
groundsheet	een grondzeil	ayn ghrontzaiyl
hammer	een hamer	ayn haamerr
hammock	een hangmat	ayn hahngmahr
haversack	een proviandtas	ayn proaveeyahnttahss
ice-bag	een ijszak	ayn aiysszahk
kerosene	petroleum	paytroaleeyurm
kettle	een ketel	ayn kayterl
knapsack	een ransel	ayn rahntserl
lamp	een lamp	ayn lahmp
lantern	een lantaarn	ayn lahntaarn
matches	lucifers	lewsseefehrs
mattress	een matras	ayn maatrahss
methylated spirits	brandspiritus	brahntspeereeturss
mosquito repellent	muggenolie	murghernoalee
nails	spijkers	spaiykerrss
pail	een emmer	ayn ehmmerr
paraffin	petroleum	paytroaleeyurm

penknife	een zakmes	ayn zahkmehss
picnic case	een picknickmand	ayn piknikmahnt
plastic bags	plastic zakjes	plehsteek zahkyerss
pot	een pot	ayn pot
primus stove	een primus	ayn preemurss
rope	een touw	ayn too°ʷw
rucksack	een rugzak	ayn rurghzahk
saucepan	een pan	ayn pahn
scissors	een schaar	ayn skhaar
screwdriver	een schroevedraaier	ayn skhrooverdraayerr
sheath knife	een dolkmes	ayn dolkmehss
sleeping bag	een slaapzak	ayn slaapzahk
stewpan	een braadpan	ayn braatpahn
string	een touw	ayn too°ʷ
table	een tafel	ayn taaferl
tent	een tent	ayn tehnt
tent peg	een haring	ayn haaring
tent pole	een tentstok	ayn tehntstok
thermos flask (bottle)	een thermosfles	ayn tehrmosflehss
tin opener	een blikopener	ayn blikoapenerr
tongs	een nijptang	ayn naiyptahng
torch	een zaklantaarn	ayn zahklahntaarn
water carrier	een waterzak	ayn ᐯaaterrzahk
wood alcohol	brandspiritus	brahntspeereeeturss

SHOPPING GUIDE

Crockery

beakers	bekers	baykerrss
cups	kopjes	kopyerss
mugs	kroezen	kroozern
plates	borden	bordern
saucers	schoteltjes	skhoaterltyerss
tumblers	bekerglazen	baykerrghlaazern

Cutlery

forks	vorken	vorkern
knives	messen	mehssern
spoons	lepels	layperlss
teaspoons	theelepeltjes	taylayperltyerss
(made of) plastic	(van) plastic	(vahn) plehsteek
(made of) stainless steel	(van) roestvrij staal	(vahn) roostvraiy staal

Chemist's—Drugstore

Chemists in Holland usually carry most of the goods you'll find in Britain or the U.S.A. The sign denoting a pharmacy is *Apotheek* (ahpoa**tayk**). In the window of an *apotheek*, you'll see a notice telling you where the nearest all-night chemist's is located.

For perfume, cosmetics and toilet articles you'll have to go to a *drogisterij* (droaghister**raiy**)—drugstore, or non-dispensing chemist's.

This section is divided into two parts:

1. Medicine, first-aid, etc.
2. Toilet articles, cosmetics, etc.

General

Where's the nearest (all-night) chemist's?	**Waar is de dichtst-bijzijnde (dienst-doende) apotheek?**	Vaar iss der dikhtst-baiyzaiynder (deenst-doonder) ahpoa**tayk**
What time does the chemist's open/close?	**Hoe laat gaat de apotheek open/dicht?**	hoo laat ghaat der ahpoa**tayk** oapern/dikht

1. Medicines—First-aid

I want something for...	**Ik wil iets tegen ... hebben.**	ik vil eets tayghern ... hehbern
a cold	**verkoudheid**	verrko^{ow}thaiyt
a cough	**hoesten**	hoostern
hay fever	**hooikoorts**	hoa^{ee}koarts
a hangover	**een kater**	ayn kaaterr
insect bites	**insektenbeten**	insehkternbaytern
sunburn	**zonnebrand**	zonnerbrahnt
travel sickness	**wagenziekte**	vaaghernzeekter
an upset stomach	**indigestie**	indeeghehstee
Can I get it without a prescription?	**Kan ik het zonder recept krijgen?**	kahn ik heht zonderr rersehpt kraiyghern
Do I have to wait?	**Moet ik erop wachten?**	moot ik ehrop vahkhtern
When should I come back?	**Wanneer zal ik terugkomen?**	vahnayr zahl ik terrurgh-koamern

FOR DOCTOR, see page 162

Can I have a/an some…?	Mag ik … van u hebben?	mahkh ik … vahn ew hehbern
antiseptic cream	antiseptische crème	ahnteesehpteesser krehm
aspirin	aspirine	ahspeereener
bandage	verband	verrbahnt
calcium tablets	calciumtabletten	kahlseeyurmtaablehtern
clinical thermometer	een koorts-thermometer	ayn koartstehrmoamayterr
contraceptives	voorbehoedmiddelen	voarberhootsmidderlern
corn plasters	likdoornpleisters	likdoarnplaiysterrss
cotton wool	watten	√ahtern
cough syrup	een hoestdrank	ayn hoostdrahnk
crêpe bandage	een zwachtelverband	ayn z√ahkhterlverrbahnt
diabetic lozenges	tabletten voor diabetici	taablehtern voar deeyaabayteessee
disinfectant	een ontsmettingsmiddel	ayn ontsmehtingsmidderl
ear drops	oordruppels	oardrurperlss
eye drops	oogdruppels	oaghdrurperlss
first-aid kit	een eerste-hulp trommel	ayn ayrster-hurlp tromerl
gargle	gorgeldrank	ghorgherldrahnk
gauze bandage	een gaasverband	ayn ghaassverrbahnt
insect repellent	een insektenwerend middel	ayn insehktern√ayrernt midderl
iodine	jodium	yoadeeyurm
laxative	laxeermiddel	lahksayrmidderl
lint	pluksel	plurkserl
nose drops	neusdruppels	nursdrurperlss
plasters	pleisters	plaiysterrss
sanitary napkins	maandverband	maantverrbahnt
sedative	pijnstillend middel	paiynstillernt midderl
sleeping pills	slaappillen	slaappillern
tampons	tampons	tahmponss
throat lozenges	tabletten voor de keel	taablehtern voar der kayl
tranquillizers	kalmerende middelen	kahlmayrernder midderlern

VERGIF	POISON
ALLEEN VOOR UITWENDIG GEBRUIK	FOR EXTERNAL USE ONLY

SHOPPING GUIDE

2. Toilet articles—Cosmetics

I'd like a/an/	Ik zou graag	ik zoᵒʷ ghraakh ...
some...	willen hebben.	Villern hehbern
acne cream	een acne zalf	ayn ahknay zahlf
after shave lotion	een after shave lotion	ayn "after-shave" loashern
astringent	een lotion met samentrekkende werking	ayn loashern meht saamerntrehkernder Vehrking
bath salts	badzout	bahtzoᵒʷt
Cologne	een eau de cologne	ayn oa der kolloñ
cream	een crème	ayn krehm
for dry/normal/ greasy skin	voor een droge/ normale/vette huid	voar ayn droagher normaaler/vehter hurᵒʷt
cleansing cream	een cleansing crème	ayn kleensing krehm
foundation cream	een basiscrème	ayn baaserskrehm
foot cream	een voetcrème	ayn vootkrehm
hand cream	een handcrème	ayn hahntkrehm
moisturizing cream	een vochthoudende crème	ayn vokhthoᵒʷdernder krehm
night cream	een nachtcrème	ayn nahkhtkrehm
cuticle cream	een nagelriem crème	ayn naagherlreem krehm
deodorant	een deodorans	ayn dayoadoarahnss
emery board	een kartonnen nagelvijl	ayn kahrtonnern naagherlvaiyl
eye pencil	een wenkbrauwpotlood	ayn Vehnkbroᵒʷpotloat
eye shadow	een oogschaduw	ayn oaghskhaadewᵒᵒ
face pack	een gezichtsmasker	ayn gherzikhtsmahskerr
face powder	poeder	pooderr
lipstick	een lippenstift	ayn lippernstift
make-up bag	een make-up tasje	ayn maykurp tahsher
make-up remover pads	make-up remover pads	maykurp reemooverr pehds
nail brush	een nagelborsteltje	ayn naagherlborsterltyer
nail clippers	een nagelschaartje	ayn naagherlskhaartyer
nail file	een nagelvijl	ayn naagherlvaiyl
nail polish	nagellak	naagherllahk
nail polish remover	een nagellak remover	ayn naagherllahk reemooverr
nail scissors	een nagelschaartje	ayn naagherlskhaartyer
paper handkerchiefs	papieren zakdoekjes	paapeerern zahkdookyerss
perfume	parfum	pahrfurm

powder	poeder	pooderr
powder puff	een poederdons	ayn pooderrdonss
razor	een scheermes	ayn skhayrmehss
razorblades	scheermesjes	skhayrmehsherss
rouge	een rouge	ayn roozher
cream/powder	crème/poeder	krehm/pooderr
shaving brush	een scheerkwast	ayn skhayrkvahst
shaving cream	een scheercrème	ayn skhayrkrehm
shaving soap	een scheerzeep	ayn skhayrzayp
soap	zeep	zayp
sponge	een spons	ayn sponss
sun tan oil/cream	een zonnebrandolie/	ayn zonnerbrahntoalee/
	-crème	-krehm
talcum powder	talkpoeder	tahlkpooderr
tissues	kleenex-tissues	kleenehks-tisshooss
toilet paper	toiletpapier	tvaalehtpaapeer
toothbrush	een tandenborstel	ayn tahndenborsterl
toothpaste	tandpasta	tahntpahstaa
tweezers	een pincet	ayn pinseht

For your hair

bobby pins	haarspelden	haarspehldern
brush	een borstel	ayn borsterl
comb	een kam	ayn kahm
curlers	haarrollers	haarrollerrss
dry shampoo	droogshampoo	droaghshahmpoa
dye	verf	vehrf
grips	schuifjes	skhurewfyerss
lacquer	haarlak	haarlahk
setting lotion	een haarversteviger	ayn haarverrstayvergherr
shampoo	shampoo	shahmpoa
for dry/greasy	voor droog/vet	voar droakh/veht
hair	haar	haar
for dandruff	tegen roos	tayghern roass

For the baby

babyfood	babyvoeding	babyvooding
bib	een slabbetje	ayn slahbertyer
dummy (comforter)	een fopspeen	ayn fopspayn
feeding bottle	een zuigfles	ayn zurewghflehss
paper nappies	wegwerp-luiers	vehghvehrp-lurewyerss
(diapers)		
plastic nappy	plastic broekjes	plehsteek brookyerss
holders		
teat	een speen	ayn spayn

SHOPPING GUIDE

Clothing

If you want to buy something specific, prepare yourself in advance. Look at the list of clothing on page 117. Get some idea of the colour, material and size you want. They're listed on the next few pages.

General

I'd like ... for a 10-year-old boy.	**Ik wil graag een ... voor een jongen van 10 jaar.**	ik vil ghraakh ayn ... voar ayn yongern vahn 10 yaar
It's for a 4-year-old girl.	**Het is voor een meisje van 4 jaar.**	heht iss voar ayn maiysher vahn 4 yaar
I want something like this.	**Ik wil iets dergelijks hebben.**	ik vil eets dehrgherlerks hehbern
I like the one in the window.	**Die in de etalage bevalt mij.**	dee in der aytaalaazher bervahlt maiy
How much is that per metre?	**Hoeveel kost het per meter?**	hoovayl kost heht pehr mayterr

1 centimetre	= 0.39 inch	1 inch	= 2.54 cm
1 metre	= 39.37 inch	1 foot	= 30.5 cm
10 metres	= 32.81 ft	1 yard	= 0.91 m

Colour

I want something in...	**Ik wil iets in het ... hebben.**	ik vil eets in heht ... hehbern
I want a darker/lighter shade.	**Ik wil het iets donkerder/lichter hebben.**	ik vil heht eets donkerrderr/likhterr hehbern
I want something to match this.	**Ik wil iets dat hierbij past hebben.**	ik vil eets daht heerbaiy pahst hehbern
I don't like the colour.	**De kleur bevalt mij niet.**	der klurr bervahlt maiy neet
I'd like it to be the same colour as...	**Ik wil het graag in dezelfde kleur hebben als...**	ik vil heht ghraakh in derzehlfder klurr hehbern ahlss

FOR CONVERSION TABLES, see pages 185–186

SHOPPING GUIDE

black	zwart	z√ahrt
blue	blauw	blo^{ow}
navy blue	marine-blauw	maareener blo^{ow}
brown	bruin	brur^{ew}n
fawn	lichtbruin	likhtbrur^{ew}n
cream	crème	krehm
green	groen	ghroon
emerald	smaragdgroen	smaarahghtghroon
olive	olijfgroen	oalaiyfghroon
grey	grijs	ghraiyss
mauve	lila	leelaa
orange	oranje	oarahñer
pink	rose	rozer
red	rood	roat
crimson	karmozijnrood	kahrmoazaiynroat
purple	paars	paarss
rust	roestkleurig	roostklurrerkh
scarlet	scharlakenrood	skhahrl<i>aa</i>kernroat
silver	zilver	zilverr
turquoise	turkoois	turrkoa^{ee}ss
violet	violet	veeyoalent
white	wit	√it
yellow	geel	ghayl
golden	goudkleurig	gho^{ow}tklurrergh
lemon	citroengeel	seetroonghayl
light	licht	likht
dark	donker	donkerr

zonder motief	gestippeld	gestreept	geruit	met een motief
(zonderr moateef)	(gherstipperlt)	(gherstraypt)	(gherrur^{ew}t)	(meht ayn moateef)

Material

Do you have anything in …?	Hebt u iets in …?	hehpt ew eets in
I want something thinner.	Ik wil iets dunners hebben.	ik √il eets durnerrss hehbern
Do you have any better quality?	Hebt u een betere kwaliteit?	hehpt ew ayn bayterrer k√aaleetaiyt

What's it made of?	**Welke stof is het?**	**ᵛehlker stof iss heht
cambric	**batist**	baatist
camel-hair	**kameelhaar**	kaamaylhaar
corduroy	**ribfluweel**	ripflewᵛayl
cotton	**katoen**	kaatoon
crêpe	**krip**	krip
denim	**gekeperd katoen**	gherkaypert kaatoon
felt	**vilt**	vilt
flannel	**flanel**	flaanehl
gabardine	**gabardine**	ghaabahrdeener
lace	**kant**	kahnt
leather	**leer**	layr
linen	**linnen**	linnern
nylon	**nylon**	naiylon
pique	**piqué**	peekay
poplin	**popeline**	poaperleener
rubber	**rubber**	rurberr
rayon	**kunstzijde**	kurnstzaiyder
silk	**zijde**	zaiyder
suède	**suède**	sewehder
taffeta	**tafzij**	tahfzaiyder
terrycloth	**badstof**	bahtstof
tulle	**tule**	tewler
velvet	**fluweel**	flewᵛayl
velveteen	**katoenfluweel**	kaatoonflewᵛayl
wool	**wol**	ᵛol
worsted	**kamgaren**	kahmghaarern

Can it be...?	**Kan het ... worden?**	kahn heht ... ᵛordern
dry-cleaned	**gestoomd**	gherstoamt
hand-washed	**met de hand ge-wassen**	meht der hahnt gherᵛahsserr
machine-washed	**in de machine gewassen**	in der maasheener gherᵛahssern

Is it...?	**is het...?**	iss heht
colourfast	**kleurecht**	klurrehkht
pure cotton	**100%-katoen**	honderrt proasehnt kaatoon
shrink resistant	**krimpvrij**	krimpvraiy
synthetic	**synthetisch**	sintayteess
wash and wear	**no-iron**	"no-iron"
wrinkle resistant	**kreukvrij**	krurkvraiy

Size

In Europe sizes vary somewhat from country to country, so the following must be taken as an approximate guide.

Ladies

Dresses/Suits						
American	8	10	12	14	16	18	20
British	30	32	34	36	38	40	42
Continental	36	38	40	42	44	46	48

Stockings							Shoes			
American } British	8	8½	9	9½	10	10½	6	7	8	9
							4½	5½	6½	7½
Continental	0	1	2	3	4	5	37	38	40	41

Gentlemen

Suits/Overcoats							Shirts			
American } British	36	38	40	42	44	46	15	16	17	18
Continental	46	48	50	52	54	56	38	41	43	45

Shoes									
American } British	5	6	7	8	8½	9	9½	10	11
Continental	38	39	41	42	43	43	44	44	45

My size is 38.	**Ik heb maat 38.**	ik hehp maat 38
I don't know the Dutch sizes.	**Ik ken de Neder-landse maten niet.**	ik kehn der nayderrlahnteer maatern neet

A good fit?

Can I try it on?	**Kan ik het aan-passen?**	kahn ik heht aanpahssern
Where's the fitting room?	**Waar is de pas-kamper?**	Vaar iss der pahskaamerr
Is there a mirror?	**Is er een spiegel?**	iss ehr ayn speegherl
Does it fit?	**Past het?**	pahst heht

FOR NUMBERS, see page 175

SHOPPING GUIDE

It fits very well.	**Het past uitstekend.**	heht pahst ur^{ew}tstaykernt
It doesn't fit.	**Het past niet.**	heht pahst neet
It's too...	**Het is te...**	heht iss ter
short/long	**kort/lang**	kort/lahng
tight/loose	**nauw/wijd**	noow/√aiyt
How long will it take to alter?	**Hoe lang duurt het om het te vermaken?**	hoo lahng dewrt heht om heht ter verrmaakern

Shoes

I'd like a pair of...	**Ik wil graag een paar ... hebben.**	ik √il ghraakh ayn paar ... hehbern
shoes/sandals	**schoenen/sandalen**	skhoonern/sahndaalern
boots/slippers	**laarzen/pantoffels**	laarzern/pahntofferlss
These are too...	**Deze zijn te...**	dayzer zaiyn ter
narrow/wide	**nauw/wijd**	no^{ow}/√aiyt
large/small	**groot/klein**	ghroat/klaiyn
They pinch my toes.	**Ze knellen aan de tenen.**	zer knehlern aan der taynern
Do you have a larger/smaller size?	**Hebt u een grotere/kleinere maat?**	hehpt ew ayn ghroaterer/klaiynerer maat
Do you have the same in ...?	**Hebt u dezelfde in het ...?**	hehpt ew derzahlfder in heht ...
brown/beige	**bruin/beige**	brur^{ew}n/behzher
black/white	**zwart/wit**	z√ahrt/√it
leather/rubber	**leer/rubber**	layr/rurberr
suede/cloth	**suède/linnen**	sewehder/linnern

Shoe repairs

Can you repair these shoes?	**Kunt u deze schoenen maken?**	kurnt ew dayzer skhoonern maakern
Can you sew this up?	**Kunt u dit stikken?**	kurnt ew dit stikkern
I'd like it/them completely resoled and heeled.	**Ik wil er graag nieuwe zolen en hakken op hebben.**	ik √il ehr ghraakh nee^{oo}√er zoalern ehn hahkern op hehbern
When will they be ready?	**Wanneer zijn ze klaar?**	√ahnayr zaiyn zer klaar

Clothes and accessories

I'd like a/an/some...	Ik wil graag ... hebben	ik √il ghraakh ... hehbern
anorak	een anorak	ayn ahnoarahk
blouse	een blouse	ayn bloozer
bra	een beha	ayn bayhaa
braces	een paar bretels	ayn paar brertehlss
briefs	een slipje	ayn slipyer
cap	een pet	ayn peht
cardigan	een vest	ayn vehst
children's clothes	kinderkleren	kinderrklayrern
coat	een jas	ayn yahss
dinner jacket	een smoking	ayn smoaking
dress	een jurk	ayn yurrk
dressing gown	een kamerjas	ayn kaamerryahss
evening dress (woman's)	een avondjurk	ayn aavontyurrk
frock	een jurk	ayn yurrk
fur coat	een bontjas	ayn bontyahss
garters (Am.)	een paar jarretels	ayn paar yahrrertehlss
girdle	een ceintuur	ayn sehntewr
gloves	een paar hand-schoenen	ayn paar hahntskhoonern
handbag	een handtas	ayn hahnttahss
handkerchief	een zakdoek	ayn zahkdook
hat	een hoed	ayn hoot
jacket	een jasje	ayn yahsyer
jeans	een spijkerbroek	ayn spaiykerrbrook
jersey	een trui	ayn trur√ew
jumper	een trui	ayn trur√ew
nightdress	een nachtjapon	ayn nahkhtyaapon
overalls	een overal	ayn oaverrahl
panties	een slipje	ayn slipyer
pants	een lange broek	ayn lahnger brook
pants suit	een broekpak	ayn brookpahk
panty-girdle	een step-in broekje	ayn stehpin brookyer
pyjamas	een pyjama	ayn peeyaamaa
raincoat	een regenjas	ayn rayghernyahss
scarf	een sjaal	ayn shaal
shirt	een overhemd	ayn oaverrhehmt
shoes	een paar schoenen	ayn paar skhoonern
shorts	een short	ayn short
skirt	een rok	ayn rok
slip	een onderjurk	ayn onderryurrk
socks	een paar sokken	ayn paar sokkern

sports jacket	een sportjasje	ayn **sport**yahssher
stockings	een paar kousen	ayn paar **ko**ᵒʷsern
suit (man's)	een kostuum	ayn kostewm
suit (woman's)	een mantelpakje	ayn **mahn**terlpahkyer
suspenders (Am.)	een paar bretels	ayn paar brer**tehl**ss
suspenders (Br.)	een paar jarretels	ayn paar yahrrer**tehl**ss
sweater	een trui	ayn trurᵉʷ
tie	een stropdas	ayn **strop**dahss
tights	een maillot	ayn **maa**yoa
top coat	een overjas	ayn **oa**verryahss
trousers	een lange broek	ayn **lahn**ger brook
umbrella	een paraplu	ayn paaraa**plew**
underpants (men)	een onderbroek	ayn **onder**brook
undershirt	een hemd	ayn hehmt
underwear	ondergoed	**onder**rghoot
vest (Am.)	een herenvest	ayn **hayr**ernvehst
vest (Br.)	een hemd	ayn hehmt
waistcoat	een vest	ayn vehst

belt	een ceintuur	ayn sehn**tewr**
buckle	een gesp	ayn ghehsp
button	een knoop	ayn knoap
collar	een kraag	ayn kraakh
elastic	een elastiek	ayn aylah**steek**
lining	een voering	ayn **voor**ing
pocket	een zak	ayn zahk
push-button	een drukknoop	ayn **drurk**-knoap
ribbon	een lint	ayn lint
safetypin	een veiligheidsspeld	ayn **vai**ylerghhaiytsspehlt
zip (zipper)	een ritssluiting	ayn **rits**slurᵉʷting

And for the beach:

bathing cap	een badmuts	ayn **baht**murtss
bath robe	een badjas	ayn **baht**yahss
straw hat	een strohoed	ayn **stroa**hoot
swimsuit	een badpak	ayn **baht**pahk
towel	een badhanddoek	ayn **baht**hahndook
trunks	een zwembroek	ayn z**v**ehmbrook

And for those handy with the needle:

crochet hook	een haakpen	ayn **haak**pehn
knitting needles	breinaalden	**braiy**naaldern
needle	een naald	ayn naalt
thimble	een vingerhoed	ayn **vinger**rhoot
thread	een draad	ayn draat

Electrical appliances and accessories—Records

The standard voltage in Holland and Belgium is 220 volts
A.C. However, plugs have different types of pins and you
may have to get a special adaptor in order to be able to use
your electrical appliances.

What's the voltage?	**Wat is de voltage?**	ѵaht iss der voltaazher
I'd like an adaptor.	**Ik wil graag een ver-loopstekker hebben.**	ik ѵil ghraakh ayn verrloapstehkerr hehbern
Do you have a battery for this?	**Hebt u een batterij hiervoor?**	hehpt ew ayn bahterraiy heervoar
This is broken. Can you repair it?	**Dit is kapot. Kunt u het repareren?**	dit iss kaapot. kurnt ew heht raypaarayrern
When will it be ready?	**Wanneer is het klaar?**	ѵahnayr iss heht klaar
I'd like a/an/some...	**Ik wil graag ... hebben.**	ik ѵil ghraakh ... hehbern

amplifier	**een versterker**	ayn verrstehrkerr
battery	**een batterij**	ayn bahterraiy
bulb	**een (gloei)lamp**	ayn (ghloo**)lahmp
hair dryer	**een haardroger**	ayn haardroagherr
iron	**een strijkijzer**	ayn straiykaiyzerr
travelling iron	**een reisstrijkijzer**	ayn raiysstraiykaiyzerr
lamp	**een lamp**	ayn lahmp
percolator	**een koffiezet-apparaat**	ayn koffeezehtahpaaraat
plug	**een stekker**	ayn stehkerr
adaptor plug	**een verloop-stekker**	ayn verrloapstehkerr
portable ...	**een draagbare ...**	ayn draaghbaarer
radio	**een radio**	ayn raadeeyoa
car radio	**een autoradio**	ayn o**toaraadeeyoa
record player	**een platenspeler**	ayn plaaternspaylerr
shaver	**een scheerapparaat**	ayn skhayrahpaaraat
speakers	**een paar luid-sprekers**	ayn paar lur**tspraykerrss
tape recorder	**een bandrecorder**	ayn bahntreekorderr
cassette tape recorder	**een cassette-recorder**	ayn kahssehterreekorderr
television	**een televisie**	ayn taylerveezee
colour television	**een kleurentele-visie**	ayn klurrerntaylerveezee
transformator	**een transformator**	ayn trahnsformaator

SHOPPING GUIDE

Music shop

Do you have any records/cassettes by…?	**Hebt u platen/ cassettes van …?**	hehpt ew plaatern/ kahssehterss vahn
Can I listen to this record/cassette?	**Kan ik deze plaat/ cassette even horen?**	kahn ik dayzer plaat/ kahssehter ayvern hoarern
I want a new stylus.	**Ik wil graag een nieuwe grammo-foonnaald hebben.**	ik vil ghraakh ayn nee°°ver ghrahmoafoan-naalt hehbern

L.P. (33 rpm)	**een langspeelplaat**	ayn lahngspaylplaat
single (45 rpm)	**een 45-toeren plaat**	ayn 45-toorern plaat
mono/stereo	**mono/stereo**	moanoa/stayreeoa

chamber music	**kamermuziek**	kaamerrmewzeek
classical music	**klassieke muziek**	klahsseeker mewzeek
folk music	**folkloristische muziek**	folkloaristeesser mewzeek
instrumental music	**instrumentale muziek**	instrewmehntaalerr mewzeek
jazz	**jazz**	jazz
light music	**lichte muziek**	likhter mewzeek
orchestral music	**orkestmuziek**	orkehstmewzeek
pop music	**popmuziek**	popmewzeek

Hairdresser's—Beauty salon

Is there a ladies' hairdresser/beauty salon in the hotel?	**Is er een dameskapper/schoonheidssalon in het hotel?**	iss ehr ayn **daa**merskahperr/**skhoan**haiytssaalon in heht **hoatehl**
Can I make an appointment for sometime on Thursday?	**Kan ik een afspraak voor donderdag maken?**	kahn ik ayn **ahf**spraak voar **donderr**dahkh **maa**kern
I'd like it shampooed and set.	**Ik wil het graag laten wassen en watergolven.**	ik **v**il heht **ghraakh laatern **v**ahssern ehn **v**aaterrgholvern

in a bun	**in een knot**	in ayn knot
a cut	**geknipt**	gherknipt
with a fringe (bangs)	**met pony**	meht **pon**nee
a permanent wave	**met permanent**	meht pehrmaa**nehnt**
with ringlets	**met krulletjes**	meht **krul**lertyerss
a re-style	**een nieuw kapsel**	ayn nee°° **kahp**serl

I want a...	**Ik wil...**	ik **v**il
blow-dry	**een brushing**	ayn "brushing"
colour rinse	**een kleurspoeling**	ayn **klurr**spooling
dye	**een haarverf**	ayn **haar**vehrf
setting lotion	**een haarversteviger**	ayn haarverr**stay**vergherr
shampoo for dry/greasy/dyed hair	**shampoo voor droog/vet/geverfd haar**	shampoa voar droakh/veht/gher**vehrft** haar
touch-up	**de wortels laten bijkleuren**	der **v**orterlss **laa**tern **baiy**klurrern

Do you have a colour chart?	**Hebt u een kleurenkaart?**	hehpt ew ayn **klurr**rernkaart
I don't want any hairspray.	**Ik wil geen haarlak.**	ik **v**il ghayn **haar**lahk
I want a...	**Ik wil een...**	ik **v**il ayn
face-pack	**gezichtsmasker**	gher**zikhts**mahskerr
manicure	**manicure**	maa**nee**kewrer
pedicure	**pedicure**	**pay**deekewrer

Under the hair-dryer, you might want to say:

It's too hot.	**Het is te heet.**	heht iss ter hayt
A bit warmer/colder, please.	**Iets warmer/kouder, alstublieft.**	eets **v**ahrmerr/ko°°derr ahlstew**bleeft**

FOR TIPPING, see page 1

Barber's

I don't speak Dutch very well.	**Ik spreek niet zo goed nederlands.**	ik sprayk neet zoa ghoot nayderrlahnts
I'm in a hurry.	**Ik heb haast.**	ik hehp haast
I want a haircut, please.	**Ik wil graag mijn haar laten knippen.**	ik vil ghraakh maiyn haar laatern knippern
I'd like a shave.	**Ik wil mij laten scheren.**	ik vil maiy laatern skhayrern
Cut it short, please.	**Knipt u het kort, alstublieft.**	knipt ew heht kort ahlstewbleeft
Not too short.	**Niet te kort.**	neet ter kort
A razor cut, please.	**Met het mes, alstublieft.**	meht heht mehss ahlstewbleeft
Don't use the clippers.	**Niet met de tondeuse, alstublieft.**	neetmeht der tondurzer ahlstewbleeft
Just a trim, please.	**Alleen bijknippen, alstublieft.**	ahlayn baiyknippern ahlstewbleeft
That's enough off.	**Zo is het kort genoeg.**	zoa iss heht kort ghernookh
A little more off the...	**Nog iets korter...**	nokh eets korterr
back	**van achteren**	vahn akhterrern
neck	**in de nek**	in der nehk
sides	**aan de zijkanten**	aan der zaiykahntern
top	**bovenop**	boavernop
I'd like a hair lotion.	**Ik wil graag haarlotion.**	ik vil ghraakh een haarloashern
I don't want any oil.	**Ik wil geen haarolie.**	ik vil ghayn haaroalee
Would you please trim my...?	**Wilt u mijn... wat bijknippen?**	vilt ew maiyn... vaht baiyknippern
beard	**baard**	baart
moustache	**snor**	snor
sideboards (sideburns)	**bakkebaarden**	bahkerbaardern
How much do I owe you?	**Hoeveel ben ik u schuldig?**	hoovayl behn ik ew skhurlderkh
This is for you.	**Dit is voor u.**	dit iss voar ew

FOR TIPPING, see page 1

Jeweller's—Watchmaker's

English	Dutch	Pronunciation
Can you repair this watch?	Kunt u dit horloge repareren?	kurnt ew dit horloazher raypahrayrern
It's going slow/ fast.	Het loopt achter/ voor.	heht loapt ahkhterr/ voar
The ... is broken.	... is kapot.	...iss kaapot
glass	het glas	heht ghlass
spring	de veer	der vayr
strap	het bandje	heht bahntyer
winder	het knopje	heht knopyer
I want this watch cleaned.	Ik wil dit horloge schoon laten maken.	ik vil dit horloazher skhoan laatern maakern
When will it be ready?	Wanneer is het klaar?	vahnayr iss heht klaar
Could I please see that?	Mag ik dat even zien, alstublieft?	mahkh ik daht ayven zeen ahlstewbleeft
I'm just looking around.	Ik kijk alleen even rond.	ik kaiyk ahlayn ayvern ront
I want a small present for...	Ik zoek een ca-deautje voor ...	ik zook ayn kaadoatyer voar
I don't want anything too expensive.	Het mag niet te duur zijn.	heht mahkh neet ter dewr zaiyn
I want something...	Ik wil iets ...	ik vil eets
better	beters	bayterss
cheaper	goedkopers	ghootkoaperrss
simpler	eenvoudigers	aynvoowdergherrss
Is this real silver?	Is dit echt zilver?	iss dit ehkht zilverr
Do you have anything in gold?	Hebt u iets in goud?	hehpt ew eets in ghoowt
How many carats is this?	Hoeveel karaats is dit?	hoovayl kaaraats iss dit

When you go to a jeweller's, you've probably got some idea of what you want beforehand. Look up the name of the article in the following lists, then find out what it is made of.

Jewellery—Watches

I'd like a/an/some...	Ik wil graag ... hebben.	ik vil ghraakh ... hehbern
bangle	een armring	ayn ahrmring
bracelet	een armband	ayn ahrmbahnt
brooch	een broche	ayn brosh
charm	een gelukshangertje	ayn gherlurkshahngerrtyer
cigarette case	een sigarettenkoker	ayn seeghaarehternkoakerr
cigarette lighter	een aansteker	ayn aanstaykerr
clip	een clip	ayn klip
clock	een klok	ayn klok
alarm clock	een wekker	ayn vehkerr
travelling clock	een reiswekkertje	ayn raiysvehkerrtyer
collar stud	een boordeknoop	ayn boarderknoap
cross	een kruis	ayn krur•wss
cuff links	een paar manchet- knopen	ayn paar mahnsheht- knoapern
cutlery	tafelzilver	taaferlzilverr
ear clips	een paar oorbellen	ayn paar oarbehlern
earrings	een paar oorbellen	ayn paar oarbehlern
jewel box	een bijouteriekistje	ayn beezhooterreekistyer
manicure set	een manicure-etui	ayn maaneekewrer aytwee
music box	een muziekdoos	ayn mewzeekdoass
napkin ring	een servetring	ayn sehrvehtring
necklace	een halsketting	ayn hahlskehting
pearl necklace	een parelsnoer	ayn paarerlsnoor
pendant	een hanger	ayn hahngerr
pin	een speld	ayn spehlt
powder compact	een poederdoos	ayn pooderrdoass
ring	een ring	ayn ring
diamond ring	een diamantring	ayn deeyaamahntring
engagement ring	een verlovingsring	ayn verrloavingsring
signet ring	een zegelring	ayn zaygherlring
wedding ring	een trouwring	ayn tro•wring
rosary	een rozenkrans	ayn roazernkrahnss
silverware	tafelzilver	taaferlzilverr
snuff box	een snuifdoos	ayn snur•wfdoass
tie clip	een dasclip	ayn dahsklip
tie pin	een dasspeld	ayn dahsspehlt
watch	een horloge	ayn horloazher
pocket watch	een zakhorloge	ayn zahkhorloazher
quartz watch	een kwartshor- loge	ayn kvahrtshorloazher
stopwatch	een stophorloge	ayn stophorloazher
wristwatch	een polshorloge	ayn polshorloazher

watch strap	**een horlogebandje**	ayn horloazherbahntyer
chain strap	**een ketting bandje**	ayn kehting bahntyer
leather strap	**een leren bandje**	ayn layrern bahntyer
What do you call this stone?	**Hoe heet deze steen?**	hoo hayt **dayzer** stayn

amber	**barnsteen**	bahrnstayn
amethyst	**amethist**	aamertist
diamond	**diamant**	deeyaamahnt
emerald	**smaragd**	smaarahkht
moonstone	**maansteen**	maanstayn
pearl	**parel**	paarerl
ruby	**robijn**	roabaiyn
sapphire	**saffier**	sahfeer
tigereye	**tijgeroog**	taiygherroakh
topaz	**topaas**	toapaas
turquoise	**turkoois**	turrkoa^{ee}ss

| What's it made of? | **Waar is het van gemaakt?** | Vaar iss heht vahn ghermaakt |

alabaster	**albast**	ahlbahst
brass	**geel koper**	ghayl **koaperr**
bronze	**brons**	bronss
chromium	**chroom**	ghroam
copper	**koper**	koaperr
coral	**koraal**	koaraal
crystal	**kristal**	kristahl
ebony	**ebbenhout**	ehbernho^{ow}t
enamel	**emaille**	aymahyer
glass	**glas**	ghlahss
cut glass	**geslepen glas**	gherslaypern ghlahss
gold	**goud**	gho^{ow}t
gold plate	**verguld**	verrghurlt
ivory	**ivoor**	eevoar
jade	**jade**	yaader
mother-of-pearl	**paarlemoer**	paarlermoor
pearl	**parel**	paarerl
pewter	**tin**	tin
platinum	**platina**	plaateenaa
silver	**zilver**	zilverr
silver plate	**verzilverd**	verrzilverrt
stainless steel	**roestvrij staal**	roostvraiy staal

Laundry—Dry cleaning

If your hotel doesn't have its own laundry or dry-cleaning service, ask the hotel receptionist:

Where's the nearest...?	Waar is de dichtst-bijzijnde...?	Vaar iss der dikhtst-baiyzaiynder
dry cleaner's	stomerij	stoamerraiy
launderette	wasserette	Vahsserrehter
laundry	wasserij	Vahsserraiy
I want these clothes...	Ik wil deze kleren laten...	ik Vil dayzer klayrern laatern
cleaned	stomen	stoamern
ironed	strijken	straiykern
pressed	persen	pehrsern
washed	wassen	Vahssern
When will it be ready?	Wanneer zijn ze klaar?	Vahnayr zaiyn zer klaar
I need it...	Ik heb ze ... nodig.	ik hehp zer ... noaderkh
today	vandaag	vahndaakh
tonight	vanavond	vahnaavont
tomorrow	morgen	morghern
before Friday	vóór vrijdag	voar vraiydahkh
Can you ... this?	Kunt u dit...?	kurnt ew dit
mend	repareren	raypaarayrern
patch	verstellen	verrstehlern
sew	naaien	naayern
Can you sew on this button?	Kunt u deze knoop aanzetten?	kurnt ew dayzer knoap aanzehtern
Can you get this stain out?	Kunt u deze vlek verwijderen?	kurnt ew dayzer vlehk verrVaiyderrern
Can this be invisibly mended?	Kan dit onzichtbaar gestopt worden?	kahn dit onzikhtbaar gherstopt Vordern
This isn't mine.	Dit is niet van mij.	dit iss neet vahn maiy
Is my laundry ready? You promised it for today.	Is mijn was klaar? U had het mij voor vandaag beloofd.	iss maiyn Vahss klaar? ew haht heht maiy voar vahndaakh berloaft

FOR DAYS OF THE WEEK, see page 181

Photography

I want an inexpensive camera.	**Ik wil een goedkoop fototoestel.**	ik vil ayn ghoot**koap** foa**toa**toostehl
Do you sell cine (movie) cameras?	**Verkoopt u filmtoestellen?**	verr**koapt** ew **film**toostehlern
May I have a prospectus?	**Mag ik een prospectus van u hebben?**	mahkh ik ayn pros**pehk**turss vahn ew **heh**bern
I would like to have some passport photos taken.	**Ik zou graag wat paspoortfoto's willen laten maken.**	ik zoo^{ºw} ghraakh vaht **pahs**poortfoatoass villern laatern maakern

Film

Film sizes aren't always indicated the same way in Europe as in the United States and Great Britain. Listed below you'll find some equivalents and translations.

I'd like a film for this camera.	**Ik wil graag een film voor dit toestel.**	ik vil ghraakh ayn film voar dit **too**stehl
black-and-white film	**een zwart-wit film**	ayn zvart-vit film
colour film	**een kleurenfilm**	ayn **klurr**ernfilm
colour slides	**een diarolletje**	ayn deeya**rol**ertyer
cartridge	**een kardoes**	ayn kahr**dooss**
cassette	**een cassette**	ayn kah**sseh**ter
roll of film	**een rolletje film**	ayn **rol**ertyer film
120	**een zes bij zes film**	ayn zehss baiy zehss film
127	**een vier bij vier film**	ayn veer baiy veer film
135	**een vierentwintig bij zesendertig film**	ayn veerehnt**vin**terkh baiy zehsehn**dehr**terkh film
8 mm	**een acht-millimeter film**	ayn ahkht**mee**leemayterr film
super 8	**een super-acht**	ayn sewperr ahkht
20/36 exposures	**met twintig/zesendertig opnamen**	meht t**vin**terkh/zehsehn**dehr**terkh opnaamern
this ASA/DIN number	**met dit ASA/DIN nummer**	meht dit aa-ehss-aa/din nurmerr
artificial light type	**voor kunstlicht**	voar **kurnst**likht
daylight type	**voor daglicht**	voar **dahgh**likht
fast	**snel**	snehl
fine grain	**fijnkorrelig**	faiyn**korr**erlerkh

Processing

How much do you charge for developing?	**Hoeveel kost het ontwikkelen?**	hoovayl kost heht ontvikkerlern
I want ... prints of each negative.	**Ik wil graag ... afdrukken van elk negatief.**	ik vil ghraakh ... ahfdrukkern vahn ehlker nayghaateef
Will you please enlarge this?	**Wilt u dit vergroten, alstublieft?**	vilt ew dit verrghroatern ahlstewbleeft
mat/glossy finish	**een matte/glanzende afdruk**	ayn mahtter/ghlahnzernder ahfdruk
with/without border	**met/zonder rand**	meht/zonderr rahnt

Accessories

I want a/some ...	**Ik wil graag...**	ik vil ghraakh
filter	**een filter**	ayn filterr
red/yellow	**rode/gele**	roader/ghayler
ultraviolet	**ultra-violette**	urltraa-veeyoalehter
flash bulbs	**een paar flitslampjes**	ayn paar flitslahmpyerss
flash cubes	**een paar flitskubes**	ayn paar flitskewberss
lens	**een lens**	ayn lehnss
lens cap	**een lensdop**	ayn lehnssdop
light meter	**een belichtingsmeter**	ayn berlikhtinghsmayterr
telephoto lens	**een telefoto lens**	ayn taylayfoatoa lehnss

Repairs

Can you repair this camera?	**Kunt u dit fototoestel repareren?**	kurnt ew dit foatoatoostehl raypaarayrern
The film is jammed.	**De film draait niet door.**	der film draaeet neet doar
There's something wrong with the...	**Er hapert iets aan...**	ehr haaperrt eets aan
exposure counter	**de opnameteller**	der opnaamertehlerr
film winder	**de terugspoelknop**	der terrughspoolknop
light meter	**de belichtingsmeter**	der berlikhtinghsmayterr
rangefinder	**de afstandsmeter**	der ahfstahntsmayterr
shutter	**de sluiter**	der slur°°terr
Could you make an estimate, please?	**Kunt u mij een prijsopgave geven, alstublieft?**	kurnt ew maiy ayn praiyssopghaaver ghayvern ahlstewbleeft

Provisions

Here's a basic list of food and drink that you might want on a picnic or for the occasional meal in your hotel room.

I'd like a/an/some...	Ik wil graag ... van u hebben.	ik vil ghraakh ... vahn ew hehbern
apple juice	appelsap	ahperlsahp
apples	appels	ahperlss
bananas	bananen	baanaanern
beer	bier	beer
biscuits (Br.)	beschuitjes	berskhur•ᵂtyerss
bread	een brood	ayn broat
butter	boter	boaterr
cheese	kaas	kaass
(grilled) chicken	een (gebakken) kip	ayn (gherbahkern) kip
chocolate	chocolade	shoakoalaader
coffee	koffie	koffee
instant coffee	instant koffie	instahnt koffee
cold cuts	vleeswaren	vlaysᚺaarern
cookies	koekjes	kookyerss
cream	room	roam
cucumber	een komkommer	ayn komkommerr
eggs	eieren	aiyyerrern
frankfurters	knakworstjes	knahkᚺorstyerss
gherkins	augurken	oᵒʷghurrkern
grapefruit	pompelmoes	pomperlmooss
grapefruit juice	pompelmoessap	pomperlmoossahp
ham	ham	hahm
hamburgers	hamburgers	hahmburrgherrss
ice-cream	ijs	aiyss
lemons	citroenen	seetroonern
lettuce	sla	slaa
liver sausage	leverworst	layverrᚺorst
milk	melk	mehlk
mineral water	mineraalwater	meenerraalᚺaaterr
mustard	mosterd	mosterrt
(olive) oil	(olijf)olie	(oalaiyf)oalee
oranges	sinaasappels	seenaasahperlss
orange juice	sinaasappelsap	seenaasahperlssahp
pepper	peper	payperr
potato crisps (chips)	chips	"chips"
potatoes	aardappels	aardahperlss
rolls	broodjes	broatyerss
salad	sla	slaa
salami	salami	saalaamee

salt	**zout**	zo°ʷt
sandwich	**een sandwich**	ayn "sandwich"
sausage	**een worst**	ayn Ʋorst
soft drink	**limonade**	leemoanaader
soup	**soep**	soop
spices	**specerijen**	spayserraiyyern
sugar	**suiker**	surᵉʷkerr
sweets	**snoep**	snoop
tea	**thee**	tay
tea bags	**theezakjes**	tayzahkyerss
tomatoes	**tomaten**	toamaatern
tomato juice	**tomatensap**	toamaaternsahp
wine	**wijn**	Ʋaiyn
yoghurt	**joghurt**	yokhurrt

And don't forget:

a bottle opener	**een flesopener**	ayn flehssoapernerr
a corkscrew	**een kurketrekker**	ayn kurrkertrehkerr
matches	**lucifers**	lewsseefehrss
(paper) napkins	**(papieren) servetjes**	(paapeerern) sehrvehtyerss
a tin (can) opener	**een blikopener**	ayn blikoapernerr

basket	**een mand**	ayn mahnd
bottle	**een fles**	ayn flehss
box	**een doos**	ayn doass
carton	**een karton**	ayn kahrton
glass	**een glas**	ayn ghlahss
packet	**een pakje**	ayn pahkyer
plastic bag	**een plastik zakje**	ayn plehsteek zahkyer
tube	**een tube**	ayn tewber

Weights and measures

1 kilogram or kilo (kg) = 1000 grams (g)

| 100 g = 3.5 oz. | ½ kg = 1.1 lb. |
| 200 g = 7.0 oz. | 1 kg = 2.2 lb. |

1 oz. = 28.35 g
1 lb. = 453.60 g

1 litre (l) = 0.88 imp. quarts = 1.06 U.S. quarts

| 1 imp. quart = 1.14 l | 1 U.S. quart = 0.95 l |
| 1 imp. gallon = 4.55 l | 1 U.S. gallon = 3.8 l |

Souvenirs

The best-known Dutch souvenirs include costumed dolls wooden shoes and blue pottery from Delft. Authentic Delft pottery also comprises white, red and multicoloured ceramics. Other high-quality products of Dutch arts and crafts are cut diamonds from Amsterdam, glass and crystal from Leerdam and silverware from Schoonhoven. In Belgium, you should look for lace, crystal and porcelain.

bulbs	**bloembollen**	bloombollern
cast-iron casseroles	**gietijzeren potten**	gheetaiyzerrern pottern
copperware	**koperwaren**	koaperr√aarern
crystal	**kristal**	kristahl
Delft earthenware	**Delfts aardewerk**	dehlfts aarder√ahrk
diamonds (cut)	**diamanten (ge-slepen)**	deeyaamahntern (gherslaypern)
dolls in local costumes	**poppen in kleder-dracht**	poppern in klayderr-drahkht
glass	**glas**	ghlahss
lace	**kant**	kahnt
pewter	**tin**	tin
silverware	**tafelzilver**	taaferlzilverr
tapestry	**een wandtapijt**	ayn √ahnttaapaiyt
wood carvings	**gesneden houten voorwerpen**	ghersnaydern hoᵒᵂtern voar√ehrpern
wooden shoes (clogs)	**een paar klompen**	ayn paar klompern

It may be best not to take bulbs out of the country yourself, since customs regulations concerning plants and bulbs are quite complex. However, Dutch flower bulb dealers are fully conversant with legal provisions and arrange shipments of bulbs all over the world.

There are also many typical Dutch sweets (candies) and items of confectionery you might wish to take back with you. Children will love *chocoladehagelslag*—shoakoa**laa**der**haag**herlslahkh (chocolate) on their bread. The spiced cakes from Groningen and Deventer as well as the Frisian *kruidkoek* are a real delight. And, finally, *Haagse hopjes* are considered the most famous of all Dutch sweets.

Tobacconist's

Cigarettes and tobacco are sold in *sigarenwinkels* (tobacconists'), supermarkets and a street kiosks.

As at home, cigarettes are generally referred to by their brand names. English and American cigarettes are available, but cigarettes produced in the Benelux countries (Holland, Belgium and Luxembourg) under special licence are very similar to American brands.

Give me a/some ..., please.	Geeft u me ..., alstublieft.	ghayft ew mer ... ahlstewbleeft
chewing tobacco	pruimtabak	prur^{ew}mtaabahk
cigars	een paar sigaren	ayn paar seeghaarern
box of cigars	een doosje sigaren	ayn doasyer seeghaarern
cigarette case	een sigarettenkoker	ayn seeghaarehternkoakerr
cigarette holder	een sigarettepijpje	ayn seeghaarehterpaipyer
cigarette lighter	een sigaretten-aansteker	ayn seeghaarehtern-aanstaykerr
cigarette paper	sigarettenpapier	seeghaarehternpaapeer
cigarettes	sigaretten	seeghaarehtern
packet of cigarettes	een pakje sigaretten	ayn pahkyer seeghaarehtern
flints	wat vuursteentjes	√aht vewrstayntyerss
lighter	een aansteker	ayn aanstaykerr
lighter fluid/gas	benzine/gas voor een aansteker	behnzeener/ghahss voar ayn aanstaykerr
matches	lucifers	lewsseefehrss
pipe	een pijp	ayn paiyp
pipe cleaners	pijpestokers	paiyperstoakerrss
pipe rack	een pijpenrek	ayn paiypernrehk
pipe tobacco	wat pijptabak	√aht paiyptaabahk
pipe tool	een pijpestopper	ayn paiyperstoakerrtyer
refill for a lighter	een vulling voor een aansteker	ayn vurling voar ayn . aanstaykerr
snuff	snuiftabak	snur^{ew}ftaabahk
tobacco pouch	een tabaksbuil	ayn taabahksbur^{ew}l
wick	een lont	ayn lont
Do you have any...?	Hebt u...?	hehpt ew
American/English cigarettes	Amerikaanse/ Engelse sigaretten	aamayreekaansser/ ehngerlsser seeghaarehtern
menthol cigarettes	menthol sigaretten	mehntol seeghaarehtern

I'll take two packets.	**Twee pakjes, alstublieft.**	t√ay pahkyers ahlstewbleeft
I'd like a carton.	**Een slof, alstublieft.**	ayn sloff ahlstewbleeft
A box of matches, please.	**Een doosje lucifers, alstublieft.**	ayn doasyer lewsseefehrss ahlstewbleeft

filter tipped	**met filter**	meht filterr
without filter	**zonder filter**	zonderr filterr
light tobacco	**lichte tabak**	likhter taabahk
dark tobacco	**donkere tabak**	donkerrer taabahk

While we're on the subject of cigarettes:

Would you like a cigarette?	**Wilt u een sigaret?**	√ilt ew ayn seeghaareht
Have one of mine.	**Neemt u er een van mij.**	naymt ew ehr ayn vahn maiy
Try one of these. They're very mild.	**Probeert u deze eens. Ze zijn heel licht.**	proabayrt ew dayzer aynss. zer zaiyn hayl likht
They're a bit strong.	**Ze zijn tamelijk zwaar.**	zer zaiyn taamerlerk z√aar

And if somebody offers you one?

Thank you.	**Dank u wel**	dahnk ew √ehl
No, thanks.	**Nee, dank u.**	nay dahnk
I don't smoke.	**Ik rook niet.**	ik roak neet
I've given it up.	**Ik rook niet meer.**	ik roak neet mayr

ROKEN SMOKERS	**ROKEN VERBODEN** NO SMOKING

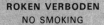

Your money: banks—currency

In Holland banks are open from 9 a.m. to 4 p.m., Monday to Friday, and sometimes in the evening too. The basic unit of currency in Holland is the *gulden*—**ghur**ldern (guilder), abbreviated to *f*, *fl* or, especially outside the country, *Hfl*. A guilder is divided into 100 *centen*—**sehn**tern (cents), Here are the different types of coins in circulation:

5 cents	een stuiver	ayn stur^{ew}verr
10 cents	een dubbeltje	ayn durberltyer
25 cents	een kwartje	ayn kⱽahrtyer
1 guilder	een gulden	ayn ghurldern
2.50 guilders	een rijksdaalder	ayn raiyksdaalderr

The different types of banknotes are:

5 guilders	vijf gulden	vaiyf ghurldern
10 guilders	tien gulden	teen ghurldern
25 guilders	vijfentwintig gulden	vaiyfehntⱽinterkh ghurldern
50 guilders	vijftig gulden	vaiyfterkh ghurldern
100 guilders	honderd gulden	honderrt ghurldern
1,000 guilders	duizend gulden	dur^{ew}zernt ghurldern

In Belgium the basic unit of currency is the *franc* (frahnk), divided into 100 *centimes* (sahn**tee**mern). There are coins of 50 centimes, 1, 5, 10 and 20 francs and banknotes of 50, 100, 500, 1,000 and 5,000 francs. Banks are open from 9 a.m. to 12.30 and from 2.30 p.m. to 3.30 p.m. (sometimes from 9 a.m. to 4 p.m.), Monday to Friday.

| Where's the nearest bank/currency exchange? | **Waar is de dichtstbijzijnde bank/het wisselkantoor?** | ⱽaar iss der dikhtstbaiyzaiynder bahnk/heht ⱽisserlkahntoar |

Where can I cash a traveller's cheque (check)?	Waar kan ik een reischeque inwisselen?	√aar kahn ik ayn raiysshehks in √isserlern
I want to change some dollars/pounds.	Ik wil graag wat dollars/ponden wisselen.	ik √il ghraakh √aht dollahrss/pondern √isserlern
What's the exchange rate?	Wat is de wissel-koers?	√aht iss der √isserlkoorss
What rate of commission do you charge?	Hoeveel provisie berekent u?	hoovayl proaveesee berraykernt ew
Can you cash a personal cheque?	Neemt u cheques aan?	naymt ew shehks aan
Here's my passport.	Hier is mijn pas-poort.	heer iss maiyn **pahs**poart
How long will it take to clear?	Hoe lang duurt de verificatie?	hoo lahng dewrt der vayreefeekaatsee
Can you wire my bank in London?	Kunt u naar mijn bank in London telegraferen?	kurnt ew naar maiyn bahnk in londern taylerghraa**fay**rern
I have...	Ik heb...	ik hehp
a letter of credit	een kredietbrief	ayn krer**deet**breef
an introduction from...	een introduktiebrief van...	ayn introa**durk**seebreef vahn
a credit card	een kredietkaart	ayn krer**deet**kaart
I'm expecting some money from New York. Has it arrived yet?	Ik verwacht geld uit New York. Is het al aange-komen?	ik verr√**ahkht** ghehlt ur^{ew}t "new york" iss heht ahl **aang**herkoamern
Please give me... notes (bills) and some small denomi-nations.	Geeft u mij ... biljet-ten en wat kleingeld, alstublieft.	ghayft ew maiy ... bily**eh**tern ehn √aht klaiyng**hel**t ahlstew**bleeft**
Give me ... large notes and the rest in small notes.	Geeft u mij ... in grote coupures en de rest in kleine cou-pures, alstublieft.	ghayft ew maiy ... in ghroater koopew**rerss** ehn der rehst in klaiyner koopew**rerss** ahlstew**bleeft**
Could you please check that again?	Kunt u dat nog eens controleren, alstublieft?	kurnt ew daht nokh aynss kontroa**lay**rern ahlstew**bleeft**

Depositing

I want to credit this to my account.	**Ik wil dit geld op mijn rekening storten.**	ik vil dit ghehlt op maiyn **raykerning stortern**
I want to credit this to Mr. ...'s account.	**Ik wil dit graag op de rekening van de Heer ... storten.**	ik vil dit ghraakh op der **raykerning** vahn der hayr **stortern**
Where should I sign?	**Waar moet ik tekenen?**	vaar moot ik **taykernern**

Currency converter

In a world of floating currencies, we can offer no more than this do-it-yourself chart. You can get a card showing current exchange rates from banks and travel agents.

	£	$
10 cents		
25 cents		
1 guilder		
10 guilders		
50 guilders		
100 guilders		
500 guilders		
1000 guilders		
10 Belgian francs		
50 Belgian francs		
100 Belgian francs		
250 Belgian francs		
500 Belgian francs		
1000 Belgian francs		

FOR NUMBERS, see page 175

At the post office

In Holland, post offices can be recognized by the letters *PTT (Post, Telegraaf, Telefoon)*. They are generally open from Monday to Friday between 8.30 a.m. and 5 p.m. On Saturdays, some post offices are open from 8.30 a.m. to noon. In Belgium opening hours are from 9 a.m. to 5 p.m.

Mailboxes *(brievenbussen)* in Holland are painted grey and red, while they are red in Belgium. The hours when mail is picked up are noted on the mailbox.

Where is the nearest post office?	**Waar is het dichtstbijzijnde postkantoor?**	∨aar iss heht dikhtstbaiyzaiynder postkahntoar
What time does the post office open/close?	**Hoe laat gaat het postkantoor open/dicht?**	hoo laat ghaat heht postkahntoar oapern/dikht
What window do I go to for stamps?	**Aan welk loket moet ik zijn voor postzegels?**	aan ∨ehlk loakeht moot ik zaiyn voar postzaygherlss
At which counter can I cash an international money order?	**Aan welk loket kan ik een internationale postwissel innen?**	aan ∨ehlk loakeht kahn ik ayn interrnahsyonaaler post∨isserl innern
I want some stamps.	**Ik wil een paar postzegels.**	ik ∨il ayn paar postzaygherlss
I want ... 30-cent stamps and ... 50-cent stamps.	**Ik wil graag ... postzegels van 30 cent en ... postzegels van 50 cent.**	if ∨il ghraakh ... postzaygherlss vahn 30 sehnt ehn ... postzaygherlss van 50 sehnt
What is the postage for a letter to Great Britain?	**Hoeveel moet er op een brief naar Engeland?**	hoovayl moot ehr op ayn breef naar ehngerlahnt
What is the postage for a postcard to the U.S.A.?	**Hoeveel moet er op een briefkaart naar de Verenigde Staten?**	hoovayl moot ehr op ayn breefkaart naar der verraynerghder staatern
Do all letters go airmail?	**Gaan alle brieven per luchtpost?**	ghaan ahler breevern pehr lurkhtpost

I want to send this parcel.	**Ik wil graag dit pakje versturen.**	ik **v**il ghraakh dit **pah**kyer verr**stew**rern
Where's the mailbox?	**Waar is de brievenbus?**	**v**aar iss de **bree**vern**burss**
I want to send this by ...	**Ik wil dit graag ... versturen.**	ik **v**il dit ghraakh ... verr**stew**rern
airmail	**per luchtpost**	pehr **lurkht**post
express (special delivery)	**per expresse**	pehr ehks**prehss**
registered mail	**aangetekend**	**aang**hertay**kernt**
Where's the poste restante (general delivery)?	**Waar is de poste restante?**	**v**aar iss der **poster** reh**stahn**ter
Is there any mail for me? My name is ...	**Is er post voor mij? Mijn naam is ...**	iss ehr post voar maiy? maiyn naam iss

POSTZEGELS	STAMPS
PAKJES	PARCELS
POSTWISSELS	MONEY ORDERS

Telegrams

Cables and telegrams are dispatched by the post office.

I want to send a telegram. May I have a form?	**Ik wil graag een telegram versturen. Mag ik een formulier, alstublieft?**	ik **v**il ghraakh ayn **tayler**ghrahm verr**stew**rern. mahgh ik ayn forme**wleer** ahlstew**bleeft**
How much is it per word?	**Hoeveel kost het per woord?**	**hoo**vayl kost heht pehr **v**oart
How long will a cable to Boston take?	**Hoe lang doet een telegram naar Boston erover?**	hoo lahng doot ayn **tayler**ghrahm naar **bostern** ehro**averr**
I'd like to reverse the charges.	**Ik wil het graag door de geadresseerde laten betalen.**	ik **v**il heht ghraakh doar der gheraadreh**ssay**rder **laatern** ber**taalern**
I'd like to send a night-letter.	**Ik zou graag een brief-telegram willen versturen.**	ik zoo**w** ghraakh ayn **breef**tayler**ghrahm v**illern verr**stew**rern

Telephoning

The telephone system is fully automatic in both Holland and Belgium, and direct calls can be made to most places in the world providing you have the correct prefix number of the relevant country and the area or dialling code (*netnummer*— **neht**nurmerr). Rates are considerably cheaper for long-distance calls made between 6 p.m. and 8 p.m. and during the weekend from 6 p.m. on Friday until 8 a.m. on Monday. Long-distance calls can be made from most telephone booths and all post offices. All public phones list directions for use in English.

General

Where's the telephone?	**Waar is de telefoon?**	ɣaar iss der taylerfoan
Where's the nearest telephone booth?	**Waar is de dichtst-bijzijnde tele-fooncel?**	ɣaar iss der dikhtst-baiyzaiynder tayler-foansehl
Could you give me some small change for the telephone?	**Kunt u mij wat kleingeld geven voor de telefoon?**	kurnt ew maiy ɣaht klaiyn-ghehlt ghayvern voar der taylerfoan
May I use your telephone?	**Mag ik uw tele-foon even gebrui-ken?**	mahkh ik ewɣ taylerfoan ayvern gherbrur^{ew}kern
Do you have a telephone directory for Amsterdam?	**Hebt u een tele-foonboek van Amsterdam?**	hehpt ew ayn taylerfoan-book vahn ahmsterrdahm
Can you help me get this number?	**Kunt u mij helpen om dit nummer te bereiken?**	kurnt ew maiy hehlpern om dit nurmerr ter berraiy-kern

Operator

Do you speak English?	**Spreekt u Engels?**	spraykt ew ehngerlss
Good morning, I want Amsterdam 123456.	**Goede morgen, ik wil graag nummer 123456 in Amster-dam.**	ghooder morghern ik ɣil ghraakh nurmerr 123456 in ahmsterrdahm

FOR NUMBERS, see page 175

| I want to place a personal (person-to-person) call. | **Ik wil graag een gesprek met voorbericht.** | ik vil ghraakh ayn ghersprehk meht voorberrikht |
| I want to reverse the charges. | **Ik wil telefoneren op kosten van de ontvanger.** | ik vil taylerfoanayrern op kostern vahn der ontvahngerr |

Speaking

Hello. This is ... speaking.	**Hallo. U spreekt met ...**	hahloa. ew spraykt meht
I want to speak to ...	**Ik wil graag ... spreken.**	ik vil ghraakh ... spraykern
I want extension ...	**Ik wil graag nummer ...**	ik vil ghraakh nurmerr
Is that ...?	**Spreek ik met ...?**	sprayk ik meht

Bad luck

| Operator, you gave me the wrong number. | **Juffrouw, u hebt mij verkeerd verbonden.** | yurfrow ew hehpt maiy verrkayrt verrbondern |
| Operator, we were cut off. | **Juffrouw, de telefoonverbinding werd verbroken.** | yurfrow der taylerfoanverrbinding vehrt verrbroakern |

Telephone alphabet

A	**Anna**	ahnaa	O	**Otto**	ottoa
B	**Bernard**	behrnahrt	P	**Pieter**	peeterr
C	**Cornelis**	kornayliss	Q	**Quadraat**	kvaadraat
D	**Dirk**	dirk	R	**Rudolf**	rewdolf
E	**Eduard**	aydewahrt	S	**Simon**	seemon
F	**Ferdinand**	fehrdeenant	T	**Teunis**	turewniss
G	**Gerard**	ghayrahrt	U	**Utrecht**	ewtrehkht
H	**Hendrik**	hehndrik	V	**Victor**	viktor
I	**Izaak**	eezahk	W	**Willem**	villerm
J	**Jan**	yahn	X	**Xantippe**	ksahntipper
K	**Karel**	kaarerl	IJ	**IJmuiden**	aiymurewdern
L	**Lodewijk**	loadervaiyk	Y	**Ypsilon**	eepserlon
M	**Marie**	maaree	Z	**Zaandam**	zaandahm
N	**Nico**	neeko			

| The connexion was bad. | **De verbinding was slecht.** | der verrbinding √ahss slehkht |
| Would you please try the number again? | **Wilt u dit nummer nog eens proberen, alstublieft?** | √ilt ew dit nurmerr nokh ayns proabayrern ahlstewbleeft |

Not there

When will he/she be back?	**Wanneer komt hij/ zij terug?**	√ahnayr komt haiy/zaiy terrurkh
Will you tell him/her I called? My name is...	**Wilt u hem/haar zeggen dat ik gebeld heb. Mijn naam is...**	√ilt ew hehm/haar zehghern daht ik gherbehlt hehp. maiyn naam iss
Would you ask him/her to call me?	**Wilt u hem/haar vragen mij terug te bellen?**	√ilt ew hehm/haar vraaghern maiy terrurgh ter behlern
Would you please take a message?	**Wilt u een bood- schap doorgeven, alstublieft?**	√ilt ew ayn boatskhahp doarghayvern ahlstewbleeft

Charges

| What was the cost of that call? | **Hoeveel heeft dit gesprek gekost?** | hoovayl hayft dit ghersprehk gherkost |
| I want to pay for the call. | **Ik wil graag het gesprek betalen.** | ik √il ghraakh heht ghersprehk bertaalern |

Er is telefoon voor u.	There's a telephone call for you.
Welk nummer belt u?	What number are you calling?
De lijn is bezet.	The line is engaged.
Er is geen gehoor.	There's no answer.
U bent verkeerd verbonden.	You've got the wrong number.
De telefoon is defekt.	The telephone is out of order.
Hij/Zij is er momenteel niet.	He's/She's out at the moment.
Zal ik het later nog eens proberen?	Shall I try again later?

The car

Filling stations

We'll start this section by considering your possible needs at a filling station. Most of them don't handle major repairs; but apart from providing you with fuel, they may be helpful in solving all kinds of minor problems.

Where's the nearest filling station?	**Waar is het dichtstbijzijnde benzinestation?**	Vaar iss heht dikhtstbaiyzaiynder behnzeenerstaasyon
I want 20 litres of petrol (gas), please.	**Twintig liter benzine, alstublieft.**	tvinterkh leeterr behnzeener ahlstewbleeft
Give me ... guilders' worth of standard/ premium.	**Voor ... gulden normaal/super.**	voar ... ghurldern normaal/sooperr
Fill it up, please.	**Vol, alstublieft.**	vol ahlstewbleeft
Please check the oil and water.	**Controleert u de olie en het water even, alstublieft?**	kontroalayrt ew der oalee ehn heht vaaterr ayvern ahlstewbleeft
Give me half a litre of oil.	**Een halve liter olie, alstublieft.**	ayn hahlver leeterr oalee ahlstewbleeft
Fill up the battery with distilled water.	**Vult u de accu even bij met gedistilleerd water.**	vurlt ew der ahkew ayvern baiy meht gherdisteelayrt vaaterr
Check the brake fluid.	**Controleert u de remvloeistof even, alstublieft?**	kontroalayrt ew der rehmvlooeestof ayvern ahlstewbleeft

Fluid measures					
litres	imp. gal.	U.S. gal.	litres	imp. gal.	U.S. gal.
5	1.1	1.3	30	6.6	7.8
10	2.2	2.6	35	7.7	9.1
15	3.3	3.9	40	8.8	10.4
20	4.4	5.2	45	9.9	11.7
25	5.5	6.5	50	11.0	13.0

FOR NUMBERS, see page 175

CAR – SERVICE STATION

Would you check the tire pressure?	**Wilt u de banden even controleren, alstublieft?**	√ilt ew der **bahndern ayvern** kontroalayvern ahlstewbleeft
1.6 front, 1.8 rear.	**Vóór 1 komma 6 en achter 1 komma 8.**	voar ayn **kommaa zehss ehn** ahkhterr ayn **kommaa ahkht**
Please check the spare tire, too.	**Controleert u ook even het reserve-wiel, alstublieft.**	kontroalayrt ew ook ayvern heht rersehrver√eel ahlstewbleeft
Can you mend this puncture (fix this flat)?	**Kunt u deze lekke band repareren?**	kurnt ew **dayzer lehker** bahnt raypaarayrern
Would you please change this tire?	**Wilt u deze band verwisselen, alstublieft?**	√ilt ew **dayzer bahnt** verr√isserlern ahlstewbleeft
Would you clean the windscreen (windshield)?	**Wilt u de voorruit schoonmaken, alstublieft?**	√ilt ew der **voorrur**ᵉʷt skhoanmaakern ahlstewbleeft
Have you a road map of this district?	**Hebt u een wegen-kaart van deze streek?**	hehpt ew ayn √ayghernkaart vahn **dayzer** strayk
Where are the toilets?	**Waar zijn de toiletten?**	√aar zaiyn der t√aalehtern

CAR – SERVICE STATION

Tire pressure is measured in Holland in kilograms per square centimetre. The following conversion chart will make sure your tires get the treatment they deserve.

Tire pressure			
lb./sq. in.	kg./cm²	lb./sq. in.	kg./cm²
10	0.7	26	1.8
12	0.8	27	1.9
15	1.1	28	2.0
18	1.3	30	2.1
20	1.4	33	2.3
21	1.5	36	2.5
23	1.6	38	2.7
24	1.7	40	2.8

Asking the way—Street directions

Excuse me.	**Neemt u mij niet kwalijk.**	naymt ew maiy neet k**v**aalerk
Do you speak English?	**Spreekt u Engels?**	spraykt ew **ehng**erlss
Can you tell me the way to …?	**Kunt u mij de weg wijzen naar …?**	kurnt ew maiy der **v**ahkh **v**aiyzern naar
Where's …	**Waar is …?**	**v**aar iss
How do I get to …?	**Hoe kom ik naar …?**	hoo kom ik naar
Where does this road lead to?	**Waar gaat deze weg heen?**	**v**aar ghaat **day**zer **v**ehkh hayn
Are we on the right road for…?	**Zitten we op de goeie weg naar…?**	zittern **v**er op der **ghoo**yer **v**ehkh naar
How far is the next village?	**Hoever is het volgende dorp?**	hoo**vehr** iss heht **volg**hernder dorp
How far is it to … from here?	**Hoever is het van hier naar…?**	hoo**vehr** iss heht vahn heer naar
Can you tell me where … is?	**Kunt u mij zeggen waar … is?**	kurnt ew maiy **zehg**hern **v**aar … iss
Where can I find this address?	**Waar is dit adres?**	**v**aar iss dit aa**drehss**
Where's this?	**Waar is dat?**	**v**aar iss daht

Miles into kilometres									
1 mile = 1.609 kilometres (km)									
miles	10	20	30	40	50	60	70	80	90	100
km	16	32	48	64	80	97	113	129	145	161

Kilometres into miles												
1 kilometre (km) = 0.62 miles												
km	10	20	30	40	50	60	70	80	90	100	110	120	130
miles	6	12	19	25	31	37	44	50	56	62	68	75	81

Can you show me on the map where I am?	**Kunt u mij op de kaart aanwijzen waar ik ben?**	kurnt ew maiy op der kaart aan√aiyzern √aar ik behn
Can you show me on the map where the university is?	**Kunt u mij op de kaart aanwijzen waar de universiteit is?**	kurnt ew maiy op der kaart aan√aiyzern √aar der ewneevehrseetaiyt iss
Can I park there?	**Kan ik daar parkeren?**	kahn ik daar pahrkayrern
Is that a one-way street?	**Is dat een straat met eenrichtingsverkeer?**	iss daht ayn straat meht aynrikhtingsverrkayr
Does the traffic got this way?	**Is het verkeer in deze richting?**	iss heht verrkayr in dayzer rikhting

U zit op de verkeerde weg.	You're on the wrong road.
U moet rechtdoor rijden.	Go straight ahead.
Het is verderop...	It's down there on the...
rechts/links	right/left
Volg deze weg tot het eerste/tweede kruispunt.	Go to the first/second crossroads.
Sla bij de stoplichten links af.	Turn to the left at the traffic lights.
Sla rechtsaf bij de volgende hoek.	Turn right at the next corner.

In the rest of this section we'll be more closely concerned with the car itself. We've divided it into two parts:

Part A contains general advice on motoring in Holland and Belgium. It's essentially for reference and is therefore to be browsed over, preferably in advance.

Part B is concerned with the practical details of accidents and breakdown. It includes a list of car parts and of things that may go wrong with them. All you have to do is to show it to the garage mechanic and get him to point to the items required.

Part A

Customs—Documentation

You will need the following documents when driving in Holland and Belgium:

- passport
- international insurance certificate (green card)
- car registration papers (log book)
- valid driving licence

Motor vehicles must carry a nationality plate or sticker. In Holland you can drive with a British or American driving licence. However, if you intend to travel through other countries, an international driving licence may prove a useful document to have. Cars may be kept in the country without special permission for a period not exceeding a year. No frontier documents are required for trailers and caravans, except for a valid registration certificate.

Here's my...	Hier is mijn...	heer iss maiyn
driving licence	**rijbewijs**	**raiyber√aiyss**
green card	**groene kaart**	**ghrooner kaart**
passport	**paspoort**	**pahspoart**
registration (log) book	**kentekenbewijs**	**kehntaykernber√aiyss**

We're staying for...	Wij blijven...	√aiy blaiyvern
three days	**3 dagen**	3 daaghern
a week	**een week**	ayn √ayk
two weeks	**2 weken**	2 √aykern
a month	**een maand**	ayn maant

| I've nothing to declare. | **Ik heb niets aan te geven.** | ik hehp neets aan ter ghayvern |

CAR—INFORMATION

A red warning triangle—for display on the road in case of breakdown or accident—is compulsory; parking lights are advisable. Crash helmets are compulsory for both riders and passengers on motorcycles and scooters. If a foreign visitor's car is fitted with seat belts, they must be worn.

Driving

In Holland, roads are classified as follows:

A. 6	*Autoweg* (oatoavehkh)—a motorway or expressway. A toll is not usually levied for motorways, but it does exist for bridges and tunnels.
E 2	European motorway. A green sign with white lettering.
N 10	National road. Usually only one traffic lane in each direction.
B-weg	Secondary road.

Roads are generally good in Holland and Belgium. Foreign drivers should take special care until they are familiar with the driving habits of the country. In Holland and Belgium you drive on the right and overtake (pass) on the left. When overtaking, you must use your indicator. Adapt your speed to road and traffic conditions, and don't get hot under the collar if local drivers seem impatient.

Pedestrians on zebra crossings (indicated by black and white stripes on the road) must be given unimpeded passage. Trams have priority over other traffic (police, ambulance and fire engines excepted). Watch out for passengers alighting at tramstops.

Unless otherwise indicated, traffic coming from the right has priority over traffic going straight on. An orange-coloured, diamond-shaped sign with a white border indicates you have the right of way. Fast-moving traffic has priority over slow-moving traffic (cyclists, mopeds, cart-drivers etc.). Cyclists require special attention in Holland. They abound!

Within cities and other populated areas the speed limit is 50 kilometres per hour (kph)—31 mph—with the exception of posted areas permitting 80 kph (44 mph). Outside built-up areas and on motorways the speed limit is 100 kph (62 mph). For cars with trailers or caravans the speed limit is 80 kph on all roads.

The police are normally quite lenient with tourists, but don't push your luck too far. For small offences you can be fined on the spot. Here are some phrases which may come in handy, but if you're in serious trouble, insist on having an interpreter.

I'm sorry, Officer, I didn't see the sign.	**Neemt u mij niet kwalijk, agent, ik heb het verkeers- bord niet gezien.**	naymt ew maiy neet k**v**aalerk aaghehnt ik hehp heht verr**kayr**sbort neet gher**zeen**
The light was green.	**Het verkeerslicht was groen.**	heht verr**kayr**slikht **v**ahss ghroon
I don't understand.	**Ik begrijp het niet.**	ik ber**ghraiyp** heht neet
How much is the fine?	**Hoeveel is de boete?**	**hoo**vayl iss der **boo**ter

Parking

As at home, parking is a headache in most cities, particularly in metropolitan areas or popular holiday resorts. Most cities have introduced parking meters and "blue zones" for which parking discs are compulsory.

Excuse me. May I park here?	**Neemt u mij niet kwalijk, mag ik hier parkeren?**	naymt ew maiy neet k**v**aalerk mahhk ik heer pahr**kayr**ern
How long can I park here?	**Hoe lang mag ik hier blijven staan?**	hoo lahng mahhk ik heer **blaiy**vern staan
Excuse me. Do you have some change for the parking meter?	**Neemt u mij niet kwalijk. Hebt u wat kleingeld voor de parkeermeter?**	naymt ew maiy neet k**v**aalerk hehpt ew **v**aht klaiyng**hehl**t voar der pahr**kayr**mayterr

Road signs

Road signs are practically standardized throughout Western Europe and are quickly learnt. The main ones are shown on pages 160 and 161.

Listed below are some written signs which you'll certainly encounter when driving in Holland and Belgium.

ALLEEN VOOR VOETGANGERS	Pedestrians only
BEPERKTE DOORRIJ-HOOGTE	Height limit
BUSHALTE	Bus stop
DOORGAAND VERKEER	Through traffic
DOORGAAND VERKEER GESTREMD	No through road
EENRICHTINGSVERKEER	One way traffic
EINDE INHAALVERBOD	End of no-pass zone
FIETSERS	(Watch out for) cyclists
FILEVORMING	Bottleneck
GEVAAR	Danger
GEVAARLIJKE BOCHT	Dangerous bend (curve)
INHAALVERBOD	No overtaking (passing)
INRIJDEN VERBODEN	No entry
LANGZAAM RIJDEN	Reduce speed
LOSSE STEENSLAG	Loose gravel
OMLEIDING	Diversion (detour)
PARKEERVERBOD	No parking
RECHTS HOUDEN	Keep right
SLECHT WEGDEK	Bad road surface
STOPLICHTEN OP 100 M	Traffic lights at 100 metres
TEGENLIGGERS	Oncoming traffic
VERKEER OVER EEN RIJBAAN	Traffic in single lane
VOETGANGERS	(Watch out for) pedestrians
WACHTVERBOD	No waiting
WEGOMLEGGING	Diversion (detour)
WERK IN UITVOERING	Roadworks (men working)
WIELRIJDERS	Cyclists
ZACHTE BERM	Soft shoulders

Part B

Accidents

This section is confined to immediate aid. The legal problems of responsibility and settlement can be taken care of later. Your first concern will be for the injured.

Is anyone hurt?	**Is er iemand gewond?**	iss ehr eemahnt gherVont
Don't move.	**Beweeg u niet.**	berVaykh ew neet
It's all right. Don't worry.	**Het is niet erg. Maakt u zich geen zorgen.**	heht iss neet ehrkh maakt ew zikh ghayn zorghern
Where's the nearest telephone?	**Waar is de dichtst-bijzijnde telefoon?**	Vaar iss der dikhtst-baiyzaiynder taylerfoan
Can I use your telephone? There's been an accident.	**Mag ik van uw telefoon gebruik maken? Er is een ongeluk gebeurd.**	mahkh ik vahn ewee taylerfoan gherbrurewk maakern? ehr iss ayn ongherlurk gherburrt
Call a doctor/an ambulance quickly.	**Waarschuw onmiddelijk een doktor/ ziekenauto.**	Vaarskhewee onmidderlerk ayn dokterr/zeeekernoowtoa
There are people injured.	**Er zijn gewonden.**	ehr zaiyn gherVondern
Help me get them out of the car.	**Helpt u mij ze uit de auto te halen.**	hehlpt ew maiy zer urewt der oowtoa ter haalern

Police—Exchange of information

Please call the police.	**Waarschuw de politie, alstublieft.**	Vaarskhewee der poaleetsee ahlstewbleeft
There's been an accident. It's about 2 km from...	**Er is een ongeluk gebeurd. Het is ongeveer 2 km van ...**	eht iss ayn ongherlurk gherburrt. heht iss onghervayr 2 keeloamayterr vahn
I'm on the Amsterdam-Utrecht road, 10 km from Amsterdam.	**Ik ben op de weg Amsterdam-Utrecht, 10 km van Amsterdam.**	ik behn op der Vehkh ahmsterrdahm-ewtrehkht 10 keeloamayterr vahn ahmsterrdahm

FOR DOCTOR, see page 162

Here's my name and address.	**Hier is mijn naam en adres.**	heer iss maiyn naam ehn **aadrehss**
Would you mind acting as a witness?	**Wilt u als getuige optreden?**	√ilt ew ahls gher**tur**ᵉʷgher optraydern
I'd like an interpreter.	**Ik wil graag een tolk.**	ik √il ghraakh ayn tolk

Remember to put out a red warning triangle if the car is out of action or impeding traffic.

B-r-e-a-k-d-o-w-n

...and that's what we'll do with this section: break it down into four phases.

1. **On the road**
   You ask where the nearest garage is.

2. **At the garage**
   You tell the mechanic what's wrong.

3. **Finding the trouble**
   He tells you what he thinks is wrong.

4. **Getting it repaired**
   You tell him to repair it and, once that's over, settle the account (or argue about it).

Phase 1—On the road

Where's the nearest garage?	**Waar is de dichtst-bijzijnde garage?**	√aar iss der dikhtst-baiyzaiynder ghaaraazher
Excuse me. My car has broken down. May I use your phone?	**Neemt u mij niet kwalijk. Ik heb auto-pech. Mag ik even opbellen?**	naymt ew maiy neet k√aalerk. ik hehp oᵒʷtoapehkh. mahkh ik ayvern opbehlern
What's the telephone number of the nearest garage?	**Wat is het telefoon-nummer van de dichtstbijzijnde garage?**	√aht iss heht taylerfoan-nurmerr vahn der dikhtst-baiyzaiynder ghaaraazher
I've had a breakdown at...	**Ik sta met motor-pech in...**	ik staa meht **mo**aterrpehkh in

Can you send a mechanic?	**Kunt u een monteur sturen?**	kurnt ew ayn monturr stewrern
Can you send a truck to tow my car?	**Kunt u een takel-wagen sturen?**	kurnt ew ayn taakerl-√aaghern stewrern
How long will you be?	**Hoe lang duurt het voordat U komt?**	hoo lahng dewrt heht voardaht ew komt

Phase 2—At the garage

Can you help me?	**Kunt u mij helpen?**	kurnt ew maiy hehlpern
I think there's something wrong with the...	**Ik denk dat er iets mis is met...**	ik dehnk daht ehr eets mis iss meht
battery	**de batterij**	der bahtterraiy
brakes	**de remmen**	der rehmern
bulbs	**de lampen**	der lahmpern
carburettor	**de carburator**	der kahrbewraator
clutch	**de koppeling**	der kopperling
cooling system	**het koelsysteem**	heht koolseestaym
contact	**het contact**	heht kontahkt
dipswitch (dimmer switch)	**de dimschakelaar**	der dimskhaakerlaar
dynamo	**de dynamo**	der deenaamoa
electrical system	**het elektrisch circuit**	heht aylehktreess sirk√eet
engine	**de motor**	der moaterr
exhaust pipe	**de uitlaatpijp**	der ur*wtlaatpaiyp
fan	**de ventilator**	der vehnteelaator
filter	**de oliefilter**	der oaleefilterr
fuel pump	**de benzinepomp**	der behnzeenerpomp
fuel tank	**de benzinetank**	der behnzeenertehnk
gears	**de versnelling**	der verrsnehling
generator	**de dynamo**	der deenaamoa
hand brake	**de handremmen**	der hahntrehmern
headlights	**de koplampen**	der koplahmpern
heating	**de verwarming**	der verr√ahrming
horn	**de claxon**	der klahkson
ignition system	**de ontsteking**	der ontstayking
indicator	**de richtingaanwijzer**	der rikhtingaan√aiyzerr
lights	**de lichten**	der likhtern
back-up lights	**de achteruitrij-lichten**	der ahkhterruir*wtraiy-likhtern
brake lights	**de remlichten**	der rehmlikhtern

rear lights	de achterlichten	der ahkhterrlikhtern
reversing lights	de achteruitrij-lichten	der ahkhterrur^{ew}traiy-likhtern
tail lights	de achterlichten	der ahkhterrlikhtern
lining and covering	de remvoering	der rehmvooring
lubrication system	de oliedruk	der oaleedrurk
muffler	de knaldemper	der knahldehmperr
parking brake	de handrem	der hahntrehm
radiator	de radiator	der raadeeyaator
reflectors	de reflectoren	der rayflehktoarern
seat	de zitting	der zitting
silencer	de knalpot	der knahlpot
sliding roof	het open dak	heht oapern dahk
sparking plugs	de bougies	der boozheess
speedometer	de snelheidsmeter	der snehlhaiytsmayterr
starter	de starter	der stahrterr
steering	de stuurinrichting	der stewrintikhting
suspension	de vering	der vayring
transmission	de versnelling	der verrsnehling
automatic transmission	de automatische versnelling	der oatomaateesser verrsnehling
turn signal	de richtingaanwijzer	der rikhtingaan**v**aiyzerr
wheels	de wielen	der **v**eelern
wipers	de ruitenwissers	der rur^{ew}ter**v**isserrss

LEFT	RIGHT
LINKS	**RECHTS**
(links)	(rehkhts)

FRONT	BACK
VOORKANT	**ACHTERKANT**
(voar)	(**ahk**terr)

It's...	Het...	heht
bad	loopt slecht	loapt slehkht
blowing	brandt door	brahnt door
blown	is doorgeslagen	iss doargherslaaghern
broken	is gebroken	iss gherbroakern
burnt	is doorgebrand	iss doargherbrahnt
cracked	is gebarsten	iss gherbahstern
defective	is kapot	iss kaapot
disconnected	is losgeraakt	iss losgherraakt
dry	is droog gelopen	iss droakh ghehloapern
frozen	is bevroren	iss berrvroarern
jammed	is geblokkeerd	iss gherblokkayrt
knocking	rammelt	rahmerlt
leaking	lekt	lehkt

loose	**heeft losgelaten**	hayft loasghehl**aa**tern
misfiring	**slaat over**	slaat **oa**verr
noisy	**maakt lawaai**	maakt laa**Vaa**••
not working	**doet het niet**	doot heht neet
overheating	**loopt warm**	loapt **V**ahrm
short-circuiting	**maakt kortsluiting**	maakt kortslur••wting
slack	**is slap**	iss slahp
slipping	**slipt**	slipt
stuck	**zit vast**	zit vahst
vibrating	**trilt**	trilt
weak	**is bezweken**	iss behz**V**ehkehrn
worn	**is versleten**	iss verr**s**laytern
The car won't start.	**De auto wil niet starten.**	der o••wtoa Vil neet **stah**rtern
It's locked and the keys are inside.	**Hij zit op slot en de sleutels zitten erin.**	haiy zit op slot ehn der slurterlss zittern ehrin
The fan belt is too slack.	**De ventilatorriem is te slap.**	der vehnteel**aa**torreem iss ter slahp
The radiator is leaking.	**De radiator lekt.**	der raadee**yaa**tor lehkt
The idling needs adjusting.	**De stationair moet bijgesteld worden.**	der staasyoa**neh**r moot baiygherstehlt **V**ordern
The clutch engages too quickly.	**De koppeling pakt te snel.**	der **kop**perling pahkt ter snehl
The steering wheel is vibrating.	**Het stuur trilt.**	heht stewr trilt
The wipers are smearing.	**De ruitewissers maken de ruit niet schoon.**	der rur••wtereisserr **maa**kern der rur••wt neet skhoan
The pneumatic suspension is weak.	**De luchtvering is slap.**	der **lurkht**vayring iss slahp

Now that you've explained what's wrong, you'll want to know how long it'll take to repair it and make your arrangements accordingly.

| How long will it take to repair? | **Hoe lang duurt de reparatie?** | how lahng dewrt der raypaar**aa**tsee |
| How long will it take to find out what's wrong? | **Wanneer weet u wat er aan mankeert?** | Vahnayr Vayt ew Vaht ehr aan mahn**kayr**t |

| Suppose I come back in half an hour? | **Zal ik over een half uur terugkomen?** | zahl ik oaverr ayn hahlf ewr terrurkhkoamern |
| Can you give me a lift into town? | **Kunt u mij een lift naar de stad geven?** | kurnt ew maiy ayn lift naar der staht ghayvern |

Phase 3—Finding the trouble

It's up to the mechanic to find the trouble and to repair it if possible. All you have to do is hand him the book and point to the text in Dutch below.

Wilt u a.u.b. op deze alfabetische lijst aanwijzen welk onderdeel defect is. Als uw klant wil weten wat eraan mankeert, wijs hem dan in de volgende lijst de term aan die hierop van toepassing is (gebroken, kortsluiting, enz.).*

accu	battery
accucellen	battery cells
accuvloeistof	battery liquid
anker van de magneet	starter armature
as	shaft
automatische transmissie (overbrenging)	automatic transmission
batterij	battery
benzinefilter	petrol (gas) filter
benzinepomp	petrol (gas) pump
bougies	sparking plugs
carburator	carburettor
cardankoppeling	universal joint
carter	crankcase
cilinder	cylinder
cilinderhoofd	cylinder head
cilinderkoppakking	cylinder head gasket
condensator	condensor
contact	contact
contactpunten	points
dimschakelaar	dipswitch (dimmer switch)

* Please look at the following alphabetical list and point to the defective item. If your customer wants to know what's wrong with it, pick the applicable term from the next list (broken, short-circuited, etc.).

CAR – REPAIRS

drukveren	pressure springs
electrisch circuit	electrical system
filter	filter
gedistilleerd water	distilled water
hoofdlagers	main bearings
injectiepomp	injection pump
koelsysteem	cooling system
kabel	cable
kabels van de bougies	sparking-plug leads
kabels van de verdeler	distributor leads
klepstoters	tappets
koolborstels	brushes
koppeling	clutch
koppelingspedaal	clutch pedal
koppelingsplaat	clutch plate
krukas	crankshaft
lagers	bearings
luchtfilter	air filter
luchtvering	pneumatic suspension
membraan	diaphragm
motor	motor
motorblok	block
nokkenas	camshaft
oliefilter	oil filter
oliepomp	oil pump
ontsteking	ignition coil
ophanging	suspension
overbrenging	transmission
pomp	pump
radiator	radiator
remblokken	brake shoes
remmen	brakes
remtrommel	brake drum
remvoering	brake lining
ringen	rings
schokbrekers	shock absorber
smeervet	grease
spoorstangeinden	track-rod ends
stabilisator	stabilizer
stangen	stems
startmotor	starter motor
stuurblok	steering column
stuurinrichting	steering
stuurhuis	steering box
stuurstang	steering post
tandheugel en tandwiel	rack and pinion

tandwielen	teeth
thermostaat	thermostat
transmissie	transmission
transmissie-as	prop shaft
ventiel	valve
ventielveer	valve spring
ventilator	fan
ventilatorriem	fan belt
verbinding	connection
verdeler	distributor
veren	springs
vering	suspension
versnelling	gear
versnellingsbak	gearbox
vlotter	float
waterpomp	water pump
wielen	wheels
zuiger	piston
zuigerringen	piston rings

De volgende lijst bevat woorden die beschrijven wat eraan de auto mankeert of wat eraan gedaan moet worden.*

aandraaien	to tighten
bevroren	frozen
bijstellen	to adjust
bijvijlen	to grind in
defekt	defective
doorgeslagen	blown
droog	dry
gebarsten	cracked
geblokkeerd	jammed
gebroken	broken
heeft speling	loose
hoog	high
kort	short
laag	low
lek	punctured/blown
lekt	leaking
los	disconnected
losser maken	to loosen

---

* The following list contains words which describe what's wrong as well as what may need to be done.

maakt kortsluiting	short-circuited
ontluchten	to bleed
opladen	to charge
opnieuw voeren	to reline
oververhitting	overheating
schoonmaken	to clean
slaat over	misfiring
slap	slack
slipt	slipping
snel	quick
speling	play
stoot	knocking
trilt	vibrating
uitbalanceren	to balance
uit elkaar halen	to strip down
vastgelopen	stuck
veranderen	to change
verbogen	warped
verbrand	burnt
verroest	rusty
versleten	worn
vervangen	to replace
vibreert	vibrating
vuil	dirty
zwak	weak

Phase 4—Getting it repaired

Have you found the trouble?	**Hebt u het defect gevonden?**	hehpt ew heht der**fehkt** gher**von**dern

Now that you know what's wrong, or at least have some idea, you'll want to find out…

Is that serious?	**Is het ernstig?**	iss heht **ehrn**sterkh
Can you repair it?	**Kunt u het repareren?**	kurnt ew heht raypaa**ray**rern
Can you do it now?	**Kunt u het meteen doen?**	kurnt ew heht mer**tayn** doon
What's it going to cost?	**Hoeveel gaat het kosten?**	**hoo**vayl ghaat heht **kos**tern
Do you have the necessary spare parts?	**Hebt u de nodige onderdelen in reserve?**	hehpt ew der **no**adergher **on**derrdaylern in rer**sehr**ver

What if he says "no"?

Why can't you do it?	**Waarom kunt u het niet doen?**	√aarom kurnt ew heht neet doon
Is it essential to have that part?	**Is dat onderdeel absoluut noodzakelijk?**	iss daht onderrdayl ahpsoalewt noatzaakerlerk
How long is it going to take to get the spare parts?	**Hoe lang duurt het voordat u die onderdelen hebt?**	hoo lahng dewrt heht voardaht u dee onderrdaylern hehpt
Where's the nearest garage that can repair it?	**Waar is de dichtstbijzijnde garage waar dit wel gerepareerd kan worden?**	√aar iss der dikhtstbaizaiynder ghaaraazher √aar dit √ehl gherraypaarayrt kahn √ordern
Can you fix it so that I can get as far as…?	**Kunt u het zo repareren dat ik naar … kan rijden?**	kurnt ew heht zoa raypaarayrern daht ik naar … kahn raiydern

Setting the bill

If you're really stuck, ask if you can leave the car at the garage. Contact the automobile association or hire another car.

Is everything fixed?	**Is het weer helemaal in orde?**	iss heht √ayr haylermaal in order
How much do I owe you?	**Hoeveel ben ik u schuldig?**	hoovayl behn ik ew skhurlderkh
This is for you.	**Dit is voor u.**	dit iss voar ew

But you may feel that the workmanship is sloppy or that you're paying for work not done. Get the bill itemized. If necessary, get it translated before you pay.

| I'd like to check the bill first. Will you itemize the work done? | **Ik wil graag eerst de rekening controleren. Wilt u al het verrichte werk in de rekening specificeren?** | ik √il ghraakh ayrst der raykerning kontroalayrern. √ilt ew ahl heht verrikhter √ehrk in der raykerning spayseefeesayrern |

If the garage still won't back down and you're sure you're right, get the help of a third party.

Some international road signs

No vehicles

No entry

No overtaking (passing)

Oncoming traffic has priority

Maximum speed limit

No parking

Caution

Intersection

Dangerous bend (curve)

Road narrows

Intersection with secondary road

Two-way traffic

Dangerous hill

Uneven road

Falling rocks

Give way (yield)

Main road,
thoroughfare

End of restriction

One-way traffic

Traffic goes
this way

Roundabout
(rotary)

Bicycles only

Pedestrians
only

Minimum speed
limit

Keep right
(left if symbol
reversed)

Parking

Hospital

Motorway
(expressway)

Motor vehicles
only

Filling station

No through road

Doctor

Frankly, how much use is a phrase book going to be to you in case of serious injury or illness? The only phrase you need in such an emergency is:

Get a doctor quickly!	**Haal vlug een dokter!**	haal vlurkh ayn **dokterr**

But there are minor aches and pains, ailments and irritations that can upset the best planned trip. Here we can help you and, perhaps, the doctor.

Some doctors will speak English well; others will know enough for your needs. But suppose there's something the doctor can't explain because of language difficulties? We've thought of that. As you'll see, this section has been arranged to enable you and the doctor to communicate. From pages 165 to 171, you'll find your part of the dialogue on the upper half of each page—the doctor's part is on the lower half.

The whole section has been divided into three parts: illness, wounds, nervous tension. Page 171 is concerned with prescriptions and fees.

General

Can you get me a doctor?	**Kunt u een dokter roepen?**	kurnt ew ayn **dokterr roopern**
Is there a doctor here?	**Is er hier een dokter?**	iss ehr heer ayn **dokterr**
Please telephone for a doctor immediately.	**Telefoneer zo vlug mogelijk een dokter, alstublieft.**	taylerfoa**nayr** zoa vlurkh **moagh**erlerk ayn **dokterr** ahlstew**bleeft**
Where's there a doctor who speaks English?	**Waar kan ik een dokter vinden die Engels spreekt?**	ⱱaar kahn ik ayn **dokterr** vindern dee **ehng**erlss spraykt
Where's the surgery (doctor's office)?	**Waar heeft de dokter zijn praktijk?**	ⱱaar hayft der **dokterr** zaiyn prahk**taiyk**

FOR PHARMACY, see page 108

What are the surgery (office) hours?	**Hoe laat is het spreekuur?**	hoo laat iss heht spraykewr
Could the doctor come and see me here?	**Zou de dokter mij hier kunnen bezoeken?**	zo^{ow} der dokterr maiy heer kurnern berzookern
What time can the doctor come?	**Hoe laat kan de dokter komen?**	hoo laat kahn der dokterr koamern

Symptoms

Use this section to tell the doctor what's wrong. Basically, what he'll require to know is:

What? (ache, pain, bruise, etc.)
Where? (arm, stomach, etc.)
How long? (have you had the trouble)

Before you visit the doctor find out the answers to these questions by glancing through the pages that follow. In this way you'll save time.

Parts of the body

ankle	de enkel	der ehnkerl
appendix	de blindedarm	der blinderdahrm
arm	de arm	der ahrm
artery	de slagader	der slahghaaderr
back	de rug	der rurkh
bladder	de blaas	der blaass
blood	het bloed	heht bloot
bone	het bot	heht bot
bowels	de darmen	der dahrmern
breast	de borstkas	der borst
cheek	de wang	der vahng
chest	de borst	der borst
chin	de kin	der kin
collar-bone	het sleutelbeen	heht slurterlbayn
ear	het oor	heht oar
elbow	de elleboog	der ehlerboakh
eye	het oog	heht oakh
face	het gezicht	heht gherzikht
finger	de vinger	der vingerr
foot	de voet	der voot
forehead	het voorhoofd	heht voarhoaft

DOCTOR

gland	de klier	der kleer
hair	het haar	heht haar
hand	de hand	der hahnt
head	het hoofd	heht hoaft
heart	het hart	heht hahrt
heel	de hiel	der heel
hip	de heup	der hurp
intestines	de ingewanden	der ingher‍vahndern
jaw	de kaak	der kaak
joint	het gewricht	heht gher‍vrikht
kidney	de nier	der neer
knee	de knie	der knee
knee cap	de knieschijf	der kneeskhaiyf
leg	het been	heht bayn
lip	de lip	der lip
liver	de lever	der layverr
lung	de long	der long
mouth	de mond	der mont
muscle	de spier	der speer
neck	de nek	der nehk
nerve	de zenuw	der zaynew°°
nervous system	het zenuwstelsel	heht zaynew°°stehlserl
nose	de neus	der nurss
rib	de rib	der rip
shoulder	de schouder	der skho‍ᵉʷderr
skin	de huid	der hur‍ᵉʷt
spine	de ruggegraat	der rurgherghraat
stomach	de maag	der maakh
tendon	de pees	der payss
thigh	de dij	der daiy
throat	de keel	der kayl
thumb	de duim	der dur‍ᵉʷm
toe	de teen	der tayn
tongue	de tong	der ting
tonsils	de amandelen	der aamahnderlern
urine	de urine	der ewreener
vein	de ader	der aaderr
wrist	de pols	der polss

LEFT/ON THE LEFT SIDE	RIGHT/ON THE RIGHT SIDE
LINKS/AAN DE LINKER-	**RECHTS/AAN DE RECH-**
KANT	**TERKANT**
(links/aan der **lin**kerrkahnt)	(rehkhts/aan der **rehkh**terrkahnt)

PATIENT
Part 1—Illness

I'm not feeling well.	**Ik voel mij niet goed.**	ik vool maiy neet ghoot
I'm ill.	**Ik ben ziek.**	ik behn zeek
I've got a pain here.	**Ik heb hier pijn.**	ik hehp heer paiyn
His/Her ... hurts.	**Zijn/Haar ... doet pijn.**	zaiyn/haar ... doot paiyn
I've got a...	**Ik heb...**	ik hehp
backache/ fever/headache/ sore throat	**hoofdpijn/rugpijn koorts/keelpijn**	hoaftpaiyn/rurghpaiyn koarts/kaylpaiyn
I suffer from travel sickness.	**Ik ben wagenziek.**	ik behn Vaaghernzeek
I'm constipated.	**Ik heb last van constipatie**	ik hehp lahst vahn konsteepaatsee
I've been vomiting.	**Ik heb overgegeven.**	ik hehp oaverrgherghayvern

DOCTOR
1—Ziekte

Wat is er aan de hand?	What's the trouble?
Waar doet het pijn?	Where does it hurt?
Hoe lang hebt u die pijn al?	How long have you had this pain?
Wat voor een soort pijn voelt u?	What sort of pain is it?
dof/hevig/bonzend voortdurend/af en toe	dull/sharp/throbbing constant/on and off
Hoe lang voelt u zich al zo?	How long have you been feeling like this?
Stroop uw mouw op, alstublieft.	Roll up your sleeve.
Kleedt u zich uit (tot het middel), alstublieft.	Please undress (to the waist).

DOCTOR

PATIENT

I feel faint.	Ik voel mij slap.	ik vool maiy slahp
I feel...	Ik ben...	ik behn
dizzy	duizelig	dur^{ew}zerlerkh
nauseous	misselijk	misserlerk
shivery	rillerig	rillerrerkh
I've/He's/She's got a/an...	Ik heb/Hij heeft/ Zij heeft...	ik hehp/haiy hayft/ zaiy hayft
abscess	een abces	ayn ahpsehss
asthma	asthma	ahstmaa
boil	een steenpuist	ayn staynpur^{ew}st
chill	kou gevat	ko^{ow} ghervaht
cold	een verkoudheid	ayn verrko^{ow}thaiyt
convulsions	stuiptrekkingen	stur^{ew}ptrehkkingern
cramps	krampen	krahmpern
diarrhoea	diarrhee	deeyaaray
fever	koorts	koarts
haemorrhoids	aambeien	aambaiyyern
hay fever	hooikoorts	hoa^{ee}koarts
hernia	een hernia	ayn hehrneeyaa
indigestion	een indigestie	ayn indeeghehstee

DOCTOR

Gaat u hier liggen, a.u.b.	Please lie down over here.
Open uw mond, alstublieft.	Open your mouth.
Diep inademen.	Breathe deeply.
Hoest u eens, alstublieft.	Cough, please.
Ik zal uw temperatuur opnemen.	I'll take your temperature.
Ik zal uw bloeddruk opmeten.	I'm going to take your blood pressure.
Is dit de eerste keer dat u hier last van hebt?	Is this the first time you've had this?
Ik zal u een injectie geven.	I'll give you an injection.
Ik wil een flesje urine/ontlasting van u hebben.	I want a specimen of your urine/stools.

DOCTOR

PATIENT

inflammation of...	**een ontsteking aan...**	ayn ont**stay**king aan
influenza	**griep**	ghreep
morning sickness	**last van misselijk- heid**	lahst vahn **miss**erlerkhaiyt
a rash	**uitslag**	ur^{ew}tslahkh
rheumatism	**reumatiek**	rurm**aa**teek
palpitations	**hartkloppingen**	**hahrt**klopingern
stiff neck	**een stijve nek**	ayn **staiy**ver nehk
sunburn	**zonnebrand**	**zonner**brahnt
sunstroke	**een zonnesteek**	ayn **zonner**stayk
tonsilitis	**een amandelon- steking**	ayn a**amahn**derlontstayking
ulcer	**een zweer**	ayn z√ayr
It's nothing serious, I hope?	**Het is toch niets ernstigs, hoop ik?**	heht iss tokh neets **ehrn**sterghss hoap ik
Is it contagious?	**Is het besmettelijk?**	iss heht ber**smeh**terlerk
I'd like you to prescribe some medicine for me.	**Ik zou graag een recept van u willen hebben.**	ik zoo^{ow} ghraakh ayn rer**sehpt** vahn ew √illern **heh**bern

DOCTOR

Het is niets ernstigs.	It's nothing to worry about.
U moet ... dagen in bed blijven.	You must stay in bed for ... days.
U hebt...	You've got...
een blindedarmontsteking	appendicitis
een gewrichtsontsteking	arthritis
een darmgriep	gastric flu
voedselvergiftiging	food poisoning
een blaasontsteking	cystitis
een oorontsteking	otitis
een longontsteking	pneumonia
voorhoofdholte-onsteking	sinusitis
een keelontsteking	throat infection
Ik stuur u naar het ziekenhuis voor een algemeen onderzoek.	I want you to go to the hospital for a general check-up.
Ik stuur u naar een specialist door.	I want you to see a specialist.

PATIENT

I'm diabetic.	**Ik ben suiker-patiënt.**	ik behn sur^{ew}kerrpaasyehnt
I've a cardiac condition.	**Ik ben hart-patiënt.**	ik behn hahrtpaasyehnt
I had a heart attack in...	**Ik heb in ... een hartaanval gehad.**	ik hehp in ... ayn hahrt-aanvahl gherhaht
I'm allergic to...	**Ik ben allergisch voor...**	ik behn aallehrgheess voar
This is my usual medicine.	**Dit medicijn gebruik ik gewoonlijk.**	dit maydeesaiyn gher-brur^{ew}k ik gher∨oanlerk
I need this medicine.	**Ik heb deze medicijn nodig.**	ik hehp dayzer maydee-saiyn noaderkh
I'm expecting a baby.	**Ik verwacht een baby.**	ik verr∨ahkht ayn baybee
Can I travel?	**Mag ik reizen?**	mahkh ik raiyzern

DOCTOR

Hoeveel insuline gebruikt u?	What dose of insulin are you taking?
Injecties of medicijnen?	Injection or oral?
Wat voor behandeling hebt u gehad?	What treatment have you been having?
Welke medicijnen neemt u in?	What medicine have you been taking?
U hebt een (lichte) hartaanval gehad.	You've had a (slight) heart attack.
... wordt niet in Nederland/België gebruikt. Dit is ongeveer hetzelfde.	We don't use ... in Holland/Belgium. This is very similar.
Wanneer verwacht u de baby?	When's the baby due?
U mag tot ... niet reizen.	You can't travel until...

PATIENT
Part 2—Wounds

I've got a/an... Could you have a look at it?	Ik heb ... Kunt u het even onderzoeken?	ik hehp ... kurnt ew heht ayvern onderzookern
blister	een blaar	ayn blaar
boil	een steenpuist	ayn staynpurᵉʷst
bruise	een kneuzing	ayn knurzing
burn	een brandwond	ayn brahntⱽont
cut	een snijwond	ayn snaiyⱽont
graze	een schaafwond	ayn skhaafⱽont
insect bite	een insektenbeet	ayn insehkternbayt
lump	een bult	ayn burlt
rash	uitslag	urᵉʷtslahkh
sting	een steek	ayn stayk
swelling	een zwelling	ayn zⱽehling
wound	een wond	ayn ⱽont
I can't move my ... It hurts.	Ik kan mijn ... niet bewegen. Het doet pijn.	ik kahn maiyn ... neet berⱽayghern. heht doot paiyn

---

DOCTOR
2—Verwondingen

Het is (niet) ontstoken.	It's (not) infected.
U hebt een hernia.	You've got a slipped disc.
Er moet een röntgenfoto gemaakt worden.	I want you to have an X-ray taken.
Het is...	It's...
gebroken/verstuikt ontwricht/gescheurd	broken/sprained dislocated/torn
U hebt een spier verrekt.	You've pulled a muscle.
Ik zal u een antiseptisch middel geven. Het is niet ernstig.	I'll give you an antiseptic. It's not serious.
Bent u tegen tetanus ingeënt?	Have you been vaccinated against tetanus?
Ik wil graag dat u over ... dagen terugkomt.	I want you to come and see me in ... days' time.

DOCTOR

PATIENT
Part 3—Nervous tension

I'm in a nervous state.	Ik ben erg nerveus.	ik gehn ehrkh nehrvurss
I'm feeling depressed.	Ik ben erg neerslachtig.	ik behn ehrkh nayrslahkhterkh
I want some sleeping pills.	Ik zou wat slaaptabletten willen hebben.	ik zoᵒʷ ∨aht slaaptaablehtern ∨illern hehbern
I can't sleep.	Ik kan niet slapen.	ik kahn neet slaapern
I'm having nightmares.	Ik heb last van nachtmerries.	ik hehp lahst vahn nahkhtmehreess
Can you prescribe a/an...?	Kunt u mij ... voorschrijven?	kurnt ew maiy ... voarskhraiyvern
anti-depressant	een anti-depressivum	ayn ahnteedayprehsseevurm
sedative	een kalmerend middel	ayn kahlmayrernt midderl
tranquillizer	een rustgevend middel	ayn rurstghayvernt midderl

---

DOCTOR
3—Nervositeit

U bent overspannen.	You're suffering from nervous tension.
U hebt rust nodig.	You need a rest.
Welke tabletten hebt u tot nu toe ingenomen?	What pills have you been taking?
Hoeveel per dag?	How many a day?
Sinds wanneer voelt u zich zo?	How long have you been feeling like this?
Ik zal u wat pillen voorschrijven.	I'll prescribe some pills.
Ik zal u een kalmerend middel geven.	I'll give you a sedative.

PATIENT

Prescriptions and dosage

What kind of medicine is this?	Wat zijn dit voor medicijnen?	√aht zaiyn dit voar maydeesaiynern
How many times a day should I take it?	Hoeveel keer per dag moet ik ze innemen?	hoovayl kayr pehr dahkh moot ik zer innaymern
Must I swallow them whole?	Moet ik ze heel doorslikken?	moot ik zer hayl doarslikkern

Fee

How much do I owe you?	Hoeveel ben ik u verschuldigd?	hoovayl behn ik ew vehrskhurlderkh
Do I pay you now or will you send me your bill?	Zal ik nu betalen of stuurt u mij de rekening?	zahl ik noo bertaalern of stewrt ew maiy der raykerning
Can you give a receipt for my health insurance?	Kunt u mij een kwitantie geven voor mijn ziekteverzekering?	kurnt ew maiy ayn k√eetahntsee ghayvern voar maiyn zeekterverrzaykerring

---

DOCTOR

Recepten en dosering

Neemt u om de ... uur ... theelepels van deze medicijn.	Take ... teaspoons of this medicine every ... hours.
Neemt u ... ... tabletten met een glas water...	Take ... pills with a glass of water...
... maal per dag voor iedere maaltijd na iedere maaltijd 's morgens 's avonds	... times a day before each meal after each meal in the morning at night

Honorarium

Ik heb liever dat u meteen betaalt.	Please pay me now.
Ik stuur u de rekening.	I'll send you the bill.

FOR NUMBERS, see page 175

Dentist

Can you recommend a good dentist?	**Kunt u mij een goede tandarts aanbevelen?**	kurnt ew maiy ayn **ghoo**der **tahnt**ahrts **aan**bervaylern
Can I make an (urgent) appointment to see Dr ...?	**Kan ik een afspraak met Dr ... maken? (Het is dringend.)**	kahn ik ayn **ahf**spraak meht **dokt**err ... **maak**ern (heht iss **dring**ernt)
Can't you possibly make it earlier than that?	**Kan het werkelijk niet eerder?**	kahn heht **v**ehrkerlerk neet **ayr**derr
I've a toothache.	**Ik heb kiespijn.**	ik hehp **kees**paiyn
I've an abscess.	**Ik heb een abces.**	ik hehp ayn ahp**sehss**
This tooth hurts.	**Deze tand doet pijn.**	**day**zer tahnt doot paiyn
at the top	**bovenaan**	**boa**vernaan
at the bottom	**onderaan**	**ond**erraan
in the front	**voorin**	**voar**in
at the back	**achterin**	**ahk**hterrin
Can you fix it temporarily?	**Kunt u er een noodvulling in doen?**	kurnt ew ehr ayn **noat**vurling in doon
Could you give me an anaesthetic?	**Kunt u het verdoven?**	kurnt ew heht verr**doa**vern
I don't want it extracted.	**Ik wil hem niet laten trekken.**	ik **v**il hehm neet **laat**ern **trehk**ern
I've lost a filling.	**Ik heb een vulling verloren.**	ik hehp ayn **vur**ling verr**loa**rern
The gum is...	**Het tandvlees...**	heht **tahnt**vlayss
bleeding	**bloedt**	bloot
very sore	**is zeer pijnlijk**	iss zayr **paiyn**lerk

Dentures

I've broken my denture.	**Ik heb mijn gebit gebroken.**	ik hehp maiyn gher**bit** gher**broa**kern
Can you repair this denture?	**Kunt u dit gebit repareren?**	kurnt ew dit gher**bit** raypaa**ray**rern
When will it be ready?	**Wanneer is het klaar?**	**v**ahnayr iss heht klaar

Optician

I've broken my glasses.	Mijn bril is gebroken.	maiyn bril iss gherbroakern
Can you repair them for me?	Kunt u het voor me repareren?	kurnt ew heht voar mer raypaarayrern
When will they be ready?	Wanneer is het klaar?	√ahnayr iss heht klaar
Can you change the lenses?	Kunt u er andere glazen inzetten?	kurnt ew ehr ahnderer ghlaazern inzehtern
I want tinted lenses.	Ik wil graag gekleurde glazen.	ik ghraakh gherklurrder ghlaazern
I'd like a spectacle case.	Ik wil graag een brillekoker.	ik √il ghraakh ayn brillerkoakerr
I'd like to have my eyesight checked.	Kunt u mijn gezichtsscherpte opmeten?	kurnt ew maiyn gherzikhtsskhehrpter opmaytern
I've lost one of my contact lenses.	Ik heb een van mijn contactlenzen verloren.	ik hehp ayn vahn maiyn kontahktlehnzern verrloarern
Could you give me another one?	Kunt u mij een andere bezorgen?	kurnt ew maiy ayn ahnderer berzorghern
I have hard/soft lenses.	Ik heb harde/zachte contactlenzen.	ik hehp hahrder/zahkhter kontaktlehnzern
Have you any contact-lens liquid?	Hebt u contact-lenzen-vloeistof?	hehpt ew kontahktlehnzern vloo••stof
A large/small bottle, please.	Een kleine/grote fles, alstublieft.	ayn klaiyner/ghroater flehss ahlstewbleeft
I'd like to buy a pair of sunglasses	Ik wil graag een zonnebril kopen.	ik √il ghraakh ayn zonnerbril koapern
May I look in a mirror?	Mag ik even in de spiegel kijken?	mahkh ik ayvern in der speegherl kaiykern
I'd like to buy a pair of binoculars.	Ik wil graag een veldkijker kopen.	ik √il ghraakh ayn vehltkaiykerr koapern
How much do I owe you?	Hoeveel ben ik u schuldig?	hoovayl behn ik ew skhurlderkh

FOR NUMBERS, see page 175

Reference section

Where do you come from?

Africa	**Afrika**	aafreekaa
Asia	**Azië**	aazeeyer
Australia	**Australië**	oastraaleeyer
Europe	**Europa**	urroapaa
North America	**Noord-Amerika**	noart aamayreekaa
South America	**Zuid-Amerika**	zurᵉʷt aamayreekaa
Austria	**Oostenrijk**	oasternraiyk
Belgium	**België**	behlgheeyer
Canada	**Canada**	kahnaadaa
Denmark	**Denemarken**	daynermahrkern
East Germany	**Oost-Duitsland**	oast durᵉʷtslahnt
England	**Engeland**	ehngerlahnt
Finland	**Finland**	finlahnt
France	**Frankrijk**	frahnkraiyk
Great Britain	**Groot-Brittannië**	ghroat-brittahneeyer
Greece	**Griekenland**	ghreekernlahnt
India	**India**	indeeyaa
Ireland	**Ierland**	eerlahnt
Israel	**Israël**	israaehl
Italy	**Italië**	eetaaleeyer
Japan	**Japan**	yaapahn
Luxembourg	**Luxemburg**	lewksermburrkh
Morocco	**Marokko**	maarokkoa
Netherlands	**Nederland**	nayderrlahnt
New Zealand	**Nieuw-Zeeland**	neeᵒᵒ zaylahnt
Norway	**Noorwegen**	noarⱽayghern
Portugal	**Portugal**	portewghahl
Scotland	**Schotland**	skhotlahnt
South Africa	**Zuid-Afrika**	zurᵉʷt aafreekaa
Soviet Union	**Sowjet-Unie**	sofyeht ewnee
Spain	**Spanje**	spahnyer
Sweden	**Zweden**	zⱽaydern
Switzerland	**Zwitserland**	zⱽitserrlahnt
Tunisia	**Tunesië**	tewnayseeyer
Turkey	**Turkije**	turrkaiyyer
United States	**Verenigde Staten**	vehraynerghder staatern
Wales	**Wales**	ⱽaylerss
West Germany	**West-Duitsland**	ⱽehst durᵉʷtslahnt
Yugoslavia	**Joegoslavië**	yooghoslaaveeyer

Numbers

0	**nul**	nurl
1	**een**	ayn
2	**twee**	t√ay
3	**drie**	dree
4	**vier**	veer
5	**vijf**	vaiyf
6	**zes**	zehss
7	**zeven**	zayvern
8	**acht**	ahkht
9	**negen**	nayghern
10	**tien**	teen
11	**elf**	ehlf
12	**twaalf**	t√aalf
13	**dertien**	dehrteen
14	**veertien**	vayrteen
15	**vijftien**	vaiyfteen
16	**zestien**	zehsteen
17	**zeventien**	zayvernteen
18	**achttien**	ahkhteen
19	**negentien**	nayghernteen
20	**twintig**	t√interkh
21	**eenentwintig**	aynernt√inerkh
22	**tweeëntwintig**	t√ayyernt√interkh
23	**drieëntwintig**	dreeyernt√interkh
24	**vierentwintig**	veerernt√interkh
25	**vijfentwintig**	vaiyfernt√interkh
26	**zesentwintig**	zehsernt√interkh
27	**zevenentwintig**	zayvernernt√interkh
28	**achtentwintig**	ahkhternt√interkh
29	**negenentwintig**	nayghernernt√interkh
30	**dertig**	dehrterkh
31	**eenendertig**	aynerndehrterkh
32	**tweeëndertig**	t√ayyerndehrterkh
33	**drieëndertig**	dreeyerndehrterkh
40	**veertig**	vayrterkh
41	**eenenveertig**	aynernvayrterkh
42	**tweeënveertig**	t√ayyernvayrterkh
43	**drieënveertig**	dreeyernvayrterkh
50	**vijftig**	vaiyfterkh
51	**eenenvijftig**	aynernvaiyfterkh
52	**tweeënvijftig**	t√ayyernvaiyfterkh
53	**drieënvijftig**	dreeyernvaiyfterkh
60	**zestig**	zehsterkh
61	**eenenzestig**	aynernsehsterkh

REFERENCE SECTION

62	tweeënzestig	t√ayyernsehsterkh
63	drieënzestig	dreeyernsehsterkh
70	zeventig	zayvernterkh
71	eenenzeventig	aynernsayvernterkh
72	tweeënzeventig	t√ayyernsayvernterkh
73	drieënzeventig	dreeyernsayvernterkh
80	tachtig	tahkhterkh
81	eenentachtig	aynerntahkhterkh
82	tweeëntachtig	t√ayyerntahkhterkh
83	drieëntachtig	dreeyerntahkhterkh
90	negentig	nayghernterkh
91	eenennegentig	aynernnayghernterkh
92	tweeënnegentig	t√ayyernnayghernterkh
93	drieënnegentig	dreeyernnayghernterkh
100	honderd	honderrt
101	honderd één	honderrt ayn
102	honderd twee	honderrt t√ay
110	honderd tien	honderrt teen
120	honderd twintig	honderrt t√interkh
130	honderd dertig	honderrt dehrterkh
140	honderd veertig	honderrt vayrterkh
150	honderd vijftig	honderrt vaiyfterkh
160	honderd zestig	honderrt sehsterkh
170	honderd zeventig	honderrt sayvernterkh
180	honderd tachtig	honderrt tahkhterkh
190	honderd negentig	honderrt nayghernterkh
200	tweehonderd	t√ayhonderrt
300	driehonderd	dreehonderrt
400	vierhonderd	veerhonderrt
500	vijfhonderd	vaiyfhonderrt
600	zeshonderd	zehshonderrt
700	zevenhonderd	zayvernhonderrt
800	achthonderd	ahkhthonderrt
900	negenhonderd	nayghernhonderrt
1000	duizend	dur^ewzernt
1100	elfhonderd	ehlfhonderrt
1200	twaalfhonderd	t√aalfhonderrt
2000	tweeduizend	t√aydur^ewzernt
5000	vijfduizend	vaiyfdur^ewzernt
10,000	tienduizend	teendur^ewzernt
50,000	vijftigduizend	vaiyfterghdur^ewzernt
100,000	honderdduizend	honderrtdur^ewzernt
1,000,000	een miljoen	ayn milyoon
1,000,000,000	een miljard	ayn milyahrt

first	**eerste**	ayrster
second	**tweede**	t√ayder
third	**derde**	dehrder
fourth	**vierde**	veerder
fifth	**vijfde**	vaiyfder
sixth	**zesde**	zehsder
seventh	**zevende**	zayverder
eighth	**achtste**	ahktster
ninth	**negende**	nayghernder
tenth	**tiende**	teender
once	**eenmaal**	aynmaal
twice	**tweemaal**	t√aymaal
three times	**driemaal**	dreemaal
a half	**een helft**	ayn hehlft
half a...	**een halve...**	ayn hahlver
half of...	**de helft van**	der hehlft vahn
half (adj.)	**half, halve**	hahlf hahlver
a quarter	**een kwart**	ayn k√ahrt
one third	**een derde**	ayn dehrder
a pair of	**een paar...**	ayn paar...
a dozen	**een dozijn...**	ayn doazaiyn
I'm 26 years old.	**Ik ben 26.**	ik behn 26
He was born in 1940.	**Hij is in 1940 geboren.**	haiy iss in 1940 gherboarern
1985	**negentien vijf- entachtig**	nayghernteen vaiyferntahkhterkh
1987	**negentien zeven- entachtig**	nayghernteen zayvernerntahkhterkh
1990	**negentien negentig**	nayghernteen nayghernterkh

Time

Het is kwart over twaalf. ('s middags)*
(heht iss kvahrt oaverr tvaalf [smiddahkhs])

Het is tien voor half twee.
(heht iss teen voar hahlf tvay)

Het is half vier.
(heht iss hahlf veer)

Het is vijf over half vijf.
(heht iss vaiyf oaverr hahlf vaiyf)

Het is kwart voor zeven.
(heht iss kvahrt voar zayvern)

Het is tien voor acht.
(heht iss teen voar ahkht)

Het is tien uur.
(heht iss teen ewr)

Het is vijf over elf.
(heht iss vaiyf oaverr ehlf)

Het is tien over twaalf. ('s nachts)**
(heht iss teen oaverr tvaalf [snahkhts])

* = 12.15 p.m. ** = 12.10 a.m.

Note: In ordinary conversation, time is expressed as shown here. However, official time uses the 24-hour clock. For instance, 13.15 corresponds to 1.15 p.m. and 20.30 to 8.30. At midnight, time returns to 0 so that 12.17 a.m. is written 0.17.

REFERENCE SECTION

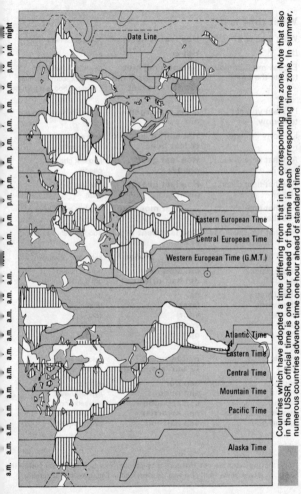

a.m. a.m. a.m. a.m. a.m. a.m. a.m. a.m. a.m. a.m. a.m. noon p.m. p.m. p.m. p.m. p.m. p.m. p.m. p.m. p.m. p.m. p.m. night

Date Line

Eastern European Time
Central European Time
Western European Time (G.M.T.)

Atlantic Time
Eastern Time
Central Time
Mountain Time
Pacific Time
Alaska Time

Countries which have adopted a time differing from that in the corresponding time zone. Note that also in the USSR, official time is one hour ahead of the time in each corresponding time zone. In summer, numerous countries advance time one hour ahead of standard time.

REFERENCE SECTION

What time is it?

What time is it?	**Hoe laat is het?**	hoo laat iss heht
It's ...	**Het is ...**	heht iss
Excuse me. Can you tell me the time?	**Neemt u mij niet kwalijk. Kunt U mij zeggen hoe laat het is?**	naymt ew maiy neet k**v**aalerk. kurnt ew maiy zeh**g**hern hoo laat heht iss
I'll meet you at ... tomorrow.	**Ik zie u morgen om ...**	ik zee ew **m**orghern om
I'm sorry I'm late.	**Het spijt me dat ik te laat ben.**	heht spaiyt mer daht ik ter laat behn
At what time does ... open?	**Hoe laat gaat ... open?**	hoo laat ghaat ... **o**apern
At what time does ... close?	**Hoe laat gaat ... dicht?**	hoo laat ghaat ... dikht
At what time should I be there?	**Hoe laat moet ik er zijn?**	hoo laat moot ik ehr zaiyn
At what time will you be there?	**Hoe laat bent u er?**	hoo laat behnt ew ehr
Can I come ...?	**Kan ik ... komen?**	kahn ik ... **ko**amern
at 8 o'clock	**om acht uur***	om ahkht ewr
at 2.30*	**om half drie***	om hahlf dree
after (prep.)	**na**	naa
afterwards	**later**	**l**aaterr
before	**voor**	voar
early	**vroeg**	vrookh
in time	**op tijd**	op taiyt
late	**laat**	laat
midnight	**middernacht**	midderrnahkht
noon	**12 uur 's middags**	12 ewr smiddahkhs
hour	**een uur**	ayn ewr
minute	**een minuut**	ayn meenewt
second	**een seconde**	ayn serkonder
quarter of an hour	**een kwartier**	ayn k**v**ahrteer
half an hour	**een half uur**	ayn hahlf ewr

REFERENCE SECTION

---

* Note that the Dutch say, not "half past" the preceding hour, but "half to" the **following** hour; in this example "half past two" is expressed in Dutch as "half to three".

Days

What day is it today?	**Welke dag is het vandaag?**	**v**ehlker dahkh iss heht vahndaakh
Sunday	**zondag**	**z**ondahkh
Monday	**maandag**	**m**aandahkh
Tuesday	**dinsdag**	**d**insdahkh
Wednesday	**woensdag**	**v**oonsdahkh
Thursday	**donderdag**	**d**onderrdahkh
Friday	**vrijdag**	**v**raiydahkh
Saturday	**zaterdag**	**z**aaterrdahkh
in the morning	**'s morgens**	smorghernss
during the day	**overdag**	oaverr**d**ahkh
in the afternoon	**'s middags**	smiddahkhs
in the evening	**'s avonds**	saavonts
at night	**'s nachts**	snahkhts
the day before yesterday	**eergisteren**	ayrghisterrern
yesterday	**gisteren**	ghisterrern
today	**vandaag**	vahndaakh
tomorrow	**morgen**	morghern
the day after tomorrow	**overmorgen**	oaverrmorghern
the day before	**de vorige dag**	der voarergher dahkh
the next day	**de volgende dag**	der volghernder dahkh
two days ago	**twee dagen geleden**	t**v**ay daaghern gherlaydern
in three days' time	**over drie dagen**	oaverr dree daaghern
last week	**verleden week**	verrlaydern **v**ayk
next week	**volgende week**	volghernder **v**ayk
for a fortnight (two weeks)	**gedurende twee weken**	gherdew**r**ernder t**v**ay **v**aykern
birthday	**de verjaardag**	der verryaardahkh
day	**de dag**	der dahkh
day off	**de vrije dag**	der vraiyyer dahkh
holiday	**de feestdag**	der faystdahkh
holidays	**de vakantie**	der vaakahntsee
month	**de maand**	der maant
vacation	**de vakantie**	der vaakahntsee
week	**de week**	der **v**ayk
weekday	**de weekdag**	der **v**aykdahkh
weekend	**het weekeinde**	heht **v**aykaiynder
working day	**de werkdag**	der **v**ehrkdahkh

Months

January	**januari**	yahne**waa**ree
February	**februari**	faybrew**aa**ree
March	**maart**	maart
April	**april**	**aa**pril
May	**mei**	maiy
June	**juni**	**yew**nee
July	**juli**	**yew**lee
August	**augustus**	o^{ow}**ghur**sturss
September	**september**	sehp**tehm**berr
October	**oktober**	ok**toa**berr
November	**november**	noa**vehm**berr
December	**december**	day**sehm**berr
since June	**sinds juni**	sints **yew**nee
during the month of August	**tijdens de maand augustus**	**taiy**dernss der maant o^{ow}**ghur**sturss
last month	**de vorige maand**	der **voar**ergher maant
next month	**de volgende maand**	der **volg**hernder maant
the month before	**de maand daarvoor**	der maant **daar**voar
the next month	**de maand daarop**	der maant **daar**op
July 1	**1 juli**	ayn **yew**lee
March 17	**17 maart**	**zay**vernteen maart

Note: The names of days and months are not capitalized in Dutch.

Letter headings are written thus:

Amsterdam, August 17, 19..	**Amsterdam, 17 augustus 19..**
Utrecht, July 1, 19..	**Utrecht, 1 juli 19..**

Seasons

spring	**de lente**	der **lehn**ter
summer	**de zomer**	der **zoa**merr
autumn	**de herfst**	der **hehrfst**
winter	**de winter**	der **v**interr
in spring	**in de lente**	in der **lehn**ter
during the summer	**in de zomer/ 's zomers**	in der **zoa**merr/**soa**merrss
in autumn	**in de herfst**	in der **hehrfst**
during the winter	**in de winter/ 's winters**	in der **v**interr/**sv**interrss

Public holidays

Listed below you'll find the dates of national holidays *(open-bare feestdag)* celebrated in Holland (NL) and Belgium (B).

January 1	**Nieuwjaarsdag**	New Years's Day	NL	B
April 30	**Koninginnedag**	Queen's Birthday	NL	
May 1	**Dag van de Arbeid**	Labour Day		B
May 5	**Bevrijdingsdag**	Liberation Day (once every 5 years: 1980, 1985 etc.)	NL	
July 21	**Nationale Feestdag**	National Day		B
August 15	**Maria Hemel-vaart**	Assumption Day		B
November 11	**Wapenstil-standsdag**	Armistice Day		B
December 25 and 26	**Kerstfeest**	Christmas and St. Stephen's Days	NL	B
Movable dates:	**Goede Vrijdag**	Good Friday	NL	
	Paasmaandag	Easter Monday	NL	B
	Hemelvaartsdag	Ascension Thursday	NL	B
	Pinkster-maandag	Whit Monday	NL	B

The year round

The climate in Holland and Belgium is quite unpredictable! Summer days may be either rainy and chilly or gloriously hot and dry. Mild—even warm—spells in spring and autumn are by no means uncommon, and winters are more often rainy and grey than outright cold. Real freeze-ups are rare.

		J	F	M	A	M	J	J	A	S	O	N	D
Amsterdam	F	39	39	42	51	57	61	67	65	57	51	42	39
	C	4	4	6	11	14	16	19	18	14	11	6	4
Days with no rain		12	13	18	16	19	18	17	17	15	13	11	12
Brussels	F	36	36	41	44	51	60	62	63	59	51	41	37
	C	2	2	5	7	11	16	17	17	15	11	5	3
Days with no rain		19	18	20	18	21	19	20	20	19	19	18	18

Common abbreviations

afz.	afzender	from…
A.N.W.B.	Wegenwacht	Dutch Touring Club
a.s.	aanstaande	next
a.u.b.	alstublieft	please
a/z	aan zee	on sea
blz.	bladzijde	page
B.T.W.	Belasting Toegevoegde Waarde	value added tax (VAT)
b.v.	bijvoorbeeld	for example
CS	Centraal Station	Central Station
Dhr.	de heer	Mr. (written)
d.w.z.	dat wil zeggen	i.e.
E.H.B.O.	Eerste Hulp bij Ongelukken	first-aid organization
enz.	enzovoort	etc.
excl.	exclusief	not included
G.G.D.	Gemeentelijke Geneeskundige Dienst	local ambulance service
GWK-bank	grenswissel-kantoren	frontier exchange offices
inl.	inlichtingen	information
j.l.	jongstleden	last
K.A.C.B.	Koninklijke Automobiel Club van België	Royal Belgian Automobile Club
K.N.A.C.	Koninklijke Nederlandse Automobiel Club	Royal Dutch Automobile Club
m.	mijnheer	Mr. (spoken)
mej.	mejuffrouw	Miss
mevr. (mw.)	mevrouw	Mrs.
N.J.H.C.	Stichting Nederlandse Jeugdherberg Centrale	Dutch Youth Hostels Organization
NL	Nederland	Netherlands
n.m.	namiddag	a.m.
no.	nummer	number
p.a. or p/a	per adres	care of
r.-k.	rooms-katholiek	Roman Catholic
v.m.	voormiddag	p.m.
z.o.z.	zie ommezijde	please turn page

REFERENCE SECTION

Conversion tables

Centimetres and inches

To change centimetres into inches, multiply by .39.

To change inches into centimetres, multiply by 2.54.

	in.	feet	yards
1 mm	0.039	0.003	0.001
1 cm	0.39	0.03	0.01
1 dm	3.94	0.32	0.10
1 m	39.40	3.28	1.09

	mm	cm	m
1 in.	25.4	2.54	0.025
1 ft.	304.8	30.48	0.304
1 yd.	914.4	91.44	0.914

(32 metres = 35 yards)

Temperature

To convert Centigrade into degrees Fahrenheit, multiply Centigrade by 1.8 and add 32.

To convert degrees Fahrenheit into Centigrade, subtract 32 from Fahrenheit and divide by 1.8.

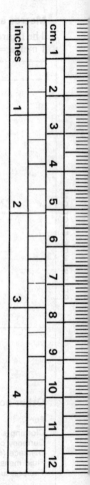

Metres and feet

The figure in the middle stands for both metres and feet, e.g.
1 metre = 3.28 ft. and 1 foot = 0.30 m.

Metres		Feet
0.30	1	3.281
0.61	2	6.563
0.91	3	9.843
1.22	4	13.124
1.52	5	16.403
1.83	6	19.686
2.13	7	22.967
2.44	8	26.248
2.74	9	29.529
3.05	10	32.810
3.35	11	36.091
3.66	12	39.372
3.96	13	42.635
4.27	14	45.934
4.57	15	49.215
4.88	16	52.496
5.18	17	55.777
5.49	18	59.058
5.79	19	62.339
6.10	20	65.620
7.62	25	82.023
15.24	50	164.046
22.86	75	246.069
30.48	100	328.092

Other conversion charts

For	see page
Clothing sizes	115
Currency converter	136
Distance (miles-kilometres)	144
Fluid measures	142
Tire pressure	143

REFERENCE SECTION

Weight conversion

The figure in the middle stands for both kilograms and pounds, e.g., 1 kilogram = 2.205 lb. and 1 pound = 0.45 kilograms.

Kilograms (kg.)		Avoirdupois pounds
0.45	1	2.205
0.90	2	4.405
1.35	3	6.614
1.80	4	8.818
2.25	5	11.023
2.70	6	13.227
3.15	7	15.432
3.60	8	17.636
4.05	9	19.840
4.50	10	22.045
6.75	15	33.068
9.00	20	44.889
11.25	25	55.113
22.50	50	110.225
33.75	75	165.338
45.00	100	220.450

REFERENCE SECTION

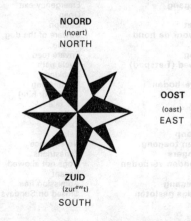

NOORD
(noart)
NORTH

WEST
(√ehst)
WEST

OOST
(oast)
EAST

ZUID
(zur^ew^t)
SOUTH

What does that sign mean?

You're sure to encounter some of these signs or notices on your trip.

Bellen, a.u.b.	Please ring
Bezet	Occupied
Dames	Ladies
Deur sluiten	Close the door
Duwen	Push
Eerst kloppen	Knock before entering
Geopend van ... tot ...	Open from ... to ...
Gereserveerd	Reserved
Gesloten	Closed
Heet	Hot
Heren	Gentlemen
Hoogspanning	High voltage
Ingang	Entrance
Inlichtingen	Information
Kassa	Cashier's (cash desk)
Koud	Cold
Levensgevaar	Danger of death
Lift	Lift (elevator)
Mannen	Men
Niet aanraken, a.u.b.	Do not touch
Niet roken	No smoking
Nooduitgang	Emergency exit
Open	Open
Opgepast	Caution
Pas op voor de hond	Beware of the dog
Privé	Private
Privéweg	Private road
Rijwielpad (fietspad)	Cycle path
Roken	Smoking
Roken verboden	No smoking
Te huur	To let (for hire)
Te koop	For sale
Trekken	Pull
Uitgang	Exit
Uitverkoop	Sales
Verboden toegang	No entrance
Voetgangers	Pedestrians
Voor honden verboden	Dogs not allowed
Vrij	Vacant
Vrije toegang	Admission free
's Zondags gesloten	Closed on Sundays

Emergency

Emergency telephone numbers for fire (*brandweer*—**brahnt**✓ayr), accidents (*ongevallen*—**o**nghervahllern) and police (*politie*—poa**leet**see) vary from place to place. For large cities which have their own telephone books, these are given on the outside back cover of the publication. In the case of smaller towns and villages which are comprised within a regional telephone book, the emergency numbers are listed immediately after the locality heading.

Be quick	**Snel**	snehl
Call the police	**Roep de politie**	roop der poa**leet**see
CAREFUL	**VOORZICHTIG**	voar**zikh**terkh
Come here	**Kom hier**	kom heer
Come in	**Binnen**	**bin**nern
Danger	**Gevaar**	gher**vaar**
FIRE	**BRAND**	brahnt
Gas	**Gas**	ghahss
GET A DOCTOR	**ROEP EEN DOKTER**	roop ayn **dok**terr
Get help quickly	**Haal snel hulp**	haal snehl hurlp
Go away	**Ga weg**	ghaa ✓ehkh
HELP	**HELP**	hehlp
I'm ill	**Ik ben ziek**	ik behn zeek
I'm lost	**Ik ben verdwaald**	ik behn verrd**✓alt**
I've lost my...	**Ik heb ... mijn verloren**	ik hehp maiyn ... verr**loar**ern
Keep your hands to yourself	**Handen thuis**	**hahn**dern tur**ew**ss
Leave me alone	**Laat me met rust**	laat mer meht rurst
Lie down	**Ga liggen**	ghaa **ligh**ern
Listen	**Luister**	**lur**ew**sterr
Listen to me	**Luister naar mij**	**lur**ew**sterr naar maiy
Look	**Kijk**	kaiyk
Look out	**Pas op**	pahss op
POLICE	**POLITIE**	poa**leet**see
Quick	**Vlug**	vlurkh
STOP	**STOP**	stop
Stop here	**Hier stoppen**	heer **stop**pern
Stop or I'll scream	**Houd op of ik gil**	ho**ow** op of ik ghil
Stop that man	**Houd die man tegen**	ho**ow** dee mahn **tay**ghern
STOP THIEF	**HOUD DE DIEF**	ho**ow** der deef
Wait a minute	**Een ogenblik**	ayn **oa**ghernblik

FOR CAR ACCIDENTS, see page 150

Index

Abbreviations	184
Arrival	22
Authors	105
Baggage	24, 71
Bank	134
Barber	122
Basic expressions	17
Beach	87
Body, parts of	163
Breakfast	34
Camping	89
equipment	106
Car	142
accidents	150
breakdown	151
driving	147
filling station	142
parking	148
parts	152
police	150
rental	26, 74
repair	155
Casino	85
Change	24, 134
Church services	79
Cinema	80
Colours	113
Complaints	35, 58
Concert	82
Countries	174
Customs control	22, 146
Dancing	83
Dating	95
Days	181
Dentist	172
Directions	25, 144, 187

Doctor	162
Drinks	59
Dry cleaning	126
Eating out	38
appetizers	44
bill (check)	58
cheese	55
complaints	58
dessert	57
drinks	59
eggs and omelets	45
fish and seafood	47
Flemish dishes	64
fruit	56
game and fowl	51
herbs and seasoning	53
Indonesian dishes	63
meat	49
ordering	40
salads	45
sauces	54
snacks	62
soups	46
vegetables	52
wine	60
Emergency	189
Friends	92
Gambling	85
Games	84
Grammar	7
Hairdresser	121
Hotel	28
breakfast	34
bill (check)	31
checking in	29
checking out	37
difficulties	35
registration	32
service	33

Introductions	92
Invitations	94
Landmarks	90
Laundry	126
Lost property	72
Materials	114, 125
Measurements	
fluids	142
km/miles	144
metric	112, 186
sizes (clothing)	115
temperature	185
tire pressure	143
weight	130, 187
Medical section	162
Menu list	43
Money	24, 134
Months	182
Movies	80
Music	82, 120
Nightclub	83
Numbers	175
Opera	82
Optician	173
Porters	24, 71
Post office	137
Pronunciation	13
Public holidays	183
Relaxing	80
Roads	147
Road signs	149, 160
Seasons	182
Shopping guide	97
barber	122
bookshop	104
chemist's	108
clothing	112
cosmetics	110
drugstore	108
dry cleaning	126
electrical appliances	119
hairdresser	121
jeweller	123
laundry	126
news-stand	104
pharmacy	108
photography	127
provisions	129
records	120
shops, list of	98
souvenirs	131
stationer	104
tobacconist	132
toiletry	110
watchmaker	123
Sightseeing	75
Signs and notices	188
Sports	74, 85–86
Taxis	27
Telegrams	138
Telephone	36, 139
alphabet	140
Temperature	183, 185
Theatre	80
Time	178, 180
Travel	65
bicycle	74
bus	73
car	142
ferryboat	72
plane	65
subway	72
tickets	69
train	66
tram (streetcar)	73
underground	72
Voltage	119

Quick reference page

Please.	**Alstublieft.**	ahlstew**bleeft**
Thank you.	**Dank u wel.**	dahnk ew √ehl
Yes/No.	**Ja/Nee.**	yaa/nay
Excuse me.	**Neemt u mij niet kwalijk.**	naymt ew maiy neet k√aalerk
Waiter, please!	**Ober!**	oaberr
How much is that?	**Hoeveel kost het?**	hoovayl kost heht
Where are the toilets?	**Waar zijn de toiletten?**	√aar zaiyn der t√aalehtern

Toilets

HEREN (hayrern)	DAMES (daamers)

Could you tell me...?	**Kunt u mij zeggen...?**	kurnt ew maiy zehghern
where/when/why	**waar/wanneer/ waarom**	√aar/√ahnayr/√aarom
What time is it?	**Hoe laat is het?**	hoo laat iss heht
Help me, please.	**Help mij, alstublieft.**	hehlp maiy ahlstew**bleeft**
Where is the ... consulate?	**Waar is het ... consulaat?**	√aar iss heht ... konsewlaat
American British Canadian	**Amerikaanse Engelse Canadese**	aamayreekaansser ehngerlsser kahnaadaysser
What does this mean?	**Wat betekent dit?**	√aht bertaykernt dit
I don't understand.	**Ik begrijp het niet.**	ik bergraiyp heht neet
Do you speak English?	**Spreekt u Engels?**	spraykt ew ehngerlss

BERLITZ® Books for travellers

TRAVEL GUIDES

They fit your pocket in both size and price. Modern, up-to-date, Berlitz gets all the information you need into 128 lively pages with colour maps and photos throughout. What to see and do, where to shop, what to eat and drink, how to save.

	ASIA, MIDDLE EAST	China (256 pages)
		Hong Kong
		India (256 pages)
		Japan (256 pages)
		Singapore
		Sri Lanka
		Thailand
		Egypt
		Jerusalem and the Holy Land
		Saudi Arabia
	AUSTRAL-ASIA	Australia (256 pages)*
		New Zealand
AFRICA	Kenya	
	Morocco	**BRITISH ISLES** — Channel Islands
	South Africa	London
	Tunisia	Ireland
		Oxford and Stratford
*in preparation		Scotland
	BELGIUM	Brussels

PHRASE BOOKS

World's bestselling phrase books feature all the expressions and vocabulary you'll need, and pronunciation throughout. 192 pages, 2 colours.

Arabic	Hebrew	Serbo-Croatian
Chinese	Hungarian	Spanish (Castilian)
Danish	Italian	Spanish (Lat. Am.)
Dutch	Japanese	Swahili
Finnish	Norwegian	Swedish
French	Polish	Turkish
German	Portuguese	European Phrase Book
Greek	Russian	European Menu Reader

FRANCE	Brittany		Costa Blanca
	France (256 pages)		Costa Brava
	French Riviera		Costa del Sol and Andalusia
	Loire Valley		Ibiza and Formentera
	Normandy*		Madrid
	Paris		Majorca and Minorca
GERMANY	Berlin	EASTERN	Budapest
	Munich	EUROPE	Dubrovnik and Southern
	The Rhine Valley		Dalmatia
AUSTRIA	Tyrol		Hungary (192 pages)
and	Vienna		Istria and Croatian Coast
SWITZER-	Switzerland (192 pages)		Moscow & Leningrad
LAND			Split and Dalmatia
GREECE,	Athens	NORTH	U.S.A. (256 pages)
CYPRUS &	Corfu	AMERICA	California
TURKEY	Crete		Florida
	Rhodes		Hawaii
	Greek Islands of the Aegean		New York
	Peloponnese		Toronto
	Salonica and Northern Greece		Montreal
	Cyprus	CARIBBEAN,	Puerto Rico
	Istanbul/Aegean Coast	LATIN	Virgin Islands
ITALY and	Florence	AMERICA	Bahamas
MALTA	Italian Adriatic		Bermuda
	Italian Riviera		French West Indies
	Italy (256 pages)*		Jamaica
	Rome		Southern Caribbean
	Sicily		Mexico City
	Venice		Rio de Janeiro
	Malta	EUROPE	Business Travel Guide –
NETHER-	Amsterdam		Europe (368 pages)
LANDS and	Copenhagen		Pocket guide to Europe
SCANDI-	Helsinki		(480 pages)
NAVIA	Oslo and Bergen		Cities of Europe (504 pages)
	Stockholm	CRUISE	Caribbean cruise guide
PORTUGAL	Algarve	GUIDES	(368 pages)
	Lisbon		Alaska cruise guide
	Madeira		(168 pages)
SPAIN	Barcelona and Costa Dorada		Handbook to Cruising
	Canary Islands		(240 pages)

In preparation

Most titles with British and U.S. destinations are available in French, German, Spanish and as many as 7 other languages.

BERLITZ

german
english
englisch
deutsch

DICTIONARIES

Bilingual with 12,500 concepts each way. Highly practical for travellers, with pronunciation shown plus menu reader, basic expressions and useful information. Over 330 pages.

Danish	Finnish	German	Norwegian	Spanish
Dutch	French	Italian	Portuguese	Swedish

Berlitz Books, a world of information in your pocket! At all leading bookshops and airport newsstands.

Imagine, in a short time from now, being able to speak an entirely new language. French, perhaps. Or Spanish. German. Or Italian.

Berlitz, the world-renowned language instruction institution, has developed these self-study programs *expressly* for those people who want to learn to speak a foreign language *fast*. And without going through the tedious, repetitive drills and grammar rule memorization that are featured in other courses.

Instead, with the Berlitz Express programs, you learn to speak *naturally*, by listening to—and then joining in on—"real-life" dialogue on cassette tapes. This helps you *absorb* correct grammar and vocabulary almost unconsciously. And because the tapes use *sound effects* to convey meaning, you can learn your new language while you're driving, biking, walking, or doing just about anything.

Each Express Program Contains:

- TWO CASSETTES TOTALLING 100 minutes of instruction and using lively *sound effects* to identify objects, actions, and situations in your new language.

- LESSON TEXT explains new words and grammar variations as you encounter them.

- BERLITZ ROTARY VERB FINDER. How do you change the expression "I go" to "I will go" or "I went" in the language you're learning? Just spin the dial and you'll have your answer for a wide variety of common verbs.

- CONVENIENT STORAGE ALBUM protects tapes, book, and Verb Finder from damage.

Dial (no charge, USA)
24 hours, 7 days a week.

In the U.S.A.

1-800-431-9003

In Great Britain

0323-638221

Refer to Dept. No. 11604. Why not give us a ring – right now!

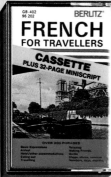

GB-402
96 202

BERLITZ®

FRENCH
FOR TRAVELLERS

CASSETTE
PLUS 32-PAGE MINISCRIPT

OVER 300 PHRASES

Basic Expressions
Arrival
Hotel/other accommodation
Eating out
Travelling

Relaxing
Making Friends
Banks
Shops, stores, services
Numbers, days, months

Treat yourself to an hour with BERLITZ®

Just listen and repeat

It's fun, not work. And you'll surprise your friends and yourself: it's so easy to pick up some basic expressions in the foreign language of your choice. These cassettes are recorded in hi-fi with four voices. Bringing native speakers into your home, they permit you to improve your accent and learn the basic phrases before you depart.

With each cassette is a helpful 32-page script, containing pronunciation tips, plus complete text of the dual-language recording.

An ideal companion for your Berlitz phrase book, pocket dictionary or travel guide. Order now!

$9.95/£5.95 (incl. VAT)

use convenient envelope attached.

11603.

From: _____

To: _____

U
t
o
C
ar
st
or

B
E
P
$
£

P
C

[ ]
[ ]
[ ]
[ ]
[ ]
[ ]
[ ]
[ ]
[ ]
[ ]
[ ]

*N
Tr
fo
no

Affix First
Class or
Air Mail
Stamp

ORDER FORM

1. Name _____

   Address _____

   _____

2. Complete the address on the adjoining envelope for either:

Berlitz Publications, Inc.
P.O. Box 506
Delran, N.J. 08370-0506

Cassell Ltd.
1 St. Anne's Road
Eastbourne
East Sussex, BN21 3UN
U.K.

3. Calculate:

In the U.S.A.

____ Programs at
$19.95 each $_____
____ Phrase Cassettes
at $9.95 each $_____
____ European Phrase
Cassettes (2) at
$14.95 per set $_____

Add $ 1.50 per order for
postage and handling $ 1.50

TOTAL $_____

(N.Y., N.J. residents add sales tax)

In the U.K.

____ Programs at
£14.95 each   £_____
____ Phrase Cassettes
at £5.95 each £_____
____ European Phrase
Cassettes (2) at
£10.95 per set £_____

Add £ 1.00 per order
for carriage   £ 1.00

TOTAL   £_____

(VAT included in all prices)

4. Indicate method of payment, please:

☐ Check or money order enclosed made payable
to Berlitz

☐ American Express   ☐ Master Charge

☐ Diners Club   ☐ Visa

Credit Card No. _____

Expiration Date _____

Interbank No. _____

(Master Charge Only. Located above your name.)

Signature _____

**Note: Credit card holders – it's faster ordering
by phone. See numbers on reverse side.**

5. Detach this order form. Insert check or money order
in envelope. Please allow up to 4 weeks for delivery.
Order Berlitz travel guides, phrase books and dictionaries
through your bookseller.

11604.